Mine Looks Purple

a novel

by Jonen Gleewell

Dedicated to you.
(You're welcome.)

Table of Contents

1. Take heed

"Is it really too much to ask," Nate said as he stepped out of the shower, "to have a boyfriend who doesn't get it on with the waiter while we're out dining?"

~"Are we still on that topic?"~ a voice replied. It was a silent voice that no-one could hear but Nate Noodascue, a captivatingly handsome young man with green eyes, athletic body and twenty-two years on the meter.

"I am still on that topic, yes."

~"You two broke up ages ago. And besides, your ex was rich. I feel you should have given him the benefit of the doubt."~

"Benefit of the doubt? They were practically doing the nasty right there on top of the table. In front of my mom, I might add."

~"Did I mention he was rich?"~

"Yes, well, I'm done with no-good boyfriends who cheat. Unless they discover a new breed of men, I plan on staying single forever."

~"Good grief."~

Nate toweled himself dry and wandered butt-naked into the kitchen. Because, he figured, Why not? He was alone at home... sort of.

"Now, where did I put that dip bowl? I'm in the mood for veggie burritos."

~"But I want fish sticks"~ the unheard voice objected.

"Tough. Burritos it is."

~"I never get to choose."~

Nate opened the fridge. "This guacamole, has it gone off, you think?"

~"What do I care? You never listen to me. And see how far it has gotten you. Here you are again on a Saturday night, a young man described by your pals as a wet dream–"~

"*The most memorable wet dream doused with a generous dose of cuteness* were the actual words, I think."

~"Aye, what I am getting at is this: You spend all your time at work, at the gym and at home. You should go out and meet people. Preferably at a seafood restaurant."~

"I said no fish sticks!"

~"They also serve other food there."~

"I'm telling you, I don't feel like going out. The last five guys were only interested in getting straight into my boxers."

~"You are far too fussy. All that romance stuff is for wusses. You want to reel in a big fish, you need to bait the hook, if you catch my drift."~

"I can't help it. I am more of a wine and dine kind of guy than a *prey and lay* one."

~"You've got them all lining up for you. Take advantage. Stop pretending to be that one magnificent pearl surrounded by a sea of bottom-feeders."~

"I'm not interested in hook-ups. Don't I have more to offer than just my body?"

~"Be glad you have a body."~

"Oops, sorry. I forgot, Jarrrvis. No offense."

~"None taken."~

Jarrrvis the dead sailor monitored his host's every move and thought all day, every day. It was in fact the only thing he could do.

~"Hey, how about some anchovies on that burrito, Cap'n?"~

"No anchovies! Why can't you just be an imaginary friend I grew out of and leave? You're like an unwanted houseguest who is hanging around for a ride to the afterlife party."

~"Hah. That's very funny. You know what would have been funnier? If I hadn't heard you think up that line these last five minutes."~

At Nate's conception, when he was still scrambled egg, something very exceptional had happened. Somehow, by astonishing circumstance, Nate was born with Jarrrvis camping out in his cranium. How a colossal foul-up like this could even have happened, neither of them had a clue.

Jarrrvis claimed he had been a real person once, three hundred years earlier, but other than that he never talked about his past life. Nate did try to bring it up from time to time.

"So tell me. What color was your hair?"

~"Mind your own damn business."~

"You mind your own mind first."

The sailor had been a whale-hunter, to be specific. He had admitted that much. Hence his obsession with the sea and everything in it. Tragically, his lifetime had been cut short in his early thirties. Exactly how, he wouldn't say. He wouldn't even explain the triple R in his name. Was he imitating the stereotypical pirate way of talking, as in *Arrr, matey*? Or, more likely, had it been a dyslexic clerk who had entered a typo in the register of births? Only Jarrrvis knew the answer to that.

For eight thousand days and counting, the sailor has been voicing his opinions and demands. It had started as early as in the delivery room when Nate got slapped on the bottom and an outraged Jarrrvis instructed the baby to ~"Clock that sadist doctor in the teeth. Then get us a pitcher of rum to drink."~

The young man had since tried to ignore the embarrassing anomaly in his brain. Easier said than done.

~"Don't be stingy with the sauce, kid. You've got two mouths to feed, so to speak."~

"No worries, I've got this covered… This is what the weekend is for, you know? I'm going to just relax and make snacks."

Nate drenched a skinned avocado in corn oil and added a big squeeze of hot chili pepper paste before mixing it by hand. He paid attention that none of the spicy salsa could splash onto him.

Suddenly, a series of loud thumps and the sound of water splashing set off tremors throughout the apartment. Something large and flesh-colored came flying out of the bathroom door and crash-landed onto the kitchen tiles.

"Yikes!" Nate screamed. He nearly toppled over in shock. The slippery avocado in his hand squirted out, ricocheted off a portrait of his mom and smashed to bits against a designer cuckoo clock.

"*Gobbling goose!* I'm here at last." She got up on her feet. Slowly. Very slowly.

The intruder was a ghastly-looking woman, eighty years of age or older, with flat, black-dyed hair. She, too, wasn't wearing an inch of clothing.

Nate stood there, wide-eyed. He definitely was not ready to see what he saw.

Cuckoo-cuckoo! The mechanical bird cast one glance at the scene and decided not to come out of its clock again for the rest of the week.

"Who the hell are you?!"

~"And why is the toilet seat stuck around your waist?"~ Jarrrvis joined in.

"Yeah! And why is my toilet seat stuck around your waist?"

The crone started coughing and wheezing. "Deary me," she finally managed, clearly dog-tired from exertion. "I flew in through the wrong window and landed in your john, didn't I? My name is Sauvetyne. Remember me?... No?... By the way, your *soulnub cluster* is blurry for some reason. How peculiar.-"

Nate blinked twice.

"-So why is this old bag standing in your kitchen, eh? Well, I'll tell you... Speaking of wrinkly bags, mind covering up?"

~"Look who's talking!"~

Nate realized he'd been dangling his junk at her and quickly cupped his hands around it. Big mistake. The chili sauce immediately set it ablaze like hell on a spit, but now he was too embarrassed to take his hands away. Sweat started gushing from his temples.

~"It burns!"~

Sauvetyne took a step closer. Her nakedness caused Nate to flinch involuntarily. "Why's your face gone red?" she asked.

~"It's going to leave a scar. A crater!"~

"Doesn't matter," she went on, raising her voice for dramatic effect. "I've come because I am *YOUR UNBORN ANCESTOR.*"

"Wha... What's that supposed to mean?"

"Your unborn ancestor. Like you, I return to this earth time and again without truly being born. We are here, but unborn."

Nate went cross-eyed. Somewhere a heating radiator gurgled. "Huh?"

~"I think I can taste the color blue. It burns so bad!"~

She whistled a bit through her dentures every time she spoke. "You are my unborn ancestor, too, brother."

'*That's insane. She can't be related to me... can she?*' he asked Jarrrvis mentally.

~"She looks like my late cousin Herbert. Only he didn't have a moustache"~ the sailor pointed out from behind Nate's eyeballs. ~"But, hello? Can we focus on what is important here? Your crotch is developing blisters."~

She further explained. "We are family. It's a terrible curse that we are both under. We are wading through the murk between the Material and the Spiritual. I've been many people: Sauvetyne, of course, but also Giddy-Rose, Toila, Emily, Wyndell and... well, a nameless ladybug."

On hearing this, Nate's brain went supernova. All he had wanted was a quiet evening alone. Now he thought he may never have children and there was one hundred and twenty pounds of raving delirium dripping toilet water on his new rug.

"You need help, lady!" he said, averting his eyes from her chest and... all the rest.

Suddenly she lurched at him, and grabbed hold of his wrist. He tightened his grip too, and instantly regretted it.

~"The burn!"~

"Voegant is tracking you down," she said, "because he wants to use us to break free from the cycle of life and death. Take heed, brother! Take heed!"

~"Is she for real?"~

"That's enough! I'm calling the police!"

~"And an ambulance."~

She squeezed his wrist harder. "–It is all about the bubbles! Don't you understand? Through the bubbles Voegant is going to seize control of your soulnub cluster. It is vital that you stand up against him or the results will be catastrophic. Pledge allegiance to the bunny and save your soul! The gap-toothed bunny, I say, the gap-toothed bunny!"

Nate had enough. He struggled himself free, plunged his unmentionables in a vase filled with water and flowers–"Man, that's better!"–and started dialing.

She opened the palm of her hand and revealed an silver object shaped like an owl. A barn owl to be exact. "Look," she said.

Nate disconnected the call. He was intrigued.

'*How does she know owls are my favorite birds?*'

~"Forget owls. The King Prawn, now that is impressive"~ Jarrrvis responded to no-one in particular, ~"It feeds on plankton and manages to spawn seventy thousand larvae every few months."~

'*Prawns? What does that have to do with anything!?*'

~"Oh, so now all of a sudden you listen to me?... Hey. She's watching you."~

Sauvetyne smiled. "Promise me you will stand up against

Voegant. Don't be deceived by his slick tongue and smoother body. Then his reign of heebie-jeebies cannot exist. We will no longer need to exist either. We'll be martyrs that time forgot." She opened up the owl. It was in fact a locket. Wedged inside sat a portrait of a man. The paint was crackled.

"This heirloom belonged to you." She pressed it into his free hand. (His other hand was still holding the vase in position.)

Nate looked at the portrait. The man was roughly ten years older than him. In no way could he even remotely pass for a family member. Nevertheless, the image triggered a heavy jolt in Nate's brain… a purple-colored jolt messing up his vision for a moment. There was no denying that. He recognized the face from somewhere, the devious eyes, the lavish locks of hair, the thin lips.

'Where have I seen him before? Why is my mind blank?'

Try as he might, he couldn't place him. He took a closer look. The man was wearing a type of soldier's uniform he'd never seen before. A bunch of letters and numbers were engraved underneath. Maybe a regiment identification number? There was a name: *Pilchett, soldier 1ˢᵗ division*. Engraved on the back of the locket were some curly words. It read *Blood nor gore shall dismay*.

"You understand now?" she asked. "You are him. You are Pilchett!"

The last trace of doubt evaporated from Nate's mind. He knew he should have listened to the little voice that had been whispering in his ear the whole time.

~"Forget the police. Call the loony bin instead."~

The sound of snoring filled the room. Nate looked over. 'She has dozed off?!'

The eighty-something woman was leaning against the kitchen countertop, asleep.

~"That's old folk for you… Get dressed and get calling."~

'Okay. Do I just leave her standing like this, without clothes on?'

~"Are you volunteering?"~

'No!'

Half an hour later when the men in white coats came to take her away, she was stirred awake and was ready to inflict pain. "This is the end, Pilchett," she yelled. "Listen to me, the whole of mankind is counting on you! I know it sounds *CRAZYYY!*" and she kicked a paramedic in the knee and knocked out one of his front teeth too. And that was after they forcibly injected her with tranquilizers. In the end, luckily, she tired out and they hogtied her into submission.

Doctor Leek Ph.D. (Head of the psychiatric ward) assured Nate that she would be taken good care of, but politely declined when Nate suggested him taking a look at the contents of his boxers. "I'm not that sort of doctor. Ahah. But slap some ointment on it, yes, and I suspect the grotesque swelling will go away. Eventually. Maybe try not to pee for a while."

…

"Finally!" Nate exhaled after returning from a trip to the drugstore. He sprawled himself across the couch. The cooling gel was bringing welcome relief.

The purple headache, sadly, had no intention of subsiding.

"I'm seeing purple again."

~"Aye. Me too."~

No doctor so far had been able to diagnose why headaches turned his vision slightly purple.

"Oh well…" he said and ate his potato chips straight out of the bag. (Understandably he was no longer in the mood for spicy burritos.) Jarrrvis kept pining for fish sticks. Normality was restored in the home of Nate Noodascue, inhabitant of the coast town called Portweald.

Little did he know that soon he was going to die under mysterious and surprisingly bubbly circumstances.

2. Bliss. It's an elusive thing.

Nate looked up at the clock on his nightstand and groaned.

"I don't feel like going to work. Do I have to get up?"

~"You're asking me? You really wanted this job."~

"Yeah, but I thought working for a multinational corporation would be more fun than it actually is."

~"Fool."~

"I guess it's true what they say: Life is a lot like a fruitcake. It looks good on the outside. Then you bite into a slice and it's full of those black raisins you never liked."

~"It's not too late to join the navy."~

"I am going to assume you are joking."

Reluctantly, Nate got out of bed, got dressed and made breakfast.

"Going to work, doing the same chores day after day, it all seems so pointless, Jarrrvis. Ever since that crazy crone broke in last week, I've not been feeling myself, you know what I mean? It's as if I'm expecting something awful to happen."

~"Or rather, someone awful."~

"I take it you are referring to my co-tenant?"

They had heard her being brought in late the night before.

"I'll drop by her room and say hi for a minute before leaving."

~"If you must."~

At first glance he thought he saw a moving pink Christmas tree topped with honey-blonde curls, but it was her, of course. The little child was busy rehearsing a routine in front of the wall-to-wall mirror.

Sharminella Buckelfluger was a beauty pageant queenie. She even had vanilla-scented business cards that read *Sharminella*

Buckelfluger, beauty pageant queenie.

"Hello and good–mm–evening, members of *this-stink-wished* jury," her voice squeaked. "My name is Sharminella and I, mm, like ponies and *banananananasplits* and, oh, I am four years old." Blink blink blink. A dam-burst worth of glitter mascara showered down her cheeks as she stretched out four digits toward the imaginary jury.

Her age was a deliberate lie. She was actually six. Her real birth certificate was buried in an archive somewhere and money had exchanged hands to keep it buried. This way Sharminella could dominate the four to six-year-old bracket for another eighteen months or so. It was a trick of the trade.

(To appear younger, a desperate queenie would sometimes even resort to injecting baby fat into the face. Anything to dazzle the judges! And if the injections upset her complexion, then no worries. None of her skin was going to be visible on stage, anyway, because kiddie pageant tradition dictated that *everything face* had to be smothered in caked-on makeup until mannequin-level smoothness was achieved. The motto to remember was: Better to draw on an eye, than to see the actual eye.)

"Morning, Sharminella. How are things?"

"Okay," she replied, hopping listlessly across the room. When she was out of the limelight, her saccharine, nine point five smile tended to evaporate. She bumped against the dressing table, which was suffocating under the weight of curling irons, lipsticks, contact lenses, dyes, tweezers, hair sprays, sequin studs, earrings, nail polish, hip padding, bronzer, hair extensions, liver spot concealer and a hundred other things. All these she used to obliterate any semblance she had to a little girl and, instead, evoke the illusion of an eerie-looking, stunted hooker version of herself.

"I'll be off to work in a minute," Nate said in a further

attempt at small-talk. "Have you planned fun things today?"

"Yes."

"Will your road manager come to visit?"

"Yes."

"What's his name again... Mr. Holafinger?"

"He better come quick or he is fired, fired, fired!"

Sharminella's life story was an unusual one. She was orphaned the month before she was born. Her intended parents had died unexpectedly and the surrogate mother–having done her part of the deal–wanted nothing to do with the baby. In the years that followed, the agency tried to get her adopted, but after every trial period she was refused and returned to sender. You just couldn't threaten a little diva like Sharminella with "Eat your spinach or no dessert!" without bearing the consequences.

So, at the tender age of four years and seven months she set herself the goal to leave the orphanage and become a self-employed *glamor entrepreneuse*. Nothing could stop her. She signed with an agent and soon was raking in the prizes. Mr. Holafinger was appointed her legal guardian–slash–road manager and two assistants were hired for makeup and dressmaking.

Obviously, Nate was wary of sharing a two-bedroom apartment with a monstrously mascara-ed kid. However, she could pay her part of the rent and he needed a roof over his head. She wasn't his first choice, but at the time she was his only choice.

'I *practactize* my special talent now," she told Nate and selected a baton.

~"I don't know if I can watch her twirl a stick again. Also, where is the talent in twirling a stick?"~

'Harpooning a whale instead is hardly appropriate for a pageant, Jarrrvis.'

~"Says you."~

The girl flung a baton. It punctured the ceiling and stayed stuck. She casually picked up another baton.

'Sharminella isn't all bad. She can be fun to have around... occasionally.'

~"Like when."~

Nate had to think for a moment.

'Like, for instance, she keeps me in the loop of the latest skin care product fads.'

~"Pfff."~

'And she invites me to her dollhouse tea parties where gossip is always freshly served.'

~"You sound like an ad."~

'Okay, I admit, since she's been elevated to pageant royalty, she's less likeable.'

~"She's a bitchy pest."~

'Hang in there. A week from now she'll be off again, touring the country.'

~"She can do a lot of damage till then."~

True, Nate agreed. When it came to dating, she was severely cramping his style. And his style already suffered from more cramps than your average nursing home.

At one time, a co-worker whom he had actually liked, had asked if he could still come up for a cup of coffee. Big mistake. The last thing the guy wanted to find was a living room doing duty as a crowded beauty parlor and a misguided child star, mostly all throat, screaming into his face "Get out! Get out! I'm waxing my legs!"

Nate sighed. The *Sharmy curse* was upon him and he knew it.

'Just seven more days...'

Sharminella was also a very light sleeper and a fierce terror if awoken in the middle of her beauty sleep, afternoon lull, power nap, after-dinner snooze or nightly dream marathon. It was unwise to incur her wrath by accidentally waking her up. Nate had no natural defense against it.

"I like your high heels with the training wheels," he said to her conversationally.

"You can't have them. Your big cankles don't fit," she threw back without missing a beat. "The shoes are mine, mine, mine!"

She ditched the baton, returned to the dressing table and started applying more layers of gunk to her face.

~"In my day, brats had to respect their elders or they'd get disciplined. You are a doormat."~

'It's not that simple. She is my roomie. She has rights too.'

~"Please. You're scared she'll scream if she doesn't get her way."~

'I'd like to avoid screaming, yes. Remember what that reporter wrote about her? He said her tantrums befit a full-blown prima donna. And you know what Holafinger calls her behind her back?'

~"That infernal midget shocker?"~

'Okay, granted, yes, he said that too, but he also calls her his cash cow.'

~"What's your point? That's she's allowed to be a brat because her prancing around on a stage brings in the big bucks?"~

'No, I mean I don't like her attitude either, but maybe she misbehaves because she doesn't have parents to tell her what's right or wrong.'

~"Everything about her is wrong."~

'Maybe her ambition is compensation for her lack of parental affection.'

~"You've lost me."~

'Maybe she aches to receive the attention and appreciation from the jury to fight her feelings of loss.'

~"Come again?"~

'*She spends all her time getting the balance between glitter, glamor and disquieting creepiness just right, so she could feel loved.*'

~"She's a brat."~

3. Stir

Far away, in a place where few humans dared to tread, the creature was stirring in the watery deep. The creature had been rudely awoken from its slumber and now craved food, food, food to slake its hollow hunger. One of its gelatinous eyes zeroed in on a prey floating on the surface. The creature shot off, rising at tremendous speed. It was unstoppable once it set out to kill. Ominous patterns started rippling on the water surface. Still, the prey carelessly stayed put, unaware that murder was on the menu. In a blur, the mouth broke through the surface and snapped shut. The water settled again, washing away the evidence... Then, a second later, the creature spit out the mosquito, for it was not to its liking. The creature was, in fact, a tiny fish called Cork.

Cork was a guppy, showcasing a jazzy orange horizontal stripe. It was both harmless and clueless. It did not plan to usurp society as we knew it in any way. Cork just did what it did best: whirling in its bowl... endlessly riding that *guppy-go-round*.

Its owner, on the other hand, was scheming to unravel the very fabric of the *Material and the Spiritual Blah-blah-blah* sometime in the chillingly near future.

"I'm getting impatient," she said to the fish while her blackened fingers were plucking away at a bothersome hair knot. "I am so near to succeeding, I can taste it!" She took a bite out of her strawberry pie, greedily, not savoring its flavors. "Long live the Barn Owl Army!"

The woman was in her late forties and had what some might call a forgettable face. Her clothes she wore loosely around her wide hips. Her hair was whitish and unkempt. When she walked, her movements somehow looked unpracticed. But as her enemies would soon find out, behind the balmy facade and casual demeanor, something far more sinister lay lurking.

"Let's see what today's statistics have in store for us, shall we?"

Statistics were her game. She used the unerring power of statistics in the same way that a fortune-teller uses a crystal ball. Her self-developed technique was based on the logic that when you read a random string of words or numbers, then that becomes statistical data. In other words, the first thing that your eye lands on *must* give you the wanted answer to the question. Only, the difficult part is to figure out what the actual question is.

She picked up a discarded lottery ticket to decipher it. "Listen to this, Cork, it says here *There's a jackpot rollover on Wednesday... Fill box to void.* So I predict that every penguin will be turned into dogfood within the next fifty years." She brushed pie crumbs off her lap. "Well, that doesn't help me in my search."

Her small living room office was stacked to the ceiling with print-outs and random publications containing countless data to help her with her work. She could barely turn around in the space without bumping into paper columns. It had taken her decades of intense number-crunching to pinpoint the whereabouts of her target, one Mr. Nate Noodascue from Portweald. He didn't know it yet but he was going to be a critical factor in the successful execution of her dark intentions.

She examined an old weather forecast. "A 98% chance of a migration pattern of rain clouds due south. Now, this I can use." The forecast told her, clear as water, that the young man would soon be taking her bait and come to her. She was almost euphoric. "Finally!" She bumped her head against the low ceiling. The expletives that ensued almost brought the ceiling thundering down.

"What's this?" The nutritional value label on the back of a potato chips bag informed her that he would not be coming alone. *5.5% trans fats*. She deduced from that, that Noodascue was going to be accompanied by five and a half others. She wondered about the half for a moment, but the statistics couldn't be wrong. She had a closer look at the packaging. Wait. She spotted a warning: *May contain nuts*.

"Here's that warning again! I must not confide in Noodascue too quickly, Corky, no matter how long I've waited for this. There is a catch. I wish I knew what. We must go about it carefully. Yes, very carefully."

She jostled herself through heaps of decaying paper toward the kitchen. Her oven was more or less the only feature that still stood out. Every other inch was taken in by patient package inserts and instruction manuals for heavy machinery.

"How about I get a nice rhubarb cake ready for him when he arrives?" She thought out loud. "Yes. I'll do just that… Now, I'd better check up on the women and see how they're progressing."

She pushed against a kitchen tile. A hidden panel opened. Behind it, a secret tunnel led to a large room with beds, on which a harem of ovulating women lay waiting.

4. Spatula

The doorbell rang the next day.

"Oh, it's here!" Sharminella whooped.

Nate went to answer the door.

"Please sign your name for receipt," a pet store's delivery boy instructed.

"A cat?"

Nate returned to the living room. "You bought a cat, Sharminella?"

"The most *sweetistest* kitty-cat," she giggled. "Is it in the hall?"

"You can't do that without consulting with me first."

She suddenly pretended she was no longer in the room.

"–Plus, we live on the third floor. You can't keep a cat cooped up inside. It needs to go out. And it will shed filthy long hairs all over the place, on my cushions, in my breakfast cereal, on my toothbrush. I mean, twiddle a stick about in its fur, you get instant candyfloss!"

~"Aye, cats on deck are bad luck"~

"–So, in view of that, I'm afraid I have no choice but to ask you kindly to–"

She had turned on the waterworks.

'She's crying, Jarrrvis. You know I can't take it when she cries."

~"Stay strong. No back-paddling now."~

But it was a lost cause. Sharminella wasn't a newbie at the negotiation table. For instance, where other kids her age were still trying to negotiate a knife and fork, she had already struck a deal to market her own brand of tableware. Nationwide available in eight colors. (All shades of pink, of course.)

"Well, I guess it can't do harm," Nate relented, "to have a

quick look before you take the animal back to the store."

The queenie instantly brightened up and galloped toward the hall, where she tore open the smaller of two boxes. The one with the air holes.

Out popped the white head of an inquisitive kitten. Its eyes were a vivid blue. The elongated ears, little nose and tongue poking out were pink. Other than that, it was completely white from head to tail. The kitten was an exquisite feline sitting on a branch of its pedigree tree so high up it would have taken an entire squad of firefighters to get it down.

Its new owner was hopping around in circles, shrieking and clapping. "Spatula! Your name is Spatula, because you are a boy. You must be my pet and my most *bestestest* friend! You follow me all day and eat nibbly-nibs."

She swooped the newcomer up in her arms and twirled it around. The tiny ball of fur was purring, undisturbed by the excitement going on around it. It was obvious the two were going to be inseparable by the end of the day.

"Listen to me, Sharminella. Having a pet is a big responsibility. I am willing to feed it daily, if needed, but I refuse to clean up the mess after it goes potty," Nate said before he could stop himself. He cursed inwardly.

~"There you go again"~ Jarrrvis spat. ~"Always giving in without putting up a fight."~

"Potty, you said potty! *Buhahahahhahahahahah!*" Sharminella taunted. Not that long ago she wasn't even housebroken, today she made fun of Nate's toddler lingo.

~"You are such a sucker."~

'*I know, I know.*'

~"Take the helm of your own ship, man."~

'*You don't like Sharminella, I don't like Sharminella, but look at it this way: She doesn't have any friends. Not really. I'm thinking, owning a pet might make her more... agreeable.*'

~"She has a legal guardian. She can play with him."~

'Mr. Holafinger is a bad influence. When he comes by it's all about the business. I often feel sorry for her.'

~"She's all alone in this cold, bad world, is that it? And your eternally selfless nature can't help but to throw out a lifeline. All hail Nate the Benevolent."~

'Yeah, but look how cute. Who could say no to that tiny pink tongue?'

~"Bah."~

'See those mini whiskers.'

Forced cohabitation with the kitten, Nate reasoned, needn't be entirely unpleasant. In fact, it might actually be fun to have the furry bundle of joy stalking around, on an ever adventurous quest for all things edible. Although, from past experience, he knew with cats this usually included the unsuspected biting in ankles from underneath couches. The *sneak-attack of the wet nose*, he called it. Or the infamous *lick and run*.

"Potty, potty, potty, potty!"

"Yes, very amusing, Sharmy. The cat can stay, but remember, you'll have to get one of your assistants to take care of its business."

"No, not. I buyed a machine for that. Special *impork delivellelly*. Oh, Spatula, you're *soooooo lovellelly*. Gimme a smoochie-moochie!"

Nate's right eyebrow sprang up the way often happened when trying to decipher Sharminella-speak. So, she bought a machine? He decided to check out the large box in the hall that read *Stroll-Make™*.

Curious about what new horror it may bring, Nate opened it. Out came the Stroll-Make DeLuxe C5 with built-in Panoramic Sound Advantage, Double Hermetic Seal and limited rubber-mouse-on-a-string option. It confused him.

~"It's an unholy marriage between a tumble dryer and a

trash-can."~

Nate scratched the top of his head. He read from the instruction booklet:

"Congratulations on purchasing a fine product of the Ponstram Corporation. Can't find the time to take your domesticated friend out for walkies? No problem. This trademarked wonder is a lifesaver for every pet owner without the luxury of a garden."

He read on.

'*It says here that it's basically a combination of an interactive litter box, treadmill and feline spa, whatever that is.*'

~"Switch it on already"~ Jarrrvis grumbled. Not only had he not gotten his way, his interest in the written word limited itself to treasure maps with a big X marking the spot.

'*There is no start button. It's sensor activated.*'

Nate plugged in the electrical cord. "Sharminella, sweety, put the hairball inside the small opening, please."

"Kitty must go in the thing now," she ordered. "Be a good kitty."

Spatula gently pawed the base of the contraption and decided it was safe to walk on. It started sniffing everything to its heart's content. With a jerk the grid belt set in motion. Slow at first, but then its speed increased.

"Kitty does not want to run so hard!"

"Don't worry, Sharminella. Probably just a start-up glitch."

"*Mrawargriiaah!*" was the protest coming from inside, and to all bystanders it was clear that Spatula meant *Just you bony ankles wait till I find the damn exit.*

"Kitty wants out!"

"I'm trying!" Nate responded, "I can't reach! It's gone too far in. Man, this belt is really too fast. It's dangerous!"

The bewildered puss was trying to flee faster, but that caused the belt to accelerate even more. Its little legs could barely keep up. True panic set in, and then panic rapidly turned into teeth-shattering, apocalyptic fear. The Stroll-Make went into overdrive. Projections were now exploding onto the inside surface.

"Rrriiraaaaaaaww!"

The flashes of trees, humping moose and dog bones were blindingly bright. Spatula clamored in despair... spurting... scratching...

A squiggly spout detached itself from inside the torture device and mindlessly released a jet of pheromones in its eyes.

"Rrriiroaaaaaaawww!" Spatula growled with absolute indignation.

Nate yanked the plug out of the wall. The machine instantly went dead and Spatula flew out, squirting a trail of airborne diarrhea in its wake.

The kitten disappeared after that, to a place where no-one would bother it. In the days that followed, late at night, Nate could hear it crawling around in the spaces behind the walls.

The kitten was, in fact, getting itself ready. For it had sensed that bad things were about to go down.

5. Spay brothel

Nate had waited in his room all day to make one phone call. *The Call of Destiny.* Vick, the handsome dude from Legal, would make or break Nate's future success in the field of *l'amour*. Nate had everything riding on the positive outcome of this call. If Vick blew him off, then he would never recover. Never.

~"I thought you said you never wanted to date again."~

'*That was before Vick's path and mine intertwined.*'

~"Good grief."~

'*Vick digs me too! Right? Or was he just humoring me?*' Nate fretted. '*No, he wasn't, otherwise he wouldn't have told me to call him... Yeah, must be... I didn't just imagine the look he gave me when I bumped into him at the coffee machine. This is it! Things are finally going to happen!*'

"... Call me some time", Vick had said. "We'll go somewhere and have fun..."

'*That's as good as saying: I want to take you out on an actual all-systems-are-go proper date!... Or is it?*'

For many years Nate had been on a journey of discovery. A search to fulfill his ultimate fantasy: hitting it off famously with an amazing stunner–*aka Vick the dude from Legal*–and spending the rest of their days together in everlasting enchantment. Money trees and lucky clovers included.

'*But is Vick what you would call a* dude, *or more like a* strapping young man?'

Doubt set in. Earlier in the day he had already dismissed *hunk, jock* and, with some reluctance, *studmuffin* as possible contenders. His brain was trying to stall for time now that destiny was calling. '*My love life is ready to blast off in four, three, two...*'

~"You'll do great. It'll be like shooting fish in a barrel"~

Nate cleared his throat and loosened up his jaw. "Ahem! Ahem! *Lu-lu-lu-luu-luuuu!*"

Nate looked at the clock. It was nine thirty p.m. No more stalling, he told himself. With cold sweat in his hands, he dialed.

'*It's ringing!*'

The point of no return.

Jarrrvis gave a few last pointers. ~"Just say your lines, stay calm, remember to smile and you'll be all right. Oh, and you've got more visible abs than a warship's got cannons, so he's going to say yes no matter what you do."~

The world was spinning underneath Nate's feet.

~"Don't mention catfish, though. Freshwater fish are conversation killers."~

"Enough about fish already!"

Riiiiiing

"Okay, here goes nothing..."

A vast expanse of space stretched out in front of his eyes.

Riiiiiing

"Feed me, Nanny!"

Nate jumped up with a start. Sharminella was standing right behind him.

~"Sharminella, the human tuning fork from hell, has crawled out of her den."~

"Not now! Go away. I'm on a call and it's important."

Riiiiiiiiiing

"My doll Bubby and me are very hungry!"

"Leave my room. Go and ask your assistant."

"No, she's, mm, on strike because I put gum in her hair. We die. We need *foooood!*"

"I said *Out! Go!*"

"*Foo-fod-fod-fod-fooood!*"

Riiiiiiiiiing

Vick picked up at the other end. "Y'ello?"

"LOOK, WILL YOU GO OUT ALREADY?!"

"..."

Nate broke off the call. Embarrassed. Nailed to the floor... "What have I done?"

~"Well, you yelled at him instead of–"~

"Yeah, yeah, I know, I know, I'm an idiot! I have no life. I'm a total screw-up. There, I confess, you got me! Happy?"

~"Hey, don't take it out on the messenger."~

Nate sniffed. "Oh well... so much for romance. I'll just die horribly alone then, shall I?"

He felt awful. He was more upset than that time when he was made to believe that a street gang of rogue dentists in his neighborhood were *root-canaling* everyone in sight.

"Ahem," she coughed.

Sharminella was still standing next to him.

"Crap!...Uh, I just was talking gibberish. Hahah. Pay no attention."

She wasn't. Her big eyes and those of her anorexic fashion doll *Bubby the Wanton Booboo* both kept staring up at him. Their made-up faces were surprisingly similar: a hint of plastic, and lots of overeagerness. (The gimmick of the Wanton Booboo series lay in the fact that if you put two Wantons side by side, they would try to pull each other's braids. It's a doll eat doll world out there.)

"Nanny Nate is silly. A silly boy," she cooed.

~"Ack! I don't think I'll ever get used to seeing her up-close."~

'Obviously, but be nice.'

For a queenie like her, there was no such thing as overkill. In her line of work moderation was strictly taboo. If her face looked like the latest creation of a half-witted cosmetics guru with shell-shock, only then it was considered the height of style in pageant land. Her fake eyelashes could usually double for the gaping mouths of flesh-eating plants. And most of her mini-outfits... Not even celebrities would want to dress up their lap dogs in things so garish.

~"Anyway, I'll cross this Vick guy off the list then, shall I? No worries. Plenty more fish in the sea... Besides, you still got me."~

Nate sighed.

"I want *fooooood*."

One more sigh for good measure.

'*This is definitely not what I signed up for...*'

~"Your own fault for indulging *Missy Hissy Fit* over here."~

'*Sometimes I wish I could just go live in the walls with Spatula and forget about everything.*'

~"What's keeping you?"~

'*The kitten hates my guts.*'

~"Well, there's that."~

Sharminella was bored of him just standing around, doing nothing. She cleared her throat. The sound of a very sharp blade cutting into steel came out.

"*EEEEEE!*"

"Oops, forgot about you for a mo' again. Tell me, what would the finicky eater like to munch today?"

"I want yummy!"

"Naturally–" He stumbled into the kitchen. She followed with the doll. "–Could you be a bit more specific?"

"I want spay brothel."

"Spay brothel?"

Nate searched through the kitchen cabinets, the fridge, the shelves, even under the sink. "Sorry, ma'am, but we seem to be all out of spray-on cheese-in-a-bottle. Pray, would ma'am care for sardines on dry toast?"

"*EEEEE!*"

The threat in Sharminella's voice was akin to that of a

foghorn. Only hers was in a higher pitch and forever wailing.

"You know, Sharminella, you treat a friend like sheep do their food: trampling on it all day," Nate protested. "Maybe you get away with it, now that you are still young, but later on people will just drop you like chop wood."

"I said *EEEEE!* and I mean it!"

"I don't care! You are not the boss of me, *Smellinella.*"

"*EEEEEE!*"

This time her screaming might have broken all the glass windows in the building so Nate was forced to give in.

"Okay, we're driving to a store and buy the things you want. Are you happy?"

"Yes."

"Mind removing your fingernails out of my leg now?"

"Love you too, Nanny," she smiled, the smile of a honey-dipped vixen.

~"She's getting on my nerves. In my day, when a girl gave a man any lip, she'd be flogged with a cane."~ a salty voice reverberated from the far reaches of Nate's brain.

"Sharminella, you do get that I am not actually your nanny, right?"

"Hurry, Nanny, hurry up!"

"Yes-yes, okay, Princess. We're moving," he said, "but just so you know, it won't be long before your manager will introduce you to the exciting world of calories. You'll be eating rice crackers and drinking tap water from then on."

"What are *calovaries?*"

"All in good time. All in good time."

...

"Unbelievable! We've been driving around for over an hour and each and every one of the stores is closed," Nate moaned.

"Not a single night store open that carries processed cheese. Is everybody off tonight?"

~"Everyone is getting off. Everyone except you."~

'*Yes, thanks for the mental note. That is very helpful.*'

"Me and Bubby are sleepy and dead from not eating and you bad nanny!" Sharminella complained, always at the ready to do her part of the skit. "I want candy."

Nate hit the brakes. "What? Now all of a sudden you want candy?"

"Yes, chocolate chewies and, mm, cookies and magic gum balls."

"That's it, young lady. It's already way past your bedtime, it's dark out and I'm taking you home this instance"… is what Nate would have liked to say, but he already felt bad about having called her Smellinella earlier. So, instead, he sighed like it was his personal catch phrase and drove on.

"Wait. There is a box. A big candy box." Sharminella was pointing out the window. The vending machine was located inside the main entrance of the Museum of Contemporary Art.

"Huh? I didn't know the museum was open this late."

~"The entrance door is ajar but only the night-lights are on."~

Nate swept the parking lot with a critical eye. It looked peaceful enough. Deserted in fact. The hood of his car got keyed once around these parts and he'd never forgotten it. Nate was fond of his car. He wasn't a tuning geek, but he wasn't impartial to a pair of camp fuzzy dice either.

Sharminella got out first, scampered across the lot and went through the open door. She gawked at the vending machine. It stood tall under a dim light, almost like a homing beacon to lost midnight snackers. The candy behind the glass was barely visible.

"Are those chocolate eggs?" Nate wondered.

"Dunno."

~"I ate a black egg once"~ Jarrrvis reminisced, ~"The cook dug it up after a year and served it with fish head soup. In my opinion, it should have stayed buried."~

'You should have too.'

~"Hey, I can hear everything you think, you know?"~

Nate paid the machine and made his selection. An egg from the top row rolled to the front of the screw wire, dropped and splashed to bits as it hit bottom.

"What the hell…?"

A marquee above the vending machine lit up. *Thank you for participating in the Stupend-o-matic art project, brought to you by Culture Vultures Inc. – Bringing culture to the masses.*

Slimy goo kept dripping out of the hatch.

"Look at this mess! I got egg yolk on my designer jeans. Why me?"

Sharminella shrieked with laughter while rubbing her tummy. When you're six, ridicule is the best dish on the menu.

"I got to wash this out. Come."

The museum restroom was located four steps in, to the left.

"Okay, listen. I'm going in the men's to clean up. Wait here outside the door. Don't wander off."

"Don't wander off."

"Don't just repeat what I say. Promise."

"I won't wander off," she replied and flashed her plated milk teeth.

Nate hoped she was being sincere. He knew firsthand that her promises were more like serving suggestions. What you got was never as appetizing as what was displayed on the packaging.

Sure enough, the moment he turned his back, she and her doll tiptoed into the exhibition rooms in search of exciting adventures. Not long thereafter, she happened upon the play corner of the museum and–"Yay!"–finally filled her tummy with cookies made out of kid-safe modeling putty.

When Nate got back from making the egg stain look less like an incontinence problem, he saw that Sharminella was gone. His heart started racing.

~"Deceitful squirt!"~

'She's probably drawing moustaches on paintings. I've got to find her.'

~"Better get cracking."~

Nate was already underway.

Wandering through the dim exhibition rooms, he was surprised that they were littered with common household objects and masonry tools. He could only distinguish these works of art from the museum furniture by their name tags. Nate had a natural-born contempt for contemporary art. Generally he deemed it a healthy attitude.

"Sharminella? Where are you? Stop playing hide and seek. We shouldn't be in here at this hour."

~"This place is weird."~

He crossed a large room with a stack of fluorescent bricks dumped on top of a foundation of squashy lemon pie. The eyesore, for lack of a better description, was called *No Title*. In fact, now that he had a good look at the tags, all the installations and thingamajigs in the room were equally called *No Title*.

"Aargh!"

~"What is *that*?"~

Unexpectedly, Nate had almost bumped into a mortally obese man wearing an earwax-colored suit. The man did not move, nor did he appear to be breathing. He was middle-aged and totally inanimate, staring straight ahead at a huge, empty canvas.

"Oh, sorry!" Nate apologized after the initial shock. "I didn't mean to freak out. It's just, I didn't think that somebody would be standing here in semidarkness."

The man's pockmarked, bloated face and tufts of fine, white hair could have easily brought to mind a potato that had been lying out on a field all winter.

"Don't want to be any trouble," Nate rambled on. "Just looking for Goldilocks and then I'll be on my way."

'*Why is he not moving?*'

~"I think it might be one of those lifelike dummies. A really, really fat one."~

Nate took a step closer to check. If it actually was a dummy, he'd feel stupid that he had almost peed his pants.

~"Please. I had to undergo that during your entire infancy."~

"Are you the watchman, Sir?" Nate tried again.

No reaction.

'*This guy's creeping me out. Is he deaf? Is he sleeping upright with his eyes open?*'

Suddenly, and without apparent stimulus, the man took a long, deep breath. A surge of air went into his mouth, and then he exhaled. He turned to Nate, not with a smile, not with an annoyed expression, not with much of anything. All he did was say flatly "Hello."

He radiated an indifference to Nate's presence so complete, he was looking straight through him. Something about his bloodshot eyes Nate found perplexing, and the teeth didn't look like his own. The top half didn't match the lower half at all.

"Welcome to my exposition," he said with all the enthusiasm of a dead turtle. "My name is Poledoris, or Doctor Brainzipper if you prefer. Some people do."

Nate raised an eyebrow with suspicion.

~"Ghost ship is setting sail. All aboard!"~

"Sorry to barge in here this late, but the door was open and I had a stain and I'm looking for a girl, and–"

"Let me give you the tour of my collection," he interrupted.

"People want this, so I'm told."

"Uh, okay then."

The man slapped his arm around Nate's neck. Though he was exceedingly overweight, he was strong; strong enough to pretty much make his wrestling opponent go anywhere he went.

"This masterpiece over here is called *No Title*," he said.

"Sorry to be a pain, Sir," Nate squealed while being dragged around the room, "but could you release me from your chokehold?"

~"Get this lunatic off of you!"~

'I'm trying! He won't cooperate!'

"Do you know I've had an artichoke accident?" Poledoris stated. "Tore my scalp right off.–"

'Artichoke accident?!'

"–I show you."

Before Nate could say no, the man placed a hand on top of his white hair and twisted it a quarter turn (similar to how someone would screw the lid off a jam jar). It was a toupee. He lifted it up. The underlying skin was now exposed. A thick, gruesome scar ran from the hairline above his right eye to his left earlobe. Seeing it nearly made Nate retch.

~"This is a nightmare!"~

Poledoris aka Doctor Brainzipper–his nickname explained–snapped the patch back in place.

"Let go of me!" Nate tried again. No such luck.

"The accident irrevocably damaged my capacity to express feelings like love, hate, compassion, penis envy, etcetera... except for narcissism. That's why I became an artist."

At this point Nate's gray matter was trying to leap out and make for the hills.

Poledoris froze again. Didn't speak, didn't move, though still kept a firm hold on his captive, who was by now considering unconditional surrender.

"Hello, uh? … Sir?"

A minute passed.

~"Well, great fun this evening is turning out to be."~

'Yeah… Do you think he really can't feel emotions like us?'

~"Maybe."~

'To feel highs nor lows, what must it be like? Can he even be called alive?'

~"Are you alive?"~

'What do you mean?'

~"This crackpot has the tact of a goat's headbutt to the groin, but has accomplished more with this exhibition than you have displayed in a whole decade."~

'Not true. I'm fairly certain I have made something artistic, recently-ish.'

~"A clay candle holder in preschool doesn't count."~

Nate was not prepared for that comeback. He'd try to swallow it down, if only his throat wasn't being choked off by said crackpot.

"Have a look at my latest creation," Poledoris commanded suddenly. "If you don't, that's fine too.-"

"Uh..."

Nate was dragged toward another wall.

"–No Title is the name of the piece. It's a recurring theme."

They both stared at the huge, white canvas.

"It's just a huge, white canvas pinned to the wall," Nate gasped.

Poledoris swooped him forward with a jerk. "Incorrect, it is not empty." He pointed at the tiniest of black spots in the center.

"Yeah, I see it now. It's a dot! That makes all the difference."

"Quite right," Poledoris replied.

~"Seriously? He didn't even pick up on the sarcasm? Okay, maybe now I'm thinking this screwball is playing a joke on you. No-one can have a jellyfish for a brain."~

Then, without a clear trigger for it, Poledoris loosened his iron grip at last.

~"Run, Cap'n!"~

Jarrrvis's captain jumped back, out of reach. He didn't leg it just yet. "I'm probably going to regret asking this, but what are those words next to your, uh, painting?"

"A continuous autocue displaying the critics' reviews of my masterpiece."

~"What a prick!"~

Poledoris read some of the autocue out loud. "An exuberant extravagance with deep-rooted existential undertones... Shamelessly exacting in its superb visionary dialogue between our visceral zeitgeist and the search for the higher divinity within... His oeuvre is an astonishing feat combining unsurpassed social commentary with avant-garde iconography. It is an open letter to trash-culture and sharply satirical."

Nate tried to take all of it in. "But it's just a big empty canvas!"

"With a dot."

"That's what I'm saying! It's just a big empty canvas with a minuscule black smudge in the middle!"

"Indeed."

"Does it carry a message for the viewing public?"

"None."

"Does it have any redeeming quality at all?"

"None."

"Then why does it hang in the museum?"

"It is Art."

Nate ran as fast as his legs could take him.

6. Arresting

Together on the couch... Things were heating up. Nate couldn't remember ever feeling more *hornirific*-that is, anxious and horny at the same time. Chester's fingers were skillfully exploring Nate's body in search of exciting new places.

Nate could hardly believe he was kissing the soft lips of Chester, the Skater with the Sexy Sideburns: a passionate kisser, muscular, great smile, brains. He had the whole package, and what a package indeed. Nate was trying not to giggle too much-except for in a manly way, of course-as Chester started nibbling on one of his earlobes, and breathing his warm breath closely in Nate's neck, and then moving further down, down, wetting his lips in anticipation.

Nate opened his eyes. A mermaid was floating by.

An actual mermaid, fishtail and all, was hovering on the ceiling. Wading through liquid air. She had long, ginger hair, covering her face and shoulders. She was sporting an impressive pair of breasts.

"The nipples are gawking at me," Nate blurted out.

~"And those are only two out of six she's showing."~

The silhouette of two arms holding a fishing rod extended out of Nate's body. The arms belonged to Jarrrvis. He happily plopped a baited hook upside down onto the ceiling surface. ~"I hope she is a biter."~

Nate woke up in bed, feeling shaken and dazed. A weak splash of morning light slipped in through the window and landed on his nose.

'*What the heck was that all about?*'

~"Why can't you dream about kelp or something? Like a normal person."~

'*Normal person he says.*'

~"Don't turn this around on me."~

'*Sorry... What an awful night.*'

~"You haven't slept properly in a week."~

'*I know... Hey, I thought we'd agree you'd stay out of my dreams. It's only fair seeing that I can't hack into yours. I'm not into mermaids.*'

~"Sorry. I was awake and got bored."~

'*What time is it anyway?*'

Nate looked at the clock. It was still early morning. '*Wait a second..!*' Alarm sensors were going off in his head. Something in the room didn't feel right, but what?

"Yikes!" he screamed in disgust. "Why are you in here?!"

Poledoris aka Doctor Brainzipper was standing at the end of the bed; His two joyless eyes locked onto a spot between Nate's legs. "You are pitching a tent," the man said and managed to deliver the statement entirely free of sexual innuendo.

In a rush, Nate got up, wrapped a bathrobe around his waist and picked up the bedside lamp as a defensive weapon. Naturally, he was upset. It was one thing to dream about bare-chested fish, but quite another to wake up to the *abominable snob-man* pointing out your arousal.

"This is breaking and entering what you're doing, you know?" he raised his voice. "I can have you arrested! I've done that kind of thing before." He tried to shoo away the intruder by repeatedly switching the lamp on and off in the man's face. Poledoris didn't budge.

"I let the mister in when he ringed the bell," Sharminella's voice explained. She was doing cartwheels back and forth in the hallway and was only visible through the open bedroom door for a second at a time. "He says he knows you. He says he goes to live in the *apartlament* next-door."

~"Next-door? Have mercy on us all."~

43

"Tell me you're not really going to be my neighbor!"

"You want a knob."

"Huh?"

Poledoris reached inside a burlap sack filled with blue doorknobs, took one out and held it up. "Knob."

Nate was momentarily lost for words. *'This is crazy! This is too much! Is a guy not allowed to have a decent night's sleep in the privacy of his own home?'*

~"Yeah! That was a prize mermaid and no mistake. Sad. She's gone now."~

Nate put the lit lamp back in its place. It cast a shadow that gave him another start. "What's that in the corner?"

"A ventriloquist's dummy."

"But... why, man? Did you put it there?"

"Yes."

Dumbstruck, Nate turned on his heel and staggered out of the room. *'I give up! I'm not even going to try and make sense of it.'*

~"Pushover."~

'Shut it.'

On the way to the bathroom he was closely followed by the bulky man in the earwax-colored suit, who started scattering doorknobs in the hallway as if sowing seeds. They dropped with a loud *clank!*

~"That's it, doorknob weirdo, keep walking. The front door is straight ahead. Use it."~

Passing the living room, Nate saw Sharminella standing on top of a suitcase. She was inside a whirlwind of activity. Two stressed-out assistants were getting her dressed and paint-spraying her makeup on. They were constantly colliding like two oafs trying to spin dinner plates on long sticks. Sharminella, herself, was sucking her thumb.

Clank!

Nate had given up learning the assistants' names. Too often they were replaced with new ones. Most of them quit after spending one hour with Little Miss Bossypants anyway.

Clank!

~"Good. She's leaving today."~

'*They are prepping her. That's her travel look.*'

~"Is she traveling on a carnival float?"~

Clank!

Nate closed the bathroom door behind him and made sure he had locked it. He reconsidered. '*Better to double-lock it.*' Still somewhat dazed and confused by the surrounding mayhem, he lifted up the toilet seat and started tinkling.

"Finally, some peace and quiet." He allowed his mind to drift off.

A paw suddenly lashed out, missing Nate's left eye by an inch.

"*Waah!*" Nate screamed and ducked.

The sneaky, white paw retracted through a knot hole in the wall panel.

"Just great! Spatula is awake too. Damn vindictive kitty!"

Nate had made five capture attempts so far. He was beginning to think that the kitten actually enjoyed living inside the walls.

He looked down at his feet. "Aww, man! I just mopped the floor in here yesterday."

~"Were you trying to write your name in snow?"~

'*No, I was making a rendition of the Mona Lisa, what do you think?*' he said frustrated. "*Spatula startled me, is all.*'

Clank!

"I'm going out to check on the mailbox, okay?" Nate informed Sharminella a short while later. "If there is any mail for you, I'll bring it in too." She couldn't hear him because her golden curls were broiling under three blow-dryers.

Outside in the hall, canvases were blocking Nate's path and he had to squeeze himself past. He quickly jumped aside for a bunch of cooks (dressed in cooking uniforms and obligatory mushroom hats) carrying stacks of lemon pie into Poledoris's apartment.

~"He is moving in today? Already?"~

'That's strange. You think he's here because he wants something from me?'

~"I just think he's clinically insane."~

'Yeah. He's a weirdo, alright, but his weirdness seems to change constantly, you know what I mean? For example, one moment he's like a tragic statue… motionless… The next moment he talks your head off with nonsense. What does he want from me? What is his deal?'

On the stairs, some movers were busy hauling crates labeled masonry tools. Nate slipped by them on his way down. "Sorry, pardon me, thank you very much, excuse me, coming through."

In the communal front garden, some tranquility descended on Nate at last. He was still in his bathrobe and a pair of slippers, not his usual getup, but he didn't care. "Breathing space… grass… flowers," he said to the world at large and inhaled deeply. "Isn't it glorious?"

~"I prefer the open sea, me. No lawns to mow."~

He opened his mailbox, the only one in the row that was hot pink and an exact cold-cast replica of a Wanton Booboo doll house. Sharminella had insisted.

'Great," Nate scoffed. 'Five identical copies of this month's Essential Garden Gnome Periodical. What could I possibly want with these?'

~"Someone wants to give you a subtle hint."~

'A hint of what?' Nate looked at the cover. 'A bearded fellow with a red pointy hat and pipe standing in someone else's yard? That's ominous. Seems to me like he is up to something with that *toadstool, too. Good thing the magazine took a picture of him for evidence later.'*

~"Don't change the subject. You know very well why you got five copies. It's because this guy... What's his name again?... has a crush on you and invents reasons to hang around your mailbox so he can spot you coming out of the building, that's why. But as usual, you fail to see that as a compliment."~

"I find him creepy. He is a stalker. He has found out where I live."

~"That's because he is your mailman!"~

"*EEEEEE!*" A gut-wrenching scream exploded from somewhere inside the building. Nate knew that such a blast could only be produced by one little girl. Without a moment's thought he darted inside, up the stairs, toppled over a crate filled with anvils and pooper-scoopers, got up and pressed on. "*Rraaarh!* Damn it! Damn double damn damn!" His heart was pounding like mad. Again, a terrifying "*EEEEEE!*" discharged from the third floor. Nate was feeling more scared than the time when he'd bought an imported pouffe and had learned that a nest of giant tropical spiders were hatching inside.

Finally, he burst through the door, panting "What's wrong?! What is it?"

Sharminella was in shock. If possible, her reflection in her small hand-mirror looked even more shocked. The assistants, the movers, the bakers and Poledoris were all huddled around her in a circle.

"My babyface... my...," she stammered and feigned falling into a faint.

Nate had totally lost his bearings, didn't understand what was happening, until an assistant whispered in his ear. "She's just noticed her first wrinkle. It's the beginning of the end."

Nate blinked.

"A wrinkle?"

"*EEEEE!*" Sharminella repeated, to make sure that this fact was thoroughly understood. If her eruption was going to register on seismographs across the globe, then as far as she was concerned, good!

Nate couldn't believe it. Specifically, he couldn't believe how ludicrous his life was. The crazy people, the stress... He couldn't deal with it anymore. It felt like his brain was imploding.

Clank!

Bob Holafinger, the road manager–slash–legal guardian stormed in. He was short and stout, and was engaged in three phone conversations at once. He brusquely interrupted all three speakers with a "I will see you in court!" and broke off the calls.

"Right! People, listen up! A crow's-foot is no joking matter. So this is what's going to happen," he said, clearly trained to handle a crisis such as this. He started shouting orders around. "Movers, open a bag of wall plaster! Baker-man, we'll need your pie scoop, pronto! You, Nate boy, get water and hot towels! Chop-chop! Look alive! We need to get Wunderkind prepped and ready for the press junket at the airport in exactly fifty-two and a half minutes. Assistants, mix the plaster and put a thin layer on Sharminella's face. This'll be the primer. Then apply a matt foundation. The crow's-foot will be blotted out. Build your way up from there. Go!"

"Yes, Sir!" they barked in unison and frantically set to work. Except for Poledoris, who apparently still had knob sowing to do.

Clank-clank!

Nate did the tasks, but on autopilot. His mind was a spindle of chaos and frustration. Breathing came fast and shallow. A panic attack wasn't far off. He grabbed his keys and wallet and walked out...

Seven hours later, Nate found himself at the Portweald police station, under arrest for *causing a brawl in a bar, in a bathrobe and a pair of slippers.*

...

"Let's run this by us one more time, shall we?"

Officers Dirks and Duncetead always got a kick out of grilling suspects. It was a form of entertainment for them. Seventeen years on the force and they had yet to crack their first case, but what they lacked in competence, they made up for in belly size.

When they heard about one Mr. Nate Noodascue being brought in for questioning, they had jumped at the opportunity to interrogate him. Apart from the charges of public intoxication and indecent exposure, there were promising witness accounts of the suspect making wild claims about home violence, extortion and possibly even manslaughter. The two wanted to squeeze a full confession out of him, and by doing so, finally get on the Chief of Police's good side...

Nate was dolefully hoping for the end of the whole ordeal. Several grueling hours of answering questions had left him with a purple-hued hangover. His clothes reeked of stink bomb. Throughout the interrogation, Jarrrvis (three sheets to the wind as well) hadn't stopped singing the same lewd sailor songs, over and over. Mercifully, the ghost voice had now fallen silent.

He knew he had hit rock-bottom. How Jarrrvis and he had gotten so drunk was a mystery to him. He'd only had one shot glass of vodka, and seven or eight other beverages he vaguely recalled having vast amounts of alcohol in them.

Where, at the time, he had thought he was lamenting his woes and insane living conditions to the bartender in a concise, articulate and coherent way, he now remembered he had in fact been yelling in anger. He had mooned the pinball machine. At some point, he may have puked into the pickled egg jar, or down some lady's cleavage. The details were fuzzy. The bartender must have ratted him out to the cops...

"So," interrogator Dirks summarized, "yesterday, Tuesday the thirteenth at a quarter to six a.m., you state you were lying in bed at your domicile, when a man in his twenties–brown hair, brown eyes, no distinguishing features–dropped out of the ceiling on a skateboard together with a mermaid–floppy fishtail, gills, naked from the waist up–and they copulated, while a dead doctor was performing plastic surgery on the Queen."

"No, you've got it all wrong! I've told you before, that part was just a dream!"

"Oh, a dream, huh?" the one called Duncetead cut in. "You clearly stated earlier that, and I quote, *the zombie doctor broke into my home and was skulking around, carrying a sack of doorknobs on his back*, end quote. It's on file, son. No point denying it."

"Well, no! Yes! I mean, the doctor is real. Actually I don't know if he's a real doctor or not, he is in the arts. He told me his scalp had been torn off by an accident. He is like brain-dead or something. And there was no surgery!"

"Okay, so it was just a zombie losing his head then. Seems like what we have here is a case of careless littering, huh Dirks?"

Booming laughter erupted from the two fat bellies. Their bellybuttons were both outies and they were bobbing in sync with it.

Nate gritted his teeth.

"Indeed, indeed," Dirks resumed. "So what you're saying is, this so-called doctor was involved in the black arts and assaulted her Majesty with doorknobs. Now that's what I call gross malpractice!"

Booming laughter again.

"She's not a queen. I said *queenie!* Look, she's a little girl. Sharminella is her name!" Nate was at his wit's end.

"A girl?" Both policemen looked at each other conspiratorially, as if a crucial lead had been unveiled. If their police department represented the long arm of the Law, then the two more likely were the big toe.

Duncetead decided to prod deeper into the psyche of the suspect. "The utensils you mentioned... talk me through them again. What did you do with them? Come-come, out with it!"

"Huh? The pie scoop you mean? They used that to apply the plastery stuff to her face."

"A-hah! A breakthrough!" Duncetead cried victoriously. "You ordered the doctor and his assistants to cover up the tracks of their weird experimentations and to plaster the girl into the wall. Isn't that exactly how it happened?"

"No-one was being plastered-in alive! Why won't you people understand?"

Nate felt his stomach wrenching into knots. Stale alcohol breath was floating on his tongue like mist over a field.

'*How did I get so low...?*'

~"It's because you hang out with freaks and don't eat enough of the recommended daily dose of pipefish."~ Jarrrvis commented. Apparently he had woken up. ~"You call yourself a man? You can't even hold your liquor."~

At this point Nate started slapping his own face.

~"Hahah. Why are you hitting yourself? You can't get at me. Everything's your fault."~

"Shut up!"

Dirks and Duncetead had seen all they needed to see. They handcuffed Nate to the desk to prevent him from hurting himself further. Noodascue was a madman, no doubt about it. Worse, he was the leader of a whole gang of depraved murderers. But he was getting tangled up tighter and tighter in his own lies. This bird was going to sing any minute now.

"Well, if no-one got plastered into a wall, what about the written statement you made about the claw trying to snatch at you in the john?"

Dirks smacked the piece of paper onto the desk, unmasking Nate for what he really was: a homicidal maniac.

"No, that was just Spatula! I swear, you've got this the wrong way around!" Nate chirped.

"Kitchenware now, 'ey?"

"The kitty! Spatula is the kitty! The kitten is Spatula! It trapped itself inside the wall space after... after..."

Nate stopped talking.

"After what?!"

"After... what we ... did ... to ... him."

"Real-eally? That *is* interesting. What exactly did you do to the poor animal? You beast!" Duncetead's short fuse had burned down to the dynamite stick and was about to explode. Maiming people was bad enough, but harming defenseless kittens was where he drew the line. "You beast!" he repeated.

"Easy now, easy now, Duncetead," Dirks took over. "Let's go back to the girl. The hot water and towels you used... She was not having a baby, was she?"

"What? No, of course not!"

"Ah good, good," Dirks observed. "Forcing a little girl to deliver a baby when she's not even pregnant, that is bordering on..."

"What kind of person do you think I am?" Nate shouted. "The towels were just to clean up her face."

The phone in the interrogation room started ringing. Duncetead answered it. "Yes, Officer Duncetead here... Hi, Chief." Both cops jumped up off their seats. The voice on the line sounded angry.

"... Allow me to explain, Sir," Duncetead began but was interrupted. Nate couldn't make out what was being said, but he picked up snatches of the conversation: *house search was an unnecessary drain on resources* and *turned up nothing*.

"You sure, Sir? But he is a sociopath, Sir!" Duncetead protested and then, addressing Nate, said "No offense meant."

This remark seemed to set off another slew of words from the other side of the line, after which Duncetead said "Yes, Sir. Right away, Sir." and the call was disconnected.

He harrumphed and pulled the chair back under his rump. Mentally he saw Victory galloping off to the horizon, where Victory's horse stopped to prance a bit and Victory enthusiastically waved goodbye at him in that special way that only tiny children with tiny hands can.

"Uh..." Duncetead added, shuffling documents around in circles and pretending to be preoccupied. His colleague Dirks, quick on the uptake, nervously tapped his pencil on the desk and looked utterly forlorn. Neither of them dared to make eye-contact. Nate had the distinct impression both cops were stalling for time while desperately trying to come up with a way not to lose face.

Silence fell. A sound vacuum collapsed on top of it.

"To summarize," Dirks said, surprised by the hoarseness of his own voice. "Your final statement then–"

~"Here it comes."~

"–The zombie doctor and his team of his assistant movers and bakers mummified the little missy queen with plaster towels and put her into the wall with a spatula called Kitten, while the mermaid and the skater were having it off on the ceiling?"

"Sure, why not?" Nate finally gave in.

"Well, I guess, uh, you're free to go then. Thank you for your co-operation."

7. Pumice?

"My life sucks!"

~"It also blows."~

Nate was jogging laps around Portweald park even though it was raining. It helped him think. Yesterday's outrageous interrogation had been a real eye-opener.

"I've made up my mind," he barked at the dark sky, "I'm not some chump people can mess with. Bullshitters, begone!"

A wet-through teenager walking her dog threw him a dirty look.

~"That's what I've been telling you. You must set your own course."~

A passing car sprayed puddle sludge over him. Nate couldn't care less.

"I'm serious! This is going to be the new me. No more weird stuff!"

~"Hear hear."~

"No more crazy people bursting into my life. I will not allow it. Only sanity. Yeah, straightforward sanity."

~"That's the ticket."~

"For too long I have been a doormat, welcoming all who enter and, in return, getting stuck with their mud."

~"You tell 'em, kid."~

"From now on, I'm going to speak up. I am the king of my castle. I am the womb in which my future self is, uh, charging ahead like a saddled bull that is empowered by all my potential and bequeathed with–yes, I've said it, bequeathed–with the flags of perseverance and circumspect greatness in the breeze of, uh, things."

~"Easy now. Don't strain yourself."~

...

Monday morning, Nate got up in a state of disoriented wariness. Exactly how he was going to bring about his own salvation, in all honesty, he didn't have a clue.

When he arrived at work, he was summoned to the CEO's office. This sort of thing was unheard of. He had only briefly met the Chief Executive Officer once on the day he was hired, when the Boss of the Department Head of Nate's direct Manager had introduced them to each other.

'*This is bad.*'

~"I don't think I remember the guy."~

'*Sure, you do. The CEO was that short, nondescript man who was ogling my feet like a covetous lover.*'

Nate pictured him in his mind for Jarrrvis's benefit.

~"That guy."~

Everyone employed at *ZPMQZ Portweald Division* (part of a multinational corporation) knew that the CEO was something of a foot fetishist. This was not a big secret. In fact, the company motto was *We take pride in business and in pedal hygiene.* It was even taken up in the mission statement, right under *We strengthen our resolve to maintain global service leader in vague niche markets of our sector, whichever that may be at any one time,* and of course the universal *We strive to make our shareholders filthy rich.*

'*He's going to fire me. I just now it. What other reason could there be? To hobnob with Management?*'

~"The foot freak isn't going to fire you.–"~

'*Thank you.*'

~"–He's got personnel for that."~

The elevator opened onto the top floor. Nate's breath caught.

'*…The Froth of Fate!…*'

There it was, obstructing the hallway: the shallow,

antibacterial water feature of legend. Employees were required to go barefoot through the disinfectant before proceeding to the CEO's office.

Rumor around the watering hole had it that many who had crossed the Froth of Fate had gotten demoted or dismissed. And some colleagues even had never made it back. The tales told had taken on mythical proportions. It was said that beyond the rippling surface awaited something worse than what had happened to Atlantis... worse than whatever went on across the river Styx... worse than athlete's foot!

Nate carefully followed the instructions written on a board. He removed his shoes and socks and placed them on the top shelf of the rack (next to the complimentary bunion care products and toenail clipper). With tucked-up trousers he waded through the oily froth.

'*Yuck! It smells of old granny undergarments.*'

~"Is that so?"~

'*Not that I've got any experience in smelling the underwear of the elderly, but I have a vivid imagination.*'

~"Too true."~

'*And just to put the record straight: some grannies probably do smell nice... maybe.*'

Through the other end, Nate dried his feet with a towel. He gave his toenails the once-over. He wiggled his toes. All ten were there. '*Good.*' Nate trudged on, the stone floor cold under his bare feet. Behind the corner, he met the equally legendary *Consuming Carpet*: a thick, wall-to-wall carpet that was slowly suffocating the space. As he continued walking over it, he noticed that the carpet patterns gradually got more elaborate and expensive-looking. By the time he was almost at the CEO's door, the carpet had reached such a massive density that it could nearly classify as a black hole. A coffee trolley could get lost in there and never be found. All the vibrancy of the surrounding colors had fled, leaving only stern black and white and grays.

The office door opened and out came a female biker in a seductive, skintight outfit and a helmet that obscured her face. Not the company's usual dress code.

She halted–her body language betraying that she was alarmed by the presence of Nate. Then she moved forward and passed by without acknowledging his existence.

Nate was equally surprised. Most of all because the woman was still wearing her biker boots.

~"Whoa! Sexy curves with an attitude. I like it. Who is she?"~

'*Don't know. Must be someone high up if she can ignore the CEO's strict no shoes, normal service policy... Weird. Do you see the logo on the back of her suit?*'

It was a barn owl with *Owl's Angels* spelled out above it.

~"Why is it weird?"~

'*The rambling hag who broke into my place had the same owl for a locket. What does it mean?*'

~"It's coincidence and it's not important."~

'*My gut feeling says it is important. Owls are important. Something bad is going to happen.*'

~"Something like you having a meeting with the CEO right now?"~

Nate swallowed nervously. Whenever he was nervous he had that annoyingly warm sensation in his stomach. "I'm doomed," he mumbled.

~"Come on, have faith in yourself. Think positive."~ Jarrrvis ventured the pep-talk of a lifetime. ~"Take control. Remember the promise you made to yourself. Barge in there with head held up high. Who knows, maybe you won't get laid-off. Take some pride."~

"You think so?"

~"I know so."~

"Right!" On impulse, Nate swung open the door, completely

forgetting to politely knock first. It banged loudly. The CEO, startled, looked up from his see-through glass desk. There was a young man standing in his doorframe, his face flushed with embarrassment. Slowly, the CEO put down his pen. Five long seconds passed.

"Pumice?"

"... Sir?" Nate replied befuddled.

"Pumice? It's a polishing stone to fight calluses."

The CEO pointed at a porous stone on the edge of the desk. Nate had to let this proposal sink in for a moment.

"Oh. Thank you, but no. I'm good, Sir."

"If you change your mind, please be my guest. It's what it is there for."

With a hand gesture, he motioned Nate to come closer and sit on a reclining chair with a pedicure basin attached to it. Reluctantly Nate did as instructed. He noticed the armrests were covered in little, white flecks for some reason. And there seemed to be an awful lot of the flecks around, on the desk, on the furniture, even a snow blizzard's worth had descended on the CEO's hair.

~"It's dandruff!"~ Jarrrvis screamed at Nate.

'It's absolutely everywhere!'

~"He even got dandruff in his eyebrows!"~

'Probably a medical condition. Nothing to be embarrassed about.' Nevertheless, Nate lifted up his feet, planning to keep them up for the duration of the conversation.

"What are you doing?"

"Nothing, Sir. Just cramps. Please continue."

"Now... Noodascue," the CEO mulled. He was one of those executive types who use long pauses as a negotiation tactic. "The reason why I called you in here..."

Again the rest of phrase hung in the air like a roof painter precariously holding on to the ledge of a twenty-story building.

"...I have been monitoring your behavior this month."

Nate sat on the edge of his seat. *'Monitoring?'* He was preparing for the worst. The CEO flipped a switch causing Nate's chair to spin upward. His feet were now at eye-level. The CEO flipped another switch, swinging Nate and his chair a quarter turn to the right. With a third switch, the wall slid open and a large screen swept into view. Every room and hall of the entire office building was being displayed in real-time on screen. Some of the camera angles appeared to be at ankle height.

"Surprised?"

~"Psychotic?"~

"Yes," Nate confirmed.

"A multinational corporation such as ours needs to stay one step ahead of the competition ... whoever they are. So it is important to constantly check up on our staff and see to it that we are all marching in the same direction... I'm sorry to say your input has fallen short of being exemplary."

"I don't follow, Sir."

"Come now. No need to play footsie with me..." The CEO pointed at the wall. "This is footage of last week Friday." Nate indeed recognized himself walking past the office cubicles of his department. "You are spotted loitering around the coffee machine for an entire nine minutes until your colleague Mr. Vick Massix from Legal arrives and has the good sense to send you back to work."

Nate wanted to say "Actually that's not what happened", but then changed his mind.

"Here's another one of three weeks ago... Clearly you are purposely making weird spastic movements, calling out to your colleagues... I dare say, almost inciting your colleagues to mutiny as well."

~"Did someone say *mutiny?*"~ Jarrrvis was paying close attention again.

"I got the hiccups, Sir."

The CEO sniffed.

"Be that as it may, ZPMQZ cannot tolerate rebellious behavior at work."

~"It's over. You are as good as fired."~

"However..."

Nate waited.

"However... the company has been looking for someone to perform a special task... A source of mine nominated you – insisted, to be specific – called you extremely well-suited for it. So if you put your best foot forward and do well, I might grant you leniency in future."

"Thank you, Sir. I, uh, I'd be very grateful, Sir." Nate was holding onto straws again. '*I wonder what the special task is.*'

~"I want to know who that source is."~

There was a knock at the door. From his high-up position Nate couldn't see who it was, but he could take a pretty good guess based on the gust of cigarette ash blowing in. Sure enough, shortly after, the large room was filling up with the familiar, dull sound of Edna vacuuming. Ever since she had been afflicted with a near-silent vacuum cleaner, somehow she had gotten it into her head to imitate the noise herself. "*Vooooo.*" No-one had the courage to address her about it.

Try to imagine the most stereotypical portrayal of a cleaning lady called Edna (apron, rubber gloves, rubber boots, rubber face...) Then picture this chain-smoking woman having to endure a rigid, no-smoking policy for eight hours a day. It wasn't a pretty sight.

"First we will proceed with an aptitude test," the CEO continued. "Answer me the following..." After a tediously long pause he said "Do you enjoy biting the heads of button mushrooms?"

The question confused Nate. "No, not really Sir."

"Have you ever found yourself fondling the edges of puzzle pieces?"

"Never, Sir."

"Have you ever used scissors to cut the extremities of a common waffle?"

"Not in recent memory, Sir."

"Really?"

"No, Sir."

"... I see."

Quietly the CEO wrote some notes down in a black pocketbook. With a sudden whoosh, Nate's chair was back on the ground. Nate himself followed a second later.

"Fine, fine," the CEO said. "Listen carefully... Our company is constantly buying and selling off subsidiaries, making it difficult to keep track of what it is that we actually produce."

Subliminally, cleaning lady Edna slid into view and set about vacuuming the profuse quantities of dandruff under the desk, around the CEO, on his shoulder pads and in his hair. "*Vooooo*," her unusual chant went.

"Yes, thank you, Edna... So, Noodascue, ZPMQZ has acquired a firm called *Cibyl Unlimited Holding* in its portfolio. And considering that our entire audit team has been missing in action since June–"

~"Excuse me?"~

"–we urgently need someone who is expendable and can go and have a look at what it is that ZPMQZ actually bought..."

Nate was dreading what was coming next.

"...That someone is you."

'*Bingo! Bless my luck.*'

~"Bad, Nate. Bad!"~ Jarrrvis felt he had to nip these negative thoughts in the bud. ~"See it as a wonderful opportunity to climb the corporate ladder. To learn the ropes. To meet new people. This is what you want: change! Setting sail on exciting new oceans. It will be a piece of cod–Sorry, cake."~

"Sorry, Sir, but me doing an audit? I don't have the training."

"I'm sure you'll pick it up as you go along. Nothing thorough, just a quick look-see in the factory… or stables… or whatever it is… will suffice. The firm is located in Pinglop."

"Pinglop, Sir?"

"I hadn't heard of it, either." He read from a file on his desk. "Pinglop is a thriving city founded by a prominent patriarch several centuries ago. The municipality of Pinglop is entirely self-sufficient and has obtained a unique degree of constitutional independence. It lies two thousand miles south from here. There are no train stations or airports nearby."

"Then how do I get there?"

"You will go by car. Cross some rivers by ferry. Drive around a mountain or two."

"With all due respect, can't I at least go two thirds of the way by plane?"

"No. The source was adamant about that. You leave tomorrow."

"What? I mean. I can't just leave, Sir. Can I?"

"Oh, I find it's easy. You lift your left foot up, put it in front like this, shift your weight half-way, then do the same for the right foot."

And with that, it was decided.

~"Who is that source he refers to? Is it that biker chick?"~

"Before I forget, Noodascue, we will not send you off empty-handed."

"Oh, good. For a moment I thought–"

"We will provide you with one egg timer, a tin of itching powder and a rubber duck."

"Rubber uh…?"

"Yes, standard issue duck. A company tradition since 1847, when the company was founded by a traveling salesman of party tricks. You must carry the items with you at all times. There is a severe sanction if you don't. Please sign here for receipt on the dotted line."

Nate signed, more confused than before. The CEO then took the three sacred items out of his drawer.

'*What use is itching powder on a trip?*'

~"He's nuts."~

"That's good quality products you got there, kid," Edna butted in from out of nowhere.

"Uh, thanks. I'm sure they are, ma'am." Nate looked at the tin. Itching powder held some unpleasant memories from his childhood, but he was too polite to refuse.

"*Vooooo.*"

'*This is too stupid for words. Can't believe I've just signed for a yellow ducky.*'

He tucked the things away in various pockets, while Edna went off to liberate some couch cushions from their flaky, white slumber.

"That is all. You may go."

"Thank you, Sir," Nate said to get the hell out of there.

"Ahem."

"Yes, Sir?"

"Haven't we forgotten to do something, Noodascue?"

"Sir?"

Five seconds passed.

"The pumice, Noodascue. The pumice."

8. The demigod

A stark-naked, blonde demigod was standing in the center of the living room when Nate returned from work. Nate shut the front door, blinked incomprehensibly, took a good look at his keychain, then at the door and concluded that this was indeed his own apartment, the one he had left this morning, abandoning all his hopes and dreams like any other working day.

~"Come again?"~

Nate quickly corrected himself. '*Used to abandon. Used to.*'

Slowly he turned the key again and–with mischievous eyes, wishing that it hadn't been a mirage–he went inside.

'*Yes!*'

The mystery guy was still hanging around and happily humming a tune. He was nothing short of orgasmic splendor: perfectly toned muscles, radiant hair with a cowlick in front. He had a magnificent tattoo of angel wings that ran across his shoulder blades. A glorious ray of sunshine fell upon his grandiose buttocks. It was as if the ray's destiny had been forged in the stars to travel many a light-year just for that purpose: illuminating a perfect pair of buttocks. In his own right, Nate was considered an Adonis by many, but to Nate this specimen was sex personified.

~"But what's he doing here? Is he one of Sharminella's assistants? Doesn't he know she's traveling?"~

'*Who cares? It's awesome!*' Nate's brain was motorcycle racing in loops inside his skull, and he giggled like a little school girl. '*Weeee!*'

~"Settle down. And start coming on to the guy already."~

"Uhm, hi... hunk?" Nate said. "Did you get lost on your way

to a locker room?"

~"Are you serious? That is your pick-up line?"~

Hunk didn't move. "I'm posing," he replied and winked, which prompted Nate–unable to stop himself–to cackle "That's a big tool you got there."

He wasn't kidding. The chiseled body of his dreams was holding up a chainsaw. This was the greatest brainteaser of all. *'What wacko would ask someone to pose like that?'*

"Wait a minute!" Suddenly the fog cleared. "Mister hunk person, you don't by any chance see a burly man lurching about, do you? Sort of like a Frankenstein monster with all the decorum of llama spitting into an overflowing chamber pot?"

"Greetings, skin meat," the familiar voice blared.

'Oh, crap! He's back.'

"The subject is modeling for me. I am inevitably on the brink of creating an artistic triumph."

Poledoris emerged from behind a pillar. He had glued three marshmallows onto a large an otherwise hopelessly empty canvas. "Finished. I shall name the painting *No Title*."

'Another questionable work of art.'

~"By a questionable man."~

"Okay, I'm off then," the yummy model said, "It has been... interesting." He quickly put on his clothes and left.

Saddened and annoyed, Nate asked "So, Poledoris, how did you manage to get in this time? Your place is next door!"

"The organism handed me possession of her key while she is away. She does not trust you alone with the kitten."

"The organism?"

~"I think he means Sharminella."~

"People have names, you know? They are individuals."

No reaction was forthcoming.

"Well, this is just great! Why do I always get stuck with the weirdos?"

The expression on Poledoris's face remained blank.

'*You see that? He didn't even flinch when I called him a weirdo. Would it kill him to act civilized? A dull disposition and towering egomania does not equal likeability.*'

Jarrrvis formulated it differently. ~"I find him about as welcome as a warm fart."~

'*Yeah, because he has the social skills of a moth hole.*'

~"I have fought primordial squid creatures that made more sense than him."~

'*If Poledoris were a documentary, the tag line would be* No really, there was no need.'

~"Hah!… The epitaph on his headstone would read *Here lies a man. Full stop.*"~

"Listen, Poledoris, I'd appreciate it if you would hand over the key to me and be off. I'm leaving on a road trip tomorrow, but there's no need for you to drop by. I cannot stress this enough. Do–not–drop–by! Stay out of my apartment. Spatula is safe in the walls and knows how to take care of himself."

~"You can say that again."~

Since the Stroll-Make incident, multitudes of bird feathers had been twirling down out of a cracked tile in the ceiling. If they were anything to go by, the kitten had devoured dozens of birds already. Mainly yellow canaries, it seemed. It was a mind-boggler to Nate where Spatula hunted them. Were his wall spaces and those of the other flats interconnected? He was reluctant to verify this with his fellow tenants… especially the bird lover on the top floor who had his own aviary.

'*Imagine. Decades from now, when this building gets bulldozed, bird skeletons are going to be spilling out of every hole. The demolishers will have to run for their lives as an avalanche of beaks and bones comes thundering down the rooms and hallways…*'

"A road trip? We go together," Poledoris said.

Nate snapped out of his daydream. "What? You are not accompanying me. No way!"

"I go with you."

"No no no! I forbid you and that is my final word!"

...

The following morning Nate rushed out to put his travel bags and dumbbells into the trunk. He was running late.

"What the hell?!"

A thief had broken a side window of his beloved car. Glass lay scattered on the driveway. Then Nate spotted him. Sitting casually in the backseat–as if it was a cab!–there he was. Poledoris said "When do we depart?"

"Get out of my car! Now, out this minute! I said no and I meant it. You have no business going to Pinglop. And you are going to pay for a new window!"

Nate was determined to stand his ground, but that ground quickly turned into treacherous quicksand because Poledoris didn't move an inch and he knew there was no way that he could wrestle him out of the car. "I order you!" he tried, but his resolve was waning.

The obnoxious neighbor stayed seated, effortlessly swallowing every piercing look in the same way a large cube of blubber would an arrow. He simply stared back, his eyes two pitch-black irises floating on lakes of bloodshot veins.

"Look, will you please step out?"

Resting his rump leisurely on broken glass fragments, the man stayed put.

~"You can have more intelligible conversations with your own navel fluff."~

Shamelessly, Poledoris belched a belch of a thousand blights. "buu*uUUUURP!*" In Nate's imagination, a green mist of stink was filling up the interior.

~"It's a good thing someone already cracked open a window. Har-har."~

Such rotting stench was inhuman, but apparently Poledoris was immune. Clearly Nate was no match against his opponent's ever-looming chokehold, indifferent gaze and toxic stomach acid.

~"Time to call the cops."~

'*And meet those two, incompetent jerks again? No, thanks!*'

"Owls."

"What did you say?"

"Owls," Poledoris repeated.

"What about owls?"

But the man wouldn't elaborate.

"Look, I have to leave now if I want to stay ahead of traffic, so tell me. What do you know about owls?"

No reaction.

"Right!"

Heaving a sigh as deep as a bottomless abyss, Nate got behind the steering wheel and started up the motor.

~"What are you doing?"~

'*Me, you and* nature's slip-up *here are going to Pinglop.*'

~"You are letting me down, kid."~

'*This is still my car. So if I decide to take him with me, I'm taking him with me.*' With stubborn pride he wiped the stray glass fragments off the dashboard and drove away, to the accompaniment of Jarrrvis sarcastically applauding Nate's bold act of rebellion.

9. Tripping

Nate hit the brakes.

He had just passed a hitchhiker on the side of the road. Not just any hitchhiker… A ray of golden sunshine was illuminating the model known as Demigod.

"Heading south?" Demigod asked smoothly when he had caught up with the parked car.

"Sure, hop in!" Nate grinned from ear to ear. Something about Demigod's lips and the way they met up in one cheeky corner of his mouth was irresistible.

~"Bravo. This is how you're supposed to do it. Be assertive. Reel him in."~

"I didn't catch your name last time. We met yesterday, remember?"

"How can I forget?" He returned the grin. "My name is Knibble with a K. Brentillion Knibble. Better just call me Brent." He moved into the passenger's seat and put his backpack and guitar case in between his legs.

"I'm Nate Noodascue."

"I'm glad you drove by, Nate. Must be fate." Brent looked over his shoulder to say hello to the backseat. "Hi again, Mr. Poledoris."

"Moist hinge."

Brent grimaced.

Nate tried to laugh it off. "Haha. Great, great stuff, Poledoris. Ahem. So, Brent, why are you traveling?"

"Oh, well, I want to make it big in the music biz, but that isn't working out. I sing and play guitar, you know. During the day I earn money doing odd jobs like modeling, carrying coffins at funerals, shoveling camel manure. Anything really. At night I usually visit clubs in search of talent scouts. But I'm through with this place. Got to seek out new adventures, meet new people. Nothing really ties me to Portweald anymore. No friends, no real home. I'm going to try my luck farther south."

Brent went on to tell about the time he and his former band *Apoplectica* had scored a moderate hit called *Crotch on the crutch* until creative differences drove them apart. The rest of the day they talked about their past successes and failures.

After some gentle prodding, Nate was persuaded to share his *I was chubby in my teens before I took up weight lifting* anecdote.

"My mother is the kind of parent who measures health by the pound. She used to force-feed me under the motto that *If you don't stow, you can't grow*. So when I was little, at mealtime I would plead *No more mashed potatoes, Mom. I'm full. I can't eat another thing!* And she would say *Nonsense. Finish your dish. It's just a swallowing technique you learn to master*. And then I'd say *But, Mommy, my tummy will explode*. Then she would go *Eat! There is still room in your lungs, isn't there?*"

~"Hahahahah."~

Brent revealed his only bodily complaint. "I suffer from a chronic case of *ear taco*. It is a condition where during the night I unknowingly sleep on one ear while it is folded up. The following morning I wake up with a red ear aching like a spicy taco."

~"I think we can do one better."~

"When I was a small boy," Nate countered, "my granny kept a novelty bar of chocolate in her candy drawer, just for me. That bar must have weighed over half a stone and was years past its expiration date. The chocolate tasted revolting. I loathed visiting her. She thought she was giving me a treat, but it was cruel punishment. No matter how many times she broke off a piece, that horrible bar never seemed to lessen in size. Sunday after Sunday I saw how the chocolate deteriorated and changed color.

First from brown to a muddy brown, then to black with mildewy stuff white on top. It grossed me out. But Mom said I should be grateful for her kindness, and that granny's eyesight wasn't what it used to be, and that at any rate, chocolate had happy hormones in them and they never hurt anybody… It hurt my teeth. The chocolate was hard as a rock. I swear, inside that petrified block I once found the fossil of a dinosaur egg."

"Heh, very funny," Brent beamed. "How sad your childhood must have been."

"You don't think it turned me into a bitter person, do you?" Nate asked, suddenly serious.

"Nah. Not really. Maybe more like sweet and sour." Brent winked at him. He was only kidding.

"Yay! Thanks Brent. This is a lot more entertaining than the lame chitchat I get at work. Most of my colleagues follow to motto *Why reach for the stars when I can reach for this beer?*"

"I'm glad to be of assistance. I'm enjoying this too," Brent said sprightly. "Look, there! A double rainbow. Must be the most vibrant one I have ever seen. Got to be a sign of something, surely."

"I agree!" Nate replied. "You know that scientists claim rainbows are basically an optic happenstance of light refracting on rainwater?"

"Pfff! How wrong are they?"

"Yep," Nate smiled back. If he tried to smile any harder, he could wear his upper lip as a unibrow. Clearly this was the beginning of something big. He was totally enamored of his passenger's charismatic personality and dazzling physique. Brent was the most positive person he had ever met. And equally, Nate struck Brent as an attractive and captivating cutie. In short, they hit it off famously.

Poledoris, too, befriended a splattered window bug whose views on the futility of existence were broadly identical to his own.

...

The three travelers halted for the night in Cabbage Cove, a farming village. It had one grubby Bed and Breakfast going by the name of *Come for the Hills, Sty for the Pigs*.

"This is the royal bedroom," the rheumatic B&B owner informed them. She shuffled into the room on her slippers.

Nate was intrigued. "Really? A member of a royal family has slept here?"

"No."

"Oh."

"It's the royal bedroom because cleaning it is a royal pain in my ass."

Brent snickered behind Nate's back.

"I see, uh…," Nate responded, "the double bed looks very welcoming after having sat upright in a car seat all day."

"The single bed kiddie room is across the hall," she continued. "My apologies, but there is a mass wedding of piglets on Spume Hills this weekend and all the regular rooms are booked. You'll have to agree among yourselves who sleeps where."

~"Mass wedding of piglets?"~

Nate's brain was still trying to compute this news, when Poledoris took a step forward, keeled over onto the double bed and shut his eyes. "I will lie here for eight hours as is customary," he said and only that. Only that and another blunt *buuurp*.

"So," the lady asked Nate and Brent, "which one of you will sleep next to him?"

The two shared a glance at each other and blurted out in unison "We'll take the kiddie room, thanks!"

"Here are the keys then. Breakfast is served from six to six thirty. The water pump is turned off till morning. And if you need to go number one or number two or number three, the outhouse is round the back-"

~"Number three? What the hell is number three?"~

"-Oh, and take this jerry can of translucent naphtha with you. To frighten off the killer badgers."

~"Come again?"~

Before Nate could ask about the unsettling smell in the hall, the lady had disappeared. On closer inspection, it turned out she had slowly sunk down to the floor. "Oh dear. Let us pick you up, ma'am." The two swiftly helped her back on her feet. "Let go of me, scoundrels," she protested. "I'm still strong and able-bodied. I gave birth to quintuplets, you know!" And with that, she shuffled away at a snail's pace. Off she went down the hallway, clumsily bumping into the flimsy walls left and right whenever her inner ear suffered from the occasional lapse of equilibrium. It was a sad yet compelling spectacle to watch.... A bit like slapstick coping with senility.

'It's not just me who thinks this place is screwy, right?'

~"I've been in worse backwaters."~

'Like where?'

~"I'm not telling."~

'Typical.'

Nate opened the door to the kiddie room. It was the size of a broom closet. In fact, it featured a real bucket with mop and a box of cracked teapots. A sad excuse for a bed was squeezed in between. Awkwardly, Nate and Brent changed into their night attire–striped briefs and white boxer short respectively–and they folded themselves onto the mattress, taking special care not to touch each other, nor the moldy, mystery stains.

~"Move a bit closer. Don't be self-conscious."~

'I'm not spooning him, if that's what you want.'

~"I guess a bit of forking's out of the question?"~

'Rude.'

"This was not exactly how I thought spending the night," Brent said, staring wide-eyed at the ceiling.

"It's my fault. I'm really sorry, I didn't know this place would be so crummy!" Nate apologized. "I could've driven another forty miles to the next B&B, I guess, but it got draughty without the side window and all and–"

"Shusssh... I'm just nagging because I'm tired," Brent interrupted the jabbering. He softly placed his finger on Nate's lips. "It's no big deal."

On contact, an electrical pulse shot through Nate's spine and blew out every synapse along the way. Usually, Nate was of the opinion that the *laying on of finger against lips* ought to be strictly reserved for fluffy romance novels, but given the circumstances, he decided to sit this one out and see what Brent was going to touch next.

"In fact," Brent continued. "I'm happy I've met you and made a new friend. You are fun to hang out with, Nate."

"Thanks," Nate cracked a smile and fumbled for something in his wallet. "Here, you can have this guitar pick. I found it ages ago and have carried it around for no reason. Now I know why. So I could give it to you."

"Wow. A red one with flames. How did you know I collect them?"

"I didn't."

Their eyes locked for the first time.

Nate had the most intense green eyes, each one like a tropical lagoon floating on an ocean of white. Brent had two whole galaxies to get lost in, not unlike those astounding images recorded by space telescopes. Nate had only known Brent for a short period of time, but he could tell Brent would be the one who put the stars on for him at night. And every time Brent thought about Nate, he could swear he'd picked up the eternal mantra of the cosmos. *Ommm.* They both uncontrollably started to blush.

On the edge of hearing, barely audible, strange grunting noises erupted from out of nowhere. The romantic tension between them snapped to bits, like a fluttering blossom being trampled on by a stampede of unhinged hippos. Or something similar.

"You hear that too? What is that?" Nate asked upset.

"I do. This isn't a bordello, is it?"

The grunting increased in volume, up to a nauseating crescendo. They put their ears against a wall to listen. Brent was the first one to figure it out. "It's hogs oinking! By the sound of it, they are stacked up by the dozens in every room!"

"They actually let the animals stay inside?" Nate was shocked.

"It's very off-putting," Brent admitted.

~"I take it this means you are not going to put out tonight?"~

'*You kidding?*'

~"I was afraid you were going to say that."~

The orchestra of grunting, oinking and squealing kept the B&B awake till daybreak. Only occasionally it was interrupted by the odd belch from the adjacent royal bedroom.

10. Ladybug

The next day, in the coast town of Portweald…

"A ladybug, you say?"

"Yes."

"Doctor Leek, she *transformed* herself into a *ladybug?*"

"Yeah, the size of, let's say, a bathtub."

"The size of a bathtub?!"

The corners of Officer Duncetead's mouth dropped. "Are you actually telling me that your mental patient turned into a giant, red beetle with black spots, and broke out?"

"Yes, yes. Aha. Indeed so," Doctor Leek confirmed. "She chewed through the window bars and undressed first. We attempted to catch Sauvetyne in mid-air, but she spat a big glob of orange liquid at one of the staff members. The smell was overwhelming. She kicked him in the good knee too, and said *Oh look, I'm circumagitating.* Then she took off.–"

Officer Duncetead stared incredulously at the young doctor who was, in his opinion, not much better than the punks that hung around the liquor store in town. Gifted genius or not.

"–The wounded staff member is in the emergency ward now for treatment, but the nurses don't want to go near him, no."

"Really? And why's that?"

"Yeah, hnn, because of the stink."

The Officer scratched his bald spot and looked at the photo on the name-tag, to check if the smart-ass in the white coat in front of him was indeed Doctor Xander Leek Ph.D. That, at least, seemed to pan out. He scanned him for crazy signs. Working in an asylum every day, he figured, some of the place was bound to rub off on personnel. Clearly, he thought, the Doctor was insane.

"This metaphysically insectival phenomenon has got my rapt attention," the Doctor marveled.

"Listen, Sir," Officer Duncetead said with an inflection around *Sir* that betrayed his feelings on the matter. "You called the station about a missing elderly person. So we get assigned to come here, at the end of our shift I don't mind telling you, even though we were in the middle of conducting important police business"... (which was code for drinking a cold beer and reading the *Dear Tittiana advice column in Tittopia Magazine*)... "So what we expect to come and do here is file a quick account of a runaway sicko, and be back at the station to clock out. Instead, you're serving us some mega-bug hooey. Can't you just say that she wore a polka dot dress and got lost at a group outing?"

"Sorry, but that's not what happened. A ladybug–"

"Yes-yes, so you've told me. A ladybug."

The thing that annoyed Officer Duncetead the most was that he was the one who was going to have to write the missing person report.

Since the reprimand he and Dirks had received following the *zombie doctor incident* (the one where a brief lapse in judgment on their part had them believing that a drunkard was the leader of a group of sociopaths) the Officers were reluctant to mention fantasy characters in reports ever again. The Chief of Police had been furious at them. Especially after he had read the two-page long description of the six-breasted mermaid. And its fold-out addendum with illustrations.

The Chief had threatened that if they made a blunder like that again, they would end up doing guard duty at the pond in Center Square. (And everyone on the force knew that only dim-witted officers were given that watch to keep them out of the way. Supposedly watching the pond was to prevent people from feeding the ducks, but no duck had been sighted at the pond in a long time. Some people said the ducks had simply moved south. Others said it had happened around the same time that old Ms. Crumbwell had bought herself a larger handbag.)

One room over, Officer Dirks was dumbstruck by the gnawed-through steel bars in the window, and the toxic orange goo on the floor. For the first time in this *mad clog dance called Life*, as he would put it, Dirks was witness to something he could not explain on the spot. Mystified, he swallowed a cupcake in whole. Awful smell in the room or no smell, a cupcake was still a cupcake, and it helped him to think.

He heard the Doctor talking to Duncetead next-door. "Undeniably, yes. Sauvetyne bit her way through bars an inch thick, excreted putrid liquids as a repellent and escaped by sprouting hymenopteran wings. She is extraordinary."

"Extraordinary, my butt," Officer Dirks mumbled to himself. He had always considered himself a normal guy with simple views. So when things got complicated, he got angry. "Who does that warty old kook think she is? She has no business attacking normal people with her civil disobedient, alien witchcraft."

A new thought hit him. A dangerous thought. "Wait a minute! What if this ladybug witch is the first of an army?... What if aliens have done something to our food and all the pensioners in the world are going to get turned into baby flesh craving ladybugs? This is serious. Someone should do something about it!" He quickly gulped down the last cupcake and wiped his greasy fingers on his uniform. "Our country is being invaded from the inside!"

In his own mind, the general public should be lucky that he was a cop. He was the best thing to happen since the invention of edible undies. Dirks would usually rely on himself, on pepper mace and on a stun gun to deal with things, but not today. Today he was facing forces greater than his own. More drastic measures were required. "This calls for immediate action!" Adrenaline rocketing through his wobbly body, Dirks started running. After two yards, he started walking at a steady pace.

"When was she admitted to the hospital?" Duncetead asked Doctor Leek.

"We brought her in two weeks ago. Sauvetyne had no papers, no background data. We kept her under heavy sedation... until this morning. Obviously a mistake."

"I see. What is her profile?"

"Compound eyes, exoskeleton, six legs, you know, two large antennae, and–"

"No, you idiot." Duncetead interrupted. "I mean to say, her human form. What is her personal description?"

"Well, octogenarian most likely, around four and a half feet tall, plump body. Hair, black like a chimney. Big yap. I classified her as a delusional vagrant."

Duncetead doodled this information onto his notepad, next to the pretzels he drew earlier. "Very well. We'll put the profile out."

Dirks arrived, wheezing. "*CALL HEADQUARTERS!* This is supernatural activity! The highest authorities need to know about it. All the old farts in the country are morphing into monsters! They will bring the end of society!" he shouted, and after a moment's reflection added "And they'll give even yuckier suck-kisses at family gatherings."

"*SHIT!*" Eyes opened to the gravity of the situation, Duncetead immediately started making the call. "Doctor, do you have any more info that could be useful? Anything at all?"

"Not much. Oh wait. One other thing I remember. Sauvetyne broke into a guy's apartment and claimed that he was her unborn ancestor. Nonsense clearly. You want the guy's name?"

"Of course, brainiac! Tell us! That may well be the lead we

need to crush this ladybug invasion! We'll all be national heroes."

"His name is Mr. Nate Noodascue."

The faces of Duncetead and Dirks turned the palest of white.

"Officer Duncetead, hold that call. Never mind."

11. Penni drops

"Oops, I accidentally damaged the paint on your car. Am in a hurry. Call me on this number..."

Nate swore under his breath. He re-read the message on the crumpled piece of paper that had been stuck under the windshield wiper. He was intrigued that the culprit had hastily jotted down the same message in three other languages on the backside, just to make sure. Judging by the squiggly handwriting tilting to the left, Nate assumed that had been written by a woman.

"Well, at least she had the decency to leave a note," Brent yawned. He was still sleep-drunk from the terrible night at the B&B *Come for the Hills, Sty for the Pigs*. In retrospect, the pun should have been a dead giveaway. Nate had a look around his car to locate the accursed dent. Nothing. Not even a minute scratch. "Call her up," Brent said.

"I would, but mobile network coverage in these parts is poor. I wouldn't be surprised if this village still uses homing pigeons."

"There's a hill round the back of the B&B. Maybe you can call from up there."

"I'm on it."

It took Nate a while to reach the top and make the call.

Riiiing-click

"Hello? This is Penni speaking. I was expecting your call," the sensual voice of a woman imparted to him. As if confessing her sins.

"Yeah, hi... uh, I got your message about the car. It said to dial you up."

"Mmmh... dial me, baby, dial me here and now! Pant pant."

~"Did she actually say *pant pant?*"~

"Uh, right, and so I did dial you," Nate replied startled. "But the thing is, I couldn't find any dents."

"Oo, it's all *goooood* baby! Penni's motor is running hot for you. Pant pant."

"Uhm, did you race up a flight of stairs just now?"

"Well, would you like to try out my stairway? Pant pant."

"Uh, no, It's just you are breathing heavily into the phone, is all."

"I am a naughty girl, aren't I? Penni should be spanked. Will you spank me?"

Lost for words, Nate exhaled deeply.

"That's the spirit, honey. Make me want it. Talk dirty to me."

"I'm sorry, but I get the impression-"

"Paaant."

"-Like I said, the distinct impression you are in fact trying to instigate-"

"Paaaaaant."

"-instigate phone sex with me!" Nate said distraught.

"Yes, yes! I'm yearning for it, loverboy. From eight till eleven thirty. Reduced rates at weekends."

~"Is this sort of scheme still a thing?"~

It was obvious to Nate that he had been bamboozled by a deceitful note, but a blurry picture was forming in the back of his mind. There was something in her sultry voice that reminded him of someone he once knew.

'*I remember her face.*'

~"I remember her hooters."~

"Penelope?"

"Y-yeah?"

"It is Penelope, right? Penelope Mangez from West Brine?"

"Yes... Who is this?"

"It's me, Nate Noodascue. We went sailing together a couple of times, on school trips."

"Hey, hi! What a coincidence. That's unbelievable. Long time no hear. How are you?"

"I am doing great, thanks… You?"

"This erotic panting-job is paying my tuition at the University of Ancient History."

"… super?" Nate responded, his brain meanwhile cascading down to his feet. "But how did you end up in a backward place like this?"

"Huh? No, actually you are calling long-distance. Other people get paid to put notes on cars. I am far away at headquarters at the moment. This way the suckers who call get charged thrice."

~"Sucker."~

"Hey, listen," she added. "I have something important to tell you. Come closer to the receiver."

"Okay."

And then Penelope Mangez whispered an incantation to Nate that he would soon hear again at the moment of his death. "*Seebil-muah-nicblimz-aumhinm-tula…*"

"Let's get on the road," Nate said as he walked down the hill at a trot. "I've got a company to audit and stuff."

"Why do your ears look red?" Brent asked.

"Never mind, never mind." Nate dove into the car and got the engine running.

"You look flushed. And you are shaking. Did you have a row with that person on the phone?"

"Not at all, actually. It was a prank number, but it turned out to be a nice girl from Portweald I used to know."

~"The nicest girls often turn out to be the naughtiest. I recall one time, there was this pretty boatswain's daughter near the coast who knew a trick or two with devilfish tentacles…"~

Nate was thinking that if ever there was a need to tune out

Jarrrvis, now certainly was.

"So we are having this warped conversation," Nate continued, "and then, for no reason, she starts saying nonsense words in a weird voice. Like reciting a voodoo curse from a bad horror movie, you know? It sounded like she was choking on a grasshopper or something. A shame really, to see someone bright and intelligent lose her marbles like that."

"Were you two close?"

"No, nothing like that. Just someone from school I used to know."

~"Girls can be fun. I've always said it, you are way too picky."~

Nate chose to ignore that remark.

"All just adds to our thrilling adventure," Brent mused.

Nate cheered up a little. "Yep. To think that not three days ago I was sitting in a stuffy office at ZPMQZ doing endless number-crunching."

They drove on, for miles and miles. The road cut right through a rocky landscape chock-full of hills. It was beautiful.

"Nate, can I ask you something?"

"Shoot."

"I noticed that you've been looking behind your shoulder and sighing every five minutes since we left. Is there a problem?"

"I don't know. It's silly, really. I can't explain, but the back window has changed somehow."

"How do you mean?"

"I don't know. I haven't washed it in a while, but it is like a lot more light is shining through. I just can't see what's different about that window. It's not the position of the sun and it's not the baggage on the roof. Am I overlooking something? It was much darker in here yesterday. Almost... like something is missing."

"We forgot Poledoris!"

~"Son of a gun! At this rate, we're never going to reach Pinglop."~

Nate felt better already. "Well... maybe leaving him behind in Cabbage Cove wasn't a bad thing."

"How so?"

"Look at it this way, Brent. Poledoris smashed my car window, forced himself on this trip. He is a bully and smells fetid. And he hogs all the good beds. Let's face it, no-one can stand the arrogant vat of protoplasm, so why should we?"

Everything Nate said was certainly true, still Brent was reluctant. "But I've never even seen him carry money. Do you reckon he can pay his way back home? Can he manage on his own?"

"It's not that *it* can't fend for itself," Nate suggested. "*It* has no natural predators."

"The big question is: will he survive?"

"Sure he will. He is a species standing at the top of his own fool chain."

"That's funny... Hey, what's that over there? Is that a cloud falling? *WATCH OUT!*"

"*SHIIIT!*"

Nate swerved the car out of the way for Poledoris, who plunged from the sky and slammed dead onto the road. The tires screamed to a halt. Brent jumped out and ran up to the fleshy heap. "*ARE YOU OKAY?*" Nate followed immediately after. "*BRENT, IS HE DEAD?*"

~"Oh well. Always sad to see a species go extinct."~

Miraculously, Poledoris crawled back onto his feet, seemingly unhurt apart from some scratches and a few rips in his suit. They gaped at him in astonishment.

"Aren't you in incredible pain?" Nate stammered. "I don't understand. How did you even get here?"

Poledoris brushed the dust off his shoulders, walked to the

car, opened the door, seated himself in the back and closed the door again. He was ready to depart.

~"That guy! Always a barrel of laughs... If life were a boob, then Poledoris would be its nipple twist."~

The man had put on his pompous face. The one that seemed to say *I have not made your acquaintance before and you are not interesting enough to be acquainted with now.*

"He does sort of look okay," Brent said.

Nate knocked on the glass. "Hey, you. Did you jump out of a low-flying plane?"

Poledoris lowered the window. He opened his mouth and several long feathers fell out. Then he spit up a bird band (used to tag birds) that Brent caught in midair. Its imprint read *Alvin – albatross* and had the logo of a zoo next to it.

'Whaaat?'

Finally, the enigma spoke... be it in the style of a nature documentary. "Many seabirds are known to pick up shells from the shoreline and drop them on the rocks, to crack them open and feast on the goo inside. How droll."

"Are you saying you got snatched up by an albatross and then dropped?" Brent yelled. "That's impossible!"

Of course, expecting a straight answer from Poledoris was like waiting for banks to start handing out free money. The travelers were stuck with Poledoris again. Nate and Brent got in the car and they set off.

~"If only there was an albatross big enough to swallow Poledoris..."~

12. Reunion

"Oh no!" Nate mewled, as his eyes met the unexpected horror. "Anything but this!"

"You know her?" Brent asked.

Deep sigh. "Yes."

"Don't you want to go over and say hello then?"

"Not particularly, no."

"Really? That sweet little child over there, sitting on the twelve suitcases at the end of the pier and sucking her thumb?"

When they squinted and focused beyond the mountain of hair, the makeup muck and the tragic fashion sense, they discerned the little girl underneath, sobbing.

"Nate, what harm could it possibly do to just go over and chat with her?"

"No. It's just not fair! She was supposed to be out of my sight for several weeks. What is she even doing here in the middle of nowhere? It doesn't make sense! You don't know her, Brent, but she's like having a plug in the ear."

~"She's a constant calamity. A cause for strife. A morale-crusher."~ Jarrrvis added. ~"An obnoxious pox on Nate's vitality! A she-demon with hive-hair sustaining its own biotope."~

'*Enough, Jarrrvis.*'

~"Guess I went overboard a bit."~

Brent tutted at him. "I call that a little harsh."

"Well, I call *that* a Sharminella!" Nate said, pointing her way accusingly.

Clearly, Brent was not with the program yet. What he saw was a sad little girl who resembled somewhat a discarded toffee apple in her rumpled red and yellow skirt and jumbo leaf-pattern hat.

"Don't get me wrong. I respect her right to exist," Nate admitted, "I do. We share an apartment. I am contractually obliged to. I just can't endure being around the spoiled kid for any long period of time… She makes me do things."

"What things?"

"Things like… For instance, having clean fingernails is great. Got nothing against it. But I couldn't bear going through another one of her nail polish *séances*."

~"Hear, hear!"~ Jarrrvis backed him up. He, too, recalled the smothering varnish fumes. Fumes with the power to put people in a trance. ~"Last time, I ended up channeling a dish of boiled escargots. It got messy."~

"And dress-up parties. Those are the worst."

"Demeaning?"

"No. She never lets me wear the good stuff."

"Ah."

"As far as I am concerned, the less I see of Sharminella, the better."

This remark did not sit well with Brent. "Are you honestly telling me that you don't feel any love for her?" A question coming out of left field.

"Oh, well, love is such a strong word. I guess if you were to say *tolerance*, you know, maybe–"

Brent didn't wait for the end of the sentence. He got out of the car. "Hiiii!" he hollered at her. Clearly Sharminella had heard him, because she quickly used her sleeve to wipe away the snot, to look more presentable.

"That is a beautiful hat you are wearing," he said, stepping onto the boardwalk of the pier. "I'm sure you've picked it out yourself. And I bet you're so clever you can tie your own shoelaces too."

She sized him up with suspicion. Any sensible person would

have turned back, but Brent bravely marched on.

"My name's Brent. What's yours?"

"Your shoes have cooties!"

"Uh... I didn't realize they did," Brent kept smiling, but a tad less certain now. "Do you like to play choo-choo train with me?"

"No, that's stupid. You stupid."

Sharminella and her ever-goggling Wanton Booboo doll Bubby both looked daggers at him. Brent made a mental note to steer clear of choo-choos for the duration of the rest of his life.

"Uh, are you alone? Where are your parents?"

"Where are yours?" the orphan snarled back and started crying again and it was all Brent's doing. He was trying to think of more nice things to say, but ran out quicker than the mascara on her cheeks. He gave it a last shot. "Did you have fun at the playground? I see you got your pretty face painted up like a clown's. It makes me laugh."

"It is pageant makeup! *EEEEEEEE!*" She was bawling now.

Brent was in over his head. Down by the car, Nate couldn't help but chuckle. He knew this was not how to walk up to a budding diva. There was protocol to be observed. An angle of approach to be maintained. Nate also thought that Brent looked very cute while he was audaciously taking on *the Sharmy*. '*He is good-looking, has got a warm personality, is intelligent and good with kids.*' Nate snickered. '*Well, kids that matter. No, allow me rephrase that: good with actual kids under normal circumstances. Sharminella is more like the pocket version of a tyrant with a sweet tooth. She's a whole category on her own. Anyway, what was I on about before I got sidetracked?*'

~"Remember Brent?"~

'*Ah yes. Brent. He is so dreamy and delicious. Mmmh!*' A warm glow spread over Nate.

Poledoris, in the backseat, had nothing to contribute to the scene.

"So, are you, mm, my new toad mangler?" Sharminella asked Brent.

Brent jumped up, thinking he might have stepped on something squishy and amphibian. "Oh, I'm sorry. No, I didn't touch your toad. Did it hop away? Is that why you are sad?"

"She means *road manager*," Nate said, finally coming to his rescue.

"Ah. Good. Phew! I knew that."

"Sure you did."

"*NANNY!*" Sharminella screamed and hugged Nate's legs ferociously. If he had been wearing shorts, he'd have gotten an instant wax job. "Don't ever leave me again! Oh! Don't you dare! Don't you dare!" Tiny fists battered away at his hip.

~"What a drama queenie."~

"Sharminella, it's *you* who stepped on that plane to do pageants, remember?"

But big tears welled up in her big eyes. For the first time ever, Nate believed them to be one hundred percent non-crocodilian. He felt ashamed of having acted like a jerk. "Of course I won't leave you, sweetheart. What happened? Right about now, you should be doing your peacock feather routine in a revue a thousand miles from here."

"Bob drived off," she said, alternating sobbing and snorting snot back up.

"He did what?"

"Drived off with the *asssasistants* and said that I am a, mm, viscous elephant–"

~"*Vicious infant* probably."~ Jarrrvis clarified.

"–and that I am bad because I, mm, always want to have things *snort* my way and then Bubby cried and Bob was *snooooort* mean to me, mm, and he said people paid him lots of money to leave and he said I am over the hill and I cried."

Watching her in this state was heartwrenching. Sharminella's bombastic finesse for theatrics easily eclipsed that of most renowned opera productions. "Your road manager deserted you here on this pier? That's cruel! Bob Holafinger had better not be around anymore or I'll, uh, I'll... I don't know what I'd do to him!"

"And I cried and cried and *sob* cried," Sharminella continued in between gushes of drippy stickiness. "And he gave me the papers and said, mm, he was not my lethal girdleman anymore."

Nate took a look at the official documents. It read *Resignation of rights in the capacity of Legal Guardian. 'Poor kid. First she was abandoned at birth, now this. She's only six!'*

~"Hated, sneered at and alone against the world!"~ Jarrrvis reacted.

'*Woah! Talk about opening a can of worms. It's not like you to get upset.*'

~"My ex-life is no-one's business. Let's just say I can relate."~

Sharminella was crushing Nate's kneecaps. She was holding on for dear life. "Cried, cried, cried, cried!"

"Sharminella, exactly how many hours have you been sitting here?" Nate asked.

"Since yester, mm, day afternoon." Her brittle voice was almost inaudible. "Bob paid for a hotel room for me so I slept there."

"Unbelievable!" He was shocked. This degree of negligence went beyond Nate's breaking point... beyond caring that Brent saw him like this. He was livid. '*Yes, she can be demanding. Yes, she is at times utterly insufferable. That doesn't justify leaving her to her fate!*'

~"Damn right!"~

"Brent, go in the grocery store and buy the biggest chocolate bar you can find!"

"Okay!"

"In fact, buy the whole display!"

"Right!"

Brent saw an opportunity and chanced throwing Lady Fortune's dice. "Can I get a sweet-and-sour gumball for myself?"

"Just take my wallet and go! Go!"

Brent hurried off.

Nate was still fuming when Brent returned with a bag of *Toothache Truffles*. The bonbons did the trick and calmed Sharminella down significantly, but Nate couldn't shake off his revulsion. "I mean, it's brutal! I can't imagine what it must have felt like," he said out of earshot of the girl.

"A defenseless imp, forsaken in the middle of nowhere," a male voice joined in, "waiting in vain in a lone room all afternoon, night and morning. A wounding experience that, no doubt, will fester into a full-fledged childhood trauma. *In cauda venenum.*"

There was a man sitting on a vintage motorcycle. The attached sidecar, where one would expect to see a seat, was for some reason a psychiatrist's couch.

"Greetings all, I am Kean Flock."

"Greetings, Kean Flock. Who the hell are you?" Nate barked back, annoyed for the interruption.

"I am a licensed psychotherapist, at Sharminella's service. Nice to meet you. I got here as fast as I could. Mr. Holafinger contacted me last night and paid up-front. I am to ensure her well-being and take her home safely. I will, of course, present myself to her under the guise of being a life coach. I must say, he did not inform me of there being bad blood. Nor did he divulge the reason for this location."

Despite Nate's state of mind, his libido was presently overruling all thoughts. Nate was pleased to discover that the psychotherapist was not a balding Freud fanatic in a grayish, cotton sweater vest. On the contrary, he was a rather fetching, tall man. Not really the type he would go for, but there was something to be said for the spiky hair, strong jawline and sharp suit. The man had an indefinable quality about him.

~"How about that! And he is probably swimming in money. Don't let this gentleman caller slip through your fingers."~

'*Are you kidding me with your gentleman caller? No-one talks like that anymore!*'

~"Come on, squirt. That's two in your basket. Start two-timing already. I used to own crooked fishing rods that didn't wait as long as you to *pull*."~

Longingly, Nate looked over at Brent, who was checking out the imitation leather couch. "So, what cool kind of outlandish gizmo is this?" he asked, pointing at the sidecar.

"Well, you used to have your ice cream trucks, soup peddlers, door-to-door dry-cleaning services. So I thought *Why not mobile shrink sessions?* I'm cornering a neglected niche in the market."

"Wow. Very original, I'm impressed!" Brent had to confess.

Nate was aware that Dr. Flock hadn't taken his eyes off him at all since he'd arrived. Nate didn't know what to make of it.

~"It means he's interested. Haul 'em in!"~

"Listen, can we forget about the couch for a sec and get back to Sharm–?" Then Nate's eye fell upon Poledoris who had slipped out of the car and was scribbling the word *BUBBLES* on the car bumper with a permanent marker.

"Hey!"

"Hello, flesh," the potbellied brute replied, opening and shutting his mouth as if trying to sieve krill out of the air.

"Stop that immediately! Vandalizing my car is not creating art! What is wrong with you?!"

For Nate this was the last straw. "You are not a gifted artist. You're a screwball, a fat freak of nature, roadkill stitched-up again! Your artistic atrocities are worthless!"

"Quite right," Poledoris said in a neutral tone. "I will sign the work and catapult it into a priceless masterpiece acclaimed by critics and the like." With a crowbar he scratched *POLEDORIS* in big letters along the length of the car.

"Stop that! I said, stop that!"

Paint curls painfully dislodged from the bodywork and twirled down screaming, their shrills inflicting a wave of goose bumps on the innocent bystanders.

~"Where did he find the crowbar?"~

It took all the strength Brent and Dr. Flock could muster to keep Nate from pouncing upon the artist. The eccentric oddity himself registered the whole skirmish in the same way as, let's say, a BLT sandwich would. He just finished up carving his name.

Eventually Nate cooled down... back to his good-natured self, but only after a drastic intervention–chains and nougat were involved–and a lot of diplomatic mediation of Dr. Flock. As it stood, Poledoris would be kept under surveillance by everyone, and Nate agreed not to grind the nutball's nuts under a steamroller. It was a fragile truce.

"Do you suffer often from violent eruptions?" the psychiatrist asked afterwards.

It was a private session. Nate–on his back on the comfy sidecar couch–somehow felt he could tell Dr. Flock everything. His deepest secrets and emotions. Well, everything except the supernatural *Jarrrvisitiation* thing.

"I normally don't get violent eruptions at all, but lately I've been feeling... out of sorts. Angry."

~"You were kicking and screaming like a caught sea monster out of hell."~

"I guess I'm under a lot of stress from work and from dealing with friends and frea–," Nate quickly corrected himself. "Acquaintances."

"Go on." Dr. Flock pushed.

"My previous breakdown happened five days ago. I got arrested by the cops for being drunk and disorderly. That was an all-time low. I made a promise to myself. I was going to change my ways… make a big contribution to the world… I was going to make out with a boyfriend!" Nate stared into the distance. "In my head there is a voice warning me every day of how dreadfully dull my life is getting. I am a complete pushover. I am a failure."

"Don't be hard on yourself. You have conquered the first obstacle, which is admitting the situation. No-one expects you to succeed immediately. The occasional relapse is inherent to the process. The important thing is to always get back on your feet and persevere."

This rather generic advice ignited a spark of hope in Nate. "You are right, of course. I have to shake off old habits that are holding me back and seize the day, so to speak!"

"Glad to see another satisfied customer. You are going to do great."

"Fantastic! I actually feel better now, Doctor Flock. How much do I owe you?"

"Free of charge," he grinned. "The first session is always on the house. Between you and me, I wouldn't mind seeing a handsome guy like yourself frequent my couch more often." While he said it, he gently massaged Nate's forearm.

"Uh, thanks."

Nate had forgotten the effect he had on people. Being a stunner came naturally to him. Sometimes he felt a bit guilty about it even. But not now. Not after the session.

'Why wouldn't I be able to snag a boyfriend (possibly Brent) with my hot body and winning personality? Any boyfriend would be very lucky to have me. (Please, please, let it be Brent.) All's fair in love and war, right? The early bird catches the worm. Come and get it while it's hot. If you got the assets, you got to flaunt the assets. And more of that kind of stuff.'

~"Attaboy!"~

"Earth to Nate. You still here? You are eons away," Nate heard a voice. A hand had moved up to massage his upper arm.

"Huh? Oh, I was daydreaming, Doctor Flock."

"Kean?"

Nate had to think of a response. "I'm flattered, but uhm, I am sort of seeing someone else right now."

"I am not following."

"Huh?"

"It's Kean. Do call me by my first name. What were you saying?"

Nate's face flushed red. He'd misunderstood. "Ah... That's what I meant, of course. I am seeing you sitting beside me, yeah." Nate retracted his arm and an embarrassing silence followed. He cleared his throat. "So... Uhm, what about Sharminella?"

"Miss Buckelfluger? I'd be delighted to take her off your hands."

"No."

"Pardon?"

"No. You are not taking Sharminella away from me," Nate said. "She needs a familiar face. She's coming with me to Pinglop, Doctor Flock." He was prepared to defend his position and braced for battle.

"That is agreeable. I spoke with the girl earlier and she expressed her wish of staying close to you. Moreover, Pinglop was where I was heading anyway, before I got Mr. Holafinger's message. I will be more than happy to tag along till we find a suitable solution for Sharminella. It all works out."

Nate's chest deflated. "Okay then. As long as we are clear."

"One more thing."

"Yes, Doctor Flock?"

"Do call me Kean, if you please. And secondly, now that

things have been smoothed over, I think you and Poledoris should apologize to each other. Make amends."

Nate shrugged in a *Do I really have to?* kind of way, but he already knew that the unyielding answer to this question has always been and always will be *Yes. Yes, you really have to.*

They found Poledoris in the company of Brent, who was trying to stack all of Sharminella's suitcases on the back of the motorcycle. A lost cause.

"Hold it. We are going to load them on my car roof. Sharmy is coming with us."

"Yaaaaay!" she cheered.

Watching Sharminella do her happy dance warmed Nate's heart like mulled wine on a cold winter night. Seeing Poledoris lick the barnacled pier post behind her, less so.

Nate considered strapping the man onto the roof rack too, next to the other inanimate objects, but then he remembered the truce.

"Poledoris, hi. Can I have a quick word? I would like to apologize for the way I behaved. I hope you have no hard feelings… Displaying any feelings would be welcome, actually… Hey, I am talking to you. Are you even listening?"

He was not. He was licking the post.

~"I guess that will have to do."~

"Well, I tried… Kean."

"Uh, Nate, I got some bad news, I'm afraid," Brent said.

"Yikes. What is it?"

"I've just heard from the ferry operator's desk that the ferryboat sank last night."

"It sank?"

"Yeah, while it was moored in the harbor. They don't know if it happened by accident or on purpose."

"That's awful!"

~"Another vessel sent to Davy Jones's locker. One day he will claim us all."~

"It gets worse. The replacement boat won't get here till next week."

"You're joking?"

"That is a setback," Kean joined in on the conversation. "We have no other option than to drive around the lake."

Nate moaned. "Driving around the lake, that's going to take an entire day. At this pace, we'll never reach Pinglop. Give me a break!"

"Well, look at it this way," Brent said, "with all the nasty surprises now behind us, the only way left to go is up."

Nate tried to keep a straight face in the presence of such credulous optimism, but he cracked up in the end. *'Brent is so cute...'*

"Yes, there is that smile! That's the Nate I like."

"Well, okay, folks," Nate smiled back. "We'd better get moving."

While Brent, Nate and Kean strapped the suitcases to the car roof, Sharminella entertained herself playing *peek-a-boutique*. (It was a game she had made up where she took her hands away from her eyes and went "Peekaboo" followed by "I see jewels!")

"I don't understand. How can one girl fill so many cases?" Brent wondered. "Maybe there is still room in the back. I'll have a look."

When he opened the trunk, out jumped Spatula–hissing and wild. Its white fur stood on end. ~"Watch it! It's out of control!"~ The creature ran up to Kean and viciously bit him in the ankle.

"*OOAARGH!*"

A shriek of joy followed. This came from Sharminella, who snatched the enraged kitten up and started petting it like there was no tomorrow. "Kitty! You're here! Meow-meow!"

"Sharmy, no! It's dangerous!"

"*Rriiroaaww!*" Spatula writhed in her arms to free itself. It climbed into her hair, then scurried down her back.

"*AAARGH!* The agony!" Kean yelled. He was hopscotching in circles around a vacant Poledoris.

Brent, luckily, still had his wits about him. "Stand still so I can see! Let me help you–" Kean slowed down. "–The bite hasn't punctured the skin, I think, but it's best to disinfect and bandage it. The first aid kit is in the car."

"I'll get it!" Nate volunteered.

Sixty seconds after the pandemonium had begun, it ended. Spatula, now the picture of innocence, sat calmly on the pavement as if nothing had happened. It stretched one leg up in the air and licked his inner thighs clean with a sandpaper tongue.

...

The escapee called Sauvetyne landed on the balcony. She was half-human, half-ladybug and completely naked. (When she flew, clothes were a hindrance to her wings so early on in life she had adopted a nudist lifestyle.)

"One… two… three!" She smashed one of the windows with a metal bar, and unlawfully entered Nate's living room. She crouched down in front of a closet and put her arm into the space underneath it.

"It's gone! Someone took it!" she said, referring to the owl locket that she had secretly kicked under the closet right before the asylum people had jumped her and drugged her.

Sauvetyne ransacked the apartment to make sure the locket wasn't hidden in another location. It wasn't. But she did find Nate's itinerary. Now she knew where he was headed. It was the very same place from which she had escaped many weeks earlier.

"Pinglop!"

...

The group of travelers had only just set off for Pinglop again, when a small explosion filled the dusty street with black smoke. Kean's motorcycle had *terminal muffler cough*. (At least, that's what the shady-looking owner of the repair shop called it when he asked to pay upfront.) The motorcycle had to be left behind for repairs, so Nate graciously offered Kean a ride in the car.

Nate drove. Brent sat next to him. On the backseat, Poledoris, Kean, Sharminella, her doll Bubby and Spatula all struggled fiercely for territory.

"Not too crowded back there?" Brent inquired.

"We can manage," Kean lied. His hamstrings were cramping up because his bandaged ankle was positioned on the back of the driver's headrest. There just enough space for everyone.

"Rrrrrrr..." Spatula softly purred in Poledoris's lap and didn't care about human discomforts. The kitten had just devoured its own body weight in secondary meat byproducts (meat from the store, not Kean's).

"Nanny Nate, what does that yellow thing mean?" Sharminella asked, pointing at a sign.

"Caution: deer crossing, fifty yards."

"Wow!" she said with feigned surprise. "That's a very very very big deer!"

~"Hah. You walked right into that one."~

"Is he your boyfriend?" she went on.

"Well, uh, Brent and I haven't really–"

"Did you show him your peepee?"

"Sharminella, I am surprised at you. You are much too young to know about that stuff."

A smile dimpled Brent's face.

Nate felt a little embarrassed, although he didn't know exactly why.

"Okay, that's enough questions for now, Princess," he said. "I am king in this car and I rule that everyone with a smaller skull than mine must be silent."

Sharminella couldn't argue with that. She didn't know what skull meant.

For a while nothing much happened. As the afternoon progressed, the outside heat was slowly seeping into the pores.

Nate was puzzled. "What I can't get my head around is how Spatula survived the last couple of days without food or water."

On cue, Poledoris produced a disgusting looking and soppy thing from his pocket. "The vertebrate has been sucking the mucus out."

The item was a sponge that Nate used to wipe dirt and bird dropping off his car. He had been meaning to throw it out. Poledoris must have found it in the trunk. They watched with revulsion how Poledoris put the moist, filth-caked sponge back in his pocket.

"Ewww! That's ewwy! You are ewwwwy, stinkyface," Sharminella said.

"My ears register a voice," Poledoris stated.

"Remarkable," Kean joined in. "I'm curious. Mr. Poledoris, on what level are you consciously aware of interpersonal communication?"

"My ears register another voice."

No-one spoke for a second.

"Ladies and gentlemen, behold, a living and breathing placenta," Kean joked. "A moral vacancy. An anthropoid ape with less than a basic grasp of the social fundamentals."

~"As dense as a doorknob, he is."~

Nate was surprised by the sarcastic edge in Kean's statement. He'd assumed a shrink would be above this kind of thing.

"Stinky-stinky stinkyface. Nah-nanana-nah."

"Settle down back there," Nate implored, and he would have added *And, by the way, your perfume smells like expensive bug spray*, but he was trying to maintain the peace.

"*Mmhu-hum-mm-hum…*" Brent had been humming the same song under his breath for twenty minutes and it was starting to annoy Nate more than anything else, if possible, but Brent had seen him being cross too often already. Nate really wanted things to go well between them. With everything that had been going on lately, the two of them hadn't been able to spend much quality time together. '*Brent is just so stunningly sexy, it hurts.*'

"A honey bee's sexual organs explode while mating the queen." This little nugget of unsolicited information came from Poledoris.

"Yes, uh, that's quite a sobering insight," Nate had to admit. He got a visual before he could stop himself.

~"Makes you wonder, doesn't it? If a Poledoris falls in the woods, does he make a sound?"~

"*Mmhmuhmm-hmm,*" Brent continued.

"My tummy flops!" Sharminella said. "I want pancakes!"

"Poledoris wants a chew toy," Poledoris said to the upholstery.

~"Oh boy. Here we go."~ Jarrrvis could sense chaos brewing.

Kean was intrigued. "Fascinating. Although Mr. Poledoris is emotionally barren, the urge of *Want* remains strong."

Poledoris burped through his nostrils.

Kean lectured on, ignoring the unorthodox rebuttal. "The extemporaneous *Want* predominates. Very similar to a cat's behavior in a way."

"*M'iw?*" Spatula interjected.

"Pancakes-pancakes-pancakes! Now!" Sharminella was working herself up to giving another bravado performance in

Antagonism.

"Be patient, Sharminella. We're stopping at a road restaurant in half an hour or so."

"No! Kitty and me want it now! *Om-nom-noms* in our tummies."

"Thirty minutes!"

"Unfair, unfair! I am killed of hunger. Bad nanny! Bad nanny!" she spouted.

"Don't do this, Sharminella. Sit quiet and behave!"

Sharminella stuck out her tongue and blew a raspberry, taking special care to get the amount of wetness just right. "*Plllfffrb!*"

"Put in psychosomatic terms, the essence of that which was once Poledoris remains *ad infinitum* bulldozed under a massive overweight block of repression."

~"Aye, he's your regular thigh-slapper."~ Jarrrvis heckled.

"Poledoris wants a chew toy."

~"What a loggerhead."~

"Mister Pollydolly? Your mouth smells like poo!" Sharminella observed with the deadly precision of a rooftop sniper.

"Poledoris wants a chew toy."

"Nanny *Naaaaate?*"

"Yes. What is it?"

"Why is Pollydolly gross?"

"Shush. It's rude to say a person is gross when that person is sitting next to you."

A thought formed in Nate's head, '*In the assumption, of course, that Brainzipper shares the same gene pool as humans.*'

~"Aye. Trying to carry a conversation with Poledoris is like having a peanut stuck up your nose. It's slightly uncomfortable and nuts."~

Nate felt the sensation of something gelatinous and sticky on his skin. He almost veered off the road.

"Poledoris wants–"

"Right! Who just threw a marshmallow down the back of my shirt? You, Sharminella?" Nate fumed.

"It was Bubby. I swear I saw her do it!"

"*Ooargh!*" Kean shouted out.

"Aack!" Nate replied.

Screech! the car tires screamed.

"Why did you kick my seat?" Nate barked with indignation.

"My apologies," Kean yelped. "Damn kitten tried to bite me. Again!"

"Spatula hates you," Sharminella said accusingly.

"I haven't done her any harm!"

"Not *her*, stupid! He is a boy cat. I can tell because he, mm, has a thingy. Now, kiss and make up!"

"I'm not kissing that feline!"

"Come, kiss Spatula!" Sharminella commanded.

"I refuse."

"Kiss and make *uuuuuuup!*"

"I strongly suggest you do what she says." Nate's stress levels were soaring.

"Kiss and make up. Right-on-the-whiskers!" Sharminella squeaked.

"Okay, fine," Kean folded, "but we are going to talk about this childish conduct as soon as I get out of this nutshell of a car." With a swift movement he picked up the furball and put his lips square onto its wet nose.

"*Grreoww!*" Spatula shot off like a spiraling bullet. Possessed. Right at that moment, the car entered a very long and very dark tunnel.

"Somebody stop that puss!"

ZOOOF (sound made by kitty at six g centrifugal force)

~"Hey, watch it!"~

"Ouch!"

"My tailbone!"

"I'm trying to drive here, people!"

"*Mmm-hmu-mmuh…*"

"Chew toy."

"Scoot over a bit."

"There's no room."

"I think I felt cat flab."

"Eeww!"

"~Whose limbs are these?"~

"Look, I'm driving here, you know!"

"Wah! What's on my chest!?"

"I think I can feel a foot, three fingers and an armpit."

"Ow, my salivary glands!"

~"Save our souls!"~

"Chew toy."

"Quit that ruckus!"

"Sharmy, get off the rear shelf and back in your seat!"

"I got you! Oh, I got you, Spatula kitty-boo!"

"…mrorrw…" (stifled complaint)

"Stop hogging the cup holders!"

"Don't think I can't see you in the rearview mirror, young lady," Nate said when finally daylight hit and the mayhem subsided.

"*Plllfffrb!*" (extra wet)

"And take your pink umbrella back out!"

"But he stinks like poo-poo!"

"A mouth is not an umbrella stand."

"But the poo-poo?"

"The answer is no, Sharminella. It's just not hygienic."

~"He does stink. His breath could kill a donkey. I think he eats dung for breakfast"~

"*Mhu-muhmm-mm…*"

"Brent, will you cut it out with the humming already? It's not helping!"

"Huh? You mean, you can hear me? I thought only I could hear that in my head!"

"Of course not. We all can."

"Really?"

"Yes."

"No, really?"

"Yes!"

"Oh crap! I've just realized something. At all those funeral wakes where I was working as a temp, the mourners could hear me humming *the Gagging Genitalia Anthem.*"

~"Still beats *99 bottles of beer on the wall.*"~

13. Scene

When sunset came round, the weary travelers found a new place to rest for the night: a trailer park located in a remote valley.

'Like a breakaway herd of giant aluminum caterpillars chomping on a grassy field, the collection of dingy trailers stand shimmering in the moonlight.'

It took Nate a few seconds to form the thought in his head.

~"Poetry in motion sickness, if you ask me."~

In a few hours' time a storm was probably going to tear up the valley, but for now it was all still open sky and muggy heat. The end of the season was nearing and even the die-hard fans of camping had already left.

"You're lucky you caught me. I am the last one here," Jilly the park owner said and she handed them the trailer keys. She was an amiable outdoorsy type of woman. "You can drive a hundred miles in any direction and not encounter a soul. It's sensational here, isn't it? Anyway, simply drop the keys in the mailbox in the morning, before you leave. Well, that's enough chatting for me. I am wrapping up. My city vacation is starting tonight. Ciao!"

Nate and Brent were sharing trailer 2A. Next-door in 2B, Kean and Sharminella were in session. To get her in touch with her inner child.

"With eyes closed, Sharminella, can you see your younger self in the mirror before you?"

"Yes."

"Now, note how sweet as sugar you were."

"A-uh! So a lot of sugar!"

"And how you got everything you needed just by being your innocent self.

"So *no-ninny-self!*"

"Very good. Memorize it, and at the next pageant, act pure and sweet like that and you're guaranteed to win over the judges."

"*Yeaaaay!*"

"That's how to exploit your inner child."

She was one pleased customer.

Before going off to bed, she completed her training for the day with a set of *feebs*. Flawless Execution of Eyelash Batting was a muscle-toning technique that involved fifty fluttering bats of one eye, followed by fifty of the other. It took Sharminella a long time because she couldn't count so high yet and didn't know when she was done. (It's tough being a queenie and honing your craft.)

"I am heading back to my trailer now, Sharminella. Rest well," Kean said, finishing up on some writing, but she was sound asleep. Kean noticed that someone was loitering underneath the window. He stepped out. "Evening, Nate. Still got plans?"

"Who, me? I thought I'd go for a stroll. It's so beautiful here. Spatula is out on the prowl and Poledoris is locked safely behind key 10F. Everyone is happy."

~"Tell it like it is, you lily-livered dolt. You're nervous about going inside for some one-on-one time with Brent."~

'*Maybe that too.*'

Kean seemed to be reading Nate's mind, because with a knowing wink he handed him a breath mint. "I noticed there is chemistry between you and Brent. It is paramount in situations such as these to make a good impression. See you in the morning."

Once again Nate was taken aback by Kean, but he was grateful for the gesture. He sucked on the mint for a while, took a deep breath and braced himself for what was to come. Inside

2A, on the sofa bed of the tiny living room, Brent was strumming on his acoustic guitar like an experienced rock musician. With his wild hair hanging over one side of his face, loose-fitting jacket, dirty T-shirt, he looked the part and oh so scrumptious. Nate brushed past the heartthrob as he came in. The trailer really was tiny.

~"Sharminella owns dollhouses that have more legroom."~

'*Not now, Jarrrvis. Please.*'

~"This place is tighter than a clam with constipation"~ Another punch line. Jarrrvis even mimicked the sound of the drums. ~"Du-dum-tissh!"~

No-one was laughing.

"What's that smell? Cleaning agent?" Brent asked.

"Spearmint. Don't like it?"

"No. I mean, yeah, it's okay."

They both grinned. Nate was trying to look sophisticated, but the silly expression wouldn't come off. It was the anticipation that had got him reeling. His brain was a powder white cloud. Great things were about to happen. Brent could feel it too. Not in the least in his pocket.

'*Tonight is teeming with endless possibilities... Outside, the swirling air is playing hide-and-go-seek in the foliage, whispering sweet little nothings to the trees... A flirtatious concerto of crickets is recording a sultry soundtrack. Several crickets even burst into flames from rubbing their dry hind legs too rigorously together, much to the delight of the fireflies. Meanwhile, fairies are stealing Brent's socks–*'

~"Stop stalling!"~

'*Oh. Sorry.*'

~"This is it, my man. The dry spell is over. Mess it up and I'll keelhaul your marbles."~

Nate was excited. Brent was excited. The sexual tension that had been floating around the previous days was so thick, it could be tapped into a coconut shell and served with a festive parasol. One slight hitch: neither of them had much experience in making the first move. Nate found himself in an awkward dilemma. *'Do I tell him "I like you a lot" or "I want you here now"? What if the words come out all tacky!... Argh! Why is speech so defective?'*

~"Aye. Defective is right. It's got that in common with most of the rest stop toilets we've encountered so far."~

'You're not helping!'

Brent looked up from his guitar. He sensed that Nate had gone awfully quiet. "You okay?"

"Yes... So, what's that you're playing?" Nate managed at last.

"This? It's a song I wrote a long time ago, called *Stuff.* I was someone else back then. But, like my aunt Tulip Sprinkles used to say: *Writing music is like home-grown therapy. It's cost-effective and it keeps you off the moonshine whiskey.*

"Aunt... Sprinkles?"

"Yes, aunt Tulip Sprinkles is her name. She manages a butterfly conservatory. You want to hear me play the song?"

"Absolutely."

And Brent started singing in a subdued but clear voice. Gently he caressed the strings with a few simple chords. Magnificent. Brutally honest. It was a melody drenched in misery, but sung by its survivor looking back and affectionately forgiving himself. It was inspiring to witness that Brent's purpose in life was to become a singer-songwriter. A strong wave of empathy rushed over Nate. He was baffled. Chills were running up and down his spine. The only thing that Nate could come up with when the last note dies out was... "I am entrails."

"You are entrails?"

~"You can go ahead and just kick yourself, Nate."~

Nate had meant to say *enthralled.* His face flared up red. For once it was Brent who raised an eyebrow. Fortunately at this moment Destiny stepped in, bleating *Right! This coy silliness has gone on long enough* and caused Nate to trip over one of his dumbbells and right into Brent's arms. Brent interpreted this as a first move and gladly obliged by pressing his delicious lips against Nate's. The jacket came off, and then his T-shirt. The tattooed angel wings flexed as the muscles underneath tensed up and then relaxed. Tiny sweat pearls glistened on his smooth back. Nate wrestled himself out of his shirt and shoes and socks. His muscular arms and six-pack were thrown into the battle. They frolicked on the sofa. Skin on skin. Two hotties making out. Sparks were flying. Their scents were melting into one sexy fragrance. All was lust and instinct and fuzzy cute love. Nothing else mattered. Even Jarrrvis had stopped giving pointers. Slowly, like defusing a bomb, Nate unbuttoned Brent's jeans. The trailer windows were steaming up. Teasingly, Brent let his lips travel from Nate's shoulder to the ear, leaving a trail of love bites along the way.

'*This is perfect. I'm drifting into heaven,*' Nate thought. '*I'm as horny as a hoot owl*' and with his beak he pecked hard in Brent's flesh.

"*YAARG!*" Brent screamed in pain. "What are you doing?"

The purple blotches in front of Nate's eyes evaporated. He was back in the room. "Huh? I am so, so sorry! I don't know what came over me," he apologized, thinking '*Strange, I imagined having a beak there for a moment.*'

He ruffled his feathers. Which was even odder. He didn't have any.

"Are you feeling okay?" Brent asked.

"Mhh? Oh, yeah sure. I'm fine. Obviously it's been a long day. I guess I'm exhausted."

"Look, if you just want to go to sleep, I... understand."

"What? No, no. I could not possibly want you more." There, he'd said it. He was radiating happiness. In response, Brent ran a hand gently through Nate's hair. "And I wouldn't want to be with anybody else but you either."

Nate tilted his head and closed his eyes again. He moved in, with his lips curled, waiting to be kissed. They ended up colliding their noses into each other's eye. A confusion of noses, cheekbones and eyebrows followed. Brent chuckled.

'His mouth really fits perfectly around his infectious smile.' Nate mused and when he looked away he realized that his head had turned around one hundred and eighty degrees. He was flying over the treetops of a forest in the nighttime. A sudden craving for raw mouse overpowered his senses. He blinked.

"Sorry, what just happened?"

"Our noses bumped, that's all," Brent said. "Those are the casualties of love, I guess."

Disoriented, Nate tried to focus on Brent's lips–Surely, they were the most addictive lips on earth–but weird, violent flashes were now bombarding his brain: gun blasts, pools of blood, hostile trees with razor-sharp treetops and the sensation of being in mortal peril... His wounded wings were a blur in the black of night... The cold wind cut mercilessly into his flesh...

He looked to one side. Two other owls were accompanying him. They, too, were shooting through the air on a matter of life and death. One of the owls shouted "We must reach the lighthouse and find a way across the ocean! We must. If we land, we are dead!"

He looked down. There, on the forest floor, hundreds of rabbits were giving chase... Their horrific, red eyes betraying their single thought: Kill.

"What the hell is happening to me?"

From a distance he heard Brent say "Uhm, Nate? Is this your first time? Don't worry. No need to panic. It's fine."

The images abruptly stopped. Nate was back in the trailer, alone with a Brent in the buff. Outside, a clear moon was dispersing soft light over the hills, and in the fields the crickets were still scraping their hind legs like a mutual bad itch.

Nate liked to think of himself as a romantic and he would normally find this scene highly idyllic, but tonight he wasn't entirely with it. "Panic? Why would I panic?... Excuse me for a sec. I need to, uh, check if I've combed my hair."

"By all means, certainly," Brent said visibly disappointed.

With half a step, Nate was inside the compact bathroom. He closed the sliding door and splashed water in his face. The last of what remained of his arousal was drained out with the sink water. "What the heck was that? I think I'm flipping out!" he ranted at the mirror, more for himself than for Jarrrvis's sake, who could hear his inner thoughts. "This is crazy!"

~"Getting cold feet? Still a little wet behind the ears? I must say, Cap'n, you look absolutely gutted."~

"This really is not the time for witty banter! You know something about this?"

~"Well, let's see. There's the birds and the bees. And something about cross-pollination... My old man gave me *the talk* three hundred years ago, so I'm a bit rusty on the details. Although, if given the chance, I'm sure I'd still know exactly how to *waggle my bobber*, if you know what I mean. Heheh."~

"I am not asking about the facts of life! What's with this freaking owl stuff? I could feel everything and smell and see everything. Like a nightmare, but hyperreal. What the hell was that? If you know anything about it, I want a straight answer!"

~"Oh, isn't it obvious? You were experiencing a vision."~

"What do you mean?"

~"It was a vision."~

"Explain!"

~"Mister Nate sees pretty pictures inside his noggin."~ Jarrrvis tried again.

Nate could swear the ghost voice was actually enjoying this.

His companion was positively gloating. ~"Aye, a vision. Either that or you ate gone-off shrimp."~

Meanwhile, outside, Spatula sat on the trailer roof and listened in on Nate's monologue through a vent. The little *Furball of Fury* twitched its tail–An indicator that it was paying close attention. Also, it kept its ears keenly perked up while only half-heartedly licking its groin.

Inside the trailer, Brent, too, was being very still so he could hear Nate through the thin, plastic wall.
"Are you deliberately holding something back?"
...
"Don't try that on me!"
...
"I demand you give me something firm I can work with."
...
Brent nodded to himself as if to say *I understand. He must be rousing the troops, so to speak. To charge over the hill.*
...
"If you keep this up, I'm coming in and dragging you out myself!"
...
Brent nodded again. *Been there. The first time is always a bit stressful.*
...
"Tell me, am I man or fowl? I don't know anymore!"
...
"And where do the army of rabbits come in?"
...
"Not what I call cute bunnies, no!"
...
Brent's eyes widened to the size of rattling maracas. Quickly

he pressed his ear flat against the wall. He shifted his body, obviously feeling very naked and exposed all of a sudden.

...

"Bloodthirsty, ravenous creatures. Do you find that sexy?"

...

Brent had always considered himself to be a laid-back, open-minded kind of guy, but clearly not every scene he felt comfortable in. "Uh, look, Nate," he said to the wall. "I like you a lot, but tonight could we maybe just go to sleep?"

...

"How would you like it if you had feathers on your ass?"

...

Brent jumped up and headed for the nearest exit.

Inside the bathroom, Nate saw his mirror image haze over. Purple. Everything became purple. The haunting visions were coming back. Nate went under...

...

I find myself standing on floorboards soaked in dark-brownish red. No matter where I turn my head, it's everywhere: blood. Sticky, nauseating blood. My wounded wings keep stinging terribly; my heart is pumping in overdrive. It must be going over four hundred beats per minute. The owl on my left, the fat one, coughs up a pellet, noisily and with considerable effort. It's stress at a critical level. The bird is rocking its body out of fear. Always rocking. He never stops.

The other one on my right–the owl wearing the military epaulets–is the leader of the three of us. He is pacing back and forth, trying to think up a plan fast. Although heavily wounded by a round bullet, the owl still clings on to life, fuelled solely by hatred.

Who am I? Man or bird? Or both? Somehow that is irrelevant. All I can think about is that this is the end. The three of us have barricaded ourselves in an old lighthouse on the edge of an ocean cliff and we are going to die.

"Hell's maw is about to devour us hair and teeth and all!" I condemn my comrades in arms. "All the sins, all the murders we have committed for our country. Today is our ruin. Today we pay the piper!"

On these words of doom, the fat one upchucks another slimy pellet. "Sauvetyne!" the owl leader bellows at him. "Stop that. You are a soldier! Soldiers have the stomach of an iron barrel. Blood nor gore shall dismay a member of the Barn Owl Army!"

"Yes, Voegant. Blood nor gore shall dismay," Sauvetyne stammers, the pangs of death very much upon him. "Forgive my cowardice, brother."

"And you, Pilchett," the blood-soaked leader called Voegant commands me. "Stop fretting and be worthy of your stripes. No driveling. No praying. No pleading for mercy. We have a war on, not a tea party... Go check at the window to see if the enemy is approaching. That is an order."

"Yes, Sir!"

I half walk, half hop over to the oval window, the only one at the top of the lighthouse with a view of the forest. The wind is holding the tower in a tight grip, blowing on it as if it's a colossal flute, creating eerie whoosh sounds and making the wooden rafters creak.

"Well? How many do you see? Before I croak I want to know who turned up to do us in."

"Owls don't croak, they screech."

"Shut up, Sauvetyne!"

"Sorry. It's nerves. I can't, can't keep myself from, I feel sick. I just–"

"Stop that gibberish!"

Carefully I look down the tower. Below, hundreds of armed animals have gathered. Not only the rabbits, but other species too. Within a second, several salvoes of hot lead come screaming through the air, missing my head by an inch. The window frame splinters and showers me with nasty woodchips and glass projectiles.

"It's the Rabbitskins," I shriek in alarm. "I recognize the uniforms. And a battalion of stinking Frogs! They are positioned on the northern flank, under the trees. They have long rifles. And, way in the back, I see Blue Partridges!"

"Blast it!" Voegant thunders, while dabbling in his own red puddle. "I don't believe it! Those armies are at war with one another. So why are they not at each other's throats?"

At this point a sneering voice from below reaches our feathered ears. "Butchers of Belony, listen to my call. We have you completely surrounded. Step outside the lighthouse, please. Slowly. And keep your wings to the ground. In single file, if possible. Jolly good."

Voegant's heart-shaped face turns red with pent-up rage. That mocking, infuriating voice can only originate from one man. The Barn Owl's archenemy. "Colonel Taytelly!"

"Captain Voegant. This is Colonel Taytelly reporting for duty. Surprised to see me? I bet you do. You left me for dead on the battlefields of Stroke-on-Piff, but I can assure you, I have a good deal of strength in me yet to kill you… and then possibly drown you if I feel like it. Basically whatever suits my fancy."

Voegant, Sauvetyne and I peek through the broken window. And there he is on the clearing in front of the lighthouse. He looks battered. One of his legs is missing, which might account for the bandages round his hips. The uniform no longer looks white and parts of the sleeves show scorch marks.

His erect rabbit ears are defying the gale. And then I spot those two upper incisors, sticking out like overconfident snake fangs, irritating the hell out of me.

"You should be flattered, you know," Taytelly shouts triumphantly. "Not every day sworn enemies put aside their differences–for a limited time only of course–to hunt down three of the most detested war criminals. It takes a special kind of hatred, yes, smoldering, festering hatred against you, the Ravagers of Quint-Pelvix and Blipstone, to bring about such an armistice–a temporary one at that. Hundreds of us have united in these woods and we all have our pistols out."

Throughout the Colonel's pompous tirade the impact of his words are somewhat spoiled by the comical appearance of his perky button nose. It wiggles up and down in delighted frivolity like all rabbit noses do when showing excitement.

"So this is how it is all going to go down, is it?" Voegant spits, a darkness shrouding his face. "Pilchett," he shouts at me. "Our army has indeed pilfered and slain many villagers to earn those titles. And good fun it was, wasn't it?"

"Yes," I reply. I am petrified now, but I know that it most certainly was good fun.

"And Sauvetyne, tell me. Did we not enjoy engaging in battle near Flipmoor and Ipstonk?"

"Of course, Voegant," Sauvetyne replies in a quivering voice. "We fought hard and won, and then we reaped the rewards."

"This is a sign, my brethren. Once we were but three stupid sons of a turnip farmer. Turnips were all we knew! We ate turnips morning, noon and night. Then the call came to defend our country. We joined the glorious Barn Owls and got our hands red. And I worked my way up the chain of command, didn't I?... What I'm saying is, everything we have seen, everything we have done, we did because it was meant to be. And now that we are trapped in this lighthouse it is time to take the next step–"

A spark of hope still?

"–to die!"

Sauvetyne turns green in the face. A vat of chills rolls over me. "What do you mean?" I yell at him, almost choking on the anger in my words. "I thought you said we had a chance of survival if we could reach the cliffs and the ocean!"

"Remember your place, soldier. I am still your superior! Yes! We will come out victorious. But I did not say we would stay alive! Not the way you think anyway." And then a creepy laugh bursts out of his beak, the laugh of a madman, well, mad nocturnal bird.

The voice from outside is back. "Surrender now and we promise you, you will get a proper military trial. I've just had a quick chat with the other commanders. Opinions, strategies and carrots were shared, and everybody now agrees death by firing squad would be most convenient and satisfactory for all. So be good chaps and come down."

"No thanks, we're good," is our reply from the besieged tower. "But thank you for asking."

This is not the response Taytelly was expecting. Agitated he hops around on the one leg, momentarily distracted by the discovery of a fresh, tasty leaf, then back concentrating on the lighthouse. "Burn it down to the ground!" the Colonel shouts at his soldiers. He is through with waiting. Many cheers fill the forest, and torches are lit to set the base of the lighthouse on fire. Within minutes fiery teeth are biting their way to the top.

In the course of those few minutes, our leader and eldest brother has explained his plan to us. It involves a rather eclectic, dark ritual.

"Don't step inside the triangle yet," we warns. "Do exactly as I say, word for word, or dammit, I swear I will kick you so hard in the back, you'll choke on your own spleen!"

"Do owls have spleens?" I ask.

"Silence!"

119

The flames have already reached our hideout. We are trapped. No escape! Dark smoke is rising up out of the cracks in the floor. *Burned alive. I'm going to be burned alive* is all that is going through my mind. Endless gallons of ocean water pounding away at the cliff wall, but none to extinguish the fire. How barbarously ironic. I'm losing my mind. "Hooh, I'm at Death's door! The pain! I won't stand the terrible pain! Help me, please, someone!"

"Concentrate, Pilchett!" Voegant reacts, not taking his eyes off what he's doing.

"We're going... to make a blood... pact?" Sauvetyne stutters.

"Blood-pact?" Voegant roars. "No, this ritual will take us far beyond petty flesh and bones. We will strike a pact bargaining with our very souls!"

I'm paralyzed with fear. "So we sell ours to the devil then?"

That wild expression is holding Voegant's face hostage again. "Selling our souls to that guy? No, Pilchett. In comparison, the devil is a milksop!"

And then my world is swallowed in a blaze of purple fire...

...

Nate had a splitting headache, a purple-colored one. Still dazed, he stumbled out of the tiny bathroom and discovered that the trailer door was flung wide-open. Brent had fled.

The storm overhead finally broke, and for the next forty-two hours it would reign over the valley.

14. Sorrow

Nate was consumed with sorrow. The only thing of Brent that remained, was one hurriedly penned-down note.

Sorry. I don't think this is going to work out. We want different things, I suppose.

I must admit this is hard on me because I really thought we had something here. Thought we might be soulmates even. Can you believe it? That was just me being a fool. I see now I was wrong. And I always follow my intuition.

I'm hitching a ride with Jilly the park owner, so don't worry about me. Thanks for everything and have a great life. You are a cool guy. Maybe I'll see you around some time. Bye.

- Brent

Brent's departure left an emptiness so large, it caught Nate by surprise. In the days that followed, Atlantean waves of loss and loneliness were crashing on the shore of his mind. "We want different things," Nate kept murmuring. "That's what he wrote. We want different things." He was inconsolable. He just couldn't help it. All his aches, all his memories of past relationships gone bad were surfacing in one continuous stream of tears. *'Brent is not coming back...'*

The rain, too, kept coming down heavily, forcing the travelers to stay put in the valley. Nate didn't care. He lay on the sofa bed, in total darkness. He crawled up in the fetal position with no intention of doing anything ever again.

Someone knocked and opened the door. The sounds of the storm rushed in.

"Nate?" the someone inquired.

No reply.

In the dark, a nose was being blown. Blowing it seemed to involve half a box of tissues.

"Nate, may we enter?" Kean asked. "And perhaps turn on the light? Sharminella is here with me. You promised her you'd braid her hair this evening. She could also use help practicing her pageant skills… We'd really appreciate it if we could come in. It's pelting with rain. We're getting muddy and drenched. My umbrella is getting wrecked."

"Yeah–sniff–come in," a hoarse voice answered.

"I'll bring some instant cauliflower soup later… It's okay, Sharminella, step inside… What?... There's no reason to be afraid." Some hushed negotiations passed between Kean and Sharminella and then there was a noise exactly like that of someone being pushed inside against her will and of a door closing behind her.

Hesitantly, Sharminella sat down on her beauty case and used the hand of her Wanton Booboo doll to flip the light switch… "*Eek!*"

Nate's eyes were swollen. His face had drooped like a wet sand castle. He made a half-hearted attempt to dry his tears and flatten his hair so as not to scare her witless. She had never seen him like this. To her, he looked like frog sick.

"You look like frog sick."

"I'm fine," Nate said with fabricated cheerfulness. "What do you say we go for some over-the-top glamorous bangs?"

"*Yaaaay!*"

"You grab the hair glue.–sniff–I'll plug in the industrial trouser press."

She rummaged through her beauty case.

"Hey, wait a second, Sharmy. Where did you get this?"

Something silvery round her neck twinkled like a mirror ball. Nate instantly recognized it.

"Hoh, this? Spatula gave it to me. I was home, mm, sleeping

in bed and he dropped it from the *air ditty-oinking gent.–*"

~"Air conditioning vent. Is she even trying to pronounce it?"~

"–It's *soooo* beautiful. And it has a, mm, funny dude. See?"

"Funny dude?"

Her delicate hand held up the barn owl locket with the soldier's portrait inside, the same locket that the crazy old woman had presented to him two weeks ago.

'*She must have left it in the apartment and the kitty found it.*'

Two weeks… It seemed a century. The things that that lunatic Sauvetyne had told him were now smacking him in the back of the head. ~"She did warn you not to get involved with the next gorgeous man to come around. How'd she phrase it? Aye, *his slick tongue and smoother body.* Well, I'll be damned. Guess she was right."~

"Are you okay, Nanny Nate?"

"Sorry… Yes–sniff–That locket was actually meant for me."

"Your neck is too ugly for it. I keep it. I keep it.

~"Take it from her. Now."~

Nate couldn't really muster the energy to make a thing out of something so trivial.

~"I think you should have it yourself."~

"You can keep it," he said to her. "It's yours."

"*Weally?*"

"Yes, *weally.*"

"*Weally weally?*"

"Yep, Sharminella. *Weally weally.*"

"*Weally weally weally weally weally weally weally?*"

Nate sighed.

"Yeah, *weally weally weally weally weally weally weally!*"

"*Yaaaay!* I give you a *smoochie-moochie.*" And she jumped up to lavish a hug on him.

"Okay. Settle down, Sharmy. We have to do your hair."

The whole procedure–including, but not limited to, finding a matching dress, spray-painting makeup on, accessorizing and applying lotions, powders and perfumes–took up the rest of the evening. Sharminella could tell that Nate's heart was not really into it.

He couldn't shake the thought that his one shot at a solid, loving relationship had been blown to bits by the freaky things that got chucked at him on a daily basis. Things like the cuckoo granny, the scary visions and the bear-sized amoeba called Poledoris. Why couldn't he simply be the likeable boy next-door, who led a normal life and had normal friends who behaved normally? Textbook normality. No such luck.

And, suddenly, there had been Brent... the answer to his prayers. And, just as sudden, Brent had left and everything was falling apart.

Under other circumstances, Jarrrvis would have commented on Nate's melodramatic flair, but–atypically–he kept silent. After all, his being an unsolicited inner critic could be misconstrued as being part of *all things freaky*. He'd risk getting heaped onto that pile, and then where would he be? No. The dead sailor, for once, played dead.

"bmb lrirm ldd."

"blurmp?"

"blwmz zbbns plf m!"

"I think it's safe to take the gas masks off, Sharminella," Nate sniffled. "The hair spray in the room is thinning out. What were you saying?"

"I'm hungry, Nanny Nate."

"You are always hungry," he said with a wan smile. "Have a look in the travel bag. I put a cheese bun in there. It's not as fresh as what you are used to, but it's still good."

"Yuck! It tastes like old slippers!"

"You haven't opened the bag! How can you even know? And

anyway, it's all there is. Life only hands out poisonous gifts."

"No, I hate *poiseanus!* I want lasagna. I want it now. *La-sa-gnaaa!*"

This was too much for Nate to bear. In tears he rushed into the bathroom and shut himself in. He had tried to stay strong, but he could conceal his grief no longer. All sluice gates swung open.

"I said lasagn–!" Sharminella stopped, confused. This was not how things usually went. She told him that. "This is not how it goes, Nate. How it goes is, I scream and pinch and, mm, stamp my foot and then we go buy what I want." But Nate wasn't listening. He was in anguish. The little girl didn't understand why he acted that way. She'd always thought that that kind of heartrending howling belonged to the realm of difficult children in toy stores. Lost in her confusion, she started crying too.

Kean entered with a tray of cauliflower soup. "What's happening here? Sharminella, why are you blubbering? Is that Nate in there?"

"Did I do some, mm, thing wrong?"

"It's not your fault. He's having a mental breakdown, that's all. His heart got broken, but it will heal, in time."

"He is *sooo* sad." And then a big thought popped into her head that was sure to set everything right. "When I am an *internatal supplemodel*, I buy a mommy and a daddy for Nate and they never leave him, mm, and the daddy cuddles and the mommy gives kisses and they all play all day with Wanton Booboo dolls, mm."

"That is a nice sentiment, Sharminella, but you are not a model yet. Now, I heard you screaming for lasagna. We have discussed this naughty behavior in our last coaching session, haven't we? Do you recall what I said about not being unruly? It would be sweet of you if you were a bit kinder to Nate. Do you promise to be sweet?"

"I promise."

"Promise who?"

"I promise, Sir."

"That's better. Good," the psychotherapist said. He liked taking full control of situations. "I'm going to have a talk with Nate now. He has got a bright future in front of him, Sharminella. Possibly one even more powerful than we can imagine. He can't be falling apart whenever a fly-by-night guy dumps him... Nate? Come out of there, please. Let's examine the facts."

"... no."

"You are experiencing bereavement. What you need is a good rest to counter the exhaustion. I bet you haven't slept at all."

Nate's body squirmed in protest. He was too tired to sleep, but being awake felt like torture. He gave in. Slowly he came out and assumed a horizontal position on the sofa bed, for the look of the thing.

"Listen, Nate, the quicker you get passed this, the better. I took the liberty of answering your calls on your behalf. The Audit Department at your company ZPMQZ requested a status report. I fibbed and said that your travels to Pinglop are taking longer due to an unexpected spell of bad weather. They connected me through to several departments and eventually I got the CEO on the line who told me to tell you to *toe the line*. Then followed an uncomfortably long pause of dead air, so I hung up."

Judging by the groans emanating from the bed, Kean gathered that that might not have been the right course of action. So he quickly added in a cheery voice "But forget about work and audits and bread on the table and everything else for now. Try to rest a bit, okay?"

Sharminella had her own ideas on what grownups must do when they have been struck by unrequited love. "Nanny Nate falled on his kissy lips and now he is sick and has to, mm, wear a high black hat and never-ever-ever smile and must dig deep holes in the ground, mm, to bury dead people in and make a big mountain of money. But who is going to tie my shoes?"

"Nate will be fine, Sharminella. And you're wearing high heels that don't have laces, so that's sorted. Be a dear and take one tablet out of that little box there and dissolve it in a glass of water."

"Yes, Sir."

If Nate's mind hadn't been elsewhere at the time, he would've been in awe of how effortlessly Kean had Sharminella do what he wanted. As instructed she opened the overhead compartment where the glasses were stored. Of course, Kean first had to help her reach by lifting her up. Sharminella then offered Nate the medicine tablet in an empty glass. No good. So, after Kean explained how to run water from the tap, she proudly walked up to her Nanny, carefully balancing the glass of fizzy liquid. Her tiny hands only spilled a third of it on the way. For the six-year-old a simple task could quickly turn into an epic odyssey. "Thank you–sniff–Princess." Nate drank the lemon-flavored medicine and instantly he sank into a long, dreamless sleep.

"*EEEEE!*"

Nate was brutally awoken.

"What's happening!?"

Bonk!

He banged his head hard against an overhanging shelf. There was panic around him. Sharminella stood on the bed, screaming her lungs out. Her runny nose was out of control, erupting with excessive bubbles of snot. Poledoris and Kean were crammed together in the kitchenette. The trailer was rocking and water gushed in from under the door.

"It's been raining nonstop! The valley can no longer process the excess water," Kean said to bring Nate up to speed. "Our plight has become precarious."

Nate shot a look out of the window. All his love troubles were temporarily forgotten. "The whole valley is flooded!"

"Precisely."

~"I may only be a whale-hunter, but going by that water coming round the hill, I bet there's a nearby river overflowing and this lunchbox is going to get hit and flushed downstream any second from now!"~

"*EEEEE!*" Sharminella contributed.

Exactly one second later the predicted flood started wreaking havoc on the trailers, dumpsters, fences, lamp-posts. Basically everything in its way.

~"Hold on tight!"~

"*M'iw-m'iw-m'iw!*"

"Spatula!"

To Nate's dismay, he spotted Sharminella's sidekick outside, on a branch in the water. It was hiding under a large leaf and meowing in despair. Without thinking twice, Nate pushed open the door. More water rushed in, carrying the strong smell of river.

"What the blazes are you doing?" Kean gnarled. "Close that door!"

~"It's only an animal. Just leave it!"~

"Got to save the kitty!... Look! There's a tangle of tree branches underneath us. The trailer is caught in it. Maybe if I walk carefully on those I can fetch Spatula."

"Ooh, please Nate, save my Spatty!" Sharminella pleaded through hyperventilated breaths.

~"Stop, you nincompoop! If your foot skids, you'll get stuck, or worse, you get pulled down in the undertow and we'll drown!"~

"Damn! Hadn't thought of that!"

Kean raised an eyebrow. "I didn't say anything. Thought of what?"

"Oh. Uhm. The water looks treacherous. Walking over to the kitten is too dangerous."

Another wail erupted. Nothing much on earth is sadder than a cat wailing. He had no more dry space to move around in. The downpour was not helping either.

"*Waaaaa!* Nate do something! I promise I am a good girl forever and ever and ever if you save kitty!" Sharminella howled. Trails of mascara were running a race to reach her trembling chin.

"We need an impromptu fishing net of some kind and a long stick," Kean suggested.

"He's more than three yards away. That'll never work. Think, people, think!" Nate urged.

~"Quickly! The water level is rising!"~

'*What can I do? I'll never forgive myself if I can't save Spatula and it breaks her heart!*'

Nate felt utterly powerless. He looked at Poledoris, who was oblivious to the unfolding drama, of course. The man still occupied the kitchenette and was poking a finger in his eye. "Mayonnaise anyone?" he blurted out.

"You think Poledoris might float like a life raft?" Nate said maddened. "He is bloated enough."

It did not seem possible, but a new cloudburst rendered visibility to practically zero. Another woebegone wail erupted from the kitten, marooned as it was in the middle of the deluge.

"Hey. Here's an idea," Nate said brainstorming out loud. "Can't we lure the animal with something? The branches should be sufficiently steady to carry his weight. We can't run across, but he can!"

"Right!"

In a frenzy they ransacked the cabinets and drawers for

anything that might interest a puss in distress. A book of cards, a pair of dungarees, a moustache comb… They found all sorts of things left by previous vacationers.

"Nothing! I can't believe this trailer is packed with junk. How many tea cozies do people need!" Nate yelled in exasperation.

"*Waaaaa!* Save kitty!"

"I think I've found something!" This came from Kean. "A length of fishing wire, but no hook, I'm afraid."

~"That's of no use! Can't angle him out of the water. Cats have no lips to speak of!"~

"Just keep searching!"

Nate went through his sports utility bag. It was soaked. "Crap! Everything in here is crap!" The egg timer and the tin of itching powder were still as useless as the day they were given to him by the CEO. Nate stuffed them in his pocket. Then he saw the third gift, the rubber duck. "Yes! Yes! We can work with this!" In a blur he fastened the fishing wire to the duck and threw it out in Spatula's direction.

The kitten's eyes immediately focused on the strange canary, tempting its hunting instincts. Nate had guessed right. The creature was so savage it would even attack a prey in the middle of a catastrophe. And fat yellow birds had always been his favorite.

"Quickly now. Jump!" Nate muttered. "Just jump!"

"Come on, *kitty-boo!* Move your, mm, butt!"

~"He's not doing it! His breed is not very fond of water by nature."~

But Jarrrvis was wrong. Just as Spatula pounced on the duck, Nate pulled in the wire. Spatula jumped again, onto the closer tree branch, and again. Within seconds Spatula was back in Sharminella's arms. "Shut the door!" Kean instructed Nate. The cold water had already reached his knee, and more was on the way. In fact, the embankment higher up chose that moment to collapse under the pressure, causing a new billow of river water to come rolling down with speed. The rickety trailers took the hit and got thrust farther into the valley.

"Grab hold of something!" Nate shouted. He was fearing the worst. (Everyone did so, except Poledoris, who sloshed about and stuck his tongue out. A mosquito landed on it.) "Look, over there! That's the parking lot, and my car. The water hasn't reached the plain yet!"

"What about it?"

"Kean, we can make an escape! We'll swim to my car!"

"Are you delirious? What if tree trunks bump into us? What if the trailer does?"

"Come on! It can't be more than twenty yards. Swimming is our only chance!"

"Is it?! The pull of the water–"

"You'd rather stay in this deathtrap? Listen, we have to risk it. There is no other way!"

Kean couldn't bring anything up against that. He nodded.

Nate now directed his attention to the scared little girl still clutching her arms around Spatula and her doll. Nate wanted to protect her. He loved her dearly. The thought surprised him. He squatted down to be on her eye level and gave her a real hug. It was something that had been long overdue. Next to them, a cavalcade of plastic teacups were bobbing merrily along.

~"Could we hurry up maybe, Mr. Noodascue?"~

"Sharminella, you promised to be good, so listen carefully. I want you to sit on my back. I'm going to swim out and you cling on the whole way like the time I was on my hands and knees cleaning the apartment and you commandeered my body and made me piggyback you to the nearest store. Remember? So you hold on tight just like then, never let go! This is very important. You swear to hold on?"

A timid "yes" was whispered through the veil of wet golden

curls.

"Good, that's settled. Kean, you take Spatula, okay?"

"Okay."

Spatula welcomed Kean gesture with a vicious scratch and a *grrralllw*.

"Damn thing hates me!"

Nate picked the kitten up. "I suppose I'll have to take him then."

"And Bubby, you can sit, mm, in my neck," Sharminella said sternly to her doll. "But keep still and be good."

~"Hurry!"~

"I want to swim to shore."

This unexpected life sign from Poledoris caught everyone off guard. Spatula leaped up at him and nestled itself in the man's toupee. The trailer suddenly lurched and tipped over. "*HOLD ON!*" Everyone and everything inside the trailer got thrown about like the contents of a washing machine.

~"We're capsizing! Abandon ship!"~

The exit door was now on the ceiling. Poledoris ripped it out of its hinges. The clattering rain immediately showered him.

Nate was relieved that somewhere inside that balloon head and ample neck flab some sort of fail-safe mechanism of self-preservation had been set in motion. Neither Nate nor Kean could have carried Poledoris across on their backs.

"Would you believe, he has some sense in him after all," Kean said. "Wasn't sure he was even viable to live! I'm contemplating writing a treatise on him for a medical journal. I'll call it *The stillborn grown man.*"

"Contemplate later! We need to get out of here, Kean. Everyone, quickly, climb through the hole. Go!"

Outside, the roar of water was deafening. What had once been a peaceful, grassy field had turned into a seething river of horror. Poledoris dove off and landed belly first in the water, with the kitten's sharp claws embedded into his eyebrows. The others followed sliding down the side of the trailer. "Three... two... one!"

"*EEEEE!*"

"You're doing great. Now, *HOLD TIGHT!*"

They dove in.

Swimming was rough–instantly–from stroke one. Due to the swaying surface and the rain, they didn't know what was up and what was down. And every few seconds something underwater bumped into them. The currents were strong and kept tugging them off course. Nate looked over his shoulder. The trailer had already disappeared from view.

~"Watch your starboard."~

'*What's that?*'

~"*YOUR RIGHT SIDE!*"~

'*Say that then! I'm nearly drowning here.*'

~"Where are lifesaving dolphins when you need them?"~

"The water is cold and a lot of, mm, mud and I'm scared!"

"Me too, Sharminella," Nate said. He was gasping for breath. "Keep holding on to me. You're doing great."

His body temperature was in free-fall and every muscle hurt like a dog bite, but he had to keep swimming. There was no other option.

~"Unbelievable, it does float!"~

'*What are you talking about? It?*'

Poledoris came up alongside Nate, kicking his short legs in a rapid, comical manner. His one eye was fixated on the parking lot, while the other, more aberrant eye kept scanning the sky for... for who-knows-what? Nate had other pressing matters to attend to.

Spatula sat on the man's head. If Nate didn't know any better, he would think that the kitten was giving navigational instructions, by swerving the tip of his tail alternately against

Poledoris's left and right ear.

"Kean? Can you hear me?... How are you holding up?"

"I'm managing."

Out of the three swimmers, Kean struggled the most. He was gulping down mouthfuls of the filthy water and regretted every drop. Mercifully, after several long minutes they reached the parking lot. Apart from some large puddles, it was still unaffected by the ravage going on around it. In the distance Nate's trailer crashed into something under the water and it sank with an understated *blop*. To add insult to injury, the rain stopped the moment the castaways dragged themselves onto land. The clouds opened up and revealed blue skies above.

~"That's irony for you."~

"We made it!" Nate wheezed. "Why would anyone set up a business in a damn flood zone? We could have died!"

~"Steady, steady. No need to lose your head."~

Soaked to the bone and shivering they got into the car. Most of their belongings were lost on the bottom of the river at the end of civilization.

Before Nate drove out the gate of what used to be a trailer park paradise, he made a point of backing the car up and dropping the trailer keys into the mailbox as instructed. Ten minutes later that mailbox was going to become the luxury home of a family of crabs, but that was not important to him. It was the principle of the matter.

He had survived his first brush with death, but it was pointless. Someone in Pinglop was making his deathbed with very unusual bedsheets…

15. Pinglop

"Well? Where the hell is it then?" Nate demanded.

It was a new day and the road had come to a dead end in the middle of a dense forest. A mountain of rock and trees obstructed their view.

"According to the map, we should be standing in Pinglop right now. I don't understand it. This is most peculiar," Kean said and readjusted his pink tights. The clothes that he had worn were wet through, so the choice was either wear the super-stretch tights out of Sharminella's only remaining suitcase or fall victim to hypothermia. Of course, on him the tights looked more like breeches that left nothing to the imagination. To protect his upper body from the elements, he had poked holes in some plastic bags and put the bags on in layers. Sadly none of Sharminella's footwear fit, so he was stuck with his own shoes and the squishy noises they made when he moved.

Nate rigorously scratched the stubble on his chin. He used both hands, in the same way a hamster washes its head... A telltale sign that lunacy was not far off.

He, too, wore multicolored tights, and a flashy blanket with sleeves that, on him, more closely resembled a hallucinogenic straitjacket. A green-and-gold sling bag completed the ensemble.

"Hold on, Kean. Hold on a minute! Are you telling me that I drove thousands of miles and put up with heartache, floods, the constant foul odor of Poledoris and pigs and then, when Pinglop comes within reach, the road *just stops dead!?* And we're all standing here dressed like morons and all you have to say about this disaster is *This is most peculiar?*... Ack! I'm so angry I could puke!"

~"Temper. It's not Kean's fault."~

'*And you shut up!*'

"I did not mean to patronize you," the psychotherapist brought up in his defense. "What I am saying is, there's bound to be an explanation."

"Huh! *Bound to be an explanation*," Nate raved on. On some level he knew he was being totally horrid, but exhaustion and anger were running the show. "This is all a bad dream... these past two weeks! This whole trip is ridiculous and I am *FED UP WITH IT!*"

~"You are out of your wits! Stop making a spectacle of yourself, Nate. No-one's amused."~

"After all I've been through, I'm not leaving till someone produces Pinglop. Come on, everyone, turn out your pockets!"

"Your behavior is inappropriate."

"I said, turn out your pockets!"

"You're clearly overstressed by this setback. Come to your senses!"

"*WHERE IS PINGLOP?*"

"Nanny Nate, you make me afraid... again," Sharminella mumbled. She was clutching Bubby to her chest.

"Right!" Kean intervened. "Mr. Poledoris, your assistance is required, please. We're going to have to use *persuasion*."

The car door swung open and the brute got out.

~"The unthinkable!"~

"*LEAVE ME ALONE!*"

Nate was determined to stand his ground, no matter how intimidated he felt by the morbidly obese man (aka Dr. Brainzipper aka *That Huge Pig Bladder On Legs)*, who was waddling straight at him with foreboding momentum.

The fact that Poledoris happened to be squeezed inside girl tights, a pair of tiny stiletto heels (with his fat toes sticking out on both sides), a poncho and a tutu (on a strategic place) only added to Nate's terror.

~"The one time the man decides to actually do what he's been told and it's to crush you."~

"Listen to reason," Kean continued. "You're in a state of psychosis. I really need you to calm down and visit your quiet place now. We intend to take you there, by force if necessary."

Nate dodged the snatching arms and escaped Kean's quick tackle attempt. He zigzagged between the trees and ran up to the rock face at the foot of the mountain.

"Show me this fabled city of wonder that is apparently so important to the corporate world that they have sacrificed my sanity for it!–"

~"Nate, you've lost the plot, man. Listen to Kean."~

"–I bet there's a secret gateway in the mountain that opens with a password, and a tunnel leading to an underground utopia inhabited by naff wood nymphs and salt-free accountants!"

~"You've lost it. You truly have."~

"Open up, mountain! I command thee!"

A startling thunderclap tore open the sky.

That was unexpected.

Encouraged by this, Nate shouted from the top of his voice "I compel thee into submission! Set wide thy doors–"

Several thunderclaps responded in botheration. And the wind picked up fiercely. Nate found himself caught in a battle of wills. His will against the boundless forces of nature. Everyone was very impressed. (Everyone except Poledoris who hadn't eaten anything edible within living memory and whose protesting stomach had become so unruly it produced the crashing sounds that they heard.)

"BY MY WORD THOU SHALT OBEY!"

The next seven seconds Nate just stood there, arms raised. A passing robin dropped a souvenir on his shoulder.

~"Bombs away! Hahahah!"~

'Oh, hilarity! How nice that my wretched life is so entertaining to you!'

~"Hey, you brought this one on yourself with that *Thou shalt obey* nonsense."~

Nate needed a few moments to let the anger cloud subside. He was well-aware that he wasn't handling things in the best way possible... The fact was, he realized, that the more easygoing, upbeat Nate of a year ago would probably see the humor in the situation and would laugh too.

"Okay, people, guess I got my comeuppance," he said sheepishly. "Sorry."

"Apology accepted."

Kean proffered a mild tranquilizer that Nate declined with a shake of the head. "Clearly Pinglop isn't here, Nate. How do you propose we proceed?–"

The sound of a hinge moving interrupted their conversation...

"–You hear that?"

"*Spatula-la-la*, where do you go?" Sharminella ran after her kitten, who had gone into some large bushes. "Nanny, come see!" she hollered.

Her pet had discovered a wishing well overgrown with ivy. The structure was in a terrible state. The bricks around the pit were mostly broken but the shingles on the roof were still intact. And hanging underneath, instead of a bucket on a rope, there was a large copper bell. Every time a gust of wind traveled through, the support beam creaked under the strain, creating the hinge noise. She picked up a wooden sign that was half-hidden in the soil. "Look. I finded something. It says *Pi... Pi... Pinglop inf...ormat...ion stall.*"

"Hah! See? I told you! I'll just press a buzzer and some steward will come show us the way into the mountain."

"Exactly how do you intend to do that? There is no buzzer or doorbell."

"Well, it's obvious, isn't it?" Nate argued. "Maybe the steward lives a long way off, but here is a big bell that makes a big sound. All we have to do is take the clapper and swing it." He swung the clapper against the inside rim, and a long, penetrating *ABOOONG* chime filled the forest.

"Everyone down to the ground!" Nate yelled suddenly. A colony of bewildered bats flew out of the bell. Sharminella screamed in horror. The bats hurled themselves smack in the face of Poledoris. (Apparently, they were unable to register him on their sensory radar.) Luckily, the bats had no intention of sticking around and they quickly took off. "What the heck was that? Are you okay?"

Poledoris's incomprehensible reaction to getting a face full of bat was "Tuna me mucho" and nothing more.

No-one spoke for a second.

~"Well, at the very least he gets points for mentioning tuna."~

'*Give it a rest, will you?*'

~"Hey, lighten up. No need to carp at my input. Get it? Carp. It's also a fish."~

'*Yeah, yeah. I get it,*' Nate snarled at the inside of his brainpan.

It took a long time for the bell chime to die out. Uncharacteristically, when it finally did, it ended with a "...*OOONG*-arghl" expression of pain.

"Who said that?" Nate asked.

"I heard it too," Kean added.

"Me too," Sharminella joined in.

"Tuna," the Maelstrom of Madness imparted, and got ignored by everyone.

They looked around. The voice seemed to have come from somewhere close-by. Strangely enough–apart from the dispossessed bats in the distant skyline–they couldn't see anything or anyone moving. Eventually the party gathered around the wishing well and looked down the pit. Even Bubby the Wanton Booboo doll took a peek. A chilly darkness scowled up at them. It made everyone's hairs stand on end. The gaping hole had a threatening quality about it.

"Ahem!"

They all looked up. The clapper was moving. It was a head! In fact, the bald head belonged to a small person with androgynous features, pointy ears and a walrus overbite. He or she was wrapped in black cloth and hanging upside down.

"*EEEEEE!*" Sharminella was horrified and screamed louder than that time when her assistant had explained what income taxes were and that she was going to have to pay them.

~"It's hideous!"~

"*PINGLOP IS THAT WAY,*" the steward(ess) shouted at them. Living inside a bell seemed to have permanently damaged his or her hearing. Nate nearly jumped out of his skin.

"Oh, uh, I'm sorry about hitting you. I didn't know you were a clapper, uhm, I mean you are not a clapper, Sir... Ma'am... no... uhm... I uh..."

"*THE BACK ENTRANCE TO PINGLOP IS OVER THERE.*"

Nate looked at the rock face, expecting to see the doors of a grand gate unlock like in an epic medieval novel.

"*OVER THERE.*"

Then Nate spotted it. It took the eyes a few moments to adjust, but once he found the base of the stairs, the whole staircase was being pieced together in his brain. Carved out in stone, a large number of very solid steps wriggled their way to the top. The mountain looked somewhat like a humongous champagne cork covered in vegetation. Along the sloping edge of the plateau, a variety of buildings, towers, domes and beautiful houses were dotted in between farmland and woods. It was an awe-inspiring sight. Rays of golden sunlight were piercing the clouds and illuminating the entire city. Nate had never seen anything like it.

"Wooow!"

~"Amazing!"~

"Astonishing!"

"Meeeeow!"

"*Buuuuurp.*"

"*PINGLOP IS OVER THERE.*"

"Yes, thank you, si'ma'm... uh, thank you for your time! Ahh, have a nice day."

~"A nice weirdo day."~

Service provided, the *bell dweller* turned around and went back to sleep.

Nate regarded the huge stairs with dread. "It's going to be a long workout. Let's start climbing. Sharminella, come sit on my shoulders. The steps are too high for your little legs."

"M'kay," she said, glad to be away from the scary person suspended over the pit.

"With any luck we'll arrive before the sun goes under. I'll leave the car parked here. Poledoris, just follow us. Are you listening, Poledoris? Hey, hello?"

Nothing.

Nate sighed. "Kean, any suggestions on how we get him to walk up the steps?"

"I'm no expert, really."

"No, but he did change into dry clothes yesterday when you asked him... Eventually he did anyway."

~"Don't remind me. The nut job is a reckless flasher. Even the kitten was traumatized."~

"Maybe if we dangle the rubber ducky in front of him, would that work?"

This was Spatula's cue to jump out of Sharminella's arms and onto Poledoris's back, and then clamber up. The kitten started navigating him again. A brush of its tail against the left ear caused him to put his left leg forward, and the same went for the right side.

"Incredible... Well, I guess that's taken care of then. Okay, people, we're moving."

After two hours of physical exertion–panting, sweating, dying–the party reached the top, not knowing that all the time the steward(ess) had meant to point out the convenient elevator located behind some firs.

Pinglop was magnificent. It was a completely self-sustaining city. Proud, prosperous and elitist. It had a state of the art public transportation network, beautiful sunflower fields, a giant hill in the middle, an excessive love of coffee, novelty shops that sold junk, et cetera, et cetera. The city had it all, but everything was a bit *off*. The roads and sidewalks were too clean for comfort, for one. The architecture was quite different from what Nate was used to in Portweald. Every street could have come straight out of a theme park advert, or maybe a fantasy novel. The houses were strikingly picturesque, and yet they were equipped with all the latest technology. Wood, colorful bricks and natural stone were the predominant building materials. Pretty, but rather humorless. Imagine a vast city built in this style. It's a culture shock.

Any moment Sharminella expected to see goblins poking their horrendous noses out of doors and windows, and growling "I smell human flesh." Her fear abated however when she caught on that the inhabitants were the same boring grownups like everywhere else. They dressed a bit differently, that was all.

"Here we are then. Pinglop," Kean smiled.

The stairs had taken a lot out of Nate... Had almost broken his back, too, but they had done little to break his temper. It had returned with a vengeance. "We'll need money for a hotel," he said. "Anyone still got money on them? I've got nothing but the borrowed clothes I'm wearing."

~"And the three company gifts in your sling bag. Don't forget those."~

'*Right. And the three idiotic company gifts. Maybe I'll use the flood as an excuse to throw them away.*'

~"You wouldn't dare. I know you. You're too much of a goody-goody."~

'*Well, maybe I'm changing.*'

"Look, Nanny! A bank," Sharminella said. "Bank has money, mm?"

"Okay. Everyone stay here. I'm getting us money."

"Nate. That's absurd," Kean objected. "Without proper credentials, how are you going to cajole them into helping you?" But Nate was already entering the bank. "Besides, your clothes look very unbecoming!" Kean called after him. "And you smell."

The whole undertaking, surprisingly, was completed in under ten minutes. Without hassle the bank manager, herself, in person, assisted Nate in setting up an account and wiring money from his home bank. This wasn't eager to please anymore. She was bent on pleasing him. Usually Nate's radiant smile and mouth-watering attractiveness was why people so readily helped him out. This time it was a mystery to him. Obviously the woman had to be blind, or a big fan of alternative fashion styles. Throughout the transaction she didn't wince even once.

"Done!" he said when he rejoined the others. "And she gave me directions to a hotel too. Follow me. It's supposed to be just around the corner, over there."

"Granted, I am impressed by how you handled the bank," Kean replied, while trying to keep up with Nate who was already ten feet ahead. "However, in the state we are in I don't see how–"

"I know that we look like mud pies crammed into *beaded*-to-death organza, but listen," Nate said sternly, "after all we went through, I'll be damned if they try to kick us out. We are going to relax in the lap of luxury tonight, if it kills me!"

And luxury was right. Pinglop's only hotel was a high profile one. It was the type of place where every soap dish, laundry hamper, carpet, shoehorn, you-name-it had the hotel logo on it. As if the hotel had a need to constantly assert itself that it existed.

The disorderly misfits walked into the lobby, where, right away, the many mirrors heralded their undesirable presence by reflecting a kaleidoscope of vulgar colors, muddy body parts, tiny moon-print pajamas, cat claws, rhinestone-encrusted scarves, tutus, tiaras and hairy underbellies. The desk clerk's initial reaction was to check her medication.

"I can see her hand hovering over the silent alarm," Kean whispered out of the corner of his mouth.

"Keep going," Nate whispered back. "Everybody smile."

They arrived at the desk.

"Hi," Nate said. "Rather ho-hum weather out, wouldn't you say?"

It only lasted a split second, but Nate had caught it in her eyes. There! A glint of... recognition had crossed her mind.

~"What was that? Nate, did you see that?"~

'I did, yeah. What's going on?'

The desk clerk moved her hand away from the alarm. Her whole demeanor had changed instantly. She smiled back at them even though smiling was clearly not in her nature. "Welcome to Voegant Resort Pinglop."

Nate was astonished. *'Voegant. That name! Just like the chief owl in my vision!'*

~"Land, ho!"~

"I'm sorry. My brain froze for a second. Did you just say *Voegant* Resort Pinglop?"

"Indeed. Are you unwell?" This was obviously a rhetorical question for her.

~"How about that? Maybe your vision wants you to be in this very hotel when whatever will happen, happens."~

"Uh, miss? I wonder. Why is the resort called that?"

This seemed to make the desk clerk nervous. Her eyes darted away, to Kean and Poledoris, in the hope of an answer from them. "I'm... I couldn't say, really. I suppose it has to be called something. Could we perhaps proceed to checking you in? Hold on. I'll get some new forms."

~"She's hiding something. Force the answer out of the wench, Nate."~

"Why the question about the name?" Kean asked while the desk clerk was in the backroom. "Why was it important? She seemed aggravated. Thought she was about to kick us to the curb."

"Just being curious, I guess. Nevermind."

"Are you certain?"

"Yeah. I'm sure."

~"She's coming back. Start grilling her."~

'I'd rather sleep in a bed tonight.'

~"Wimp."~

He ignored the gibe and glanced over his shoulder. Sharminella was getting restless. Kean was gazing at him. And Poledoris was pirouetting about like a ballerina impersonating a bean bag chair, or maybe a bean bag chair impersonating a ballerina. He did it *en pointe* even. The whirling made the desk clerk more skittish than she already was.

"Is your stay in Pinglop business or pleasure?" the desk clerk asked out of force of habit.

"Business, actually."

Her mouth formed around the shape of an O, but no sound came out.

"I'm here to audit a company," Nate felt compelled to add.

She looked him up and down. He could tell she was thinking *Is it auditing a drug lab?* Nate realized again just how exhausted he felt. After exchanging the usual information and him paying a substantial advance, she summarized. "So, I have booked three single-bed rooms for you... uh... gentlemen. And board at *Hadley Petting* for your cat Pustula–"

"Spatula."

"Mrrreow!" the kitten complained. It got hoisted into a cat carrier and locked in before it got wise to what was going on.

"–For the charming young lady, I'll get the staff to install the kiddie bed in your room, Mr. Noodascue. Just go up the stairs here and then to the left. Enjoy your stay."

Sharminella tried to pull herself up over the desk. She was displeased. "Bubby and I want *brittle sweet!*"

"I won't pay for that, Sharmy," said Nate, "It's either a kiddie bed or sleeping in a baby box."

"*Sweeet! Sweeet!*"

"I'm sure we can find some confectionary for the girl," the desk clerk cut in to be helpful–and to be rid of them. "I can ask the kitchen boy to fetch some *macarons aux pruneaux.*"

"She means she wants a bridal suite," Nate explained to the woman. "One with a deluxe living room and walk-in wardrobe, and no, she can't have one."

This was not what Sharminella wanted to hear. Her body weight was fifty percent blonde ringlets and fifty percent attitude, and she knew how to use this to full effect.

"I want, I want! Or I scream!"

"I said no, Sharminella."

"I want, I want, I want!"

"Don't mind her," Nate said to the desk clerk, "She's teething."

"No, 'm not!"

"You are."

"Am not!"

"Are too!"

"Am not!"

"Yeah, you are!"

~"Tsk. Stop this, please. You two are behaving like bickering fishwives."~

"*Noooooooooooooooot!*"

"*Toooooooooooooooooo!*"

"*Not-not-not-not-nooooot!*"

"*Tooo-tooo-tooo-to-loo-tooo!*"

A sardonic grin spread over Nate's face. He plotted a scheme to win the argument. If executed to the letter, it was highly effective, but he wouldn't get nominated for any fair play cup anytime soon. "Sharminella," he began in a velvet voice, "if you don't do as I say, I will tell everyone I know about a secret that an assistant has told me. Something about what really happened at the *Kidneys for Kids* fundraiser talent show last year. I vaguely recall an incident involving a certain girl... Alas, if only my poor brain could remember her name. Started with S–"

Sharminella's eyes shot venomous death rays at him. She knew where this was heading.

"–A little prizefighter who found herself inconvenienced by unfortunate gusts of explosive diarrhea mere moments before going onto the stage and not knowing what to do. Oh, her name is on the tip of my tongue. Such torture!"

Sharminella was the complete opposite of extremely happy. Her body was shaking. The desk clerk took a tentative step back and was ready to hit the floor if this was going to blow up. Nate knew he was skating on very thin ice, but in brave defiance he continued. "And, ah yes, then I might also tell everyone about Valerie Fallouse, the front runner who was also at the talent show, and about how this *S girl* switched Valerie's show-and-tell basket with her own, and caused Valerie to be disqualified in disgrace for delivering a basket full of, let's say, *steamy brown cookies* to the jury table."

Sharminella was breaking out in violent hives. "You wouldn't dare tell! You wouldn't dare!" She was seething in her own skin.

"Oh yes, I would!" Nate bit back, savoring the moment.

He got her. He knew blabbing was inexcusable and considered a hostile move. An act of war. Like pointing a piece of blanched broccoli directly under her nose. This would not be forgotten. Not in a million years. This one would linger.

"*EEEEE!*" Sharminella screamed and stormed off to the elevator.

Kean shook his head. "I get that you are still wobbly after the ordeal of the last couple of days, Nate. Nevertheless, was this verbal aggression really necessary?"

"I can't help myself. I feel so frazzled and empty."

~"You probably don't want to hear this, but it's okay to forget about Brent."~

'*If only I could.*'

"Enough warmongering for one day. Let's head up to the rooms," Kean suggested. "A long, warm bath will do wonders."

Later, Nate called the boutique on the first floor, to bring up some easy fitting clothes for everyone. The sparkly tights had started to chafe. He did hope that ZPMQZ were going to reimburse him for all the expenses. Hazard pay would not have been out of place either.

The evening was spent quietly and without incident. Though Sharminella and Nate didn't exchange one word.

The next day he would finally start his audit of Cibyl Unlimited Holding, the whole reason for him coming to Pinglop. Kean had agreed to take Sharminella and Poledoris off his back for the day, and Spatula would stay at *Hadley Petting* cat hotel.

The following morning all the hotel guests discovered to their consternation that someone had inexplicably removed the doorknobs from their doors.

16. Minimalistic shopping

"Listen, Sharminella, I need you to do something for me," Kean said. He was in a hurry. "Nate went off to work and I have appointments with my associates at the *Pinglop Psychotherapists and Plumbing Utilities* convention. You wouldn't like it. The convention is about to commence, so I'm sure you and your doll can keep yourselves busy on your own. See that clock tower over there? Just be back here at five, right? I know you can do that because you are a big girl now."

"You say I am fat?" Sharminella shrieked and rammed the heel of her pump down on his foot.

"Ouch! That's not what I meant," Kean yelped. "I meant to say you already look like a smart girl of seven even though you are only six."

Again, her heel slammed down on the other foot in punishment.

"Ouch! That's going to leave a mark," Kean gnarled through his teeth. "I don't have time to deal with this now... You see that arrow sign there?"

"Yeah."

"That will take you to the park. It has a playground with a sandbox. Why not have Poledoris tag along and see if planting those knobs of his will make them grow into knob trees or something? Remember, we reconvene here at five p.m.! As many fingers as are on your hand."

Now he turned to talk to Poledoris.

"You just... behave."

And with that, Kean was off. Sharminella had to fend for herself again, but at least this time she was stranded at the entrance of a shopping mall. One of the more classy ones too.

Plus she had Poledoris for a stooge. As long as she was seen in the company of an adult, she could go into any store she liked and buy whatever she wanted. No-one would start asking pesky questions such as *Are you lost and can't find your mommy anymore?* or *Would you like to take a nice seat next to the lavatory lady with the bad breath who's wearing a hideous woolen sweater until your parents come and collect you?*

The little girl didn't like it when they treated her like a little girl. Yesterday, Nate hadn't even bothered to ask her if her credit card had been saved from the flood. She felt that he didn't take a VIP of her stature seriously. Because of that, she hadn't offered him any financial help. Even less so after he'd been too cheap to cough up for a suite.

No, by comparison, shopping malls welcomed her with open arms. In the sacred palaces of capitalism her *Big Spenders* card was never refused anything. Her two devilish little eyes started to twinkle. A shopping spree would definitely lift her spirits.

She knew that she had to find a way to persuade her stooge, so she opened with a topic that was about him rather than about herself.

"Pollydolly, why do you have chipmunk cheeks? Do you store your nuts in there?"

The artist was staring directly into the sun. "Curious nose mustard jar," he professed and nothing else.

That was the strange thing about him. Who knew what went on in his head? Maybe he believed he was a condiment, or a bull with gender confusion faintly reeking of rancid cantaloupes. It was anyone's guess. Long stretches of time passed where he was docile and mute, and then all of a sudden he'd turn obnoxious, stalking hapless victims and haranguing them with talk of "the merits of our modern zeitgeist's deeper appreciation of literary idiosyncrasies in graphically suggestive outsider art and their socio-economic implications in an analytic society preoccupied with symbolic narrative dynamism juxtaposing the devotional immersion in the alchemy of abstraction as a catalyst signifier to convey verisimilitude in metaphysical dimensions and a radish."

A number of people claimed he was a true genius. That number, incidentally, was naught.

In his room earlier that morning, Poledoris had put on regular clothes, but had insisted on wearing Sharminella's Halloween hat, namely a plastic fruit basket hat ten sizes too small. Then he had wedged a large paper parasol into it. No-one was foolish enough to try and take it off of him.

"Hello? *Hellooooo?* You listening? Me and Bubby want to do shopping in shops," Sharminella clamored.

"Nose," he replied and walked toward the mall.

"*Yaaaay!*"

Happy to have secured a stooge, Sharminella started her spree purchasing an expensive white dress, which she then took to a store specialized in printing slogans on textile. In her own somewhat incoherent way she instructed the storekeeper to grace the front of the dress with the words *I am Salmonella. I am the best bootee pagan weenie of ever and ever much batter than that stewpit Valerie Phallus, so there! And I love my doll Butty- not Butty-Boobie the wonton poopoo!* Then she proudly put on the dress and marched up and down the walkway, saying from the top of her voice "Good, now everyone knows who is the *bestestest.* Me is!"

In a plus-size clothing outlet she bought Poledoris a vest with lettering on the back *This body is *hot* like goat cheese!*

Then they went into a pet store where Sharminella wanted to adopt a small turtle, one gerbil (cute), two piranhas (vicious), interlocking stick insects, a baby ostrich still halfway out of its egg, an unidentified litter of furry creatures with fleshy pale snouts, a gray parrot that could mimic the words *Polly wanna thin crisp wafer made of flour and water,* or when it thought no-one was listening *I'm all about the cracker*, a handful of garden snails in a glass terrarium, four zebra finches and a complimentary bucket of fishing bait. But the sale fell through because the angry cashier kicked them both out for trying to feed plastic bananas to the puppies in the window display.

After several lavish helpings of strawberry and caramel ice cream at a bistro called *Le Trough*, Poledoris zeroed in on an art gallery called *We Invented Sliced Bread*. Abruptly he got up from the table. Sharminella resisted at first, "Not that way, Pollydolly! I want to go to candy store!" but to no avail. She bit him in the ankle, pulled at his thumbs and sprayed lemonade at him through the gab in her milk teeth, but Poledoris's non-mind was made up. Reluctantly Sharminella trailed after him.

She had a great dislike of this type of gallery. There were no clothes, no cosmetic products, no toys, no candy, little to no color. Just barely a handful of boring paintings on walls. It was one of those places promoting *minimalistic shopping*. (It's that thing where the store is so exclusive that the articles themselves are excluded from the store. It's all about what you *can't* find there.)

And inside, a slender saleswoman was waiting in her web. It was in her job description to be, at all times, in high heels and in a patronizing mood. This particular one even boasted an air of contained rudeness. So the showroom had to be for a very select clientele indeed. The saleswoman was what some might call *past her prime*, though she would never admit it herself. Plastic surgery had made her cheekbones stick out and she was constantly pouting her lips to accentuate the collapsed cheeks. It gave her that unfaltering expression of both suction and disapproval. She was eyeballing Sharminella and Poledoris as they entered, believing that that in itself could shoo the riffraff and their appalling attire out of her place of business. She managed to keep her distrustful gaze locked on them both, even though he was checking out the paintings on the left and Sharminella was running behind a corner on the right, groaning *"Boring, boring, boring"* to get Poledoris to leave with her. She pulled out her Magic Wanton Booboo Wand and rattled its shiny plastic diamonds inside the star at every painting in protest. *"Boring, boring, boring, boring."*

In a choleric fashion the saleswoman came toddling up to the girl. (She had to toddle, in fact. Her tight-fitting dress was not intended for people with knee joints.) She tutted "What is this? Kids are not allowed to make such noises. I can tell you are trouble. You should be held on a leash, really. This is a proper gallery for serious art connoisseurs. No window shopping and no skipping!"

Sharminella looked up. All she could see of the woman was a deep blue pillar of fabric with a head on top.

"What is it, curious child? Stop examining me like that. Don't you know it is impolite to stare?"

"Miss? I have a question," Sharminella asked all sincere and syrupy.

"Well then? Hurry up. What is the question?"

"Why does your face look like five potatoes in a nylon stocking?"

The woman's head exploded with rage. "Ow! Never have I been so insulted in my life! You intolerable little chit! I blame poor upbringing."

"Waaah! You are hurting me! Let me go! Let me go, witch!"

She had grabbed hold of Sharminella's elbow and was lifting her up with a firm grip. "It's obvious your father does not care he's raising a daughter devoid of the basics of etiquette! Where is that man! I shall give him a piece of my mind!" She turned around and discovered that the paintings had disappeared from the walls. "Where are the limited edition *Cupernivals?*" In a panic she let go of Sharminella and toddled back to the register like a drunken sausage yelling "Mall security, mall security!" She hit the silent alarm button. Then she spotted Poledoris on the floor. He was spraying a thick layer of fire extinguisher foam on a painting and pressing another painting on top of it. Then he pulled out a jar of mustard and a knife from somewhere on his person and set about smearing the back of the upper canvas with an ample spread. On this a third painting went. Like a sandwich.

The woman could not believe her eyes. "Those are original Cupernivals!" She screamed. "What the blazes do you think you are doing?"

Poledoris didn't even look up. He replied "Dryrot tastebud splurge" and then his body stopped operating like a wind-up puppet running out of spring.

"Vandals! Help! I've called mall security on you. You will regret this!"

Sharminella cut in "And I call Nanny Nate on you! I tell him you hurt me!"

The woman paused mid-rant. "Nanny Nate?... What? What did you just say?"

"Nanny Nate will punish you!"

The woman's tone of voice changed into fragrant flowers. "Would that be Nate as in Nate Noodascue? Young male, green eyes, auditor?"

"Yes. Nanny! When Nate comes he kicks your butt till it is black and blue, mm, like your ugly clothes!"

"So," the woman said, eerily calm now. "You must be the little brat that accompanies him."

"No, *you* are the brat that *acornpaneers* him!"

The woman clenched her fist. Around her finger she wore a ring in the shape of an owl. She jabbed it hard into Poledoris's shoulder blade. To this, the man had no discernable response other than a sluggish chain reaction of wobbly flesh. "And you," the woman told him, "I assume you are the zombie then." She waved a hand in front of his face. He didn't move, not even a little. He was totally lethargic. His focus was scattered into nothingness. "Are you breathing?" She leaned in to verify. Poledoris grabbed her, and grinded her into a chokehold against his chest.

"My name is Poledoris. Some call me Doctor Brainzipper. I've been told people like expositions."

"*Arghl!*"

He paraded her around in her own gallery. The woman screamed for him to unhand her. "This is assault!" Poledoris didn't listen. The viselike grip stayed and she had no choice but to undergo the physical and intellectual abuse. Occasionally Poledoris stopped at a blank wall, where a painting used to hang, and elaborated on its "esthetic particularities in post-fictive space."

"Let me go!"

Around and around they went, with Sharminella cheerfully bringing up the rear, twirling her magic wand like a baton and humming a march band tune. When the novelty wore off, the girl dragged the fire extinguisher along and strayed curly foam worms in the air left and right. It was a celebration.

Then a uniformed man, clearly mall security, turned up. "Problems here, miss?" The procession halted. All three shot a look at the security guard like they had just been caught in the act. Sharminella thought for sure the witch was going to rat them out.

"No-no... No problems. But thank you for checking up," the saleswoman's head replied awkwardly from inside the unyielding arm.

"The silent alarm went off."

"That was my mistake. My... customer is simply a bit... perspicuous in his ways. We are accustomed to some degree of, uh, eccentricity in our clientele."

The guard saw Poledoris's fruit basket and parasol combo hat and the goat cheese loving vest and concluded that eccentric must mean insane nutter.

"Well, okay then. As you wish. You know how to reach us if you need any assistance, ma'am." The guard left with a confused frown on his face.

"Now," Poledoris continued. "Did I tell you I had an artichoke accident? Tore my scalp right off. I will show you."

With one swift motion he unscrewed his toupee patch.

"Want to see the stitches?"

17. Cibyl

"House number three, Quaint Street. This must be the place."

The Cibyl Unlimited Holding residence was a massive six-storey building that really upheld the grandeur of Pinglop. The same red bricks and abundant use of wood, so typical of the city, made it stand out against the steel blue sky. Broad steps carved out in natural stone graced the climb up to a portico (which Nate remembered from his school days was basically a porch lined with a set of tall columns and a stone roof). An impressive oak door completed the picture. All very nice except for one thing.

~"Doesn't exactly look like an office building to me, Nate."~

"You can say that again." Nate was taken aback by the statues perched on top of the facade. "More like an ode to inter-species breeding. An orgy in bronze and stone."

~"Finally. My kind of art."~

The statues clearly depicted elaborate scenes of dragons doing it with wild-maned horses, serpents engaging in sexual relations with lions, nudes dancing around and playing flute, and a mammoth with its tusks raised high, as if defying anyone who had a problem with that.

"I'm not knocking the orgy, but what do women with flutes have to do with running a business?"

~"Dramatic license?"~

"I guess I'll go have a closer look."

~"Correct me if I'm wrong, but I seem to remember the house number was five, not three."~

Nate checked the instructions the CEO had given him. They had survived the flood, although most of the ink was unreadable now. "You're right! It does say five! How is that possible?

There's only one building on this side and it's this one."

He crossed the street, but there all the houses were evenly numbered. "Okay, I give up," he sighed. "Number five doesn't exist."

~"Crab! Shrimp!"~

"Yes, *hah-hah*, Jarrrvis…"

~"I'm just messing with you. Hey, what is that hovel over there? About four hundred yards behind the building. You see it?"~

"That can't be Cibyl Unlimited. The employees would be packed in like sardines."

~"Leave the fish references to me, please."~

"It's probably just a shack for cows to hide under or something."

~"A cow shack with a smoking chimney? Guess again."~

"Holy smoke! You're right. Okay, I'm on it."

Nate walked down the gravel path at a brisk tempo. Somewhere halfway, he passed a signpost with *Cibyl Unlimited Holding. Quaint Street Nr. 5* on it. At least now he knew he was at the right address.

"What's that noise?"

Without warning, a biker in black came roaring past him, fast as lightning. Nate jumped out of the way, "Hey, watch it!" but the biker didn't slow down. On the contrary, she accelerated.

~"How rude!"~

The back of the helmet had an *Owl's Angels* print on it, Nate saw. The same that he'd seen before, back in Portweald, when a sexy, female biker had come out of the CEO's office and had seemed visibly alarmed by his presence.

Confusion set in. "It couldn't be the same person, could it?"

~"This is bizarre. Too many coincidences of late, if you ask me."~

Nate picked up the pace. The biker had already reached the

shack. She got off the motorcycle. Then she did something that left Nate speechless. Baffled. Thunderstruck…

The Owl's Angel took off her helmet.

···

Meanwhile, Spatula was plotting its breakout from the cheerless basement of the Hadley Petting cat hotel. The kitten had been closely monitoring Mr. Hadley Bog to find a lapse of security, and it had found it.

The elderly caretaker was so enamored of his guest's white fur and adorable pink nose that he had grown too emotionally attached. A serious misjudgment which Spatula planned to exploit. It did not want to stay cooped up in a cage and miss out on the action.

No, the precious little snowflake really wanted to be there in the flesh when Nate Noodascue was getting murdered.

So, in execution of the escape plan, it loaded up on giblets and chased its own tail till the induced nausea resulted in a pool of vomit. Then it faked being unconscious.

Predictably, the caretaker (sick with worry) took the kitten out of the cage to have a better look… which was when it bit the man's hand, jumped off, onto a stack of crates… through an open window… to freedom.

And this was lucky, because one minute later three pregnant women entered Hadley Petting with the intention of doing the kitten great bodily harm.

···

'It can't be her, can it?' Nate thought while running the long path toward her.

The biker was a brunette with long hair. Very attractive in a conventional way. Nothing out of the ordinary in itself, but what really knocked Nate's socks off was that, although she had aged a bit, she was undeniably–most definitely–someone whom Nate would never in a million years have guessed was going to turn up here, so far from home.

"*PENELOPE!*"

Nate was really sprinting now… his feet digging deep into the gravel.

'*She can't hear me.*'

~"Or only pretends not to, maybe. Wowza, she's still hot! I'd like to wreck my ship on that siren's cliff and no mistake."~

"How's it possible that she's the biker? What is she up to?"

Now that Nate was halfway there, he could see that the cow shack was actually a very shabby dwelling, severely tilting to the left and covered in moss. The door swung open for Penelope (without her having to knock) and she disappeared behind the closing door, mere moments before Nate arrived. Completely true to form, he didn't bother to knock. He burst in.

A rhubarb cake. That was the first thing he saw. He wasn't expecting cake.

~"What's going on in here?"~

Penelope had vanished into thin air, and there wasn't much thin air to go around as it was. The room was swamped, it seemed, with every single publication released since the invention of the printing press. It was a tree-hugger's nightmare.

"I've been expecting you," a shape greeted him from somewhere behind the tall stacks of paper. (The dank vapors emanating off them made Nate's sense of smell shut down in protest.) "Are you a rhubarb lover, Mr. Noodascue? There's a seventy-four percent chance that you are."

The cake did look welcoming, but he resisted. "Where is she? The biker chick who just entered. Brown hair, tall–"

~"Good at panting over the phone."~

'Exactly! She was the one doing the phone scam, but now I'm thinking maybe she's been spying on me!'

The shape rose from her makeshift origami chair. (For, the room had no real furniture to speak of.) She was a middle-aged woman with wild, uncombed hair that was white like spun sugar. It looked weird on her. She wore a gray skirt and a knitted jacket. On the whole, quite a scruffy appearance. Nate ignored her and crawled over the volumes of books, paper pulp and packing materials of various consumer products, that were all battling for supremacy in the tight space.

"*PENELOPE?*"

"There's just me and my data, dear," she told him. "Oh, and my fish Cork, of course! You are the first person to walk in for days."

~"She's lying!"~

"Penelope? Show yourself. It's me, Nate Noodascue. Penelope Mangez?"

"I have told you there is no-one here but us."

"Don't think you can fool me! I know she walked in here not ten seconds ago. She arrived on that motorcycle!" And to prove it, he pointed with conviction at the parked vehicle outside the window... at the parked vehicle that Nate now realized had also inexplicably disappeared.

Her mild smile was gone too. "You cheeky little devil! What a nerve you've got barging into my house and giving orders! Now sit your butt down somewhere and listen!"

Nate promptly plumped himself down amid the reek of printing ink. She had that kind of uncompromising schoolteacher's tone in her voice that made everyone obey instantly. Clearly, beneath the woman's bland look, a charismatic personality was calling the shots.

"I'm not crazy. I know I'm not. I did see her," he mumbled and crossed his arms.

~"Of course you're not crazy. I saw her too with your very own eyes."~

Nate decided, for now, to go along with the charade.

"That's better," the woman said in an artificially jolly voice. "You must have had a tiring journey. I expected you a lot earlier, mind you, but there is no real harm done, I suppose. By the way, call me Cibyl."

A queer sensation shot up Nate's spine. "Have we, uh,.. have we met before?"

"I don't know. You tell me."

She watched him trying to make up his mind.

Something about her did seem familiar. Vaguely familiar, at least. She radiated a kind of... qualmish vibe... that he had encountered before, but from whom and where? In any case, the memories were too indistinct to break through the fog.

~"She reminds me of that wacky Sauvetyne person."~

'I know what you mean. But she was a ranting madwoman. This lady is obviously not her... Damn brain. Why can't I place her?'

"Daydreaming, honey?"

"Sorry, Mrs... uh, Cibyl... I think I was wrong. We haven't met," he said. "So, I take it you are the Chairwoman of Cibyl Unlimited Holding then?"

"Correct. I am the founder–"

~"... and only employee, apparently."~

"–I like being my own boss. It suits me."

Casually, while she spoke, she fed some flakes to her guppy Cork. It was swimming in a bowl precariously positioned on top of a paper stack.

'Look at how blackened her fingers are.'

~"Must be from thumbing through endless pages."~

"You think you're here to check out your company's latest acquisition, whereas in reality it is my holding that has bought

ZPMQZ. You're here because I sent for you."

Once again Nate didn't know what to make of her statements. "That doesn't make any sense!"

~"Ah! Cibyl was the hidden source! I remember the CEO saying your name came recommended."~

'And then I suppose Penelope was her messenger?'

~"It's positively raining epiphanies today."~

"I'll start at the beginning," Cibyl said. "Grab the third document from the top of that paper pile behind you, please. That will make things clearer. Yeah, that one."

Nate read the document out loud. "*How to become a professional bodybuilder using Pump-Dump™ creatine suppositories with vitamin K?*... I'm afraid I don't understand. And I'm also slightly alarmed."

"What? Oh no-no, I meant the fourth document. And the one underneath that too. It's the founder's share of Cibyl Unlimited and an official document proving my majority stake in ZPMQZ–"

~"She's just got that lying around?"~

"–I must confess the audit was just a ruse to get you to come to Pinglop."

"Yeah, I figured that out. Why couldn't you just ring me up and ask? Why be sneaky about it?"

"I wanted to make sure you'd come without knowing in advance about the big plans that await you. You might have said no."

"And what would those big plans be exactly?"

"Only world domination, kiddo. What else?"

"World domination, huh? As in *the world is my oyster* kind of thing?"

~"I prefer mussels, me."~

"I'm talking about actually ruling the world of business," Cybil elaborated.

Nate looked her sternly in the eye for signs of an ulterior motive. *'There is something else, something she's not telling me.'*

~"Ruling the world isn't enough for you?"~

"Listen, Cibyl. Not that I'm not grateful or anything, but maybe you've got the wrong guy."

She pushed him back down onto the seat. "I'm thrilled that you are here, Nate. That's what's important. You see that arch?"

"I see the arch."

The thing was made entirely out of legal papers and started at the foot of the door and curved all the way to where a dining table once had met its papery death.

"Those papers contain all the multinationals currently in the holding's portfolio. They represent billions in yearly profit. And let's not forget the power they bring. I want you involved, Nate. Here by my side, as my business partner."

"Huh? But I'm not a corporate person!" he objected. "I've never set foot in a meeting room. I don't even know what products ZPMQZ trades in. I just check numbers all day."

~"No-one at ZPMQZ actually knows what market they're in. It's all just *buy low, sell high*. Don't talk yourself out of a promotion, Nate."~

"I'm no businessman, nothing special. What could you possibly need me for?"

Cork slowly sucked the air out of a bubble. Metaphorically speaking, the fish could not have been more on the money.

"Such passion in a young man's body. Deary me," Cibyl replied. "Have some cake first and settle in. I baked it especially for you. Eat up and I will tell you everything."

She picked up a slice of cake with her stained, fish-feed fingers and presented it to him on a plate. Nate took the opportunity to study her hairline. *'It doesn't look like a wig. Must be her real hair then.'*

~"I know what you're thinking. Did Penelope disguise herself as Cibyl? She can't have. Besides, the woman is obviously a head shorter. Try to explain that she chopped her legs off. You can't."~

'*I suppose,*' Nate sulked.

"On my eighteenth birthday I took control of a very old company and grew it into the giant it is today," she said. "You'd be surprised to hear which well-known corporations I currently possess. And all my success I owe to *cibylation.*"

"Sibilation?"

"Yes. Cibylation, the science of filtering relevant information out of everyday statistics. When carried out correctly, it can be used to predict when market shares will go up or down, when it's a good day to go hiking, or what sports team is going to win the next championship."

"But that's all just information you can find on the news!"

"Yes, but cibylation goes far deeper than that. For instance, to accurately predict how long it would take to, let's say, roast chestnuts on an open fire, I select a book at random and interpret the first numbers I see."

~"Probably a cookbook."~

"The instructions on the packaging can tell you the cooking time too, you know?"

"Ah, fair enough. But can the instructions tell you the location of lost persons? Can it tell you their names?"

"No, ma'am."

"Yes, it can! That's how I found you. Over a period of decades I pored over data to find out who you were and where you lived."

"Why were you looking for me? I don't even know you."

"I'll come to that part in a minute... It took so long to find you because cibylation is not as simple as all that. The key is to read the statistics correctly. Mind and soul must be completely aligned. More importantly, you have to pose the correct question first. When the question is vague or only a half-truth, the result will be as well. Cibylation is the equivalent of asking *Is 47569082 the winning lottery number next week?* Tricky, but not impossible."

~"Well, let's try a question. If there'd be such a thing as an International Most Self-deluded Nutcase List, where in the charts would this woman be? Hands down, all the statistics say she is *my special number one with a bullet.*"~

"I've brought you here because you are unique. One of a kind. Destined for greatness. You do not know it yet, but we both have gifts and abilities no other person in this world has got. If you trust yourself and if you trust me, I'll help you shake the mediocre life you're leading. You have a brightness in your soul larger than the cosmos itself. Your potential is boundless!"

~"The next thing she'll say is *You are the Chosen One* or something. Mark my words."~

"You are the Chosen One."

~"Told you."~

"Plus, you are cute to boot. Your training starts tomorrow."

"Training?"

"I still have things to prepare. Come back then. Around, say, fiveish."

"Five a.m. in the morning?"

"Of course."

"Uh, fine. I guess I'll call the office to inform them–"

"Now, away with you! Shoo! I have much to do still."

Nate was jostled out of the place. Bemused he asked "In preparation for tomorrow, do you want me to go ahead and grow a long beard, dress up in bardic clothes, and save humanity from an oncoming meteor?"

And with that, the door slammed shut in his face.

18. Tubbing

One courageous toe went in first, to scout. The bath was hot and inviting, so he submerged himself completely. Nate loved taking long soaks after going for a run. The water felt like a snug embrace. The foam made his chiseled chest glisten in the candle light. He rolled up a hotel towel to support his head and neck and sagged a bit deeper to let the heat do the work. His shoulders relaxed. For the first time since long, so did his mind.

~"Can't beat a bath to soothe the senses."~

"Yeah… even the Chosen One needs some downtime."

~"Imagine: Nate, supreme superhuman with boundless potential."~

"Hah. It's just too grotesque and laughable to believe."

With a smile on his face he dozed off.

Ten minutes later someone knocked on the door. A voice asked "Are you decent?"

"That would depend on whether you judge my fondness of smelling my own farts to be lewd or not," Nate blurted out without giving it a second's thought.

"What I meant to convey was, can I come in?"

The voice was Kean's. Nate recognized it now. '*Hmm, can he come in?*'

He surprised himself: The answer was Yes. The idea did sound appealing. So he quickly rearranged some islands of floating foam and he covered his nipples with his fingers. (His mother had taught him that.)

"You may enter, please."

Kean stepped in and gulped. "My! Such an erotic display of supple muscle tissue. You really are stunning, aren't you?"

Nate blushed, which only added to his sexiness. People had

been paying him compliments forever... gym members, partygoers at beach parties, the driving license examiner during his exam... but only a few had ever been so out-front with it as Kean. (Psychotherapists do not beat around the bush.)

"Listen, I'd very much like to have a heart-to-heart with you about what happened at the check-in yesterday night, and earlier... Well, possibly during the whole trip."

"Sure, why not? Pull up a wastebasket."

"Good. By the way, I've brought you some luscious bath oil. It's also lavender scented."

"Great, but I've already put some in."

"I see that. But this oil will rejuvenate your skin and make it glow."

"Okay, I'll give it a try."

Kean was halfway in the act of pouring from the bottle when he saw something out of the ordinary.

"Yuck! What is that protuberance?"

"Huh?"

"That vile lump, right over there behind the tub. A decaying sheepskin rugs or something? It's repugnant!"

"Oh that. That's just Poledoris facedown on the floor."

"It is?" Kean inquired, trying to look at it from a different angle. His brain was mapping out the anatomical bits and pieces... Arms and legs spread out and so on.

"Yep. Noticed him when I was drawing the bath. I was really looking forward to relax, so I've decided to ignore the fact that he's there."

A bowl of yoghurt that Kean had eaten earlier instantly congealed into putrid stomach cheese. "He is so... so utterly... nude."

"In the buff, stark-naked, bare... Showing brain."

~"I thought he was a rotting sea cow at first."~

"Yes, but *why* is his posterior exposed?"

"Well, I guess he just can't be arsed to consider their fellow man. Best not to stare at it too long. It might think itself important and do a trick."

"As a psychotherapist, I know that suppressing memories is detrimental, but now that I've seen this–" Then Kean picked up on another detail and was even more distraught. "What are those little things in the folds of his back? Is he sprouting tiny mushrooms?! I think I'm going to heave!"

"Breathe, Doctor Flock, breathe."

Luckily, after a few deep breaths Kean succeeded in keeping down his lunch. "How can you remain calm like that? Him lying there is really uncalled for. Keeping that man around can't be hygienic."

Kean sloshed half of the expensive bath oil into the water, which he hadn't gotten round to doing, but now it was to ward off Poledoris's evil aroma.

"No-one can tell Poledoris what to do, Kean… except maybe you can. I've tried reasoning with him. I've tried baby talk, sign language, pig Latin. Eventually even Morse code. Nothing worked! He's too stubborn."

~"Keeping him around is a health risk. He should come with biohazard markings."~

"His eyes are wide-open," Kean saw. "Is he dead?"

"No. I've already checked for vital signs. Held a small mirror under his nose. I've always wanted to try stuff like that… He's fine."

"Ah. And what's the purpose of those dozen tea bags tied to his armpit hair?"

"Don't know, Kean. Haven't bothered to ask him."

~"That's no way to treat chamomile!"~

"Oh well, I guess that's what passes for normal to him," Kean relented.

"Yep."

Nate realized he liked seeing Kean not so in charge of things for once. In this new light, Kean seemed more likeable. Attractive even.

"Hold on!" Kean said. "What is that blotch of orange goo on the ceiling?"

"Barf, maybe?"

"Is it? How the hell did he manage to do that?"

"Beats me. It's a mystery. Even more so, considering we never see *Mister Projectile Vomiting* actually eat. Goo or otherwise."

"How very true."

"Anyway, what is it you wanted to tell me?"

"Well, Nate, don't take this the wrong way, but it strikes me that you have not been enjoying yourself. You have anxieties you struggle to control. You need to quote-unquote *mellow out* a bit, as they say."

"Who? Me? Why would I want to mellow out now? People tell me I am phenomenal. It was confirmed to me only this morning by a paper-crazy recluse. Can't argue with that! Taking the backseat now would be absurd, surely," Nate joked.

"All the same. Since your fling with that Brent guy went belly-up, your predominant knee-jerk reaction is passive-aggressiveness toward Sharminella and cynicism toward everyone else. At times you are downright obstructionistic. In effect you are perpetuating a downward spiral into despair. Diagnosis: a misanthropic construct maintained by self-loathing."

The energy in the room suddenly changed. Nate realized that Kean's words, mumbo jumbo as it all was, contained a big grain of truth that could be ground into flour and baked into humble pie. And it was never fun getting served humble pie.

"–And Sharminella is still a prepubescent child. She deserves to be in a stable environment where she can shine. You are more than a roomie to her. You are a constant in her life. The one familiar face. Ergo, you have to take on responsibility. She has no relatives, no close acquaintances. After my sessions with her, it is clear that she thinks the world of you. You are her substitute big brother."

"Really? Wow! Must say, I'm surprised. I always assumed she thinks of me as her obedient slave."

"Basically that's one and the same thing." Now it was Kean's turn to grin. "Until she reaches the age of seven she will be self-absorbed and believe she is the center of the universe. That's the way it goes. Spend more time with her. You can be a great, positive influence on her."

That was bull's-eye again and Nate knew it.

"Thanks. I appreciate it. I'll keep that advice in mind."

"You are welcome. Seeing that I like you, I won't charge you money for this introductory session."

"Ah."

~"Gee. That's super."~

"Meantime, you should decide where *you* want your destiny to take you. No-one can force you to gain an insight into the Life of Nate. The choices are entirely your own to make. But even a blind man can see that you have great potential. It is undeniable."

"Are you going to start too? About my incredible powers and stuff?"

~"Aye, Nate. Who died and made you God?"~

Kean twirled his finger in the bath water, creating a tiny vortex. "I am not kidding. From the moment I met you, I could sense it. You are preordained to have a huge impact on all of us, the whole of society. Don't ask me how I know, I just do! So grab those opportunities with both hands when they cross your path and make them your own. If you don't, you will pass upon formidable experiences.-"

"Sure thing."

"–When you are ready to set your goals, I will be here to support you. I believe in you."

~"Bravo! Don't know about you, but I feel a new man. That psychobabble really does work. Even though, I must admit, I found the middle part a bit boring. But on the whole, thanks to those platitudes even I now realize I can fulfill my lifelong dream of becoming a famous trapeze artist. All I have to do is get out your head and grow my own body."~

'Jarrrvis, always wisecracking.'

"Nanny?"

Sharminella came rope-skipping into the bathroom. (She was wearing a petite cowgirl getup. The costume included a broad-brimmed felt hat, tiny boots with jangly spurs, and the whip she used for skipping.) Luckily, Nate had the presence of mind to quickly cover up the more offensive parts of Poledoris with a towel, or three.

"Oh, hi, Princess. How was your day?"

"*Weeee!* I had much fun today! I did shopping and then shopping and then, mm, I did more shopping." Once Sharminella's motor-mouth was running there was no slowing her down. "And then I saw a sign for a pageant so I said I wanted to compete also and we go inside and I had many fun on stage. There was lamps, mm, and colors flashing and a pink catwalk and no jury, and the boys in the *audulence* was really cheering all the dancers, and the dancing girls on stage let me dance in the middle, but they didn't want to wear their ribbons, they took them off, and I tried to, mm, climb the pole like the girls, but it was so slippy and, mm, I didn't win, but that's okay because the first price was something that is a boob job, and Nanny always tells me that I am still too young to have a job anyway."

"You went inside a *strip joint!?*" Nate exploded.

Sharminella looks surprised by Nate's nuclear reaction.

"Don't be angry, Nanny Nate, because it makes your nose hairs stick out of your nose."

"Is this true, Kean? A strip joint! She wanted to go into a strip joint and you allowed her?"

"Now hold on a sec. I was not present when that occurred. I was invited to a seminar, so I agreed with Poledoris that he'd baby-sit her in my place–"

"*What?* You traded with Poledoris? With the human marsh monster?" Nate bellowed. He couldn't believe what he was hearing. "Sharminella, sweety, would you do me a favor and go outside for a moment, close the door and put your hands over your ears? Would you do that for me, pretty please?"

Sharminella did so without protest, because she remembered the same look on his face from back when they were at the wishing well and he got all kooky and cranky. She pushed the door shut behind her. Nate had rage in his eyes. Foamy water splashed out of the tub and out of his mouth. "So are you telling me you left Sharminella alone, all day, with Poledoris?! She could have been injured or abducted or... or... I'm furious!"

"Well, now, in my defense–"

"I can't believe it! You have the nerve to come in here and lecture me about taking up responsibility for her upbringing and *la-de-da*, and all the while you know you handed her over to... to, uh–"

~"Mr. Inertia."~

"–Mr. Inertia!"

"Now, there's no need to put it like that. Granted, he is somewhat of an aberration, but I'm sure he can rise to the occasion if the need–"

"Look at him! Just look at him! He's passed-out on the floor. Where are his clothes?!" Nate grabbed a towel and stood up from the tub. "How many aberrations do *you* trust to guard over your family? I mean, it's ludicrous! I think those are actual aquarium snails moving about on his butt!" Nate was livid. "No-one even wonders how the snails got there in the first place. They just figure it's typically Poledoris. For crying out loud! The man is a danger to himself and his surroundings and you left Sharminella in his care! Explain yourself, *VOEGANT!*"

Voegant? This last sentence came as a total surprise to Kean.

Nate had snapped. Full mental breakdown. He felt his sense of touch leaving him. Purple blotches were blooming. His head was spinning. Blood pressure dropped rapidly. Steam seemed to be filling up the entire room. It was all out of control. He was aware of his body sinking back into the water.

Through the blur, out the other side, a familiar scene came into sharp focus: The owls were back. The heat was back. Purple flames were blazing up all around him. The last thing he could hear himself say, was "I'm not feeling too well. I think I'm, no, I'm pretty sure I'm about to pass out any second n–"

...

Have mercy on us all. Let me rephrase that: Have mercy on *me!* I don't want to be burned alive! Such pain is unbearable. Screw my brethren! I have to get out of this burning cage! I'd take them both on in a dirty fight if it would mean I could escape this deathtrap. I want out! I am aching to fly to safety but I know that if I did, I'd get shot out of the sky. Panic is making it too difficult to think clearly. The flames have reached the lower rafters. My flesh is going to perish in a savage roar of fire and I don't know how to stop it. *I'm too important to die!*

My mind is haunted by these thoughts as I stand here beside my brethren, looking out the broken oval window... Three heavily wounded owls. Owls, as in birds that eat mice and that can turn their heads around and upside down. But, somehow, we are men too. Barn Owl soldiers caught up in a rotten war.

Our blood is spilling onto the floorboards.

Below, at the foot of the ramshackle lighthouse, our enemy Colonel Taytelly and his armies have gathered to kill us. The Frogs, the Blue Partridges and the Rabbitskins, they all have come to see us dead. There must be three hundred of them, maybe even double that. They wave their flags of war and banners from behind the protective cover of trees and bushes.

The Colonel is the pompous white rabbit with the overbite hopping around on the clearing. If I keep looking at him long enough, suddenly the man within is distilled out of the image. He's obviously a military man. Half-starved and skinny, but proud nonetheless. His hair is silvery white. And one of his legs is missing. What remains is a stump quickly patched up in filthy bandages. Two upper incisors are sticking out from under his curly moustache. The hatred in his reddened eyes is completely justified. In the name of our country we have committed many atrocities. And because of it, we walk the Earth on borrowed time. Hellish fire is consuming the lighthouse and soon the three of us along with it. I'm shivering.

I barely recognize my own human face in the broken window glass. Petrified bulging eyes. Dark unruly eyebrows. Sweat gushes down my temples. Once an attractive trait with the ladies, now my rebellious locks are rumpled and covered in grime. I am not the same Pilchett of yore.

I look over at my brethren. Sauvetyne is his plump, unintelligible self. The red nose he owes to beer-binging, the pink cheeks to whoremongering.

Voegant, my older brother and superior in rank, has a military face, stern and frightening. Remarkably, he is the only one who can still muster up some air of authority in the threadbare Barn Owl uniform and ridiculous epaulettes. The more so knowing that he is mortally wounded in the chest.

"I said we will triumph!" he screeches. His creepy vibe and

violent black-and-yellow eyes penetrate my entire being. "So do as I command! I promise a future with all the riches and power your tiny, backward minds can imagine. We will have revenge on our petty adversaries and reshape this miserable world into one by our own design!"

Voegant has obviously lost it.

"So you say we will triumph if we perform a dark ritual?" I ask, unable to hide my disbelieve.

"Yes, Pilchett."

"By betting our s-souls?" Sauvetyne stutters.

"Yes! Now shut up, you two. We must complete the ritual without making any mistakes if we want to prevail. I must concentrate. Everything must be executed with deadly precision for it to work."

"Please don't say *execute* and *dead*. It makes me weak at the knees," Sauvetyne shudders.

"Shut up!"

Sauvetyne is struggling to keep his owl/man body in check. He sinks his head deep inside his breast plumage that in some indefinable way resembles a scrawny winter coat. A coat that I know for a fact is what Sauvetyne is actually wearing. He starts making gagging noises again. Voegant does not take any notice. Two forward toes of his talon are cutting deep into the wooden floor. He's making an intricate carving. "What we need inside the pattern is a candle, or an oil lamp," he wheezes. Here and there little hot flames already come poking up through the knotholes. "That will do."

These blood-soaked planks are all that separate us from death. Every passing minute the deafening inferno is moving in closer. The fuming stench alone–a mixture of combusted wood and our own spilled blood–is enough to asphyxiate. The very air is boiling now. I'm thinking, whatever Voegant's master-plan is, it had better be good. I have to get out of here!

Voegant's has carved a slightly irregular circle within another circle about the size of a cartwheel. And inside that, there is something resembling a crude phallic shape. I can sense Sauvetyne is going to make a moronic remark about it any second now.

"It l-looks... hah!" Sauvetyne gibbers, "looks j-just like a man's peck–"

"It's an eight laying on its back!" Voegant cuts in with a growl. "The symbol of infinity. And the lance shape drawn above it represents the eternal rebirth of the souls. With this ritual we will be able to break away from forced rebirth."

The man is mad!

"Stay outside these marks," he warns us. "Whatever you do, do not taint it with your ignorant presence just yet. I don't know what would happen. I will cut the throat of anyone who dares! Follow my instructions to the letter."

"How do you know it will work?" I ask.

"All these damn questions, Pilchett! I learned of it while I was in the foreign legion, long before you two got yourself enrolled."

Voegant is silent for a moment to bite away the pain in his chest. "When you cross strange places and black jungles for months on end, you quickly learn to pick up a thing or two about survival. Those places were rife with things both fascinating and malefic. One time I caught a disease in the vast jungle of Kimbaliss. I fell into a coma. A medicine man was called in. Four days I floated between the living world and the one beyond. I experienced that my soul, anyone's soul, is just a nugget of soul matter. A pathetic handful of soul taken out of a larger bag of soul stuff. To keep on living, all you need is to make sure your pittance of soul stuff is kept inside your body and doesn't go wandering off. That medicine man has taught me how."

"Is it witchcraft?" Sauvetyne whispers in my ear.

"No, probably a magic much, much darker," I reply through outbursts of coughing. "Like toll collector craft or something." It's getting harder to breathe. "We're wasting valuable time! Can we get on with it, Voegant?"

"Hand over your identification tags, or anything that has your name on it."

"We're owls. We don't have hands," I say.

"Well, you'll just have to wing it then, won't you!"

He quickly collects our lockets and tosses them out the window.

"When we enter the circles, it's better not to wear anything that can tie us down to our names of birth. It's a fragile ritual. Come stand around. This is the jump into the unknown, my faithful brethren. The big leap. Blood nor gore shall dismay a member of the Barn Owl Army."

Sauvetyne and I both chime in, but we are not so sure about the faithful part considering the fact that the lighthouse is ablaze and *we are still inside!*

Voegant steadies himself. He has lost a lot of blood. He reaches for something in his pocket and ceremoniously holds it up.

"This will leech the power off our enemies and enforce our victory."

The item is fuzzy and white, kind of... "A lucky rabbit foot?!" I say incredulously.

"Better!" Voegant answers me with a sadistic smile. "The lucky rabbit foot of our nemesis, Colonel Taytelly!"

"Where did you get that?"

"Bit it off during battle."

Sauvetyne and I manage a small "Hurrah!" as Voegant drops the foot inside the center circle. On some level I know it is in fact a human foot, but my eyes only see the fur and blood.

He starts his incantation: *"SEEBIL-MUAH-NICBLIMZ-*

AUMHINM-TULA..."

He motions us to repeat the words.

"*SEEBIL-MUAH-NICBLIMZ-AUMHINM-TULA!*"

Nothing happens, except for some purple smoke swirling out of the circles.

"All very interesting, but I don't understand how it'll get us out of here!"

"You dare to defy me?!" Voegant's eyes are filled with strange lust and aggression.

"Of course not!"

Sauvetyne flinches. He's making a strenuous effort to keep down his last meal.

"So then, do you two idiots trust me?"

"Y-yes, we do," I say. "You've always had our best interest at heart, Voegant."

"Do you trust me enough that you'd do everything and anything!"

"*YES!*" I shout, "Get us out of here!"

"Very well then. Everyone stop muttering. This is very tricky and dangerous. Now, look alive!" He starts laughing out loud, a booming laugh that nearly drowns out the crackling of the surrounding wood. He truly is insane.

"So what do we do next?" I ask.

Everything that follows happens very quickly.

"Next step is to *DIE!*"

Without warning, Voegant shoots Sauvetyne in the gut with one of his pistols. *BANG!*

Cringing in agony, my younger brother topples over. He hits the occult circles, which causes a column of purple sparks and magic to burst up from them.

"You see," Voegant yells, "we can't come back *IF WE DON'T LEAVE FIRST, CAN WE?*–"

I'm shocked. Some of Sauvetyne's feathers... fingers... have lashed me in the face.

"–You're next, Pilchett. Don't worry. This is not the end."

"No! Don't do it! Wait, I–"

BANG!

A surge of indescribable pain hits my head like I've been blown apart by a cannon. Disbelieve. I look down. Everything's turning red. I taste iron in my mouth. My legs give way and I fall on top of Sauvetyne... Everything looks purple... I watch Voegant with the expression of *why?*

He presses the barrel against his temple. Purple flames are singeing his flesh. A fraction of a second before the shot goes off, Sauvetyne barfs up one last owl pellet.

BANG!

"Nooooooo! Fool! That pellet will taint the ritual!" Voegant screams in terror. He's keeling over, desperately trying to reach out and catch the falling ball of skins and bones before it hits the circles, but his hands don't listen.

My last breath is leaving my body. It is too late.

Sauvetyne has spewed.

Sauvetyne has spoiled things for everyone...

...

A very loud fire alarm went off.

Sharminella rushed into the bathroom, her arms violently up in the air. "*What happippening?!*" Talking made her vinegar-and-mud face mask crackle like paint on a creepy porcelain doll. She witnessed the scene and gulped: Nate was lying unconscious on the floor, his nose pressed into the toilet rug. Kean was hovering over him.

"It's probably nothing," Kean said above the noise in an attempt to shush her, but Sharminella was on the brink of going off into hysterics. First the alarm, now this. Her young brain couldn't compute what it was seeing. Nate wasn't usually so fleshy and wet, and not at all so kissy-kissy with polyester rug fabric. This was all very unusual. She yelled "You killed my nanny!"

"I did no such thing!" Kean raised his voice even more to be heard. The fire alarm was wailing on relentlessly. "Nate, uh, felt a sudden desire to go *nappy-nap!*–"

The goldilocked menace threw him The Dirty Look.

"–What I meant to say is, he wanted some sleepy time and he was too exhausted to put on his jammies! Yes, that's all it is, I'm sure of it. Just an invigorating catnap!"

Sharminella inhaled... A volcano of nastiness was about to erupt over Kean.

"*Dream-drunk* then?" he desperately tried to convince her everything was okay, "*Snoozy-woobles?... Gape-gob-goolies?*"

"I am going to *SCREAM!*"

"Oh, screw this! I am your senior, Sharminella. I don't need to justify myself to a six-year-old. *You* have to listen to *me!* So calm down! I said that Nate will be fine and you have to believe me. He is just out of it and that is all."

"Then why is he that much wet?!"

"Maybe he drools a lot in his sleep. What do I know?"

Sharminella was not amused. She placed her feet in a firm position on the floor and lifted her body to inflict *M.A.D.* (maximum acoustic destruction). "The hotel burns and Nate is dead! *EEEEEEEEEEEEEEEEEE!*"

Kean clasped his hands over his ears. "Right! We're vacating the hotel! Come now. No arguing."

In an act of bravery beyond the call of duty, Kean wrapped Nate in a flower-pattern bathrobe hanging from a hook, hoisted him over the shoulder and carried him down the stairs and out of the lobby. Sharminella followed closely behind. Poledoris, apparently vertical again, quickly overtook both of them by sliding down the handrail, wearing nothing but his birthday suit and proclaiming "Sweaty toilet seats and gristle in twilight douse the gravy boat of the House of Popsy-wopsy. Add the zest of one lime."

In the grand scheme of things, Poledoris couldn't have been more beside the point.

19. Albatross

"What a relief!"

Out on the street, Kean immediately understood that the siren was not the fire alarm of the hotel. It could be heard over the entire city. Just as sudden as it had begun, the siren ceased. Sharminella was still spooked, even crying a little. Searching for consolation she wrapped herself tightly around her coach's neck.

Poledoris was prancing around *au naturel*. Being exposed to the open air, the fungus around his butt crack promptly blossomed tiny asparagus-like shoots.

Surprisingly, none of the passers-by paid him any attention. Without exception they were all young women (maybe there were thirty of them, including the hotel desk clerk), who came walking out of their houses and places of business... Some were visibly pregnant. Others were popping pickled gherkins in their mouths like they were candy, which may very well have been an indication of pregnancy... The blushing women all headed toward Quaint Street, where they thronged up the large steps of the nameless building with the stone wildlife creatures humping on the rooftop. As soon as the congregation of gherkin-craving conceivers had entered the building, the grand door shut behind. A second siren went off, shorter this time, and the streets of Pinglop were deserted again.

Nate didn't catch any of this strange activity going on around him, because he only now opened his eyes.

"Ah, Nate. Good. You are back in the land of the living."

"What happened, Kean? Is Sharminella okay?"

"She's right here. She'll be fine. More importantly, are you alright?"

"What happened?"

"You fainted in the tub and immediately woke up again in a trance-like state. I called out your name several times. You couldn't hear me at all. Then you tried to walk about in the way of a wobbling duck unaccustomed to human legs, garbled nonsensical words and finally crash-landed as if shot in the solar plexus. I hope you don't mind my asking, but... have you been sniffing glue?"

"Huh?"

Nate was only half-listening, because his mind was racing. He needed to figure out the meaning of the visions and soon. They made him paranoid... Was he ill?... Was he going mad?

"Nate, concentrate please. How many fingers am I holding up? Are you hemorrhaging?"

'Jarrrvis, you there?'

~"I'm here, Cap'n. I saw the vision, of course. Can't recall anything of what Kean said... He's giving you a weird look. Better pretend you meant it to happen."~

'Oh.'

Nate started wildly flapping his arms about, like an actor hamming it up for the cheap seats. "Hahaha! I was just pulling a prank on you. Aren't I the sneaky one! Thanks for caring, Kean. I'm fine. Yes, sirree. One hundred percent okay."

"You mean, you were toying with me?"

"Yeah. I'm feeling jaunty. In fact, hah, I am as chipper as... as a machine that grinds up logs."

It was blatantly obvious that Nate was not okay at all. Still, Kean didn't press the issue. Maybe because a few minutes earlier Nate had been furious at him for neglecting his baby-sit duties.

"Ahem," Nate continued. "Would you excuse me for one moment?" And before Kean could object, Nate hurried back inside.

'I need to talk to you, in private.'

~"Don't we always?"~

'You know what I mean. Somewhere without people watching.'

Unfortunately, no such place was presently available. A huddle of businessmen in the lobby was complaining about the vulgar streaking habits of Poledoris. The desk clerk was away, so the porter had to bear the brunt of their discontent. When Nate walked by, the businessmen stared and pointed, condemning him by association. The housekeeping staff was already busy disinfecting the handrail, effectively blocking the staircase. And the elevator had a line of people waiting in front of it. Nate ducked behind a fireplace near the far wall of the lobby. He was restless. "That's twice now that those horrible visions have happened," he huffed. "My head's a mess! For crying out loud, Jarrrvis, can you tell me what's going on?"

~"Well, let's recap the important facts that have happened to you so far, shall we?"~

"Go!"

~"When you were twelve years old, you and Timmy used to play a game called *If you show me yours, I'll show you mine* after basketball practice. More recently, you were twice assailed by phantasmagorical visions involving trigger-happy hooters. And now Nate *the Chosen One* Noodascue is crouching behind a cheesy fireplace in a fancy hotel far away from home, and trampling on dust bunnies. That's about it."~

"Har-har! Tell me something I don't know."

~"A starfish can turn its stomach inside out. Not exactly relevant, but there you go."~

"Double har-har."

~"You've navigated through some rough seas, I'll grant you that."~

"You know very well I have. I'm an open book to you. It's not fair! I don't have a clue what you are thinking unless you share it with me! Could I get some help here, please?"

~"You're panicking."~

"Obviously! The fire, the rabbit colonel, that bizarre owl ritual. I feel sick! Maybe you enjoyed that little sneak preview of my death–after all, you've died once already–but I haven't!"

~"My own death was nothing like that freak show!"~

"Okay-okay. I'm sorry. Didn't mean to sound disrespectful–"

~"Too little, too late."~

"–But if I *am* to be brutally murdered by a mob of pyromaniac farm animals, is it really too much to ask that *you give a damn!?* I'm in a deep crisis and you are acting like a jerk. Who are you anyway? Why did you insist on holing up in my head like a hibernating runt? I have put up with you since forever and in return you have been loathsome, mean, condescending... Worst of all, you are a stranger. I know next to nothing about you other than that you used to get off *chasing blowholes.* For all we know, I may be turning into dead owl soon, and then where would you be? I mean, don't you care?!"

~"Let me tell you something, mister."~ Jarrrvis bit back. ~"I was a damn good whaler in my day! Had I known you'd become so much trouble, I would have hunted down the powers that be, whoever they are, and twisted their arms, or flippers or whatever, and force them to reassign me to the first creature that came crawling out of the sea!"~

"Yeah, right!"

~"I bet even mud fish are more fun to be around with than you!"~

"Pffuh!"

~"The fact of the matter is, I have no clue why I'm stuck with you either, but you better show me respect. I'm a real person. Having you at the helm isn't exactly smooth sailing."~

"Yes, well, but–"

~"And the truth is I *do* care! I may not tell you much, but I have my reasons for that. Doesn't mean I want to see you harmed. You are my buddy!"~

Nate deflated. He was unable to speak. A sense of guilt washed over him. "Sorry. I guess I got carried away for a moment. I take back everything I've just said."

~"No problem. Water under the bridge."~

"So are we good?"

~"We're good."~

Nate felt put at ease in some way. Their little spat had cleared the air. "Thanks. You're right, I am panicking, Jarrrvis. It's all so very confusing. For instance, in the vision, my reflection in the glass was the same man as in the locket Sharminella wears around her neck. Did I subconsciously add that face to the mix or is there something more behind it? And another thing I've figured out, of course, is that the Barn Owl soldiers are also owls because that's their coat of arms. The Rabbitskins are rabbits and so on, but where do I come in? How will I get involved?"

~"My guess is, we won't know till it happens. Visions are cryptic. Maybe it's just symbolic for you becoming a man or something, and nothing more. What's that called again? A rite of passage? Maybe the feathers are a metaphor for growing pubes and the lighthouse represents your manhood."~

"Huh?"

~"Let's deal with things as they come. I don't see what you can do otherwise. Take a load off."~

Nate pondered upon this. "I think I agree. After all the weird stuff I've encountered so far, how bad could it get, right?"

~"You vowed to not be a pushover any longer."~

"Exactly. I'm no pushover. So I say *Bring it on!*" And on that thought, Nate decided to worry no more.

~"That's my Nate! Now, what about Kean?"~

"What about him? Do you mean, will I forgive him for leaving Sharminella in the care of the *Landslide of Odiousness* all day? For crying out loud, she was pole dancing in a strip joint!"

~"Of course you should forgive him."~

"Why?"

~"He made a serious error of judgment, true, but he also made sure you and Sharminella got safely out of a burning hotel."~

"A hotel that wasn't on fire."

~"A technicality."~

"I don't know, Jarrrvis. Kean let me down."

~"Doesn't matter after the developments of the past few days, surely."~

"I'm not following."

~"I'm talking about your eyes wandering off. About the slight stammer when he asks you something. I won't even mention how your mind was undressing him at breakfast this morning. You have some very naughty ideas. Very creative ones too. A peppershaker, two napkin rings and apricot jam. Who would have thought!"~

Nate blushed. "Hmm, yep. There is that. I don't know why I have feelings for him. He isn't really my type, but I've been thinking about him. Kean's got this dark attraction going on."

~"Plus, this one is here. Not like what's-his-face... Brent."~

"Don't mention Brent. It still hurts."

~"Oops."~

"Kean is intelligent. Self-confident. Handsome in an *I am naked under my clothes* kind of way."

~"What's that mean?"~

"I'm not sure what I mean by that... I suppose what I'm saying is, Kean has a feral magnetism that my brain's trying to figure out."

~"Tell it like it is: He's probably real kinky in the sack. He looks the sort."~

"Have you noticed how he's always flirting with me?"

~"Well, ask him out then. Dare I say it: on a date?"~

"You think he'll say yes?"

~"He will. You have my blessing. He's a hero after all. A good catch."~

"What's the worst thing that can happen, right? I'm going to ask him out right now."

~"You do that. And don't fret. I've got your back, kid."~

Nate met up with Kean, Sharminella and Bubby the Wanton Booboo doll out on the street. He found them staring at something overhead. Poledoris was climbing up the drainpipe of one of the gingerbread houses and mooning everyone below in the process.

~"I see the circus is back in town."~

"What's he doing?"

"It is anyone's guess. He simply took off," Kean explained.

~"He thinks he's a tightrope walker now. Look."~

Poledoris stepped onto a wire strung between two houses and attempted to walk across it. The wire held up festive banners emblazoned with the Pinglop logo. It was the silhouette of an owl.

~"Have you noticed?"~

'Yep. Barn owl.'

"Get down from there!" Kean shouted. "You are going to break your neck."

As if on cue, halfway across, Poledoris's colossal gut tipped the balance and he plunged. Sharminella screamed, but not out of fear. Captivated she watched as, in the nick of time, Poledoris grabbed hold of the wire with his big toe. It was unreal how the one toe was capable of carrying his entire weight. He let his arms droop, and allowed the rest of the body to go limp. What happened next was… nothing. He just hung there in that topsy-turvy state.

"Oh, Pollydolly is waiting," Sharminella gasped. She clapped her tiny little hands together. Soft chuckles escaped from her ruby lipstick lips. She was expecting a show.

And sure enough, before long, something loomed on the horizon, a whopper of a mean-looking bird, its wingspan easily surpassing twelve feet. It was an old albatross out to settle an old score. Poledoris was ready for it, but not as ready as he could have been, because in a blink the albatross was upon him, attacking without restraint... using the hook at the end of its bill to peck into the flesh... its webbed feet kicking him in the gonads, repeatedly. Both Nate and Kean contorted their legs in sympathy.

"An albatross? Here?"

"It appears so."

~"In a way it reminds me of trampling grapes in a barrel... but now in midair, and in a groin."~

Poledoris was not in the least concerned about his posterity. He slapped the bird around a bit with his unscrewed toupee.

~"Ouch, Cap'n. This is painful simply to watch... Yet, strangely mesmerizing too."~

Despite the blows, the bird didn't let up. And neither did Poledoris. They really went at it, wrapped up in their titanic battle of the testicles. *Albatross v. the pinnacle of provocation.*

"That's classic Poledoris!" Nate smiled satisfied. "I never can tell what misadventures the ogre is getting into, from one moment to the next."

"Any idea what he could have done to make that bird so pugnacious?" Kean asked casually.

"Pugnacious? If you're asking me why they're fighting, I don't know, but to put it in your lingo: whenever Poledoris is involved, the *why* is circumstantial by default."

Nate was actually teasing him now. Kean returned the smile. Their quarrel about the way the psychotherapist talked seemed long forgotten.

Meanwhile, the spectacle above their heads was gathering a

crowd of offended Pinglop denizens and the same businessmen from the hotel. Nate expected an outbreak of policemen to come and arrest Poledoris. Unfortunately that never happened, but he did briefly catch a glimpse of a patrol car in a side street... before it drove off.

'*Weird city.*'

~"Their loss. More for us to enjoy, I say. This is epic drama. Bird against beast!"~

'*Awesome. I just came up with bird against birdbrain.*'

~"Even better."~

The fight continued for another hour. Inevitably, it deteriorated into a stalemate. Both having exerted themselves to the limit, Poledoris could only manage one punch every ten wheezes, and the albatross had landed on the wire and sporadically snapped at its opponent's toe hairs. All of it was boring Sharminella. She swirled her finger through her golden locks and popped bubble gum bubbles. "Boo!... So many boo!"

"Oh, well. I'm heading back to my bathroom," Nate informed her and Kean. "It's getting a bit chilly in this bathrobe, and I guess we've seen everything there is to see here."

"Wait."

"What is it, Sharmy?"

"Nanny?"

"Yes?"

"I, uh.."

"What is that look on your face?" Nate said with suspicion. "Are you... shy all of a sudden?"

"Uh... Bubby wants to ask something... Please?"

Nate was genuinely moved. Not that long ago she would have shouted orders at him. '*She even said please and actually meant it!*' Lately there had been definite signs of improvement.

"Okay, Princess. Why don't we let Bubby whisper in my ear what it is that Bubby wants to ask me?"

Sharminella held up the plastic doll and Nate pretended to listen like a scientist concentrating hard on something. He even mimicked stroking a long pointy beard.

"So Bubby wants to ask if, mm, Nate wants to take me to an ambush park *tomomomow*. Kean says it's only, mm, ten *mimes* away from here. *Pleaaaaaase?*"

Sharminella showed Nate a flyer with dates and events being held at a place called *Gambolodrome*.

"An amusement park? Sure, but why would you... I mean, *Bubby*, do *you* think that your friend Sharminella would want to go with us too? She doesn't like roller-coasters. Or other children."

"Yes, but there's also a talent show also and, mm, maybe she can give a stage *pur foam ants?*"

~"Ah! The cat's out of the bag."~

Sharminella set off her huge eyelashes... the batting effectively turning her eyes into strobe lights. Impossible to resist.

"Hah. Okay, you got it. We're going to the Gambolodrome tomorrow."

"*Weeee!* Nate is the best nanny in forever time!"

"Great. Except for the nanny part. I'm not a nanny. Want to race me back to our rooms?"

"Yeah."

"I shall count us down."

"Yeah."

"Ready, Sharmy?"

"Yeah."

"On the count of three we go. Three–" and Nate started running, shouting gleefully over his shoulder "The last one back inside is a rotten wannabe child prodigy!"

Sharminella, her legs already in hot pursuit, shouted the war cry back at him, her dodgy articulation making it sound more like *cotton wallaby chilled porridge.* She knew Nate was going to cheat, because she'd taught him that trick. The race was on. Halfway to the hotel entrance, though, Nate turned around.

"Ah, Kean, before I forget," he casually said in a shaky voice that gave everything away, "I've been meaning to ask you, if you've got nothing planned in your calendar for tomorrow evening–and this is of course entirely without obligation, and feel free to say so if you have better things to do–but if it doesn't put you out and you're okay with it–and knowing of course that everyone needs to *fuel up* so to speak in any case, usually thrice a day in fact, to sustain healthy organs like the bowels, and brain and, uh, birth canal.–Why birth canal? You don't have a birth canal. Forget that I said birth canal.–But so, I mean, if you don't mind the idea, and if it suits you, then…"

"Then?"

"Then would you perhaps like to go to dinner with me?"

~"on a date!"~

"… like, on a date?"

"I would be delighted."

"Tomorrow evening then."

"Tomorrow it is."

"Cool."

Red in the face, Nate promptly left the spot, the spot where his dignity had left him ten seconds earlier.

~"Birth canal. Smooth."~

20. Poledangerous

Officers Dirks and Duncetead were standing in the office of the Chief of Police once again. It was an understatement to claim that the report they had handed in on the escapee from Portweald's psychiatric hospital was *not going down well.*

"This report is horseshit!" the Chief spat. He'd never been much for subtlety. He was seated behind his desk (on a rickety chair that he refused to trade in for a more esthetically pleasing version on the basis that it would constitute a wasteful expenditure on the taxpayer's back). The Chief reread the paragraph with growing exasperation.

"Are you kidding me with this?... I quote, *The old woman turned into a giant ladybug and took off.* What did I tell you about including fantasy characters?"

"But I changed that part," Dirks tried in self-defense.

"I can see that, yes. You crossed out *giant ladybug* and wrote *old woman* above it in handwriting. So is that what you are saying, Officer? That the old woman turned herself into an old woman? Quite a feat!"

"Uh…"

"Then you typed that *She bit her way through the inch-thick bars in the window* and you crossed that out too and wrote *She probably used a can opener on the inch-thick bars.* A lot of the sentences have been altered, in fact. I won't even begin to comment on how her *venom spewing* was a typo and that you meant to type *spilling jelly* all along.

"Sir, we–"

"You two are a disgrace to your badges and uniforms! Seventeen years in service, and you both have yet to solve a single case, let alone write a decent report."

Fuming he shoved the report off his desk. It bounced off Duncetead's ample paunch... a paunch precariously balancing on a pair of relatively skinny legs... a paunch commemorating all those fallen deep-fried chicken wings of bygone buffets.

In an attempt to relax, the Chief stepped out of his office and drank a swig of water from the cooler.

Long ago, when he'd been just a regular cop, before he got promoted to his elevated position, he had taken the round-the-clock cacophony of the police station for granted. Nowadays he reveled in these rare moments by the water cooler, where he could soak up the sounds of distress calls coming in, the ramblings of vagrants and, invariably, the complaints of a streetwalker having lost a hair extension on his or her free ride to jail. The sounds soothed him. How he missed being on the frontline of the law. He missed the graveyard shifts. The camaraderie. The time when cops were cops, not the jokers he had to manage today...

"See how that vein was throbbing on his forehead?" Dirks whispered to Duncetead.

"It looked like a worm dancing on a hotplate," Duncetead mouthed back.

"I didn't say you two could talk."

The Chief was back.

"Sorry, Sir," Duncetead said out loud.

"Stand up straight and pay attention for once," he scolded them. "And–give me strength–I can see your navels hanging out from under your shirts! I expect everyone under my supervision to maintain an impeccable physical appearance."

"Yessir!" They saluted and clacked their heels together.

clack

"Tuck in your shirts."

"Yessir!"

clack

196

"Not each other's shirt, nitwits! Tuck in *your own!*"

"Yessir!"

clack

"And please refrain from saluting. This is not the army. And if it's at all possible, take up jogging. You both look one wicker basket short of a hot air balloon."

The Chief of Police could be very intimidating. Over his thirty-year long career he had overcome many things: rowdy protest marches, prison escapes, natural disasters, budget cuts. During it all he had managed to keep a calm and clear head, but there was just something about the presence of Officers Dirks and Duncetead that made his orifices bleed humanity after a minute.

"I have decided I'm going to give you one last chance to redeem yourselves. You better not mess this one up!"

"Thank you, Sir," Dirks stuttered. "We'll make good." He even made a little curtsy before he could stop himself. "Please don't put us on guard duty at the duck pond."

"Don't grovel. It's unbecoming of a policeman... Now, pay attention, I have here the three files that Officer Pittles was investigating. Three crimes linked to a same suspect. Now, as you may have heard, Pittles is going in for surgery to have his eleventh toe amputated. So, since Human Resources is breathing down my neck about how I should show myself more accommodating, and thus, since your colleague is going to be on sick leave for the next five weeks, no less, I am counting on you to take over the suspect's arrest. Clear so far?"

"Yessir!"

"Pittles has delivered excellent work. He's found a clear link between the recent break-in at our local Museum of Contemporary Art and two group abduction cases on the other side of the country. The suspect is going by the moniker Poledoris."

"Poledoris, huh?" Duncetead said. "What kind of a twerpy name is that?"

"We haven't been able to establish his real identity yet, Officer Duncetead. Nor do we know from under what rock he came crawling. One thing is certain: This Poledoris is a deranged criminal. He somehow managed to bypass surveillance cameras, but he's been described as in his mid-forties, corpulent, dead behind the eyes. In my mind, the characteristics of the worst kind of sociopath. He is dangerous. *Poledangerous.*"

"Is he armed? Any concealed weapons?"

"No, but he can be extremely persuasive on a psychological level. And his physical strength is off the charts."

"What crimes did he commit, Sir?"

"I was just coming to that, Officer Dirks. Based on witness accounts we have reason to believe that this was the same jackass who last summer impersonated a cruise ship captain. It was all over the news. He commandeered *The Popjoy Princess*, a ship crammed with pensioners on vacation, and he ran it straight into a garbage island. The depravity this man will have others endure is outrageous. After the ship hit the island, he forced dozens of helpless senior citizens, wearing nothing but their bathing suits, to disembark onto the garbage heaps. Some of them suffering from dementia were so greatly perturbed by the sudden change of scenery that they started searching for their pills and dentures and things in the stinking trash. Stop grinning, Officer Duncetead! This is serious!–"

"Sorry, Sir."

"–A reporter captured the devastation through the words of a cabin boy who saw it happen. I quote, *I thought we had sailed over the edge and into the netherworld. Seeing those withered ghouls... shocked, adrenalized... crawling over a landscape of intolerable stench and decay was a sight that will haunt me till the day I die.*"

"Hilarious," Duncetead coughed through his fist to Dirks.

"Don't test me!" the Chief snapped. "I don't care for your attitude."

"Sorry, Sir. I will try to contain myself, Sir."

"See that you do! Now, the most incredible part is that this Poledoris disappeared off the island without a trace. No raft was missing. They searched everywhere, but he was simply… gone."

"I remember the story," Dirks said enthused, "because I saw the B-movie they made about it called *Geriatric Popjoy of Doom–the shipwreck chronicles.*"

"I saw *Attack of the Saucy Wreckage Women*," Duncetead added with equal enthusiasm. "Entertaining, but clearly a knock-off. *Tittopia Magazine* only gave it two out of five boinks."

"In the movie," Dirks continued smiling, "the captain gave the old-timers a tour around the island like he was a museum guide, pausing at broken bottles and rusty bedsprings and things."

"That rumor was never substantiated," the Chief cut in annoyed. "We only deal in facts here. Anyway. Three months after the cruise ship debacle he resurfaced in a zoo. At night he slipped inside the park and wreaked havoc. We've got some blurry surveillance footage of him trying to mate the koalas with the sloths. He glued tubular bells onto a tortoise's shell. When the creature moved, the bells chimed. I won't even mention what he did to the albatross."

"What *did* he do to the albatross?"

"I said, I won't mention it!"

"I'm wondering, Sir," Dirks asked. "How do we know what his moniker is?"

"I'll tell you. He drugged a dozen pink flamingos, knotted them together by their necks and then *signed* the atrocity *Poledoris* by squeezing the ink out of an octopus. And there is more. Poledoris hotwired a vehicle shaped like a steam train that was normally used to take kids around the safari park section. He wrestled a bunch of zoo animals inside the compartments and drove them into the city. He stopped in front of a theater where an award ceremony was being held. The celebrities on the red carpet found themselves posing with giraffes, snakes, anteaters, et cetera.–"

"Ha! That's justice," Dirks remarked. "If you ask me, those lazy moneygrubbing celebrities got what they deserved."

"–No, it is not *justice*, Officer. It borders on animal cruelty."

"Now, Sir, I wouldn't go so far as to say they are animals."

"I'm talking about cruelty *to the zoo creatures,* not the celebrities!" the Chief shouted. His two lamebrained subjects were more than he could deal with. It took him counting down from ten before he could continue his narrative. "It was not until an orangutan stormed the stage, ate the wig of the presenting actress and pooped on a lifetime achievement award that Security realized there was something wrong. By then Poledoris was long gone. The theater crowd thought it was all part of a brilliant show. The organizers of the event and the zoo prefer to keep it that way and have requested a discrete investigation."

The Chief walked out into the hall (and was instantly gratified by the erratic hubbub of his fellow lawmen hard at work keeping the lid on criminality in their coast town.)

"Bernadette?"

"Yes, Sir?" a perky voice answered from somewhere behind a row of ferns.

"Would you be a dear and call that pilot and ask him to come round, let's say, within an hour? In fact, the sooner the better. Thanks. My men are ready."

"No problem. I'm calling him now."

The Chief caught the mystified looks on Dirks and

Duncetead's bloated faces, but he wasn't going to explain about the pilot just yet. A little payback for all the things they put him through.

"And that brings us to case three: Portweald. On the first of this month, late in the evening, Poledoris broke into our museum and stole several works and vandalized several others. Surveillance cameras, unfortunately, were out due to maintenance work, but we can be fairly certain it was him because he left his signature tag all over. The financial damage is negligible, in my opinion–they are contemporary art paintings and installations, not really worth the materials used–but it is a crime nonetheless. The breakthrough we needed finally came when Pittles asked around in a local supply store. The day after the break-in a man who fits the description to a T instructed canvases to be delivered to his residence in an apartment house on Snollygoster Street. He slipped up!"

"Hooray!" Dirks cheered.

"Hooray!" Duncetead echoed, but he was engrossed in his own world of thought. He'd been picking his nose and was displeased with what he found there.

"Hooray indeed. Officer Pittles chatted with the janitor of the apartment house. Poledoris was last seen seated in the car of the next-door neighbor, possibly an accomplice, who told the janitor that he was leaving on a business trip to some place called Pongo... No, Pinglop, that's it. Earlier today, a patrol car there sighted two persons who match the description of Poledoris and the neighbor."

"So when will the miscreant come back?" Dirks asked.

"*Suspect*, please... I have arranged special clearance for you both to leave Portweald and apprehend him and the likely accomplice. A special helicopter will pick you up and fly to Pinglop. So take the arrest warrants, facial composites and so forth, and go and catch them. You will be out of my hair... I mean, out of my jurisdiction for days, maybe even weeks," the Chief smirked with an undeniable amount of malicious pleasure.

This new information hit the two like a bomb.

"I must protest urgently, Sir!" Dirks insisted. "My wife is cooking meatloaf for supper tonight and she'll get cross if I'm not there to refuse to eat it.–"

"I have a weak pancreas!" Duncetead cut in, sweating like a ham roast, "And I have a medical condition. My podiatrist forbids me to fly."

"Podiatrist? That's a physician for feet."

"Yes, Chief. I get cold feet quickly."

"You will depart in an hour! No more nonsense. Go home, pack clean underwear and take off. That is an order! Now, off with you. Happy travels."

Duncetead shoved his colleague and whispered "This is all your fault, Dirks!"

"Yours!" Dirks retaliated by slapping Duncetead on the back of his balding head.

"Behave!"

"Sorry, Sir," they murmured disgruntled.

"I want this middle-aged thug caught before he starts killing people. Remember, go by the book. And I don't want to read any more tripe about monster beetles shooting venom in the report. Is that understood?"

"Yes, mister Chief, Sir!" Duncetead blurted out.

"You can read up on the three cases during the flight."

"Uh, one small thing, Sir," Dirks said... with a lurking dread that he knew the answer to the next question already.

"What is it, Officer?"

"That neighbor, would his name by any chance be Nate Noodascue?"

"Extraordinary! How did you know?"

Dirks and Duncetead looked at each other in misery.

"I had a hunch, Sir."

"Good to see that brain has not turned into a donut hole just yet... I gather, since you already met Noodascue, interrogated him on a drunk and disorderly charge, had him at your fingertips *and let him walk*, you both are best placed to sort this mess out. In your own interests, return with Poledoris and the neighbor and I might consider not kicking you off the force."

"Thank you, Sir!"

clack

"No saluting, I said... and no curtsying either!"

Dirks quickly got up off his knee.

"Now, dismissed!"

21. Splinters

Pinglop. Before dawn.

Uncharacteristically, Nate was already up, had completed his squat exercises, and had showered and eaten room service.

"Jarrrvis, are you awake?" he asked, yawning heavily.

~"I woke up a minute ago. What did we have for breakfast?"~

"Fruit and a croissant."

~"You could have ordered kippers for me, you know?"~

"Kippers and croissants do not go together."

~"I never get to choose."~

At four thirty-five a.m. Nate left the room for his appointment. Cibyl was going to train him today. Train him in what exactly? He'd spent the better part of the night speculating.

"Good morning." Kean shot past Nate and bounded up the steps of the hotel's winding staircase.

"Oh, hi. Good morning," Nate said surprised. He didn't expect to run into his date-to-be at this time of day. Well, *brush into* was more accurate. Kean was already out of view. "Hey, your fly is undone. Do you know that?"

Kean halted on the top floor. "Is it? That is disconcerting. I suddenly realize I have been networking among renowned psychotherapists looking like this for hours."

"You mean, you haven't even gone to bed yet? You don't seem at all tired."

"I have good genes. Though I might take a little nap later on. I will see you at dinner?"

"Yeah, till then… Oh, and if possible, try to prevent Poledoris from eating any more pencils. I could hear his voice coming through the wall. He sat on the john all night groaning *Splinters!*"

"Will do, Nate. I'll keep an eye on him." He could only just about see the backside of Nate descending the stairs.

"Thanks," Nate's voice answered from below.

"Incidentally, it is not just pencils he has consumed. Wax crayons too."

Now it was Nate's turn to halt on the landing. "Crayons? How do you figure?"

"Well, my suspicion was aroused when I saw Sharminella leaving the oddball's room carrying an empty box of crayons and a funnel. I think she may have been stuffing red crayons in the troglodyte's mouth."

"Caught her red-handed, so to speak," Nate said before he could stop himself. Was that normal behavior for a six-year-old? He was beginning to question his co-tenant's mental health. And a follow-up question was already elbowing itself to the front of his mind. '*What if I am partially to blame?*'

~"How do you mean?"~

'*Be honest. Wouldn't you say that I've been enabling her?*'

~"Enabling *Verminella?* Of course you have. All these newfangled child rearing notions are flawed. In my day, kids plowed the field and knew to keep out of the way of the adults, lest they'd feel the boot of discipline against their backsides."~

'*That is frowned upon nowadays, Jarrrvis. At her age she should be playing hopscotch with other children and, I dunno, building sandcastles instead of building a career. The pressure is too much and she's acting up.*'

~"Hence, the boot to the butt."~

'*There will be no boot to the butt!... Anyway, the wax crayons thing is totally unacceptable, but it's not too late for her to change. Somewhere deep beneath that glitzy pretense there hides the pure soul of a brave little girl.*'

~"Pure soul?"~ Jarrrvis scoffed. ~"You're assuming she placed the funnel in Poledoris's mouth and not somewhere else."~

'Go ahead. Laugh it up. If I can't make her see that what she did was wrong, she'll grow up to be a cruel and miserable she-devil whom everyone detests.'

~"Isn't she already?"~

'Side-splittingly amusing, Jarrrvis.'

~"Well, you know what they say: You can't choose your own children."~

'And that's the thing. Why do I have to do it? I'm not even her legal guardian. Why can't I just walk away? And while we're at it, why can't I get rid of Poledoris too? My life would be so much simpler.'

~"I can see the headlines already: Poledoris, the ingrown toenail of Nate's existence, surgically removed. Nate to watch home movie in peace. A nation rejoices."~

Nate sighed, then shouted "Kean, you still there? Will you do me a favor?"

After a few moments, Kean stepped out into the stairwell again. "Anything for you, Nate."

"At your next coaching session, will you make clear to her that it's strictly forbidden to feed the poledorilla?"

~"Hahah. Good one."~

"I have already made a note of it."

"I hope that after the experience, Poledoris will never eat pencils and crayons again. Well… at least for a while."

"How true," Kean replied. "He is a bonanza of blunders. Where are you heading?"

"An appointment with Cibyl. You know, that crazy chairwoman I told you about. My training starts in half an hour.

~"Aye. The theme is How to fulfill your transcendental destiny in three queasy steps."~

"Oh, before I forget, Kean. Just so you know, Sharminella is going to practice her new routine in front of the mirror in her room. And for this afternoon I promised I'd take her to a talent show at an amusement park."

"That is convenient, but I won't be here anyway. I am giving a lecture at the seminar. The topic is *Psychotherapy for plumbers: sanitary or just a pipe dream?*"

"Okay, have fun… if you can. See you at dinner tonight."

An early sun was rising off the rim of the plateau and coloring the meadows and picturesque streets in a blend of misty yellows. The view was sensational but, instead, Nate had been closely watching the Pinglopians on his way to Cibyl's headquarters.

~"I don't see her either."~

'Penelope? No, she's not here… All these folks are out and about and it's barely five in the morning. Why are they not in their beds?'

~"Strange city."~

After a ten-minute walk, Nate politely knocked on the door of the shack.

"Come on in, honey. I was just taking a rum cake out of the oven."

~"Rum? I live for rum!"~

Cibyl was still wearing her scruffy jacket and the same gray skirt. Her white hair was even more unruly and odd-looking than the last time they'd met.

'If it'd be possible to make popcorn out of a couple of hairy coconuts, I bet that thing on her head would be the result.'

~"There! Did you see that?"~

'See what?'

~"I swear, just now a moment ago, it shape-shifted ever so slightly when it was on the edge of your field of vision."~

'What was?'

~"Her hair."~

'Her popcocornuts *shape-shifted?*'

~"If you wish."~

'*How can you be sure that what you saw was not her wig sliding off her head? I mean, nowadays they can make a very convincing wig.*'

~"I thought we established that she doesn't wear a wig."~

'*Maybe her hair is possessed by space aliens.*'

~"You're not going to take what I saw seriously then?"~

'*What you* thought *you saw? No, I am not.*'

"Nate, are you coming?"

"Sorry. Coming."

Nate followed Cibyl into the kitchen, by skillfully performing a pelvis-intensive dance to negotiate his body around the columns of stacked paper forever on the brink of collapse.

He coughed a few times.

~"Bah! Anyone brought their gas mask? Why doesn't she throw those musty old publications out?"~

'*We know why already. She uses it for fortune-telling.*'

~"I'd use it to build a fire."~

'*Me too. Who can live like this? Hardly a place for a business hotshot. Maybe she's a delusional hoarder. Or maybe she's planning to paper-mâché the hell out of an arts and crafts project.*'

~"Aye… Hey, I was wondering, Nate."~

'*Shoot.*'

~"Do you believe in that cibylation stuff?"~

'*I haven't decided yet. My first impression was not to trust her at all, but you can't deny she has a way with people. She seems so…*'

~"Dowdy."~

'*I was going to say* determined *when she's talking, but yes, dowdy too.*'

The quirky host put her cooling cake into a picnic basket.

Napkins and some forks had already been packed. "Here. Hold Cork for me, Nate, would you?" She dumped the bowl into his hands. The orange-striped fish was spiraling around inside. Water splashed over the rim. "It's going to be a beautiful day. What do you say we go outside and start your training with a leisurely picnic?"

"Uh, okay I guess," Nate replied a bit startled.

"It's time for walkies, Count Corkinston," Cibyl told the little fish. She tapped one of her ink-stained fingers against the glass and blew it an affectionate kiss. (*It* being the fish, not the finger.) Cork experienced this as two giant distorted lips intent on sipping up its watery house and its life altogether.

Uncanny, really, how frighteningly similar Nate's future was to Cork's predicament… once the dowdy woman would get her way.

Fifteen minutes later, they were swiftly heading in the direction of Hill Street. Nate had had to step to one side a couple of times to avoid collisions with other pedestrians. Not Cibyl, though. Somehow she knew how to get around unobstructed. Nate constantly had to catch up.

"Today is the annual arts and crafts fair," she brought him up to speed, "with lots of activities and wholesome entertainment.-"

~"She really is planning to paper-mâché things to death."~

"-Cibyl Unlimited is sponsoring the event. It's my way of giving back to the community for the taxes it has to pay."

"Wait. You own the city?"

"Of course. Pinglop is my private little pastime. But rest assured, I'll be happy to put both the city and my entire business conglomerate under our mutual management."

Nate gave her one of his characteristic frowns.

"Oh deary me. I don't need to *cibylate* alphabet soup to know that you are still not with the program."

"I'm sorry, Cibyl. No offense, but I struggle with the thought of you owning a business empire."

~"...or a fashion sense, evidently."~

"No need to apologize. Listen, I have an idea. Set me an impossible challenge. Ask for anything you want and I will get it for you in no time. Should pose no problem for a tycoon like myself, right?"

~"Quick. Ask for a cool million in unmarked non-sequential bills!"~ Jarrrvis whispered conspiratorially.

"Really? Uh, okay, let's see. How about making it rain lotus petals from the sky? That would be an awesome sight," Nate said half-jokingly.

"Is that all?"

"Isn't that enough?"

Without delay the strange woman ran into the nearest house to make some calls. Two minutes later she was back out with a confident smile on her face. "Thirty minutes. Consider it done."

~"Well, pickle my mackerel! I'm sticking around to see this."~

"I have a question, Cibyl. You are a tycoon, but where are your office buildings?" He could no longer curb his curiosity. "So far, in Pinglop, I've only seen residences, small stores and so on. No offices."

"All in good time, Nate."

At the end of the lane they took a sharp left turn. They entered Hill Street, a wide stretch of cobblestones that sloped at a very steep angle. On both sides were diagonal storefronts adorned with wooden panels carved in the shape of owls and colorful brickwork in typical Pinglop style.

A traffic circle halfway down the street was bustling with onlookers (predominantly pregnant ones) who were crowding around the world's largest rice pudding. To sate their voracious appetite they were yoo-hooing and pleading for a taste, but the chef de cuisine refused.

'*They remind me of a pack of wild animals, but with swollen ankles.*'

~"Aye, never come between twenty unstable preggies and their eating frenzy."~

Overhead a banner cheerfully proclaimed *Rice to the occasion-breaking the pudding record!* The dessert itself was truly monumental. Nate imagined that the chef must have unearthed someone's swimming pool to serve as the bowl. When the sous-chefs started sprinkling on bags of brown sugar, the women looked like they were about to charge the crowd control barriers.

"Ignore them, Nate. They are of no importance."

Cibyl kept carving a downward path through the throng of people. The furrows on her forehead deepened. She had serious matters to discuss. "It is time for you to see the big picture. Infinite power will be yours, but you need to wake up and become *conscious*. Right now, you are worthless to me."

~"She dives right in, doesn't she?"~

'*Yeah. Let's go from nice to nasty in the blink of an eye. What does she mean by* conscious, *you think?*'

~"Ask her."~

"What do you mean by conscious?"

No response.

They came across a tall ladder. The man standing on it-a caricature of a ringmaster with a greasy goatee-was busy stacking sleeping pigs on top of each other, back to belly, into the general shape of a pyramid. So far he had stacked seven layers of pig. A placard explained the curious undertaking. *Otis the Hypnotist will dauntlessly attempt to annihilate the hog stacking record! Otis the Hypnotist keeps the animals in check by way of hypnosis.*

~"Good to see he's not wasting his talents."~

"Today is all about making you see that which *is* and that which *can be*," Cibyl continued her monologue. "Constraints are just things that happen to other people. What *we* are after is the ultimate conquest of the *Material and the Spiritual Blah-blah-blah—*"

~"*Blah-blah-blah?* That's proper terminology, is it?"~

"—Once you've opened your eyes, we will tackle the how. How to go about reaching these goals. But first, we begin with our initiation."

"Initiation? That's not a euphemism for fraternity hazing, is it? Because I promised my mom I would never allow my pubes to be dyed green again. It gave her quite a scare when she was doing my laundry."

"It has nothing to do with hazing," she quickly dismissed the remark. "You are one out of one hundred billion, scrumptious. You just haven't realized yet. You are a stubborn nonbeliever. This is going to change when you learn to manipulate soulnubs."

"Soulnubs?"

Cibyl had put on *the face.* The one that said *Don't interrupt.* So Nate decided to stop asking questions. For now.

They made their way through the press of people, to the other side of the circle where the vegetable stalls were. On a wagon, a wide range of pumpkins of different types and sizes were neatly put on display. In the back lay the largest pumpkin Nate had ever seen. *Nipple Nellie,* as they'd called it, weighed over eleven hundred pounds. Not the world record, but still impressive.

"I have the gift of cibylation, but it still took me many decades to track you down, Nate. Your soul signature is somehow hidden from sight. It annoys me to no end. Cibylation has pointed you out, so I should trust it. Still, there is something I'm missing." She muttered something to herself in reassurance before continuing. "Guess I'll have to jog your slumbering memory. Drag it out of you..." She looked up at him again. "Why does your soulnub cluster keeps being so cloudy?"

"Why is my what?"

So much for not asking questions.

"I need to be sure that it is really you! You see, I can't risk revealing the master-plan to the Col–." She bit her tongue. "To our enemy."

~"Colonel? As in *Colonel Taytelly?*"~

Instantly, Nate burned to ask her if that was who she'd meant, and what she knew about his visions, and also if she'd made that slip deliberately because it had seemed to come out somewhat forced. Instead, he opted to play it cool and he put on a poker face. "Enemy?"

"Yes. All in good time. With the enemy out of the way we'll become legends. Temples will be built to our glorification. Major cities will rise up around our thrones."

"I see," Nate said, not seeing at all.

The tiny fish swallowed another air bubble...

A bit further down Hill Street a painter was drawing mythological beings on a two hundred by two hundred inch canvas. The elaborate composition depicted sexually aroused satyrs riding on centaurs while attacking harpies; topless water nymphs and screaming sirens engaged in a dirty mud fight; winged hippocampi chasing a gluttonous sphinx who had unjustly appropriated all the ambrosia for herself.

~"I seem to be detecting a running theme in Pinglopian art."~

'*It's over the top ridiculous is what it is. What's wrong with a still life of a vase and some peaches?*'

~"This painting's got nice peaches too, if you know what I mean. I'd like to rinse 'em in water and eat 'em."~ Jarrrvis quipped lecherously.

'Yeah, I bet.'

"Nate?"

"Sorry, Cibyl. I got distracted."

"Let me ask you: How often do you find yourself in a weird situation? How often do weird things cross your path?"

"Where do I even start?"

"Don't answer. I'm being rhetorical."

"Oh."

"These things happen to you because you're more than the absent-minded Adonis I see before me. A scorpion among dung beetles cannot content itself with rolling dung up a hill. No, it is ruler of its environment. And you, too, are a scorpion."

Nate wanted to say his star sign is Aquarius actually, but Cibyl was already two sentences ahead.

"Your potential is exponential. You are trying to fit into a world that is ordinary, but your supreme authority is evident. It is time you claim your birthright."

~"Could she explain to me the part about the dung beetles again?"~

They breezed past two glaziers who were very slowly carrying large sheets of glass into a house one at a time. The sheets were, of course, engraved with the Pinglop owl logo.

Cibyl and Nate stopped at the foot of the cobbled street, where a stone wall circled a hill covered with natural vegetation. The wall might once have been part of a bastion or a fort, but today the little that remained of it was overgrown with weeds. The branches of trees and bushes growing out of the wall provided shade to a row of benches huddling up against it. Cibyl motioned Nate to join her on a bench and eat from the cake. She herself liked to take large bites and relish it by chewing with her mouth open. She offered him a cup of refreshing and most unwanted celery juice.

"Thanks. I'm good."

~"Now is your chance to pry some answers out of her, Nate."~

He cleared his throat. "Hey, uhm, so if I understand you correctly, all this information about me becoming a great ruler in the future, you got from cibylation?"

"I guarantee it. I'm an expert. Cibylation is never wrong, but the right interpretation of the result is crucial... I've got an idea. Let's do a test and see what comes up. Give me a scrap of printed text and I'll cibylate it for you."

Nate rummaged through his pockets. The little box of itching powder and the egg timer he had gotten on loan from the CEO unfortunately didn't have any text on them. He searched through his wallet.

"What's that annular bulge there?"

Nate's face instantly reddened into the kind of vivid red that could rock the socks off a boiled lobster. (Why a lobster would bother to wear socks is entirely beside the point, and in all fairness, cooks sometimes put little chef's hats on turkey legs and nobody says anything about that.)

"Don't be shy. Show it to me, dear," Cibyl encouraged him.

"This is actually the condom my dad gave me at my party when I turned eighteen," Nate confessed. "I keep it as a memento of the two most embarrassing minutes of my life."

~"The more so given the fact that the condom was already past its expiration date when he gave it to you and it implied that your father had been waiting two years for you to finally start dating."~

"It'll do. That's the main principle of cibylation. Whatever your eye lands on first *must* give you the reply to your question. So, condom wrapper, enlighten me. When will Nate be converted into a believer?... Now, let's have a look."

The first thing she saw was the serial reference *SG-OOP-OPPP-N*. She concentrated hard. "It's a cryptic reply." Then her

215

eyes lit up and she smiled.

"What is it? What does it say?"

"You'll find out in a minute, but we'd better go sit on that bench over there!" Cibyl quickly packed up and moved.

"Why? What's wrong with this bench?"

"Nothing's wrong with the bench itself, but unless you insist on eating pumpkin spread with the cake you'd better come over here and sit tight. The show is about to begin."

"The show?"

She pointed at a swallow passing overhead. With swift agility and skill the bird skimmed the rooftops on its way to its nest underneath the eaves of the perfume store. Then, disaster struck.

A flash of sunlight reflecting off the glaziers' sheet of glass caught the swallow unawares and caused the bird to miss its entry and crash head-on into the face of an otorhinolaryngologist (a type of doctor) who on that precise moment had decided to open her dormer window *to let fresh air in* but who got a mouthful of swallow instead.

As it happened, she was a schooled opera singer as well, so her ensuing ear-piercing scream snapped a dozen of the top pigs on the stack out of their hypnotic daze. The pigs kicked and squealed to get down, and in turn the whole structure started swaying dangerously. Onlookers gasped, took a step back. Some were drumming to move away.

The otorhinolaryngologist, meanwhile, puked out of the window, right into the neck of the painter underneath. Rattled by the sudden spell of acid rain he knocked over three large paint buckets, lost his balance and was knocked out cold. The glaziers suddenly had to face the challenge of trying not to slip on a big splash of paint. They performed a weird waltz, desperately juggling the sheet of glass in-between them, leaping out of the way of incoming women fleeing the mayhem above.

The glaziers failed and the glass was dropped. It crashed into a million sharp pieces.

Behind them, higher up, the pig pyramid finally collapsed in an overwhelming barrage of grunts and outcries. Some pigs fell onto bales of hay that cushioned their fall, many of them plunged into the rice pudding which burst out of its container and propelled itself down the street like a torrent of hog-flavored lava.

As the laws of disaster dictate, at this precise moment, a wheel of the pumpkin wagon broke off and dozens of pumpkins, big and small, tumbled off and kept rolling on, slow at first but then quickly gaining momentum. They spun through the sticky paint and through the charts of glass, transforming them into lethal weapons.

Halfway down, the orange blitz met up with the pudding raid, to form one giant killer wave of mass destruction. People were running for their lives. They dashed into stores left and right, took refuge in trees or jumped over walls, anything to escape the cataclysmic dessert.

And then, when no-one could have contrived a scenario worse than this, *Nipple Nellie*–the quintessential embodiment of pumpkinhood–came thundering down after, squashing everything in its path. It accelerated on the slippery street surface, blasted a hole through the big canvas (missing the prone painter by an inch) and took a last sprint.

Finally, it crashed violently and terminally into the empty bench on which Nate and Cibyl had been sitting earlier.

FWRACKK!

Nate's jaw dropped. There was nothing but pumpkin pulp and wood debris left.

~"Hot halibut tits!"~ Jarrrvis let slip. It was an old fisherman's expression.

"You look a bit pale, Nate," Cibyl said unperturbed. "Don't

you get enough roughage in your diet?"

Nate was speechless.

"Would you perhaps like some finger sandwiches?"

"We... we could have been crushed. If we had still been sitting on that bench we'd be killed. You saved us."

~"The whole street is a war zone!"~

"A-huh. Good thing I cibylated it as I did, right?"

For a grand finale, a squadron of biplanes cleaved the sky, spelling out letters in multicolored smoke: *N A T E.*

Then a million lotus petals were released from the planes. Petals that gently twirled and floated down to the city of Pinglop, to the turmoil below.

Cibyl smiled. "And now," she said, "you are a believer."

22. Twinkle twinkle

"That's the thing with living on a globe, Nate. You can run away from yourself, as far as your legs can carry you, but inevitably you will cross a point where every step farther is one step back to base."

At the top of the hill amid the bushes, Nate's bare feet were standing in the lukewarm water of Pinglop's natural spring. Cibyl was seated on the trunk of a fallen tree and watched him with her penetrating stare... scanned him for clues to his awakening powers. Up the street, the commotion had subsided and luckily no-one seemed to have suffered injuries save for minor bumps and bruises. Nate had blocked all that out of his mind. A sense of serenity had descended upon him.

His eyes followed the course of the spring water flowing down the hill, dividing into a multitude of brooks across a patchwork of fields, idling along curvy roads and the little groups of houses huddling together like football players.

In the far distance–no matter which direction Nate faced–he could see the rim of the high plateau on which the city was built. Beyond it, the ground fell away and there was just air. A steel-blue nothingness held Pinglop in a tight embrace. For all he knew, the outside world might not have existed anymore. The effect was enhanced by the fact that the plateau drooped nearer to the rim, like melting cheese on a slice of round bread.

"I, I'm starting to see what you mean. I think... The water is different somehow. It's strange." Nate focused on the water around his feet again.

"Go on, Nate," Cibyl smiled. "How is it strange?"

"It's like a puddle teeming with massive quantities of shimmering lights..." and then, dumbstruck by the sensation, he added "It is so beautiful!"

"Well done! This spring is the lifeline of the farmlands. They bring a form of energy to it. They are soulnubs. They do not just exist in pools. You, me, my fish Cork... every living being great and small on this planet possess a helping of it to sustain us. It is Life itself."

"It's gorgeous!"

It was a thrill for Nate to realize that he might finally come to understand his higher purpose. A purpose of which he had not even been aware until Cibyl had mentioned it a day earlier.

~"Seeing this water fills my maritime heart with memories of tropical beaches, the aurora borealis at sea and of other wonders. Like the invention of the sushi roll."~

'Sorry, what?'

~"Never mind. Just trying to be poetic here."~

'Poetic... you?'

"Now, Nate, I want you to look closely at Cork. What do you see?"

"There is a... ball inside Cork. Like a soap bubble, but with the same shiny stuff swirling around in it."

"Good! Very good. If he didn't have that, he'd be dead. All the soulnubs gather together in a soul cluster. Try something bigger."

A squirrel came scurrying down a nearby tree, saw the humans and froze midway, hanging upside down.

"Its cluster seems larger," Nate marveled.

"That's right, sugar. The squirrel is more evolved than the fish. Hence, more soulnubs."

Soulnubs. Clusters. Bubbles... Nate tried to remember when and in what context he'd heard about those things before, but he was too excited to give it much thought. He was enraptured by this new insight. This skill. His brain registered the bubbly image as if it was superimposed on what he was looking at. It didn't matter if that what he was looking at happened to be a squirrel or something else, the bubble was really there. Nate felt like, up until now, he had only been shown movie trailers and now finally he got to see the big picture.

"This is really cool. When I was a boy, I would sometimes look into the sun with closed eyes and I'd see minuscule specks floating on my eyeballs and I always thought that I'd found a way to enter another dimension or something. Well, now I know for sure. I was right all along. There is this other dimension!"

"We are making progress. Good. Now, look at me, Nate. Who do you see? Really concentrate. Not what. *Who* do you see?"

Nate did his best but couldn't distill a similar bubble from her.

"It's too hard. I'm sorry. I just can't do it," he said crestfallen.

"Nate Noodascue–just–can't–do–it!" Cibyl professed to the sky mockingly. "Relax. No need to beat yourself up over it. Everything is practice. Try yourself first, perhaps. Might be easier."

"How do I do that? I can't see my whole body."

"That's irrelevant. You don't think you're watching with your eyes now, do you? Your sight comes from within. But if you think it will help, look at your reflection in the water."

"Nope. It's not working... Maybe if I try a smaller challenge first?" He scanned the trees and bushes. They all had a bubble, though theirs didn't light up as brightly. Every blade of grass had one too. To see them, he had to scrunch up his face.

Nate sensed the presence of something hiding a few yards away. It had an unusually large cluster in comparison to its size. "There's an animal over there. I think it's watching us." With his *regular* eyes he caught a glimpse of it. Two white ears popped up and then it darted away.

"A rabbit."

~"For a split-second I could have sworn that it was Spatula."~

'Can't be. Spatula is at the pet hotel.' Nate dismissed the thought. "It was just a rabbit with white fur."

"*A WHITE RABBIT?*" Cibyl shouted. Before Nate could respond, she was off, sprinting after the animal in a fury, holding up her skirt to run faster through the grass. Within seconds she had covered a quarter of the hillside. "*A WHITE RABBIT!*" A few seconds later and she was completely out of view, leaving both Nate and the squirrel wondering *What just happened?* After several minutes she still hadn't returned. "I've decided I don't like Cibyl. I think she's keeping things from me."

~"You *think?*"~

"I'm going to try my reflection again. Might as well." Nate cleared his thoughts and concentrated. "Here goes..."

A shape was slowly forming in his chest. A bubble. It expanded beyond the confines of his body, wider and wider, while inside innumerable soulnub particles were swirling around and multiplying. Nate was pleased with himself. '*Wow! It just keeps on growing.*' And then the soulnubs really materialized before his mind's eye. They were more radiant and breathtaking than any he had seen so far. To put the cherry on the cake, there were clearly not one, but two distinguishable soul clusters inside the bubble. The clusters sporadically interlocked and released again.

Nate stood agape. Aghast. And even a bit agog.

This was a very big deal.

Finally, here was proof.

'*I can see you, Jarrrvis! You really are inside of me!*'

~"Of course I am. Who do you think has been buoying you up all these years?"~

Nate stumbled, literally taken aback by this discovery of the century. He fell on his butt. A prickly thistle rewarded his arm with a bleeding cut.

"*Aaagh-wah-wah!* Crap crap triple crap with crap on top!"

He wanted all sorts of bad things to happen to the thistle. He wanted it to rot, to be yanked out of the ground, to die. And while he was cursing, a tiny string of nub particles was leaving the plant's bubble and dancing into Nate's own. In no time its bubble was emptied out and the plant wilted lifelessly to the ground. Nate stopped. He was shocked. At the same time he felt reinvigorated. Sweat dripped off his forehead. His hands were tingling. Somehow Nate felt healthier... more *spacious* for lack of a better word.

"Excellent progress!" A voice praised him. "I see now it was wrong to doubt myself."

Cibyl was back, more savage-looking, with broken twigs sticking out of her hair and skirt, with patches of grass stains and mud here and there, but apparently rabbit-free. She struggled to let a happy smile crowbar its way through her tense muscles. She failed stupendously. "Sorry I ran off like that. I was hoping to catch the rabbit for supper. It got away. Pity." It was obvious that she was very upset. "Anyway. I saw how you took those soulnubs. Well done. This is the confirmation I was waiting for."

"Hm. Thanks." Thoughts of guilt played ping-pong with Nate's conscience. "I didn't mean to kill that plant like that. I didn't even think I could kill a plant like that," he said baffled. "I knew it was a wrong thing to do and still I did it anyway."

~"Who knew you were a vindictive person like me. Heh-heh. Chin up. It's just a weed. No harm done."~

"You and me, we belong to a handful of folks who have this ability, Nate. Others have to eat fresh food to absorb the soulnubs. From birth, their soul clusters grow, but they are ultimately limited to their natural size. *We* are different. If we absorb more consciously we can keep on absorbing, perhaps indefinitely. Now can you see your potential? With ever-enlarging soul clusters we will move up to a higher evolutionary

223

level. We become true leaders."

~"Amazing!"~

For Nate this was a lot of information to compute. "Hold on a minute." An unsettling idea had just entered his head. "This was just a plant I took from. Could I do it to animals too? Or to people?"

"Why? Who do you hold a grudge against?–"

~"One particular large blob of man-beast springs to mind."~

"–Who would you like to kill?"

"No-one," he told her quickly, feeling extra guilty for even thinking such thoughts.

"Relax, Nate. It's extremely difficult to invade another person's soul cluster. You'll find that a real bullet does the trick better... What you *can* do, is silently put suggestions into someone's head. For that you need to bring yourself into resonance with his or her soulnub flux. In layman terms I call that *applying charisma*."

"Could I use it, let's say, to get someone to fall head over heels in love with me?"

"Love? Hah. Who's got time for that? I guess you could, yes, when you're running out of chat-up lines." Cibyl was rather unsympathetic about the subject of love, which displeased Nate. "Back to business," she said. "Were you able to see your own soul bubble in the water surface?"

Nate looked at his feet. His toes had wrinkled up from being submerged for so long. They resembled ugly grapes, only hairier. "Yes, I have. It's magnificent. Can you see me like that too?"

The question seemed to have hit a nerve with Cibyl. "Only fractions of it at a time. This is bugging me, I don't mind you knowing. I have trouble locking onto the image properly."

Nate hesitated.

Perhaps now, at long last, the right opportunity had arrived to share his secret with someone. The secret that there was a voice–*a spare soul*–called Jarrrvis bunking in his body. That there were two intertwining clusters inside of him.

Somewhere in his yearly years he'd decided to never tell anyone about his affliction, because when he kept murmuring things to his 'imaginary' friend, the people around him no longer found it cute. They found it worrying. But now... maybe he could somehow help Cibyl see Jarrrvis too. She might be open to that. Maybe. If only she didn't seem so untrustworthy. Nate made up his mind. '*This is not the right time. Her own fault for not believing in the really important stuff, like love.*'

~"Be a man, not a mollusk! Do ourselves a big favor and tell her. I think it's a great idea. She is going to make us very rich and powerful. Let me repeat that: very rich and powerful!"~

'*Sorry. It's my life and my body. You've already had yours.*'

~"That's a low blow!"~

'*I'm calling the shots.*'

~"Fine. But I strongly suggest you reconsider."~

"-ate! Nate! You are daydreaming. Listen when I'm talking to you," Cibyl said annoyed. "Concentrate and try to spot my cluster."

"Oops! Sorry. Okay, hold on."

Nate turned his newly acquired skills on Cibyl. It was easier than before. Her bubble inflated to a size markedly larger than his own and was packed with glorious soulnub particles. It was impossible to ever grow tired of watching this phenomenon. "Hurray!" Nate cheered in total awe. "Success."

She observed him... deliberated her next step. "This concludes today's lesson," she said.

"Huh? We're done?"

"Yes, I have to leave you now. Something urgent has come up that cannot wait. I'll see you tomorrow morning at my house. Five a.m. sharp. You're in for a big surprise. Do not be late."

Before the end of her sentence was spoken, she'd turned around and was speedily descending the hill.

"And she's off again. That woman only knows one exit."

~"Yep. Not to mention her weird behavior around rabbits."~

"Especially white ones... And what's up with you, Jarrrvis? One moment you distrust Cibyl, the next you want me to go along with her."

~"What can I say? Maybe she's just misunderstood. And, come to think of it, isn't she entitled to keep her private business private like everybody else? Just look at what you've learned from her today. I'm totally blown out of the water by it. I know you're feeling it too because I feel everything you feel. Seeing myself as a soul cluster did me a world of good."~

Nate smiled. "I'm happy too. Now I know I'm not just crazy in the head."

~"Thanks for showing me to myself."~

"You're welcome." They may have had their differences, but his partnership with Jarrrvis had never been better. "Now let's go find Poledoris and use these new powers to brainwash him into braying like a donkey."

23. Show

Poledoris was temporarily let off the hook because the moment Nate returned to Voegant Resort he was accosted by a brat dressed in a garment at the depth of fashion. (The *height of fashion* and Sharminella had never seen eye to eye.)

"Nanny, when do we go to *gabomobamadomnitay?* You sweared, but now it is very much late! Can we go? *Can-we-can-we-can-we-can-we?*"

"Sharminella, you're garbling syllables," he responded with an air of aloofness. "I think you'll find it's pronounced *Gambolodrome Matinee.*"

~"You completely forgot about the talent show."~

'*Only for a second.*'

"So we going? I want to *goooooooo!*"

"We'll leave in ten minutes."

Her little face lit up. "*Yaaaaaaay!* I go pack all my *accessessossies.*"

~"*Accessories to murder*, no doubt."~

Sharminella gathered her things. She was overexcited, fussing whether she should enter the competition in the pink boots with the golden flower stickers or the pink ballet flats with the brocade laces, and so forth and so on. When she reached full PHM (Preshow Hyperactive Mode), you engaged her at your own risk.

It didn't bother Nate in the least. He was in a good mood and even found her fluttering about endearing. He watched Sharminella in *cluster vision*, by lack of a better description, while she made faces in a mirror. Her bubble had not yet extended outside the body but it certainly was immensely pretty. '*Hooray. I still got it!*'

"My nose is too big, Nanny. Do I need *spastic seajelly?*"

"No, Sharm, you don't need plastic surgery. You have the most delicate little button mushroom nose I have ever seen."

(The nose under scrutiny was in fact about the size of a raisin.)

"*EEEE!* You call my nose a shroom!"

"Please don't shout so loud at me in your squeaky voice."

"I don't have a squeaky voice!" Sharminella squeaked.

"Of course you don't. Silly me. Come, put on your shoes. I'll carry the dresses and the beauty case. We're off to the amusement park."

"*Weeee!*"

~"Can't we practice a bit with nub particles instead? Last time I checked you were not Sharminella's personal assistant. It's not your job. You're spoiling the kid rotten. In my day, when something was rotten, it got pulled."~

'Jarrrvis, that's a terrible thing to say.'

~"Sharminella is a terrible thing too! And correct me if I'm wrong, but you've often said so yourself."~

Nate mumbled a whole cannonade of curse words. The problem with that was, of course, that Jarrrvis could hear every one of them.

On leaving the hotel, Nate and Sharminella were being hailed by Hadley Bog of *Hadley Petting*... "Sir, terrible news! Hello?"... The elderly caretaker was trying to catch up with them in the street. "Your cat is missing. Sir, wait up!" His legs shuffled toward them as fast as the arthritis would allow. To draw their attention, he waved the bandaged hand that Spatula had bitten... "Sir, it's important!"... He urgently wanted to tell Nate that after the kitten's breakout, three pregnant women had shown up and threatened to do him harm if he dared to contact its owner. They had taken off with his registry book, too, but later–in the doctor's office–the caretaker had remembered that Nate had mentioned that he was a guest at the hotel, so the man came walking here. Unfortunately, none of this news could be passed on because Nate and Sharminella boarded a streetcar and were soon rumbling away.

The two swiftly reached the edge of Pinglop city and took the elevator down to the base of the mountain (instead of the endless stairs). His car was still parked near the wishing well–slash–information stall. The heavy copper bell was gently rocking. Nate put his ear against it. Someone was snoring inside, causing the bell to hum. Nate picked up a stick and struck it against the rim.

"THE ENTRANCE TO PINGLOP IS OVER THERE."

"*I KNOW!*" Nate shouted back at the bell. "*BUT COULD YOU PLEASE TELL ME THE DIRECTION TO GAMBOLODROME?*"

"YES, I CAN," the androgynous person replied. "AND THERE IS NO NEED TO SHOUT."

The clapper moved. Its black cloth slunk down onto the ledge and assumed the shape of the svelte steward(ess).

(S)he smiled benignly. Nate and Sharminella stared in horror at the walrus overbite. They had sort of forgotten that it had a certain vampiric quality about it. The little queenie yipped and quickly hid behind Nanny's legs. Nate almost swallowed his own tongue. He wanted to hide too but, alas, all the legs were taken.

"ALLOW ME TO BE YOUR GUIDE."

"You, uh, you are not going to fly us there, are you?"

"COME AGAIN?"

"*ARE YOU GOING TO FLY US THERE?*" Nate blared.

"FLY? NONSENSE. I'LL GO BY MOTOR SCOOTER. YOU FOLLOW IN YOUR CAR. AND PLEASE STOP SHOUTING."

(S)he rolled out a tiny vehicle that was tucked away behind

some ferns and kick-started it. Large columns of black smoke shot out the back.

~"That thing's supposed to be a scooter? More like a can of beans on wheels."~

"RIGHT. LET ME PUT ON MY POT HELMET AND WE'RE OFF."

The person did so, leaving one long pointy ear sticking out from the side.

"Hop in the car, Sharmy. Everything's fine," Nate said, trying to reassure himself as much as her. "Who's up for a pleasant ride in nature?"

As it turned out, a pleasant ride it was not. Once underway, Nate had difficulty keeping up. Driving on the narrow roads proved tricky, whereas the scooter simply zipped straight through with reckless abandon.

'Why the hell does it have to be at full throttle?'

~"Go slower then."~

'Can't. If I fall behind, we might get lost in the forest.'

~"Look out!"~

Nate stepped on the brake just in time to avert slamming into an uprooted tree.

"ANOTHER TEN MILES AND WE'LL BE THERE. I KNOW A SHORTCUT."

The daredevil dove in between some shrubs. Nate followed helter-skelter. The new road was even worse. Potholes were lurking everywhere, jolting the car left and right.

~"We're in deep water now."~

"This is madness! Driving here is not off-road but *off-reason!*"

In the passenger's seat Sharminella was having a ball. She didn't understand the danger. "*Weeee! Go faster! Go faaaaster!*" She imagined she was inside a real-life racing game.

"Don't distract me, Princess. Nanny is tailgating the scooter demon from hell!"

The car slalomed around large boulders, floored it over smelly bogs and through what might have been a recreational nudist camp for deer. (Who knew what they got up to when they thought no-one was looking.) The car nearly collided with a fawn. ~"Watch it!"~ Nate's quick reflexes took over and, fortunately, he was back in the clear.

'The car can't take much longer of this. It's breaking apart.'

Just when the onslaught reached critical mass, a row of trees pulled aside like a curtain and Nate was driving on a lovely grassy field bathing in sunlight. In the distance he could see the enclosure of the amusement park. The batty guide slowed up next to him.

"I AM TURNING BACK HERE. I GET A HEADACHE WHEN I'M UPSIDE DOWN. ENJOY THE PARK. IF YOU FEEL LIKE TAKING THE SCENIC ROUTE BACK TO PINGLOP, YOU CAN FOLLOW THAT ROAD OVER THERE."

Nate dreaded it, but he looked over anyway.

~"Lo and behold! A perfectly decent road. Look, it is fittingly level and has a nice stripe in the middle to separate the lanes. My! It even has its own delightful little signpost pointing the way to Pinglop."~

'Have you finished?'

"BYE."

"Yeah, bye-bye," Nate grimaced as he waved the rider off. "Thanks for the spine-breaking torment. And thanks for not feasting on our blood."

"Let's-go-let's-go-let's-go!" Sharminella fretted. "The show is starting and I still need, mm, to try on outfits and makeup."

"I'm right behind you, Princess. We still have hours of time."

"Only hours?" She trotted across the parking lot. "Come on,

Nanny. Move!"

~"I don't understand what there is to try out. She's already wearing her blue dress."~

'Turquoise tube gown.'

~"Turquoise tube gown, I stand corrected. And what about her face? That heavy makeup makes her look like she's been in a tragic accident involving red lipstick, a tin of salmon mousse and an eye infection."~

'No argument there.'

~"Why can't she just wear one thing and be done with it?"~

'It doesn't work that way. Frightening as it may be, in her line of business, preparation and attention to detail are what separate the golden tiara winners from the aluminum foil amateurs.'

~"How do you know so much about that stuff?"~

'I picked up a thing or two hanging out with her.'

~"I make the same hours as you do, remember? And I haven't got a clue what she's talking about half of the time."~

'Yeah... I think maybe I'm the only person Sharminella knows who really gets her.'

~"Deep, man. Deep."~

'Don't mock me.'

The amusement park, ironically, wasn't very amusing. Walking around in it, Nate found out that there were only a handful of attractions, and clearly, the big event of the year had been the introduction of a new seesaw. A sad seesaw at that, for it had a counterweight on one side, so at any given time only one lonely kid could sit on the free seat.

And a goose had pooped on that seat.

And it was green poop.

But every summer the park came alive when it hosted the Gambolodrome Festival, drawing enthusiasts from all over the country. The talent show, located in the outdoor arena, was just one of its many activities.

Performing at a big venue like this didn't fluster Sharminella one bit. She was an orphan. Toughened up by the experience, it had made her–if not exactly street-smart–then at least *smarting*–that is, a pain in the ass to work with. This was immediately apparent when she entered the backstage and started bullying everyone on her path in a way that usually only *divadom royalty* knew how to pull off. (The ploy involves: verbally attacking a random stranger without advance warning and in full view of others, complaining bombastically, and acting as if you are rightfully doing so. The trick is to never discriminate in who you bully, and never, ever, leave them time to think *Hold on a minute. We didn't book anyone famous!*)

"*Where is my dressing room!*" Sharminella barked at people. "How am I to, mm, prepare without a private room? It's filthy in here. I'm calling my agent Myrtle. Wait till she hears about these *sheniniganishigans*." Her little head was a red ball of furry set to explode. Immediately three stagehands came running up to deeply apologize and grovel and appease her with a chair to sit on and a glass of water with ice cubes in it. One higher-ranking stagehand personally went searching for a fruit basket. Nate was amazed by how they tripped over themselves to carry out her every whim.

"Cover that lamp over there! Nothing but soft light to *accencutuciate* my cheekbones!... Are you trying to poison me with this pear?... Yuck! This brownie is *room tempesture!*"

The stagehands blamed each other under their breath for not having been briefed beforehand. It didn't occur to them that she might be pretending. From the way she behaved, they simply assumed that she had to be a high-profile VIP. Within a matter of minutes the six-year-old had secured her own exclusive dressing room taking up two thirds of the backstage. The other contestants (magicians, contortionists, dancers, ventriloquists and stand-up comedians) had been shunned to a table next to the toilet stalls. Their confidence evaporated whenever she opened her mouth. The queenie had no qualms whatsoever about using scare tactics to psych out the competition. Their dreams were going to get crushed today, because her mind was set on taking home first prize. A first prize, incidentally, that was probably just a two-in-one spice rack and medicine cabinet donated by a local retailer, but still. Somewhere in a corner a mime was quietly pseudo-sobbing.

Sharminella had them in her pocket. All of them, except the triplets... Three identical sisters aged nine who kept leering at her. They didn't look browbeaten at all. Perhaps they had become immune to browbeating when they had started plucking their eyebrows and drawing them back on with a marker. Sharminella was definitely going to keep eye on them. Sure, they looked innocent enough in their cutesy little uniforms (candy-colored shoulder dresses, gaudy jewelry, knee-socks with bold blue stripes and large bows in their blond ringlets of hair), but she wasn't born yesterday. Though she did not have the vocabulary yet, she knew them for what they were: opportunistic, backbiting, malcontent, snooty, malicious, angel-faced bitches... exactly like herself, but without the talent, obviously. The triplets put the *sass* into *character assassination*. They would go all the way in the competition unless she destroyed them.

"Don't you people don't know who I am that I am?" Sharminella shouted at a guy who unwittingly stood too close to her. "I am the *worldily renownered* Sharminella Buckelfluger! The Nightingale of Vaudevilly Nights. The Temptress of the Theater Stretch!"

Nate couldn't remember how often he had watched her recite these identical lines before. When she started, victims found it impossible to get a thought in edgewise. The brain shut down. Star-struck.

~"Look at them. Stunned by the poison of a puffer fish."~

'*I know. She's memorized the whole prima donna routine word for word, straight out of the old musical movie.*'

~"Not only the words, the moves too."~

Copying the leading actress from the movie, Sharminella liberally sprayed perfume onto her silk, see-through robe trimmed with pink feathers. The fact that the perfume from the tiny phial made her reek like a turpentine factory was irrelevant. Being larger-than-life was what it was all about. Everything needed more pizazz. (Not the pepperoni kind, as Sharminella had first thought. No, the flamboyant, razzle-dazzle kind you drown a crowd in.)

It wasn't easy for a little girl to play the role of an embittered forty-something theatrical star. She didn't always say the lines when they were appropriate, and she didn't always know what they exactly meant, but pretending to be an egocentric and spiteful celebrity when you're not, was so inconceivable to most people that her bluff seldom failed.

"Hey listen, Sharminella," Nate said, "It's another two hours before you'll go on stage. I'm taking a walk around the festival tents, okay? I'm sure you and your menservants can cope."

~"I would say so. She's got two boys massaging her feet!"~

Sharminella dropped the phial with a dramatic gesture. It clattered to the ground. "Go ahead. Abandon me again on this moonlight beach. I shan't be needing your two-timing tricks no more. O my shatted heart will just live for my fans and applause from now on. I beg you, Quinton, don't leave!... And tell Abigayle, tell her... just tell her from me, mm, that I have finally seen the zitty clouds over Maycox Station and I can die *happipily–*"

"Right."

"–So get the hell out of my spotlight, buster! And don't touch my weave. You'll never work in this town again. I still have vents in high places. So what are you going to do about it, big shot? Pinch me for luck, or punch me a black eye?"

~"Do it."~

"*EEE! You pinched me!*" Sharminella screamed. "Why you do that, Nanny?"

"Well, you told me too," Nate chuckled. "Okay, okay. I'm sorry, Miss Buckelfuger. An international idol like yourself must be under a lot of pressure. I'll leave you to it."

"I shall forgive you, Quinton Twangson, for the sake of the Performing Arse and your child I once carried."

"I'm crossing my fingers."

"*Yaaay!* Now cross your toes."

"I'm crossing my toes. See you later, Sharmy. I'm sure you're going to win."

She threw him a couple of air kisses. "*Muah, muah, muah!*"

While leaving the backstage, Nate heard her finishing up the remaining bits and pieces of the act.

"Where are my lotions and *oinkments*? You people don't know how to read a rider? And I want a vase with fresh flowers! No lilies!... Never in my dirty-two-year long career have I, mm, seen such a *shamples* and such a blundering mess. This is very poor. I'm calling Mywrtle... I've had ex-husbands I had killed for less."

...

Nate followed the direction of the distant booms... monumental drumbeats heralding a grand happening. He quickened his pace. Walking to a big concert was always invigorating. There was nothing like it. That sense of fellowship shared with other music lovers all heading to the same show, knowing you're coming within earshot of great music, dancing and excessive noise exposure. Nate enjoyed the pleasant rush of adrenaline, spurred on by the rumble of the party people already there. It didn't even particularly matter what genre the band was playing. As long as they were passionate about their music and banged out a good beat, Nate was more than happy.

~"You think there'll be a steamed winkle stand?"~

'*What's that?... On second thought, I don't want to know.*'

The venue was a former opera house that had undergone considerable modification. The floor of the dress circle area was lit up in every color and shape imaginable. Underneath the ceiling there was enough lighting equipment to be seen from space, and all the walls were lined with mirrors. So it gave the impression that the place was packed with people, but somehow the coziness of the former theater was kept intact.

~"Woah! Look at those balconies!"~

'*Don't be rude.*'

~"No. I mean, those gilded balconies overhead."~

'*Sorry.*'

The original balconies had been ripped out and put back in between giant elevator tubes spiraling around one another like a double helix. On every level, right up to the ceiling, partygoers were shaking their hips and having a great time. The high ceiling itself was adorned with the painting of a buxom opera singer astride a flaming chariot. Right behind her, there was the figure of a running man with a bucket of water seemingly exclaiming *A woman driver in a burning vehicle. Make way!*'

The upper circle of the theater featured a fountain spewing mass quantities of foam and a water slide down. The mezzanine had huge horizontal fans blowing upward, with teenagers floating above it, literally dancing on air. Many people had come dressed in the most outrageous getups. Whiffs of sweat, beer and suspicious tobacco took Nate back to when he used to frequent concerts.

An underground band called *Monkey Canoodles* was playing

some new type of rock. Nate couldn't quite make out the lyrics, but they sounded something like *Kiwi peel skin claptrap oh, yeah varmint nosebleed lullaby...* followed by the obscure refrain *Edelweiss, just a bunch of hairy maggots eating a soybean.*

~"Total nonsense, if you ask me."~

'*Who knows! Maybe they're quoting from Poledoris's memoires*', Nate joked.

The audience was lapping it up, though. This was one magnificent party. "The band," a fan explained to him, "is the stuff of legend. Once at a gig they played a song so experimental and different that it instantly got banned in every club. Allegedly it contained one exceptional guitar riff that resonated perfectly with the natural vibrations of the human bowels and amplified them. One third into the number and everyone was soiling their pants.-"

"You mean...?"

~"*They all crapped themselves?*"~

"-Ironically, that song was called *Let it rip*," the fan said enthused.

"Wow... and *eww!*" Nate smiled back.

~"Why are we here? You know I don't like this kind of music."~

'*You don't like any kind of music. Period,*' Nate countered.

~"Not true. I enjoy a nice tune. Once in a while. When it's played on a stone jug."~

'*That only has one note!*'

~"Correction. I used to do one note up and one note down. That's all I needed. Kids nowadays are never satisfied."~

After an hour the band finished the set and walked off, but the audience was roaring for more. Sure enough, shortly after, *Monkey Canoodles* returned for the encore in a cloud of stage smoke.

"Thanks! We appreciate it. For our last number we'd like to

call onto the stage a very talented friend who we've recently met. An all-round nice guy. He's going to sing a new song that we composed together. Give him a hand of applause!"

Not everyone in the audience was pleased. They preferred something familiar they knew how to nod their heads to. A guy with a guitar joined the band members. It was hard to see his face through all the smoke.

"Hi. This song goes out to the most amazing person I've ever met... even though things didn't work out between us. It's fittingly called *On a date with my soulmate*. Get ready. Okay? Hit it!"

The intro immediately drew everyone's attention. It was upbeat and catchy. First it was only his guitar playing and then the other musicians came running up behind. Despite the initial doubts people found themselves humming along and tapping their feet to the rhythm. The enthusiasm and simplicity of the music struck a powerful chord in everyone, making them feel more alive somehow, more energetic. The guest guitarist sang the vocals with such heartfelt integrity and lingering love that he took the place by storm. A surge of excitement swept through the theater, throwing everyone a happy punch. The song was a celebration of joy and creativity. An instant feel-good hit. An irresistible anthem to dance and sing along to from the top of your lungs. The crowd went wild. Everyone was ecstatic. All thanks to this one all-round nice guy whom Nate thought he'd never see again. His jaw dropped to the floor. His heart leapt.

24. Pony tricks

Meanwhile, Sharminella was displeased. Very displeased. She badly wanted to be the sixth contestant to go on, because while she was painting her nails, Bubby the doll confided in her that whoever was sixth in the line-up was going to win the talent show.

So she bickered with the crew members to let her switch places, but they wouldn't budge. She then tried–in chronological order–lying, screaming, threatening, bribing, pleading, abusive language, biting of legs, flirtatious seduction, emotional blackmail, pretending to be terminally ill with the dying wish to go on sixth... none of which had any effect. Worse, the organization got wise to her not being the chain-smoking, gin-swilling, man-eating, multi-divorced, international superstar she made out to be.

As a result, Sharminella watched in the wings of the outdoor arena and grumbled at lucky number six who–horror!–was wooing the judges with his pony act. The local stock farmer had taught a young pony how to count. Without fail it gave one right answer after the other by way of banging together two cymbals tied to its ears. The queenie was not impressed. "*Pffuh!* I could do that when I was four," she complained to a stagehand. "And I got no sugar cubes for it either."

The judges, however, couldn't get enough of it. They chuckled admiringly at the man and his noble companion.

ding–ding–ding–ding–ding

"Five is correct!" he said into the mike.

applause

"How many fingers am I holding up?"

ding–ding–ding–ding–ding–ding–ding

"Seven. Correct!"

The farmer took another bow. And, it turned out, he had more up his sleeve. An impressive choreography of woolly blurs burst into view. He had trained three dozen sheep to roller-skate in a conga line, making figures of eight. The stressful baaing of the sheep provided the musical underscoring. Randomly the pony accompanied this by lashing its tail against tambourines strapped to its thighs. The spectators were *oohing* and *aahing* with delight. They gasped every time the figure of eight was on a collision course with itself, and every time, miraculously, the sheep narrowly avoided each other in flawlessly executed near-misses. One after the other they limboed underneath the pony's flank. The spectators were *eehing* and *iiihing* and *uuuhing*.

Sharminella couldn't stand it any longer. She was seething. The stinky animals were stealing away first prize! What was more, the hateful triplet girls were pointing and laughing at her. "I must be six!" She stomped onto the stage. A crew member called after her... "Watch out! You're on too soon!"... but she stubbornly ignored it. Her routine was going to start now, no matter what!

It was a nursery rhyme with lots of arm movements and impersonations, guaranteed to spring sweet tears of endearment and melt hearts. On many an occasion, panels of judges had surrendered unconditionally on seeing the girl–*shy, yet arresting... innocent, yet glamorous*–perform her surefire exploitative act.

> "Once upon a time there was a happy toad."
> ("Pssst! Little one...")
> "Hopping up and down, mm, along a castle moat."
> ("Get off the stage, kid.")
> "*Stop*, there came a voice. *Passing isn't free.*
> 'Twas a bleating goat. *This field belongs to me.*"
> (*Baaaa! Baaaa!*)

These judges, however, were puzzled by the unexpected apparition of a child donned in a wedding cake-like monstrosity, babbling something inaudibly amid the roller-skating herd. They watched as she stretched her arms and bounced around like a bloated water balloon. It was impossible to tell whether she was crying out for help or if it was supposed to be *symbolism*.

"Stay away, filthy beasts!" Sharminella shouted, "You're *ruininining* everything!" but said beasts kept whirling around her regardless. Sheep only know how to do one thing at a time and, there and then, that thing was to follow the woolly butt directly in front without a care where–or on whom–they trod.

To make matters worse, the pony was eyeballing her in a funny way.

A Buckelfluger, however, never flinched. *The show must go on.* She was determined to maintain her poise and, simultaneously, whack sheep on the chin to ward them off. Basically she was trying not to get bitten or trampled on, while looking fabulous at it. Truth be told, the queenie had encountered tougher competition than this in the past. Defiantly she soldiered on with the nursery rhyme.

> "*Good*, replied the toad. *I'll pay you with a pearl.*
> *Would that be enough, mm, for you to leave me be?*"
> *(ding-ding-ding-ding)*
> "*Yes*, replied the goat. *A pearl will bring me glee.*"
> *("Four is the correct answer!")*
> "So the toad cleared its throat,
> and out came, you see..."
> *(Baaaa! Baaaa!)*
> "the biggest pearls there ever were.
> Not one, in fact, but three!"

Sheep droppings were raining down everywhere, including on her lilac, open toe mules. Somehow she managed to stifle multiple shrieks. The farmer should have gotten her out of harm's way, but–maddeningly–he was the only person in the arena who hadn't noticed what was going on next to him. He was hard-of-hearing and the pony was blocking the view. Everyone else held their breath and gawped at the child in danger of being crushed in a whirlwind of wool.

Her rivals, the triplets, took action. "If she can go on early, then we can too!" They shuffled onto the stage on top of large circus balls. The girls (tragically named Mismeraldina, Opaquinizza and Cinderellupina) had an acrobatic act.

Sharminella, never to be upstaged, struck back by adding tap-dancing to the rhyme. She tapped so energetically that it caused chips to shoot off the boards.

Worse challenges were coming up for her… first of which were the icky strings of pony drivel trickling down her neck. She dealt with it. Trying not to crack. "I am a provisional!" she reminded herself, "but if horsey doesn't stop *I'M GOING TO SCREAM!*"

The sisters gave each other the nod. They knew that merely balancing on balls was not going to cut it against a tap-dance.

The first one, Mismeraldina, drew a knife… several knives… and started juggling. The sheep didn't mind that.

Opaquinizza was into fire-breathing, which did make the sheep very nervous, especially every time they came skating too close to the flame bursts.

The third sister broke out into yodeling… *"Yodel-odel-odel-layde-hoo!"*… and the whole herd went nuts.

(BAA! BAAAA! BAAA!)

Instantly the conga line dispersed, their flight response kicking in. In the melee that followed, the sheep were seen bumping into each other, dashing into the wings, or jumping over the orchestra pit and charging up the aisles. The triplets got knocked off of their circus gear. The farmer and audience members had to join forces to round up the livestock. Cinderellupina was still yodeling when they carried her off on a stretcher.

But throughout it all, at center stage, one little girl had not moved from her spot. One girl who was burning inside with fury. One special queenie with an eyeballing pony beside her, continuously driveling down her back. She was bent on finishing the routine she had practiced. She was going to see this through to the end. At all costs. If it killed her.

"*Now,* said the toad. *You listen up to me!*"

("Someone fetch a medic!")

"*This first pearl is a shiner, so give it to your mum!*"

(BAA! BAAA! BAAARGH!)

"*The next one even finer. So keep it, don't be dumb!*"

"*No need to be a whiner–HORSEY, YOU CAN STICK IT UP YOUR B–*"

BRRATCHOO!

A gigantic gob of snot hit her square in the face.

"*EEEEEEEEEEEEEE!*"

It proceeded to slide down and cover her from head to toe.

"*EEEEEEEEEEEEEE!*" She elaborated.

"*EEEEEEEEEEEEEE!*" She was stuck in a loop and couldn't stop.

A stagehand threw a bucket of ice-cold water over her. It had the instant effect of hand-washing a cat in a sink. Her hair fell flat. The wedding-cake dress collapsed. What was left was a scrawny creature, soaked and shivering.

There was the sound of a door opening and of someone sashaying into the spotlight. She was tall, beautiful... A brunette.

"Come," Penelope Mangez beckoned. "Follow me,

Sharminella. I've got a big surprise to show you..."

...

"Brent! Brent! It's me!" Nate hollered, but the rock music and the concert crowd were too loud for him to be heard.

The temperature inside the former opera house had increased significantly. The mirror walls were steaming up. Everyone was dancing, singing along, moving as one. In fact they were going bananas. By the time the chorus kicked in again, people were truly enraptured by the explosive power of the irresistible song and its charismatic singer. Nate couldn't believe it. Brent was standing right there on the stage. His blonde demigod was bringing joy to hundreds. Nate's love was reignited.

'*I must get closer!*'

~"Forget him, Nate. You two are too different. He said it himself in his Dear John letter."~

'*I must talk to him!*'

~"You had a few laughs together and then he dumped you. Leave it at that."~

'*You must be joking! I have felt so miserable without him.*'

~"Fine, don't listen to me then. All I'll say is, Kean is a much better match than Brent."~

'*Who?*'

~"You're cracking me up here. Doesn't matter. The place is packed. There's no way you can slip past all these party folk anyway."~

'*Oh, yeah? Just watch me. You wanted to experiment with nub particles, you got it! I'm going to plant a thought in these people's minds by way of telepathy. Just like Cibyl said I could.*'

~"Suit yourself."~

Nate inhaled and concentrated hard on the thought. '*Kindly step aside. Make room. Let me paaaassss... uh, abracadabra?*'

245

The glimmering cluster bubbles of the three rowdy women in front of him materialized. Nate willed his own bubble to *lean into* them. Their edges started rippling. Some of his particles jumped over to the other bubbles, which was pretty, but other than that nothing much happened. The crowd didn't part at all. Its only effect was, it temporarily gave Nate a purple headache.

~"The results are in. Common sense one, supernatural persuasion zero."~

'What's this?'

A ray of purple blinded him. He squinted. Something onstage was reflecting light directly into his eyes... Something that was attached to the headstock of Brent's guitar. '*It's the guitar pick I gave him!*'

The reflection swerved to the right. He saw an empty space there, so he quickly stepped forward to fill it. The ray now shone on his left shoulder. Again, this time on his left, Nate saw a gap and moved in. He was impressed. In fact, there was a zigzag line running all the way up to his heartthrob. Other people were shaking their butts right through it, not noticing at all. Every time Nate reached a new spot, the person obstructing the purple line promptly decided to step aside and Nate got closer to his goal.

"This is amazing!" Nate blurted out. '*The line anticipates where everyone is* not *going to stand* before *they aren't standing there, Jarrrvis. You think I am doing this?*'

~"My horoscope predicted this very thing. The planets Venus, Jupiter and Saturn are aligning, you see."~

'Really?'

~"No, of course not. But it's obviously you who's doing this, Knud."~

'Who the hell is Knud?'

~"Just the name of a daft seagull I kept for a pet."~

'What's that got to do with anything?'

~"Nothing at all. Just whipping up your brain like a meringue."~

'*You know, I don't like you toying with me like that , especially when I'm-*'

Suddenly, many hands grabbed his legs and back and butt. Before he realized what was going on, he was crowd-surfing over a sea of heads... to right in front of the stage, where he was gently dropped off.

"Er, thanks, I guess."

~"Getting felt up a bit on the way over was a nice bonus."~

Here, nearer to the stage, the concertgoers were noticeably younger. They were mainly teenagers letting it all out and bumping into each other for fun. Everyone was in high spirits.

Brent had spotted him. He looked stumped for a moment. Then his face brightened and he gave a smile that could melt icebergs. Possibly a whole ice age too if need be. He waved and pointed at Nate, Then he pointed at himself and gave the thumbs-up to indicate that this electrifying love song was about the two of them. He promptly put down his guitar, leapt into the press of people and waded through them until he found Nate. They joined each other in a dance. A slow dance even though the band was speeding up. The center of the crowd transformed into a circle pit–a revolving wall of torsos, limbs and screaming heads, with the two of them in the middle, untouched and safe. The eye of the storm.

Dancing with Brent felt so... effortless. Nate's mind was floating on clouds. Whenever Cupid's arrow struck, he always turned into an incurable romantic. At last, his lost love was here, close to him, holding his warm body wrapped around him. Chest to chest. Their hearts were soon thumping in perfect synchrony.

~"You and rock star. Who'd have guessed? I thought that ship had sailed."~

247

'*Almost too good to be true, but this is really happening. I'm so happy. It is all poetry. Sheer poetry...*'

With some final bangs on the drums the concert reached its brilliant conclusion and thunderous applause followed. The two were still hugging. Someone yelled "Kiss him already, you fool!" (It was that sort of a crowd.) Brent seemed to want to but hesitated. Nate was quicker and kissed his Romeo square on the lips until both their ears turned red. Another round of applause and whistling erupted. Fireworks were shooting through Nate's entire being. They looked deep into each other's eyes.

'*He still has those astounding galaxies to get lost in.*'

~"Obviously... Now say something."~

They kept looking at each other. Finding the right opening line had never been their forte.

~"Say anything."~

"You still have the guitar pick." Nate finally managed.

"Hey, of course I do. It was a cool gift. By the way, I'm psyched to see you!"

"Same here."

"I know somewhere where we can talk. I have so much to tell you."

"Okay."

Holding onto Nate's hand, he led him up some stairs to a balcony. The view was awesome. Below them, dance music was blasting through the speakers. The party was back in full swing.

"This calls for a celebration," Brent said. "First, have a drink."

Nate accepted the glass and emptied it in one gulp, not realizing that it was strong liquor. It had him almost coughing up a lung.

"Listen, Nate. I've been feeling really bad about that night when I ran off without saying proper goodbye and... perhaps more to the point, I've been thinking a lot and I know I made a horrible mistake. I didn't want to desert you in that trailer, but... well, you could say I just got a bit... scared."

"Scared? Why?" Nate hiccupped through the alcohol burn.

"Well, I sort of overheard you while you were in that bathroom. Actually, it wasn't difficult to catch everything you were saying. You were basically yelling."

"Yelling, yeah. That. I was... in a bad place."

Nate vividly remembered the first vision. A disturbing montage of owls dying and rabbit soldiers with torches.

~"Don't forget the pools of blood."~

'*Thank you for that!*'

"So I was wondering," Brent stammered. "Maybe we could, you know, try again? Start over?"

"Are you saying you'd like to go on a date with me?"

"Ahuh! I have big plans for us. I want to sweep you off your feet."

"I'd love to be swept! Uh, when?"

"Is *now* any good?"

"Yep."

A tidal wave of relief washed over them.

"Great! I must warn you, though. I just might be tempted to kiss you... well, *again*."

Nate and Brent moved closer.

"*HALT! DESIST!*"

Sauvetyne plunged from the sky. The naked crone flapped her big insect wings but it was of no use. Much like a ball in a pinball machine she smacked into every wall and pillar she passed during her uncoordinated descent.

~"What the hell?"~

People stared up in surprise, thinking she was part of a stunt show or perhaps an optical illusion done with special effects. After all, an undressed, giant ladybug granny couldn't just pop into being and start trashing the place. Spinning and tumbling she made her way down, ultimately crash-landing on the balcony where the two lovebirds stood.

"Not you again! How in the world did you find me?"

"Stand back, Pilchett!" Sauvetyne bawled at him. "You're in grave danger!"

She had shaken off most of her ladybug traits as easily as snapping her fingers. The see-through wings and the dotted red covers had disappeared. Apart from two antennas on her forehead, she now was just the very wrinkly old woman.

~"Here's another disturbing vision I can do without."~

"Leave him alone, Voegant!" Sauvetyne spit at Brent and put herself in between the two to block him off.

"*Vowgaunt?*" Brent said perturbed. His eyes were almost rolling out of their sockets. "Who's that? You must be mistaking me for someone else. My name is Brent."

The crone was all worked up and swaying unsteadily. "Why are you here, Pilchett? Why did you not heed my warning? *Holy ding-donk!* I bet that Voegant has been slipping you filthy elixirs, right under your nose! Am I too late? He hasn't given you anything to drink or eat, has he? *HAS HE?*"

She whistled through her dentures when she spoke. Nate had forgotten about that. But then, he didn't recall her having the antennas. Twitching antennas. It was unsightly.

"I had one drink! And that's entirely beside the point! Why do you keep harassing me?"

~"Well said! What's she talking about anyway. Brent is not my favorite person, but he doesn't look a bit like that Voegant character."~

Sauvetyne was breathing heavily… her rotund body sagging under its own weight. When Nate tried to move away from her, she wouldn't let him.

"Keep back! This despicable bastard has grown stronger, more powerful since I escaped from his clutches. I can't even make out his enlarged soul signature anymore. He's found a way to conceal it!"

"This is ridiculous!" Brent said visibly hurt. "Nate, I don't know who this woman is. I've never seen her before in my life!"

"Nor in any previous life?" Sauvetyne scoffed.

The question startled Brent. "Believe me, Nate. I don't know what's going on here, but I don't want to harm you at all."

"Hah!" Sauvetyne wheezed. "Liar! Smooth-talker! I'm not afraid of you anymore, Voegant. Hide behind the shape of another birth all you want, but you can't fool me. Pilchett will refuse to go through with your evil plans!"

"Is this some kind of bad joke, ma'am?" Brent asked upset. "Because I don't find it funny."

"You don't get to say anything, tricky trickster you!"

Several onlookers had gathered on the balcony to follow the spectacle. A couple of safety guards were on their way...

'*Typical! Just typical,*' Nate thought while the love of his life and the bane of his being were bickering. '*Just when I get a lucky break, madness comes dropping from the sky.*'

"That is enough!" he cut in. "You want to know what I think? Ever since you turned up in my apartment, everything's a disaster! I've had it with you!... Ah yes, things are suddenly starting to make sense to me... You put some sort of spell on me with that locket, didn't you? It's messing up my head with crazy owl crap."

"It's not a spell. It's real. Absolutely real, Pilchett! *Gobbling goose!* You must have realized by now that this man is dangerous."

"Beat it! I never want to see you again. Take your stupid spell and *GO AWAY!*"

"Curse you, Voegant! You've brainwashed him already!"

Sauvetyne attacked. Brent parried the blows, but he was on the receiving end of some nasty bitch-slaps and punches. The eighty-year-old could still do serious damage.

"Ouch! Stop that! Security! Get her off of me!" Brent called out. "For all I care, take her to some cellar with a big lock on the door!"

The safety guards quickly overpowered her and dragged her away, but not before she got to kick one of them hard on the chin-bone. It was her specialty.

"Don't let his charm trick you, Pilchett!" Sauvetyne cried out from the hall. "He is evil! I know it's crazy, but you've got to *believe meeeee!*"

Now that the show was over, the onlookers headed back to what they had been doing.

"You okay?"

"I'll be fine," Brent returned a wan smile. "Only a scratch and maybe a bruise or two."

Nate softly blew over the surface of the scratched skin. Somehow this would make it hurt less. It was something he had started doing a while back when Sharminella had grazed her knee. Nate froze in mid-pout. Luckily Brent didn't seem to find the blowing weird or childish. Or maybe he was too polite to mention it.

"Who was that anyway?" Brent asked instead. "And were that antennas on her head?"

"Yep. It's an unlikely story. I'm not sure I'm ready to tell you yet."

Brent let this sink in. "Fair enough. I think I can respect that."

"Brent?"

"Yes?"

"Your tattoo… Those are angel wings, right? Not owl wings?"

"Of course."

"So you have no idea what she was ranting about? I mean, the woman is obviously insane and all, but she was talking about some things. She seems to know about... stuff. What I guess I want to ask you is–"

"You can trust me, Nate. All I want to do is be with you. Just be with you and maybe hug you a little. And perhaps kiss those delicious lips of yours."

These sweet words finally broke the ice again. Brent was coming on hard, and he had the object of his affection soon buzzing on a fresh batch of endorphins. Nate didn't mind that Brent made a move on him and dropped the matter of Sauvetyne altogether. All his doubts were wiped off the table.

"That would be very accommodating," Nate replied, feigning gratitude in the vernacular of a decorous gentleman.

Brent played along. "Moreover, dear Sir, I wish to stipulate quite clearly that I aspire to spend more *quality time* with you in the immediate future. Kindly note the inverted commas there."

"Forthright, aren't you?"

"Let's sync our calendars. Are you free *the rest of your life?*" Brent said with naughty eyes and an accompanying suggestive eyebrow.

~"I can't believe you're seriously thinking about hooking up with this guy again."~

'Ssst, *if you don't like what my eyes are seeing, then close your... whatever it is that you can close in there.*'

No response.

'*Great. I'll take that as a sign.*'

Brent grumbled.

"What's wrong?"

"Ack! I forgot... The band is playing a corporate gig later today and they've asked me to join them. This sucks! I really hate to run off on you, but I swear, tomorrow I'll be all yours.–"

"But I want you now." Nate kissed him. A long, passionate kiss followed by some shorter, nibbly kisses. All equally wonderful.

"Oh my, I do believe I am blushing, young master Noodascue."

"Verily."

"Hey, I've got an idea… I don't need to leave just now, and there is this cozy attic above the stage next to the fly tower where we can be alone. Just us two... It has a big couch."

"What are we waiting for?" Nate grinned. He got the hint. "Let's go."

They reached the attic and straightaway they were kissing, cuddling… craving more. Hurriedly they removed their shoes, took off their clothes. And then things really took off.

And after an hour, when Nate was about to roll over on his back, smiling–he couldn't seem to stop smiling and marvel at how this was the most intense one-on-one time he had ever spent, Brent made a come-on for round two. Yummy! Nate couldn't believe his luck. Some earthshaking lovemaking was going down here. *Everything you read in trashy romance novels is true!* His fantasy guy, in real life, was so passionate and perfect. So excessively hot. He was a bewildering muscle machine, pressing his face against the side of Nate's warm neck, breathing in the scent of his skin. An aphrodisiac. Brent spooned him, running one hand through his lover's hair to massage the nape of the neck, while the other hand moved down the herculean chest, passing every rock-hard ab. He wetted his lips before moving further down. A sunbeam busting through a dormer window flooded the angel wings tattoo on his back. The sun, it seemed, was always out to catch him.

It was day outside. But if it had been dark Nate and Brent would have seen a most astounding Milky Way stretching across the firmament, shining fiercely in all its brilliance through eons of empty space. Nate didn't have to imagine it being there, because it was already here, filling the room! He saw a dazzling array of colors. Hundreds of illuminated particle strings were streaming back and forth between Brent's soulnub bubble and his own. It was mind-blowingly beautiful.

"Nate, I've been thinking."

"What? Just *now* you mean?"

"Yeah."

"You were *thinking* right in the middle of what we're doing?"

"Yes. I don't want us to be apart again. I didn't like it and I missed everything about you so much. That smile. The off-the-wall conversations... Your limber bod. All of it."

~"Everyone duck! He looks like he is about to pop a question."~

"Do you want me to be your boyfriend?"

'*To be your boyfriend...*'

The message put Nate's brain in overdrive.

'*He wants us to be boyfriends!*'

~"Aye. I heard. By all means, don't give a damn about the fact I don't like the cut of his jib."~

"Are you kidding? Yes! Of course, Brent. Nothing would make me happier."

~"Hook, line and sinker! I believe congratulations are in order."~

The two sealed the deal with another steamy kiss. And then, for good measure, with a whole lot more that would have made Cupid's cheeks blush pinker than his other pair of cheeks.

Nate's ultimate wish had come true. Never ever was he going to find another Brent as amazing as this Brent. '*He is perfect, gorgeous, creative, full of life... And he is honest.*'

...

Meanwhile, deep in the nether regions of a dark building, Sauvetyne found herself chained to a cold and uncaring floor. A very large bell jar with tiny air holes had been lowered over her body. The jar was there to make sure that even if she did manage to get out of the chains by morphing her body into that of the ladybug hybrid, the impenetrable, toxin-resistant material of the bell would stop her escape. Sauvetyne hadn't actually mastered how and when to produce the toxic repellent but she as hell wasn't going to share that information.

Apart from handing her rags to cover her body, she had been shown no mercy for her elderly state. Her knees hurt from being dragged here after Brent had sent her off. The rough flagstones were cutting into her flesh.

"Don't know what's worse," she spat with contempt, "the pain in my old bones or me having to look at your vile face again!"

Her captor was gloating. "O Sauvetyne. Helpless, worn-out Sauvetyne. Did you really believe you could win?" Penelope Mangez said, relishing every word. "You come flying back into my Master's territory, thinking you can defy him? Hah! You're pathetic. Voegant is already making preparations to perform the ritual. Yes, you have lost, Sauvetyne. Voegant is unstoppable!"

25. Supper with Kean

'This is just super,' Nate complained.

~"Strange. I thought this was *supper*."~

'Really not funny. Pfffh!'

It was hours later and Nate was seated opposite Kean at a table in Pinglop's fanciest restaurant. A sad salad had been pleading to have its croutons eaten for the last ten minutes, but Nate had no appetite. The date so far had been tedious. Awkward. Disastrous.

'Why am I here again?'

~"You've made your bed, now you've got to tippytoe out of that bed and sneak into another one."~

'I've just had the most fabulous time with my boyfriend. Note: boyfriend. So why would I want to get chummy with a conceited psychotherapist? For crying out loud, Jarrrvis, I'm still radiating an after sex glow!'

~"You were the one who asked Kean out, in case you've forgotten. Just because you got it on with someone else, all of a sudden Kean isn't worth your time anymore? I'm very disappointed."~

'You're not making any sense. Why shouldn't I just get up and leave?'

~"Because it isn't like you to go back on your promise. Plus, you've been flirting with Kean as much as he has with you. You like him."~

'I can't really understand what I saw in him. He is attractive, yes, but everything else? I'd much rather be snuggling up in Brent's arms right now.'

~"There's something about that guitar guy that I don't like."~

'Don't say that. There is nothing wrong with him. He is

perfection. I shouldn't be sitting here with Kean. I'll think up some quick excuse and go back to my hotel room. That'd be okay, right? I mean, Kean and I don't know each other that well.'

~"You survived a flood together."~

'That could have happened with anyone.'

~"Admit it. Kean is the one for you. You even let him see you naked in the bathroom. You're a tease."~

'I was unconscious at the time! And, besides, Brent has seen a lot more.'

~"I'm sticking to my opinion. Kean is in. Brent should be out."~

The coach politely coughed. "Dissatisfactory wine, don't you think?"

"Sorry? Oh, uhm. Haven't tasted yet."

'He said dissatisfactory. He's talking like a stuffy professor again!'

"You seem a bit preoccupied, Nate."

"Yeah. It's just… I've had a very long day. I've been up since four this morning."

Another pressing silence descended on the table. Kean didn't seem to be enjoying himself either. The finger food he'd recommended for a starter turned out to be, in his words, akin to chewing tree bark. It didn't help the overall mood.

'Mental note to self: never go on blah dates ever again! I don't have to put myself through this. I have someone now.'

~"It doesn't have to be blah. Make an effort. Try small talk."~

Nate placed his hand on top of Kean's and let it rest there. It took him a moment to register what his hand was up to.

'Why the hell am I doing that!'

~"Don't ask me. You moved. Not me."~

'That's so weird. It didn't even feel like I was moving my hand.'

~"Maybe you like Kean more than you know."~

'No! I don't want it there! O-oh, he's looking at me. Jarrrvis,

258

what do I do? What do I do?!'

~"Pull out! Pull out!"~

Nate retracted his arm at lightning speed and garbled an apology. The coach was visibly confused.

"So, Kean, uh... Cibyl, you know, the boss lady of Cibyl Unlimited Holding has taught me an incredibly nifty, uh, trick. If you're interested."

"A trick?"

Nate quickly thought it over. "I guess there's no harm in telling you this, seeing as you were so supportive to me saying that I have *great potential* and so on."

"Of course. You can tell me anything. What did she teach you?"

Nate waited a second for effect.

"I can see the stuff that people are made off."

"You mean skin and bone and alike?"

"No, I mean–What's that called again? Uh, oh yeah, the *astral body*. It's sort of like reading auras, but way cooler."

"Would you read mine now?"

"Yeah, okay."

A meaningful expression formed on Kean's face. Like he knew something. Or maybe he wasn't a believer of this sort of thing and was merely humoring the gullible person in front of him.

"Here goes." Nate concentrated, but before Kean's bubble could appear, a rumbling vibration set the wine glasses and cutlery off dancing. Something was approaching. Something scary. The tablecloth swooshed up and out from under the table, there it was. In all its scary blondness.

"Never creep up on us, Sharminella."

"*Sowry.*"

Sharminella was wearing casual chic. For her that meant a mini version of a skirt suit inlaid with a thousand little sequins.

She accessorized this with a flashy trophy of the same height as herself. The plaque read *First prize winner Gambolodrome talent competition.*

"That's right. You'd better be sorry," Nate huffed.

"But it was *sooOOOooh* boring in my room."

'*Boring? You should try sitting at this table,*' Nate thought, but instead he said "Don't tell me Poledoris is under there too?"

"No."

"Swear it?"

"Swear."

"Double swear?"

"Double swear or grow toe hair." She giggled at her own grossness.

"Phew, I guess, at least that is a blessing."

"Hear, hear!" Kean agreed. "That egregious cave dweller is hard to elude."

~"What he said."~

"Pollydolly is your *garden angel.*"

"Hah!" Nate chuckled heartily at her remark. "Poledoris my guardian angel? That'll be the day! Next thing you'll be telling me those doorknobs of his are fairy godmothers in disguise."

"Can I stay, Nanny? I don't want to be in my room. There is nothing to do. So can I be here? *Pleas-a-weas-a-weas-y?*"

"Well, okay then. And just so you know, you shouldn't be walking out all by yourself. It's not safe. Remember that."

"I will, Nanny."

"Good. Now you might as well grab a seat and eat something with us."

In his head, Nate was kissing her feet and singing her praises for showing up out of the blue. Anything to help drag this date to its waiting grave.

"Sit down here, Sharmy. That's okay with you too, right, Kean?" Nate asked him while he waved to get the attention of the waitress. "Could you bring us something from the kiddie menu, please? Thanks."

Nate watched Kean's face. It said it all. *Professor S. Tuffy* was hoping to have an intimate meal for two, without the *pocket-size ogress* fidgeting and slurping orange juice through a straw, but he was being polite about it. "Sharminella, tell me how it went at the competition. Did you remember to apply the seven rules of self-assertion as we've discussed?"

She didn't answer him. Instead she said "I don't like ponies anymore."

"Why is that?" Kean asked with measured interest.

"It blowed chunks all over me! And the judges didn't want me to win, but I screamed till they gave me the trophy, because I must win because I am much better than everyone and, mm, better than those stupid three-the-same girls because they are stupid losers and they have stupid names, mm, and they all have the same stupid face! I am an *uringenial!*"

"Original," he corrected her.

"Hold on. Back up there, Sharminella," Nate said. "You didn't actually win? Is that why they were all giving us dirty looks when I came to pick you up? You didn't mention any of this to me. What the heck did you do? And a pony blew chunks over you?"

"I hate that pony. Bad pony! It sneezed his yucky-yuck on me. But then, mm, a beautiful lady took me to a beautiful room and gave me candy and she let me chose from her *jewellellewry* she said I can keep!"

"What lady?"

Suddenly a bulging belly obstructed his field of vision. It belonged to the waitress, sliding an assortment of pizza squares onto the table.

"Pardon me," Nate stopped her. "Someone seems to have already taken bites out of these."

"Bites?"

"Yes, it looks like a jigsaw puzzle."

There was a pregnant pause.

A small piece of anchovy tail fin was still sticking out of the corner of her mouth. Everyone stared at the waitress. She caught Kean's cold glare. "I'm so sorry, Sir," she flushed red. "I'll get a new plate right away!"

She raced off to the kitchen, supporting her belly.

"Why are so many women in Pinglop expecting a baby?" Nate wondered.

"Haven't noticed," the coach said noncommittally.

~"Maybe it's something in the water."~

"Anyway. Sharminella, who was this lady who gave you jewelry?"

"O, she was *soooo* nice. She has, mm, shiny brown hair! And she wanted to know things about you."

"About me?"

"Yes, she said *Nate have another name?* And I say *Yes, he is Nanny!* And she says *No, I mean, does he use the name pill shed?*"

"Pilchett?"

"Yes, pill shed. And then she asks if you can do strange things like look like other people. But I said no."

"Look like other people?"

~"Penelope!"~

Nate felt vulnerable and paranoid. Someone was coming up behind him! He jumped up with a start. For a moment he was about to wrestle the intruder down to the ground. Luckily he realized it was just the waitress bringing a pizza.

"Sorry. I got spooked for a moment… Ahem, thank you."

The waitress hurried away.

"Did she tell you who she was? Did you see a motorcycle?"

"Don't know," Sharminella said and tucked her mail-ordered row of teeth into a pizza slice. She didn't notice how Nate had gone pale. Kean had. "This woman, this brunette," he said. "You know her well?"

"No, I don't."

"Really? She seemed to call you by your name."

"Ah, oh, uh... Yeah, I do know her. Sort of. She's always pulling pranks. I ignore her."

This reply didn't seem to satisfy Kean. He had a concerned wrinkle on his forehead.

Nate's mind was buzzing. *'I think you're right, Jarrrvis. It was Penelope. She's stalking me. And now she approached Sharminella to find out things about Pilchett? What does she know about the visions? What the hell does she want of me?'* So many unanswered questions. He hated that he couldn't think clearly. He'd drunk too much of the red wine that Kean was so fond of. His skull felt tingly and numb, like he'd walked through a big cobweb.

~"I bet that she'll be contacting you directly soon enough. Her talking to *Missy Loudmouth* here was just a shot across the bow."~

'You think so?'

~"I do. Things seem to be escalating. When Penelope Mangez surfaces, we'll sit down with her and have a mighty good chat."~

'Damn right. No-one kidnaps Sharminella! At least, not without my approval first.'

Speaking of the little imp, Nate noticed she was not doing anything. That is, not doing anything *on an industrial scale*. From experience he knew that when she was gaping at the ceiling, it meant that her hands under the table were busier than a magician fiddling inside a top hat.

"What're you up to?"

"Me? Nothing."

"Are you feeding your food to someone?"

There was the sound of a crunch.

"*OO-AARRGH!*" Kean shouted. "That vicious thing bit me *again!*"

Spatula appeared, hissing and growling, with its fangs out. The fur on its arched back crackled when it moved. Kean tried to grab Spatula, but got a static shock that painfully cramped up his hand. The kitten jumped in Sharminella's arms and hid inside her open jacket, protected from the man screaming hell and fire at it. "*DAMN THING! HATEFUL FOUL CREATURE!*" he went on and on shouting abuse. The whole restaurant was watching him. "*IT SHOULD BE CANED WITH A STICK! STARVED TO DEATH!*"

"Calm down! Will you calm down?" Nate urged. "You're acting like a total jackass!"

A horrified headwaiter blew in and ordered the troublemaker to leave immediately. The coach, mercifully, made a quick exit. "I'm going to dress this wound," he said without even bothering to look back. "Goodnight!"

Sharminella was on the brink of tears. She'd been in the line of fire. Nate had to make a conscious effort to push down his anger, because tending to the little girl was more important. He gave her a long comforting hug, which she eagerly accepted.

"There, there, Princess. The big jerk is gone and good riddance! It's over. Now, drink from the banana shake. You'll soon feel better."

"Stinky, stinky, stinky man!" Sharminella muttered. "He gave Spatty the *hibbly-jibbly-spibblies!* I hate him! He's so fired! I fire him five times!"

"Yes! I completely agree. You know, I think he would have really hurt Spatula, if given the chance. But did you see how he got an electric shock when he tried to catch Spatula? That was awesome, right?"

"Mm," she mumbled, "awesome…"

"And weird. I had no idea that that could even happen with

cats. Must be static buildup from rubbing against synthetic carpet or something. Hey, how about from now on we'll call him *Sparkula?*"

"*Sparkula,*" she repeated, "but only on weekends."

'*Thank goodness, she still knows how to smile… I can't imagine what I even saw in that prick. What he did was unforgiveable. Worst psychotherapist ever!*'

~"I must admit I don't understand why he flew off the handle either."~

"Nanny?"

"Yes, Sharmy?"

"What do I do now?"

"Don't you worry. I'm going to take care of you till we get home. And then I'll help you find a new legal guardian. And a new life coach, I guess."

"Really?"

"I promise. You deserve to be treated better. Flock can get stuffed."

"*Thanky,*" she said, still sniffing a bit. She eased her frightened pet out of her jacket and into a bread roll basket. His pointy white ears lay flat in the neck. Spatula's head was more eyes than face. Two sky-blue peepers looked up expectantly at her. Sharminella started licking one of his paws.

"Hey, that's not clean! What are you doing?"

"Am licking."

"I can see that, but why?"

"Spatty licks himself when he is, mm, sad. Maybe because he tastes like candy and then he licks and he is happy again."

Nate's heart melted. Every so often he caught a glimpse of the endearing little girl behind the tantrums and the glitz, and in those brief moments it was all he could do not to weep with relief.

"It's nice that you want to help, but it's best to put him in your jacket for now. I don't think this restaurant allows animals."

She obediently returned her pet to the warm pocket after giving him a peck on the nose.

"Hold on a sec. I just realize, why is Spatula not at *Hadley Petting?*"

"Spatty sitted at the window of my room when we got back from the contest."

"That's not good. Did Mr. Bog set it free? What kind of business is he running? And how did Spatula find you?"

"Dunno," she said yawning.

"Come. Let's head to the hotel. It's your bedtime. And I still have stuff to do, like, going over to Hadley and sort this out."

"Can kitty stay with me, *pleeeease*? He is so full of scared. I don't want kitty be alone in a cage."

Nate knew he could never say no to her when she was as sweet as pie. Double so when she was actually being sincere. "Alright then. Just make sure no-one of the staff sees you."

"*Weeee!*" Sharminella cheered.

Spatula slowly blinked at Nate, as if to say *Thanks, man. 'Preciate it.*

"Well, look at that!" he smiled. "Isn't it funny how sometimes cats are just like people?"

...

Nate woke up with a terminal case of *turnip breath*. It was five thirty a.m. the morning after, and an alarm clock was drilling a hole in his head.

~"Good morning, sunshine. Took you long enough."~

"*Ooww*, why do I feel so queasy?" he moaned. "Did I get food poisoning from the restaurant?"

~"How about eleven plates of turnip? Would that do it?"~

"Huh?"

Nate looked around the bed. Plates populated the floor, the chairs, the desk. Even the lampshade was topped with a plate of turnip leftovers.

~"So you don't remember ordering room service?"~ Jarrrvis teased. ~"You couldn't get enough of the stuff last night. The look on the attendant's face when he delivered plate after plate! You ordered baked turnip, smoked turnip, fried turnip and last but not least–and this is a direct quote–*Get me raw turnip. The biggest one you can find!* You were insatiable. Before you blacked out, that is."~

"What is wrong with me? I don't remember anything!"

~"Believe me. It happened."~

Nate's stomach was a burning balloon of turnip-fuming magma. He swallowed a couple of times to keep it all down. "What prolonged *brainfart* made me decide to binge-eat like that? I must've been deranged!"

~"Ah yes, the folly of the turnip gorger."~

"I mean, I don't even like turnips! Why didn't you stop me?"

~"Hah! Don't blame me for what you gulp down the hatch, dummy. You know how stubborn you can get."~

"*Ooorgh!* Don't you just want to die too?"

~"I just think today is going to be great."~ Jarrrvis replied. He was enjoying a private joke. ~"Did I mention I'm feeling great? Like a fish in the water. Things are looking up."~

"Okay, well, I'm glad at least one of us is having fun. I just want to lie here and vegetate till New Year's."

~"Can't. You're meeting Cibyl today. And I for one am looking forward to your next lesson."~

Something suggestive of a woodpecker was tapping on the door of the adjoining room.

"Three knocks are usually enough, Sharminella. Come in," Nate said miserably.

The cheery kid had trouble getting through the doorway, due to her chrome green, multilayered hoop skirt and massive, platinum blonde hair extensions. She had to push and pull at the fabric. Once clear, she hopped onto the bed and bounced up and down, up and down, warbling an old pop song about how it was good to *only wear brown from the navel down–or your baby will leave you for a clown.* (Not exactly profound lyrics, but people get away with a lot in pop music.)

~"Good grief."~

'*Jarrrvis, tell me, why must she be so hyperactive at this hour?*'

~"It's probably a gland thing."~

'*There should be a law against this degree of cheerfulness before breakfast. Allow me to rephrase: breakfast under normal circumstances. I don't plan on eating again until the next millennium.*'

Nate's face was nearly as green as her outfit. "Stop, please!" he groaned. "Settle down, Princess. I'm not feeling well. Thank you… So what's up with this *Hoop Skirt of Impending Doom?*"

"What, this? I just threw that on, Nanny," Sharminella tittered. "I change, mm, into something more dressed up when I get ready."

~"*Something more dressed up* she says!"~

"Ready for what?"

She pressed a brochure into his hands. "Me and Bubby doll booked a whole day in the beauty spa," she burbled, "It's here in the hotel and we get skin scrubbles, faecals, extreme laxation, body detusk, hairball tea massage, deep skin *exifolilolationing*, manures and pedicues! *Weeee!*"

~"Pardon?"~

"Rather you than me, Sharmy. Suits me fine. I'm going to be out anyway and won't need to baby-sit… I mean… hang around with you then. Now, how about a hug?"

"Huggie-time!"

Ten minutes later Nate left for his next Cibyl lesson. It started at six. When he walked past Kean's room he saw the door was wide-open. A maid was changing the bedsheets. She said that the gentleman had checked out in the middle of the night.

'*Kean bailed on us. Just like that?*'

~"Aye, Cap'n. Appears so."~

'*To think you wanted me to choose him over Brent.*'

~"Everyone is not who they seem... so it seems."~

'*Well, I'm glad!*'

~"Hey, look! Poledoris's room is empty too..."~

'*Uh.*'

~"Well? Aren't you going to say something?"~

'*Hurray?*'

26. Cluster shock

A mess of greasy hair greeted Nate at the door of the shack. Cibyl's face in the middle of it looked wary and tired.

"Hi, Cibyl."

She didn't speak. Instead she beckoned him in by crooking her finger. Her hands, Nate noticed, were now completely blackened from leafing through countless publications.

~"She hasn't had time to bake rum cake?"~

'*Okay by me. Half-digested turnip tends not to go well with frosting.*'

Her room, which before had still featured some furniture and arches composed out of stacked books and paper, was now reduced to a mass aggregation of paper cuts in waiting. The stink rising off of it had only increased.

"I've been very busy since our meeting yesterday. I'm trying to figure out how I can get you to, let's say, open up more. There is something I'm overlooking."

"Did you catch much sleep?" Nate asked conversationally.

"Sleep? I never sleep, precious. A waste of my time. Soulnub wielders like us don't need to.–"

'*That explains it. I was wondering where her bed was.*'

"–And, by the way, you don't look so hot either this morning. Sit your butt down somewhere, I'll be with you in a jiffy. I've nearly finished cibylating this children's book called *Zany-zu Pineapple Goes To The Beach*."

Slowly she turned the last page. A pop-up of a treasure chest on a beach unfolded. The pineapple and its friend *Loopy-Lu the Flying Lizard* had little cardboard arms that could move up and down with excitement. She read the caption: *Look out! Loopy-Lu says. But it is too late. The chest breaks in two. What do they see?*

It is the hidden treasure. Mash potatoes and peas. I like peas, Loopy-Lu says. It is healthy. And I like mash, Zany-zu says. It makes me grow. And so they eat. And they eat. Until there is nothing left.

Cibyl stared at it in deep concentration. "Mash," she said intrigued. "How does mash come into it?" She searched around until she located a small device under a pile. It had a red warning light blinking. "Mash it is," she stated, her expression deadly serious for a moment. "I'm sorry. It seems I've got some business to attend to first." Swiftly she maneuvered her body through a labyrinth of musty encyclopedias. She climbed down a ladder through a hole in the floor that people wouldn't even notice was there until they broke a leg. "I'll be in the basement for a little while."

~"Ask to go with her!"~

"Am I supposed to just wait here?"

"Yes. Feed Cork for me, will you? His food is next to the bowl. His favorite, *Regular Coral Flakes*."

...

Nate didn't know it, but someone had followed him on his walk to Cibyl's place. That someone had had to duck behind trees, trash cans and a wet dog to evade detection. Brent had his reasons.

He stealthily entered the shack through an unlocked kitchen window and swam upstream against a current of postage stamps sliding out. Nate was unaware of his presence.

In a recess of the kitchen, Brent saw there was a loose panel giving secret access to stone steps going down. He crawled through the opening, closed the panel shut behind him and started his descent. One hundred worn-down steps later it led him into a long, claustrophobic tunnel that circled in on itself, not unlike a coiled snake.

He pressed on, his every move echoing loudly off the sandstone slabs underfoot. Farther up ahead, something was happening, because a frightened voice came clashing through the stale air. "Help! Is anyone there? I need help!" Beyond the last tunnel curve he reached the source of the voice. It was Kean Flock, tied-down to a chair in a space that could only be described as a dungeon... filthy and fetid, with a ceiling dripping who-knows-what. Sauvetyne was there too, ten feet away, imprisoned in the large glass bell jar and unconscious.

"Brent! Is that really you? Thank heavens!" Kean said through a coughing fit. "I've discovered a most sinister plot. It's huge! I've tried to protect Nate, but the Pinglopian Militia came after me. You know who I mean? Those pregnant harpies. They jumped me in my sleep, beat me up. You won't believe how many people form part of the conspiracy. We can't be sure whom to trust! I'll explain everything while we escape. Quick, untie me."

Brent was about to say something, but he got distracted by the soft hand caressing his chin. Penelope gazed into the demigod's eyes and winked at him. "Untie the shrink?" she smiled knowingly. "Nah. We are not going to do that. Are we, Brent?"

...

"This way."

"Sorry?"

Cibyl had finally returned. The top half of her body was sticking out of the hole in the floor. "I said *This way*, Nate. Hold on tight to the ladder and watch where you tread. It's dark where we're going."

He followed her down a spiraling ladder with a seemingly

endless number of rungs.

"How deep does this thing even go?"

"Curious, eh?... Good."

Nate let his fingers brush along the walls around him. All the way down, the walls were massive pillars composed of pages so old that they'd begun to look like petrified tree trunks. Millions of pages in every shape and color imaginable made up the foundations of the shack.

"Wow!"

"There's more to come, gorgeous. Above ground was just the tip of the iceberg."

Now that Nate's eyes were adjusted to the gloom, he saw they were passing by entryways into crypts cluttered with dog calendars, foreign crossword books, recipes, music scores, blueprints, old propaganda pamphlets, ancient parchment and papyrus scrolls. It was a journey back into time.

"These are natural caves that have served as storage space for hundreds of years. There used to be a fortress above us, but now only the network of tunnels remains. Ah, here we are. Cross over onto the landing, please."

She opened a heavy door emblazoned with the owl silhouette. They went through it, straight into an office space complete with employees and desks and the obligatory cheap coffee smell.

~"Pickle my mackerel!"~

"Where are we?"

"Follow me down this aisle to the right."

The office was enormous. Nate couldn't even see the back wall, because it was too far away. The employees were busy doing the usual drudgery: making noisy calls, typing things up and stressing about finishing tasks against impossible deadlines, but those of them who noticed Cibyl marching past all came running up to greet her. *Toadying up* would be more accurate. If they had prostrated themselves any deeper, they would have sunk through the carpet. She mostly ignored them, deeming their displays unworthy of her attention. Nate tagged along, feeling embarrassed on their behalf.

"This is Cibyl Unlimited Holding HQ. This is your future."

Cibyl opened a door with a nameplate *Chairwoman* on it and invited him in. Once inside, Nate took a strained breath. '*Unbelievable.*'

The luxurious room was decorated in a style often mockingly referred to as *in the best possible taste that too much money can buy*, meaning there was a certain cutoff point beyond where throwing more money at it changed *adding further refinement* into *making bold choices*. And here, that cutoff point had certainly come and gone.

Bizarrely, the interior designers–possibly afflicted with bovine fever–had had the idea to sheet every available surface in the room with gold foil. Even smaller items such as the stapler had undergone the gold treatment.

"This is where I take important meetings," Cibyl continued, clearly unconcerned about how out of place she looked in her threadbare cardigan and with the *comb-free zone* that was her hair.

~"Take a look at that ugly thing."~

'*I think it used to be a desk.*'

"You like what I did with the place, Nate?"

~"If you get off on living inside a pharaoh casket, then yes."~

"The concept is very, uh... consistent, isn't it?"

To add insult to injury, precious stones had gotten hot-glued onto the abused furniture with a devil-may-care attitude of a two-year-old. The chair behind the desk, for all intents and purposes, was a throne. A throne on which to reign.

'*Preposterous. I bet the showiness is all about rubbing people's noses in her status.*'

~"Sure, the place doesn't do much in the way of curing a

headache, heh-heh, but I certainly could get used to the perks."~
Jarrrvis hinted as Nate's eyes landed on the gilded liquor cabinet
and, more to the point, on the bottles of rum.

"How about some tea, Nate?" Cibyl inquired.

~"*Tea?*"~

On cue, a butler swooped in with a fresh pot on a tray. "One
lump or two, Miss Cibyl?"

"Three."

The butler was very uncomfortable, Nate could tell. When the
man spoke, there was desperation in his voice. And after he
poured two trembling jets of the brew into the cups, he rushed
out, letting a few involuntary *nn-nnh* noises escape his clenched
teeth.

'*What was that? How tough a boss must she be if her personnel
are that afraid of her?*'

~"I guess we're about to find out."~

Cibyl stirred her drink with determined twists of the wrist.
When she was done stirring, she shook off the drop hanging
from the spoon and placed the spoon on the saucer. "Thirty-
three thousand and seventy-four Pinglopians currently work at
Headquarters around the clock. We are now on floor minus
eight. I didn't want to deface the city with office buildings so I
had the stories built underground. Inside the mountain."

"That's impressive."

"At dawn, stone shutters open and let natural light in. They
close again at sundown. My statistics show it makes the work
force eleven point seven percent more productive."

~"A woman with vision!"~

She took a sip of her tea. "Now, on the subject of our
partnership–"

The terrified butler returned. He wheezed.

"Yeah? What is it?"

"Don't mean to interrupt, Miss Cibyl, but this message

arrived last night. It is marked top urgent. The mailroom would like to express their most sincere apologies for the delay."

"Oh, do they?" she said coldly. "Who's it from?"

"Uh, Mr. Noodascue, here present, miss."

Nate was confused. "From me? I didn't send any message."

~"*Are you sure 'bout that?*"~

"Okay, let's see it. Give it to me and get out," she commanded.

The man handed her the piece of paper and left. Cibyl's eyes darted over the first lines. Her face lit up. "*FANTASTIC!*" She read on, faster and faster. "It can't be this *simple!*" She crumpled the paper up in a ball. "I can't believe it!" She alternately laughed and cursed.

"What's on the paper? What does it say?"

"Yes, dammit! Of course!" she roared. "I've been *BLIND!*"

She turned to Nate and stared. A piercing stare on a crazed face. "I've been so stupid! It's a totally impossible phenomenon, and yet–"

"Please, tell me what you mean, Cibyl. I didn't write that note."

"Stupid, so stupid of me. For the longest time I couldn't figure it out! And now..." She paced the floor with a sense of exhilaration. "It's so obvious when I think about it! All the clues are there. Right in front of my eyes the whole time!"

She stopped. Straightened up, and walked over to her office door. She pushed it shut with a *click*. She turned around and smiled benevolently.

"This calls for a toast, my dear. Today you will become a god."

"You still haven't answered my question!"

Cibyl went to the bar and picked up a crystal decanter from the back of the liquor cabinet. "Shush. Everything will be explained in a minute." She poured a fizzy green drink in a shot glass and presented it to Nate. "How about some crème de menthe to commemorate this important day?"

"Thanks, but no. I'm not in the mood for alcohol right now."

"We must celebrate!" she said sternly and held the shot glass closer to his face. The green liquid smelled sweet and artificial under his nose.

~"Don't turn down a drink, Nate. That's rude."~

"No, really, I'd rather not. It's still early. Can't I just have some orange juice instead?"

"No, you can't. Drink!"

Cibyl used that tone in her voice again. The one you didn't want to disobey. There was more. Something in her personality had changed, making her seem callous. She no longer struck Nate as a person who would keep a pet fish.

'This is too weird. What do I do, Jarrrvis?'

~"Nate, chum. She's hardly going to make you ill with expensive booze she drinks herself."~

'No. Something's not right here!'

Even though Nate did not want to, his arm was already rising.

~"Bottoms up!"~

"I... uh... no..."

His hand had somehow taken hold of the glass and was slowly bringing it to his lips. He took a sip, then downed the shot in one. It had a horrible tang. Something like two parts crème de menthe, one part baby sick.

"Bravo!" Cibyl cheered. "Well done. How are you feeling now?"

Nate smashed the glass. A bloodcurdling three seconds followed where the whole of his being shook without actually moving. 'What's happening? Am I having a panic attack. An aneurysm?' His blood pressure dropped and his senses–smell, touch, hearing, sight, taste–were ebbing away.

"*HELL YEAH! I FEEL CRACKING AWESOME!*" he yelled

out.

'*Wait a minute!*' Nate thought. '*Why did I just say that?*'

"It's working! I can walk. It's all flooding back. I am free!"

'*And why did I say that?*'

Cibyl was watching him with utmost fascination. "It's as you said in your message: simply a matter of finding the right mix of substances."

They shook each other firmly by the hand. An air of melancholy and pride filled up the room. An alliance dating back three centuries had been revived.

"United again at last," Nate stated solemnly, and thought '*I AM LOSING MY MIND!*'

"So what name are you going by these days?" Cibyl asked him.

"I've been going by the name of Jarrrvis," Nate's mouth replied. "But, of course, I prefer Pilchett."

Nate screamed ~"*WHAT?!*"~ but only in silence, seeing that he was now the ghost voice. ~"This is wrong!"~

'*Hi, Noodascue. SURPRRRISE!*' Jarrrvis responded mentally and then out loud with a smile from ear to ear he said "Now I am in control!"

Nate was shocked.

Something was up with his mouth. It was changing. His healthy teeth turned yellow and crooked. The lips got thinner and the skin around them became a shade grayer. His ears were up next. Within a few heartbeats his face was not fully his own anymore.

~"WHAT IS HAPPENING?!"~

"Well done!" Cibyl said smugly. "Pilchett, thanks to your note I understand now why you were so difficult to track down, even with extensive help from cibylation. A shame I couldn't spot you quicker."

"Yeah, why didn't you realize I was with him the moment he

arrived? I could have stayed trapped inside this landlubber for another sixty years. Waiting was torture!"

"We have our oafish brother to blame for that, as well you know."

"I certainly do," newly-named Pilchett said with unconcealed bitterness and he spat on the gold-embroidered rug for emphasis.

"The soul bubble of this Noodascue body is just one big fog to me," she continued, "because there are two clusters. A dominant one and a subservient one. Stupid me, I didn't pick up on that."

Nate found himself speechless as well as bodiless. The Earth had dropped away from under him and now he was in free fall.

"Can you believe I got born with this chump?" Pilchett scoffed. "Twenty-two years I've been a whisper in the cracks of his maudlin mind."

~"Hey!"~

"Twenty-two years of putting up with a pushover and his whining about *Why do guys only want me for my mouth-watering glutes?* and nonsense like *I'm holding out for love with a capital L.* Bah, what a loser!"

~"Turn me back! Give me my body back so I can kick the crap out of… myself!"~

'*Oh, boo-hoo! Too late! I've boarded your vessel and dropped anchor, kid.*'

~"*BASTARD!*"~

'*Up yours!*'

Nate felt horrendous. A gruesome fate lay before him and he never even saw it coming. His arms and legs no longer responded to his instructions, yet somehow they made obscene gestures. His ability to speak was gone, but he was talking filth. He was a puppet controlled without wires, held captive in his own body by the one he believed would always be, literally, on his side. Jarrrvis, his buddy. His accidental soulmate.

~"You screwed me over, man! I trusted you. You're doing nothing to stop this. You're just standing here picking *my* nose with *my* pinky!"~

'*The name's Pilchett. Keep up, numskull.*'

"Is he still in there?" Cibyl wondered.

"Yep."

"What's it like? Is he an itch you can't scratch? A voice in the void kind of thing?"

~"*LYING BACKSTABBERS!*"~

"Raving like a drunk pirate, yep. Heh-heh-heh. Serves him right. Me, I'm going to enjoy myself. Grow large. *Overindulge* a bit. I got the hump from not having humped in ages, if you catch my drift. No more second-rate experiences. From now on everything'll be firsthand." To enforce the macho statement he cupped his package firmly in his fist. "So I say bring on those delicious turnips and harlots!"

~"I hate you! You're a liar!"~

"You will get your harlots," Cibyl said. "I'll have them lining up for you day and night, night and day to pleasure your every whim. And we'll get rid of Noodascue soon enough."

"That's great, because I'm super horny and I've got some vices to reacquaint myself with. Heh-heh."

"That's the soldier I remember! Blood nor gore shall dismay the members of the Barn Owl Army!"

"Blood nor gore shall dismay!" Pilchett chanted back.

~"Drop dead!"~

"But before we party, you know what we have to do."

"I can guess."

"Yes. Everything is ready. Follow me."

They promptly walked out of the room and headed for an elevator.

~"Do what? What does she mean?"~

Pilchett didn't want Nate to know yet, but he couldn't shield his thoughts. They loomed up inside, whether he wanted them to or not. And Nate was right there to snatch them up.

'*...ritual...*'

~"A ritual?"~ Realization dawned on Nate. ~"You mean the owl ritual! From the visions? It is really going to happen?"~

'*...no...*'

~"No?"~

'*...It has already happened...*'

~"What?"~

'*Blast!*'

~"Hah! You can't keep anything from me. The tables have turned. I only have to ask. I'm picking your... my brain and you can't stop me."~

'*Shut up! Shut up! Shut up!*'

In the course of traveling across the office space, Cibyl transformed herself completely, and not a single one of the employees looking on found this in the least bit unusual. They probably wouldn't have dared. She was no longer a drab, middle-aged woman. Instead the unflattering clothes were now being worn by a thickset, grim man in his thirties. He had a military face... The face that had been haunting Nate.

"Voegant!" Pilchett said with a lump in Nate's throat, "I'm honored to see your true self again after so long."

~"Hell! What's next?"~

The two stepped inside an elevator. "Family should stick together," the elder brother of the two replied with a self-satisfied smile. His voice was sharp as a knife and revealed a calculated ruthlessness that was less obvious in his Cibyl form. "You know, I can switch effortlessly from one incarnation into one of the other ones ever since... the botch-up."

~"The botch-up?"~

Pilchett's mind flashed with memories:

Three soldiers–and former turnip farmers–are about to perish in a burning lighthouse. Voegant says he knows a way out, but Sauvetyne vomits on the occult circles and ruins the dark ritual.

Pilchett finds himself returning to life again and again. And in each life he desperately tries to trace his brothers, whom he hopes must be out there... somewhere... alive again in new bodies and searching for him too.

He discovers the glitch: He always gets *stuck inside someone else*.

Vivid memories of seven people, both women and men, are passing in review. Each of them existing in a different time... Every one of them victim to the same affliction.

And despite Pilchett's struggle to make them do his bidding... to make them look for his brothers... they invariably wind up in a mental institution or worse.

Point in case, the sixth person: a sailor gone mad. To be more precise, a whale-hunter with a speech impediment who pronounces his name *Jarrrvis*. He is paddling his rowboat on the ocean. Pilchett is inside his head screaming and pleading to turn back to shore, but Jarrrvis is determined to destroy the demon that possesses him and he keeps on rowing toward the horizon... To their demise.

Lastly, the seventh and most recent birth: The blurry shape of a doctor in a delivery room spanking Nate's bottom, with Pilchett shouting ~"Hey! That hurt, you maniac!"~

Pilchett makes up his mind there and then. This time he will go about it differently. He's going to pretend to be a clueless sailor... until the day that Voegant reached out to him.

And that was it. The next synaptic signal Nate was aware of was hearing Voegant speak. "You're coming along nicely, Pilchy. Take a look at yourself."

The elevator doors sliding shut acted as perfect mirrors. Pilchett watched in awe how all of his facial features were breaking through Nate's: his tick unruly eyebrows, collapsed cheeks, bulging eyes, etcetera.

"That's me. That's really me!" Pilchett cheered.

The body was changing too. He was a shifting checkerboard alternating athletic muscle tissue with scrawny parts.

"It's the effect of the potion. Now that I know what substances to give you, you will quickly become *fully* Pilchett again."

The door closed and the elevator went down.

Pilchett was admiring himself. "I've waited so bloody long for this moment. This is great, Voegant, but why all the stealth and secrecy?"

"I couldn't risk exposing my intentions to Noodascue before I knew for certain what his deal was. Cibylation warned me there'd be a catch and that I had to tread lightly. Now we know the reason, of course. He wasn't you. You didn't have your own body... We still have to be careful, though. Taytelly, our enemy, is at large."

"How is that possible? Didn't he die?"

"No. He was the rabbit I tried to rush yesterday, but he jumped down a hole and got away."

~"The white rabbit is an actual person?"~

"But how can he be alive after three hundred years? He should be dead!"

"We used his damn foot in the ritual, didn't we? That's a mistake I won't be making again. So he's back too. Plus, for all we know he might be able to assume the shapes of other incarnations as well, not just the rabbit's. He could be any person."

"But he's alone now, right? No army to hide behind. What real damage can he do?"

"That's true. And after the ritual is done over again–properly, the way it should've been all along–not even a thousand armies will be able to stop us."

~"Why? What happens after?"~

'... eternal life....'

~"WHAT?"~

This was when Nate decided he had enough.

("*What am I going to do?... Okay, think, Nate... I have an advantage over Pilchett... a small one, yes... I can pick up every single one of his thoughts, but he can't hear mine unless I willingly communicate them... so, how does that help me?... I've got it! The element of surprise.*")

He concentrated hard on his right arm. ("*Move, won't you!*") At first nothing happened. Then... ("*Yes!*")... a quiver... a tiny spasm. By exerting all the will power he could muster he got the arm to move up a little. Slowly, very slowly, his left arm rose into position too. Luckily, Pilchett and Voegant were so wrapped up in conversation that they didn't notice. To escape he'd have to act at exactly the right moment. Every second waiting seemed to last an hour. Finally, the elevator stopped and the doors opened. Two hands rushed up and violently shoved Voegant out. Quickly he slammed the close button. The elevator went up to the ground floor.

"No! Go back!" Pilchett fumed. "Stop that! I am in command!"

~"Hah! Maybe of your mouth, but I still seem to run the arm department and, well... *Looky here!*... the legs too!"~

To Pilchett's consternation, that was true. Nate was dancing a jig in provocation, even though the movements looked awkward and uncoordinated because the ankles belonged to Pilchett.

'*Dumb fool. Face it, you're pooped! The place will be teeming with security in a minute. You have nowhere to go!*'

~"We'll see!"~

Nate thought he had this figured out now: The body parts that he focused on morphed back into his own, and the brain functions to control each part were to be conquered separately.

"Surrender!"

~"Not likely!"~

He bolted out of the elevator. There was a guard, but he was unprepared. Nate knocked him to the ground. "*MORON, YOU LET ME RUN OVER YOU!*" Pilchett yelled at the man, but Nate had no intention of turning back to apologize. He thundered through the hall and through a door marked *Way out*. Behind it, there was a stairwell linking all the floors. ("*Do I go up or down?*") His mind was racing. It was hard to think straight, especially since his mouth kept bellowing "*HELP, I'M HERE! CATCH ME!*"

And more trouble was coming his way. The clatter of boots three levels down made it perfectly clear that guards were already hot on his trail. "We're closing in!" one of them shouted.

("*Up it is then.*")

"*I'M UNARMED!*"

~"Yeah, and *unlegged* too."~

Nate charged up the flight of stairs. He rolled into another vast office space, scrambled back to his feet and broke into a sprint, dodging startled accountants on his path. He knocked over potted plants, chairs, filing cabinets... anything within reach to slow down the pursuers. "*I'VE SPILLED TACKS ON THE FLOOR. WATCH YOUR STEP!*" Cutting corners, sliding over desks, he did everything to gain precious seconds. ("*I need a miracle and fast!*") A guard had entered the aisle and was heading in his direction. Nate dove out of sight. The guard ran straight on, unaware of his target who was gasping for breath and whose heart was pounding so hard it put dents in his ribcage.

Pilchett was gloating. "*Just give up. The countdown has*

started." Then he shouted *"I AM IN THE STAFF LOUNGE, BEHIND THE FERNS!"*

~"Quiet!"~

"GET ME MORE POTION!"

~"I said quiet!"~

Nate tore a sleeve off of his shirt and rammed it in the mouth, even though he himself was in dire need of the oxygen. ~"I warned you."~

Pilchett's inner voice, unfortunately, had no off-switch. *'Gag me all you want, you're going down! The tide is coming in. It's inevitable!'*

Breath or no breath, the options of a fugitive were limited. He made a break for it again. This meant more race-walking through departments and corridors, and trying not to raise the suspicion of the employees. A lost cause. The sleeve cuff dangling from his reddened face and the muffled screaming emanating from it were the first things they noticed, like a red flag to a bull. More guards were showing up every passing minute, and so every minute it was getting harder to outsmart them. How much longer he could beat the odds, he didn't know.

The odds were certainly stacked against him: The physical exertion was taking its toll, and the concentration needed to keep from blinking out of existence was tremendous... but he had no choice. He knew he had to stay out of Cibyl's clutches, whatever it took. He had to. One wrong turn and it was game over.

("*Crap!*")

He discovered too late that he had led himself into in a large storage area, and two grisly men were obstructing its only exit. They hadn't spotted him squatting behind some boxes labeled *sauerkraut*, but it would only be a matter of time. He crawled to the far wall, while keeping his hands clasped over the mouth to further block any sounds coming out of it. In the near-dark, he bruised his thumb on a metal floor grid. Underneath the grid, there was a long shaft. (*"Too small to fit through. Just my luck."*) How deep it ran, he couldn't make out, but gathering from the stale air flowing out, very deep. A jumble of noise and whooshing of air floated up. Bits of a faint conversation too. An angry person with a creaky voice seemed to be doing most of the talking.

"... needed... Sauvetyne... travel.... away... inside him... your name?..."

(*"It's the mad woman!"*) Nate could immediately picture her in his mind. She was probably spewing her migraine-inducing vitriol at someone... Kicking up a fuss... He was glad he was not at the receiving end for once. (*"Although,"*) he wondered, (*"Would I be in the mess I'm in now if I had listened to her convoluted stories all along? For whatever reason–"*) He stopped his line of thought. Another voice was coming in clear. A male voice that shocked him.

"Yes.... Knibble... ambush... Noodascue..."

~"Brent? That's my Brent!"~

"... secret... harm him... Nate... idiot..."

Undeniably it was Brent. Nate couldn't believe it. Double-crossed by his own boyfriend? Another dagger in the back. His brain was close to short-circuiting. Pilchett seemed genuinely surprised. '*Well, what do you know? Cherished darling Brent is an agent of Voegant's too. Slippery eel.*'

~"Please! Anybody but not him!"~

'*Heh-heh, he fooled even me with the big innocent eyes and his* I swear I've never seen her before in my life *and his* Trust me. All I want is to be with you. *Hah! Ow, how sad for poor little Nate. Everyone has turned against you. Hahahah.*'

Nate's eyes started to water. He wanted to scream with rage, wail days on end in a deep depression. He wanted to thrash the place, demolish the whole mountain with his bare hands. He couldn't. The enemy would've been on him instantly.

~"No! It's not true. Brent is different. There must be another explanation."~

'*Simpleton!*'

He pressed his ear hard against the grid. Something was happening below. A metal screak followed by louder talking "*...drink!... let loose...*" and the crackles of something electric. Piercing glances shot in Nate's direction. The guards had heard the noise too. One was telling the other one to go over and investigate.

~"Crap-crap-crap-crap! A diversion. I need a diversion. Quick!"~

'*Hey, don't look at me, sucker.*'

He rummaged through his sweat-soaked clothes for much needed inspiration. ~"Yes! I can use this."~ It was the egg timer given to him by the CEO.

'*What can you possibly do with that? Unless you want to teach those hard-boiled men how to cook the perfect egg.*'

~"Watch me."~

He set the timer five seconds ahead. Then, when the guards weren't looking, he threw the thing like a hot grenade to the opposite side of the storage area.

'*The CEO will want his egg back.*'

~"Well, you know where he can stick it!"~

TRIIIIIIIIIIING! The ploy worked. The guards immediately turned on their heels and went to check it out. Nate catapulted himself through the doorway as fast as his still faithful legs could carry him. He ran straight into a maze of service tunnels. Having lost all sense of direction, the situation was truly getting hopeless. Still he pushed on. He was determined to get away from Voegant's mountain, away from Brent's betrayal, away from the turnip-guzzling soldier who had been plotting his prison break since birth.

Nate came to a full stop. ~"Not again!"~ Another dead end. Practically all the space in the room was taken up by the machine of the central air conditioning system. The converging air ducts brought with them the sounds of people running and yelling. Some seemed to come from awfully close-by. There was barking too.

'Dogs. They've got dogs. Time to kiss your ass goodbye.'

He saw a small rusty door in a corner. ~"Not yet."~ He forced the latch open. The door gave way and revealed a narrow recess going up. He squeezed inside and climbed what must have been well over one hundred steps. He swung open another door. Blinding sunlight hit his eyes. He stumbled on, wheezing hard through the nose and ignoring the stitch in his side. Passing out seemed a real possibility.

~"Where is this?"~

Around him, creatures were engaged in what could only be described as wild, drunken revelry. Aroused leopards were trying to make out with creatures half-woman half-warthog. Bare-chested he-men were toasting war victories, spilling wine cups over a unicorn prancing on the shell of a monumental clam. Giant pythons and dragons were engrossed in carnal pleasures. And the mammoth. Of course, Nate remembered the bronze mammoth sculpture. The towering colossus looked very imposing up-close.

~"I'm on Quaint Street?"~

Nate moved to the other side of the roof. He knew where he was now: on top of the large building with the broad steps and columns on the portico... The palace version of a gingerbread house...

He had a quick look over the ridge and there it was, Cibyl's miserable shed. On the other side he could see Hill Street.

~"Someone down there must be able to help me."~

Lots of people were crowding the sidewalks, going about their business, but none of them looked up.

~"How many of you are loyal to Cibyl? How many will betray me out of fear?"~

'Leave it, kid. This isn't drama school.'

Nate's eyes searched desperately among the humdrum of pedestrians. What he needed was a friendly face. A firefighter perhaps. Anyone would have done really.

~"Yes!"~

A helicopter passed over low. Nate started waving his arms about, jumping up and down, hoping against hope that it was coming to his rescue. He had no choice, he thought. If the helicopter carried Voegant's henchmen, he was done for. If not, he might escape this nightmare after all.

The helicopter just kept going round in circles above his head. ~"Are those police officers?"~ He could make out two figures in the backseats. Two pudgy men in uniform. They were looking out of the window and pointing. ~"Why doesn't the pilot try to land?"~ He gasped. ~"Maybe they're just waving back hello. But I'm in danger!"~

In an attempt to get closer, Nate cleared a low wall that separated one section of the roof from the other. A devastatingly loud siren went off right next to where he stood. It scared him witless. His ears popped and a headache hit him in the back of the head like a purple brick. The blare of sirens could be heard all over the city. The pedestrians quickly disappeared into their houses. Then a swarm of attractive women (pregnant ones) came filing up the broad steps of the building and they went inside, oblivious of Nate's presence six stories up. The sirens stopped and the grand door closed with the sounds of hinges screeching. The streets were deserted once again.

The helicopter had flown away, to find whatever it was looking for elsewhere. Nate felt abandoned, helplessly alone. He had no way of contacting Brent–and even if he could, would he still want to talk to the guy? It was all too much to bear. (*"Crap!"*) He felt he could really do with a dose of Sharminella right about now. Her chuckles would greatly lift his spirits.

'*Enjoying the view?*'

~"Why did I come to Pinglop? I hate this place! I want my friends and be safe at home. *I WANT OFF THIS ROOF!*"~

'*Give up already, you pathetic little gnat!*' Pilchett said as encouragement.

Nate had never been so frightened in his life. The only thing keeping him from crashing were the shots of adrenaline in his veins mixed with righteous anger. What he needed was a brave knight to come to his aid. A hero. One who stepped up to the plate. A man's man. Someone with the strength of ten...

Poledoris, sadly, had the stench of tuna. The general consensus was that he had no redeeming qualities. Unless as a paperweight. He was traipsing through the empty Hill Street... his roaming eyes searching the skies... Perhaps the memory of his scuffle with the albatross still lingered in his cerebral goo, because he looked more shifty than usual. At least he had put on clothes today, which counted as a small blessing on humanity.

Nate leapt up like a mad monkey, swinging his arms up over his head. Poledoris (as ever bringing to mind a stray cow wandering into a living room, slobbering cow spit all over the dressing table) did spot him on the roof right away, but unfortunately this didn't seem to provoke any kind of response in the man.

Disaster.

'*What are you planning to do now, Noodascue? Jump off?*'

~"I'd push *you* off if I could!"~

Nate centered all his will on reclaiming what was his. Within seconds the unhealthy gums and teeth turned back into the familiar clean pearly whites. His throat and vocal cords followed quickly after.

Pilchett wanted to shout ~"Hey! How do you do that?"~ and discovered that he couldn't anymore. He was only a thought.

Nate took the gag out of his mouth. "*I'M IN GREAT DANGER! EVIL PEOPLE ARE AFTER ME. CALL THE POLICE! CALL THE ARMY! I PROMISE I'LL TAKE BACK EVERY SNIDE REMARK I EVER SAID ABOUT YOU. JUST GET ME OUT OF HERE! HELLO? DO YOU UNDERSTAND?*"

Poledoris, the human equivalent of frothing at the mouth, didn't move an inch.

~"Hah! That's classic! Look at that idiot. He just keeps staring up like a dead fish on a slab."~

It infuriated Nate.

~"Heheheh. What did you expect? You're defeated. It's time to walk the plank."~

Disaster struck again. Pilchett, of course, was catching on. He had figured out how he too could take over body parts by directing his attention on them in a certain way. Nate was caught off guard. Pilchett had already regained mastery of the hips, nose, some glands, most of the digestive tract and one butt cheek before Nate got wise.

"*WE'LL SEE ABOUT THAT!*"

An internal tug of war erupted and the writhing body parts–especially the limbs–were conquered and then reconquered, back and forth. They were like strategic landmarks from which to beset the neighboring anatomy. Nate threw himself into the fight completely. So did Pilchett. The stakes were high. In the past they had coexisted. Now, when this was over, only one man's body would be left standing.

From the point of view of Poledoris, the flesh and bones of Nate appeared to be expanding and deflating underneath the skin like boiling porridge.

Poledoris also saw a woman step into the scene. The tall brunette edged her way forward. She was wielding a gun. Her movements were precise and determined. She was about to shoot.

27. It gets worse.

Meanwhile, down in the foul dungeon, Sauvetyne was reacquainting herself with Brent. "What calamity! Wading through the murk, I am, between what is the Flesh and what is the Divine."

She seemed to have decided that Brent was not her brother Voegant *two-faced criminal deviant* after all. Instead of trying to hit him, she'd been yapping away in her shrill voice without end. "Pledge allegiance to the gap-toothed bunny, I say. It's all about the bubbles!"

Maybe she was talking to him, maybe to imaginary pixies. Only she knew for sure. Brent had no choice but to listen to her ramblings, seeing that he was the heavily chained prisoner standing next to her.

A lot was going through his mind.

Like him, the crone was chained to the floor. She was also inside a glass dome that he would usually associate with something you put expensive cheeses under. Only this dome was a lot bigger and dirtier. He didn't understand why she was in there, but he was too concerned about his own welfare to give it much thought. There was no knowing what was going to happen next. All his pleading and shouting for his release had fallen on deaf ears.

Kean, whom he'd found strapped to a chair a while back, had been yanked away shortly after. Brent couldn't bear to think what the woman who called herself Penelope had done to the poor guy. It was easy to imagine that this dungeon had been a torture chamber a few hundred years back. Still was, probably. He shuddered. '*What have I gotten myself into?*'

It had started out innocently enough. Brent thought he would stalk his boyfriend to find out the cause behind the strange behavior. '*Perhaps he has an anxiety disorder,*' he recalled telling himself. '*Such as an irrational fear of fruit flies. Or perhaps some embarrassing secret from his youth, like, maybe when he was nine, bullies made him march down the neighborhood playing the oboe in the nude. Nothing insurmountable.*' He was going to help Nate overcome it. '*But this? This is deadly serious. He must be in deep over his head. Thank you for dragging me into your hell...*'

"Let darkness be gone. The whole of mankind is counting on the boy," Sauvetyne uttered to the flagstones.

Brent sighed. '*I guess he didn't want any of this to happen on purpose. I love him. I love him at least a hundred times more than I love my guitar... It's hard keeping a grudge when you're crazy in love.*'

The two prisoners were alone most of the time, except every half hour when a jailor entered the dungeon and forced Sauvetyne to drink from a cup. For his safety the cup was mounted on the end of a stick that he shoved into the bell jar through a hatch. She always protested, but she was no match against the stings of his electroshock gun. Usually much of the green liquid was spilled in the process. The jailor didn't relent until he decided she had drunk enough.

The potions made her drowsy, and they had flattened her jet-black hair like a hairy dog after a rainstorm. Not that her overall look had been great to begin with. The clothes that she'd been given, were showing rents. Wrinkly old skin bulged out in improper places. She looked worn-out, but not beaten.

During her more lucid periods she had explained a lot to her fellow prisoner... in her own way. A mental adjustment was required to follow it all. A lobotomy might have helped too. Brent didn't know how much of what she had told him so far was real, if anything. He couldn't really ask her. She just kept jabbering nonstop, not bothering with the fact that a conversation required two people.

From what he could surmise, her name was *Sofa-teen-with-a-y* and her evil brother wanted to dig his claws into her soul. Plus the brother wanted the pilchard living inside Nate to execute some sort of devious, world-threatening plan.

"Swilling swine! Forcing elixirs on me so I can't change into the ladybug and burst out of here," she ranted, "A glass prison wouldn't hold out long against my bug bite if I wasn't so tired!"

"You can bite through ten inch thick glass?" Brent asked incredulously into one of the air holes, but his question was ignored.

"Voegant traced me to my current life. I was relieved at first, until he made his despicable intentions clear. He wants to amass huge powers! I said *No! I've seen enough of your atrocities during the war. To shatter into oblivion is the only thing I want.*"

"What do you mean by current life–?"

"He locked me up, but I escaped. *Hah-haah!* He didn't know then that I could bite through steel doors, you see? I found out that Voegant thought he had at last tracked down the location of Pilchett. But he was wary. Something in his statistics warned him against direct contact. So he chose a careful approach. He doesn't know what I know about Noodascue. Merry mirth!... And it has to stay that way," she said conspiratorially and tapped her ugly nose. A nose that only a mycophile (a wild mushroom buff) could love.

Brent had no idea with she meant by that, but suppressed the urge to interrupt her because she was finally making some sense. Sort of.

"I flew to Portweald to warn Pilchett and persuade him to disobey our vile brother. Instead I found Noodascue. His soul cluster was blurry, so I wrongfully assumed he was Pilchett and that he had just forgotten his past. But I've figured it out since... the big secret... There are two people in one body! Noodascue and Pilchett. Something must have gone wrong during the unbirth."

"Sorry, did you say *unbirth*?"

The old woman looked up at Brent in surprise, as if she'd been rudely awoken from an afternoon nap.

"Of course, the unbirth! Don't you know anything?"

"Well–"

"The unbirth is the complete opposite to the birth of the soul," she said sharply, as if he was a willful ignoramus.

"Birth of the soul?"

Sauvetyne heaved a sigh, annoyance registering on her face. In other circumstances it might have been mistaken for cramps. "Okay... All living organisms–mammals, plants, insects, bacteria–have soulnubs. Higher beings have more nubs than lower ones, obviously."

"Obviously," Brent nodded hurriedly.

"A tree might need a spoonful of soulnubs, so to speak. An ant merely a pinpoint. But each needs exactly enough to be able to live."

"That's an intriguing theory–" Brent started and was cut off again.

"When a living being dies, the soulnubs fall apart and the being loses any recollection of its former life... You know that organic matter decays, right?"

"Right, but–"

"Equally, the soulnub cluster deteriorates and the particles get scattered, to be recycled again in countless other organisms. It's part of the circle of life."

"What about people who recollect parts of a former life then, eh?" Brent asked. He thought he had her cornered.

"I suppose that can happen," she snapped with a petulant toss of the head. "When enough particles keep clinging onto each other after death and end up in the new soul cluster. The newborn may recall details of the departed's life, but they are nothing more than memories."

"Okay, but what then is an unbirth?"

"*Oooh!*" she flared up again, "It is of the utmost importance that Voegant doesn't discover Noodascue's secret! Dear o dear, he must believe it is a dead end! Otherwise he will whack your lover like a piñata."

"He must leave Nate alone! He hasn't done anybody any harm. Who is this guy? I will–"

"Shush!" She motioned. Her antennas were feeling around. "I smell the guard. He's coming back. We must escape before it is too late!"

Sauvetyne unleashed every last bit of energy she had left in her. Brent watched with astonishment–quickly followed by horror–how the old woman bent over as if to produce a difficult bowel movement and then exploded into the shape of an enormous cockroach… correction: *ladybug.* She had turned around, revealing the black dots on her red wing covers. Having completed the transformation she started exuding toxins from her greasy joints.

Sadly, the glass remained unaffected.

…

"You're going to shoot me, huh? Just like that?"

"Just like that," she replied.

The last time that Nate had seen her up-close was at his graduation. Today, Mangez still had the perfectly proportioned figure that he remembered, but she had matured into a cold-blooded femme fatale-slash-biker chick.

~"Hubba-hubba!"~

"Nice gun. It really brings out your high forehead," he taunted. "And I see you've swapped the pigtails for a pole up your backside."

~"You're a sore loser, Nate."~

She walked toward the low wall that divided the roof in separate parts. Nate was standing fifty feet behind it. He didn't dare take another step in fear of tasting hot lead, but he sure wasn't going to let her catch him either. To be fair, how much percent of his body and how much of Pilchett's there was to be caught was anyone's guess at this point. Nonetheless, the fact remained that a deadly weapon was being aimed at his head. In her tight bodysuit and impossibly high heels she was a mankiller in every sense of the word.

She spoke into her mouthpiece to someone. "Target found. What do you want me to do?... Shoot him? Yes, dear. Understood... What's that you say? Ooh, I will. Hihih, Snoozlywoozlywolfie, you're a naughty boy–"

(For some unfathomable reason, Voegant insisted that his lady friends call him Snoozlywoozlywolfie even though he was as cuddly as a crocodile with toothache.)

"–I want your baby so bad, Voegant... Mmh, you what? Your lustful hands on my sexy thighs?... Pant pant... Oh yeah, give it to me! *Give it to meeee!* Spank me. More! It turns me on... *Paaaant*... Okay, okay, I'll take care of him for you. Alpha One out."

~"Heheh. Saucy beasts! I'm glad to see my brother is getting himself some prime tail."~

Nate's mind was racing. The dirty talk had given him a few seconds to consider his options. Sadly he concluded that he didn't have any. '*Except maybe one, but how to use it?*' He kept a straight face, more to convince himself than to deceive her.

~"You can't possibly think it will work."~

Pilchett, of course, already knew what he was thinking.

"So the freaky tyrant wants to see me dead. What are you waiting for, Penelope?"

"You remember me well, even though we haven't met since our school days." She was toying with him, postponing the execution. "I didn't expect you to recognize the sound of my voice over the phone, but you did."

Nate felt exhausted and angry. People had been scheming behind his back, been using him, ridiculing him. Jarrrvis–Pilchett rather–had been feeding him red herrings. And most sickening of all, Brent might have been the biggest lying crook of them all. Nate wanted answers. Even if it was only to take them to his grave.

"You tricked me into calling you. You left a note saying you damaged my car. Why? How's making prank phone calls part of the precious master-plan?"

He wanted to do air quotes around master-plan but he no longer had motor control over his fingers. Now it looked like he was just raising two fists.

"*Seebil-muah-nicblimz-aumhinm-tula!*"

"That's what you said then. So what?"

"The words are the incantation of the ritual. Wise up, Noodascue! You should have understood that by now. Voegant wanted to see if it would trigger some memories in you."

~"It did... in me! I just neglected to tell you, stupid."~

'*Hateful bastard!*'

Time to play his ace. Nate knew he couldn't slip up now.

"I don't believe you're really going to use your gun. Otherwise you would have done it already. Well? Try it then. Point-blank me," he defied her. He was beyond fear.

"Shooting you is the general idea," she replied and casually brushed some strands of hair out of her face. "Don't want you running off when I come closer."

"Yeah, but if you hit me, you'll kill Pilchett too! And all three brothers are needed to redo the ritual and attain eternal life, right? So Voegant would get nothing either! Nothing!"

"Kill? Not yet. Just incapacitate you. I'm going to shoot your legs."

"*PILCHETT WILL FEEL THE PAIN TOO! EXCRUCIATING PAIN!*" Nate yelped.

She just grinned back. His ace was a useless wild card, turning him into the joker.

~"Do it! I want him to squirm. Shoot the pathetic failure!"~ Pilchett raged. ~"I've been shot before. The suffering means nothing compared to the glory of being reborn and harnessing endless power!"~

Clack! She cocked the gun and aimed for his legs.

"You prefer I take your left or your right, Noodascue?"

"Hey, ho, wait. I don't–"

~"Blood nor gore shall dismay!"~

"Fine, I will choose which one then."

~"*BLOOD NOR GORE SHALL DISMAY!*"~

"No, I... Hold on... Can't we–?"

"Enough talk."

~"*BLOOD NOR GORE–*"~

BANG!

Nate doubled up. Explosions coursed through his whole being, ravaging it from the inside out. His skin was set alight. Muscles violently contracted. Pilchett underwent the same crushing agony. The two snaked in and out of each other at lightning speed. For an infinity of six seconds their existence was anguish personified. A high-pitched static throbbed inside their brains. Overwhelming nausea collapsed on them like a breaking wave. Six seconds passed where they had no identity. There was only pain. Nothing but inhuman pain. They couldn't breathe, move, think. Their hearts stopped.

A series of jolts and then Nate was back. The stench of his burning flesh hit him between the eyes. Black blotches pulsated in front of his face. He realized that he was on the ground. He tried to look at his lower body. His left shinbone had a hole in it. "I've been sh-sh-shot," he stammered incredulously. The wound was bleeding hard, but it was a clean shot. The bullet was still in there. Or not. He couldn't tell. He felt as if he'd been blown away entirely. He threw up.

Penelope moved in slowly. Her high-heeled shoes clearly weren't designed to walk on the layer of pebble stones covering the roof. She climbed over the low wall.

Nate was alert. The most alert he'd ever been. His arms and legs scrambled to get up. He yowled. Trying to stand on the leg proved a big mistake.

He looked around. Where could he go? He saw a long rain gutter hanging next to the steep, shingled roof behind him, with a fire escape ladder at the end of it. The gutter was barely broad enough and seemed unsuited to support his weight... but, he figured, why get stuck on details when you've got a bullet in your leg? So he went for it. *'If I can cross that, I just might get away.'*

Despite the vastness of unabating hurt and the threat of passing out, Nate staggered onward, dragging the immobilized leg behind him. Pilchett was too weak to comment.

"Stay!" she roared.

"No."

"Stand still or I'll shoot the other leg!"

"*NO!*"

Nate didn't turn around. He stubbornly kept going. The gutter was two steps away.

"Have it your way then."

Clack!

He dreaded what was coming next... *the bang*... but instead, high-pitched shrieks and hisses were what followed. He looked over his shoulder. Something white was attacking her face with its claws and pointy teeth.

"Get off! Get off, vicious thing!"

"Spatula?"

"*Aargg!* Get off!"

"*MHRRRI-AAW!*"

Penelope violently shook her head and trashed her arms to get the maddened creature out of her hair, but Spatula was clever enough not to linger in one spot. Her actions caused her to drop the gun. It fell into a chimney. "*SHIT!*"

'*I've still got a fighting chance,*' Nate thought. With his back flat against the shingles he shuffled sideways onto the gutter, little bit by little bit, and biting away the pain. The wind had taken up and was blowing into the open wound. It was unbearable, but he had to keep moving. Dizziness was distorting his vision. The gutter seemed to alternately float up and drop. He knew he mustn't look down, because it would spin his already unsteady sense of balance into mortal vertigo.

There were new developments going on behind him. He heard Penelope's voice. "Pick up, Voegant!" She was speaking into the mouthpiece and with her other hand she tried to extract the gun inside the chimney that was just beyond arm's reach.

'*Where's the kitten? Tell me she hasn't killed Spat-!*' The moment he thought it, a white blur overtook him and bounded ahead. After sniffing a drainpipe rigorously, the kitten sat itself down next to it and started calling Nate in that singsong way of a cat, each meow sounding like a question mark.

"Move," Nate implored. "You're obstructing. I don't have the strength."

"*M'iw?... M'iw-m'iw?*" the tiny mouth uttered. His whiskers vibrated in the wind.

"Aside. Please. I'm in terrible shape."

"*M'iw-m'iw-m'iw?*"

It was preposterous. He couldn't believe that at a time like this he was being pestered by a fuzzball that on most days probably couldn't even distinguish between what was its fuzzy front and what was its fuzzy rear. Sharminella's pet categorically refused to move. '*What the hell do I do now?! Picking it up is not a good idea, because the fur might give off an electric shock. And that in turn might resuscitate Pilchett.*'

Nate sighed heavily. There was only one thing he could do: maneuver *over* the kitten. He did so with considerable effort. A new waterfall of pain washed over him... Once the obstacle had been cleared, however, the kitten simply pattered ahead again, sniffed around, and then looked up as if to say *Don't just stand there. Follow me.*

Nate groaned. No more distractions. His only focus was the fire escape. His freedom was getting closer with every step.

~"Miss me much, jackass?"~

Pilchett had taken hold of the one working leg. He'd loomed up from out of nowhere. Nate stopped dead in his tracks.

"I've got the gun, Noodascue. Stand still!"

"*CRAAAP!* Can't I get a break?"

"I shoot you, then I shoot the cat."

Penelope was coming for him, causing the gutter to bob under the added weight. Her face was marred with scars and cuts. Blood, dirt and hair caked together in an unsightly mess. She took aim. "Okay, I got him at gunpoint. He won't get away from me, darling."

Meanwhile, on the internal battlefield, Nate and Pilchett had resumed their deadly game of tick-tack-toe, wrestling for supremacy of the central nervous system, the limbs, organs, veins... Every inch. Every cell. The surprise attack had gained the Barn Owl soldier a tactical advantage, but Nate was going all-out now, tricking his opponent into seizing the appendix while he himself reinforced his hold on the hip joints.

Unfortunately, this trick only worked once. His thoughts were being wiretapped, of course, and countermeasures were taken against his next moves before he could even do them. The other way round, Nate couldn't hear anything of what Pilchett was planning.

Nate was losing ground fast. The knees, the tailbone, the neck muscles... One after the other, they became enemy territory.

"It's time to call it quits," Penelope said. She was right behind him.

"Don't shoot. It's me. I am Pilchett. I am back in my body. The idiot has lost too much energy to put up resistance."

"Turn your back around so I can see you. Why do you still have Noodascue's hair color?"

"That's just a remnant. You can lower the gun, Penelope. See? I'm not trying to flee anymore."

~"Liar! He is lying!"~

"Turn around. Now!"

~"You're a phony!"~

He didn't move. Through the tears, through the pain he tried to summon all his will power, gather all his wits... Whatever they threw at him, he was determined to fight back. He'd be damned before he allowed his body to get hijacked. He was going to reach that fire escape no – matter – what.

"You know, I don't believe that you are Voegant's brother at all. Say bye-bye to the other leg... Yes, Snoozlywoozlywolfie, I'm glad you are listening. Do I make you proud of me? Hih, I know you'll enjoy this as much as I do, darling."

A deafening crack. Nate had been shot again. Then he realized he had not.

He turned around. Penelope had crashed through the bottom of the gutter, right where the drainpipe used to be. She clung on to the rim like grim death. A piece of shingle dislodged and hit her on the head. She plummeted six stories, screaming all the way down. A second later, it was over.

Spatula was the first to take action by tugging at his shoelace. Nate had every intention of walking on, but a clenched fist was beating his nose, really pelting it. ~"How do you like that, eh? And that!"~ Nate tried parrying the blows. It was impossible. The skinny arm wasn't very strong, but it belonged to a mind reader.

"Dammit! That's not fair!"

The fist changed direction right before it hit, inflicting real damage.

~"Hahahah! This is so much fun!... Ooh, I feel the pain too, you know."~

"That's right!" Nate said and hit his own face. "*Aaaah!*"

~"Why are you hitting yourself, stupid? Are you stupid?"~

Nate quickly reconsidered and went back to trying to pin down the other arm. Suddenly from below–*POW!*–*an* uppercut. Nate hadn't expected an attack coming from the knee of the wounded leg. They both screamed... The torment was back... full-blown... The convulsions nearly caused him to fall off the roof. This was the moment Pilchett had been waiting for. While Nate was busy holding down the leg, the other arm dove into a pocket, flicked open the small box of itching powder with a thumb and emptied the contents down Nate's back.

~"Gotcha!"~

Within seconds the allergic reaction was racing through the body.

~"Unless you take a shower right now, you won't be able to stand at all in a minute!"~

Checkmate.

His eyelids were already puffing up. Nate had lost and he knew it. Still, he kept walking. The fire escape was so tantalizingly close.

'*... Ignore the pain...*'

He reached out his hand. He could grab the ladder in his mind.

'*... Just a few more steps. I'm going to make it...*'

Then darkness followed. Right before he passed out, Voegant's guards came filing out onto the roof. Nate never did have a chance.

28. The lair

"Bring me another bag of ice to reduce the swelling," Voegant snarled as he pulled a smoking jacket over his sweaty back, thus shielding the world from a hairy backside not unlike the gray-pink, unkempt skin of an aging hog.

"Yes, Snoozlywoozlywolfie."

"And bring me another wild boar roast in brown gravy, and more sugary pies. More! I'm in mourning. My beloved Penelope, my first in line, is dead. O, hot double-jointed Penni. Murdered!..." He wiped his mouth on his sleeve. "But let's not dwell on the past. Duty calls. The seed of destiny must flow. We're at the dawn of a new age!"

"Yes, Snoozlywoozlywolfie," the desk clerk of the Resort hotel cooed and hurried off in her negligee to fetch the ice bag. Her legs were still wobbly from the eleven minute nookie with her Master. A full minute longer than any of her rivals. A sign of Voegant's preference, surely. She was thrilled. To get ahead in the competition, her strategy was total inaction–that is, just lying flat on her back and *being given it* by him.

It had been eight hours since Nate got captured, and Voegant had been busy impregnating every last member of his harem.

Nate and his fellow travelers had encountered some of these devotees already: the desk clerk who had turned a blind eye to Poledoris's bare-skinned frivolity; the overtly friendly bank manager who had helped him with his money problems when they arrived wet and broke in Pinglop; the stern art dealer from *We Invented Sliced Bread* who ran afoul of Poledoris and Sharminella, but didn't press charges; the pregnant anchovy-crazed waitress from the restaurant; and some of the women present in the crowd at the fair screaming at the world's largest rice pudding. All of them had been briefed in advance and had followed their Master's strict instructions. "Do not hinder Noodascue in any way," he had commanded. "The future of the new age depends on it."

Tonight was the culmination of three hundred years of preparation. The ritual was going to take place here, in his inner sanctum. A *sex lair* was a better description. The round, high-ceilinged room had no windows except for an oval one right under the cornice. Faint sunlight fell through it and blended with the veil of opium incense inside.

There were comfy chaises longues and cozy nooks and padded benches in a hierarchical formation. The round wall was covered with red plush and adorned with curtains and golden tassels. The occasional saucy painting showed groups of full-figured laundresses with pale complexions who, in all fairness, should be catching bronchitis from skinny-dipping in those cold mountain streams.

The devotees had draped themselves over the furniture and any other available surface. (No tea table with crooked legs went unused in this place.) They had applied bright red lipstick and wore see-through nighties to seduce their leader. Occasionally they strutted around like turkeys in heat. From experience they knew that was what he liked.

The unforeseen departure of Penelope, the alpha woman, had upset the hierarchy. Now every devotee was vying for the Master's attention in the hope that he would deem her womb worthy of *the child…* The supreme being.

The *luckies* (the ones who were already expecting) practiced their abdominal breathing. They scowled openly at those who awaited the result of their home pregnancy tests. And they, in turn, scowled at those who had just had one-on-one time with Voegant and who were doing handstands to expedite the greatly desired bun in the oven.

In the center of the lair, on a king-size bed mounted three steps up on a dais, the Barn Owl captain was taking a break from his sextravaganza. Gorging himself on red meat and booze, he was a glutton who knew that this was to be his last meal.

He fed some meat morsels to Cork, whose bowl stood on a pedestal next to the bed. Like its Master, the fish didn't care for chewing.

Every inch of Voegant's thickset body was aching–especially his groin where the sting of pain had a real zing to it–but he paid it no mind. Everything was falling into place for him. The Cibyl Unlimited Holding conglomerate was ready for the transition period.

"Everything is ready for the transition period," the desk clerk said as she returned with the bag of ice.

"Good. Good. Put it down there. *Ooooh, that's cold!*"

Voegant had made arrangements for the immediate future. He had appointed half a dozen stooges to run his businesses on the backburner, because he himself was going to be indisposed for a couple of years. He was going to be a baby again.

"The stooges are ready to run the business on the backburner."

"Don't bore me telling me things I already know," Voegant said harshly. "Shut up."

The desk clerk turned white. "Please accept my apologies, Snoozlywoozlywolfie."

Voegant grunted at her. "Less talk, more pampering. Start by massaging my sore feet. In the years ahead, I won't be in the position to do much myself. It'll be a while before I'll be able to preside over Board meetings without the need for a booster seat. A minor inconvenience I'll have to suffer for the last time. After that, the limit is the sky!"

"Don't you mean–?"

"Silence! You persist in speaking out of turn in my presence?"

"I'm deeply sorry! Didn't want to speak out of turn." She dropped to her knees. "Please forgive–"

"Your weakness is unappealing. You've lost your first dibs status and you fall back to reserves."

"No, please, I'll do anything!"

"Guards!"

"*Snoozlywoozlywolfie, noooo!*"

The guards shooed the woman away. She was made to sit on the least comfortable footstool somewhere in the back. She sobbed loudly. The others were stuck for words... but not for long. They all got to move one chaise closer to the center, closer to their Master, and that was what counted.

Voegant liked seeing them grovel. Rightfully so. After all, wasn't his elevated position his *unbirthright?* Secretly he mocked his wannabe courtesans. Only in a fleeting thought kind of way, though. He didn't spend much time thinking about them, because they were just a necessary step in the proceedings. Like breaking eggs to make an omelet.

"Look at them, sad bunch," he said to Cork under his breath. "Gullible women and runaway wives imagining they're players in an erotic game of musical chairs. In the end the only remaining seat is the one I'll be sitting on... Soon I won't need anyone at all... no more figureheads, no more benchwarmers..."

Whereas, in the past, with each incarnation, he had to keep the shares of his conglomerate in a bank vault and wait until he came of age to reclaim his seat of power, after the ritual he would never have to again.

"Every country will want to sit at my table," he smiled at the fish. "And those who can't afford to, will fight for the scraps underneath... *Ah yes, nearly forgot...*" He'd been mulling over a loose thread. "There's the matter of Pilchett. Sauvetyne won't cooperate, so he's out, but Pilchett seems eager. I've already promised him a place by my side, as my equal. But is he perhaps too eager? Is he trustworthy? What a shame he's still the same sly brother. Could–"

His thoughts were interrupted by the arrival of Brent and Sauvetyne. They were being led through a hidden door connected to the dungeon. The crone didn't look like a crone anymore, nor like a huge insect. The elixirs that were forced on her had locked her solidly into her original, male Sauvetyne body. He, now, looked every bit the pudgy farmer he'd once been. Sweat dangled off his forehead like condensation on a wheel of cheese. All the feistiness of his female incarnation seemed to have been washed out of him.

Brent didn't feel particularly relaxed either.

The guards tied them both to a stripper pole (one of the few anachronistic concessions to the lair) that stood next to the bed. The ropes cut into their bruised wrists.

A woman with long, press on fingernails ripped off Brent's dirty shirt, just for the look of the thing. His muscles glistened under the silk lanterns.

"What you doing that for?"

"Shush, lover boy," she said as she sashayed away. "I just hate to see things go to waste. Nice wing tattoo on your back, by the way. Reminds me of the swans Master Voegant shoots for sport."

Brent was alarmed. "Waste? Why'd you say waste?"

Maybe it was for the best that he didn't get an answer. He looked around furtively. Unfortunately, there were no sharp objects nearby against which he could discretely rub the ropes and cut himself loose–except for perhaps the woman's razor-sharp tongue.

'Even if I succeed, then what?' He wondered. 'What can one rock musician and a granny-man-something do against these psycho criminals?...'

He noticed the large engraving on the floor, underneath their feet, covering the entire dais. It was made up of a circle within a larger irregular circle, a bit like the outline of a bean. And in the middle sat the symbol for infinity with some crude lines coming out of it, like uprising steam. Brent had no clue what the engraving was supposed to represent.

The interior door opened. Three devotees rolled Pilchett into the lair. He was seated in a wheelchair, and though he was treated like a king–with the devotees in frilly lingerie feeding him double-salted rollmops–for security reasons he was still handcuffed. Voegant didn't want to take any chances, not even after he'd made his brother drink copious amounts of the green liquid.

His leg wound had been cleaned up and tied-off with a makeshift tourniquet. And he had swallowed a bucket of painkillers to take the edge off, but that was it. No use going under the knife when the ritual was about to render his scraggy flesh obsolete in less than an hour.

"Hey, sexy! Come here." Pilchett whistled at his appointed assistant–a pinup girl in high heels. "How about another serving of gherkins and brine?" he said and let his eyes linger on her cleavage. "And if you play your cards right, perhaps I might show you my collection of tadpoles. Hint-hint. You know you want me to."

The woman blinked twice. Her faith had already been tested to the extreme today. She was totally devoted to Voegant *the future ruler of the world*, that went without saying, but when she had joined the cult it wasn't to get felt-up by the Master's lecherous brother as well.

Her charge couldn't care less. He firmly squeezed her buttocks without bothering to wipe the fish juices from his hands. She nearly choked with indignation. His broad smile revealed bits of fillet stuck in his dental graveyard. He was completely satisfied. He, too, had been busy boinking to his heart's content. Nothing like a centuries-long dry spell to wet a man's appetite.

"Ah, there you are... Magnificent," Voegant welcomed him back. "Come. Our victory awaits."

Pilchett's shrewd little eyes landed on the captives. The first one was a squat man whom Pilchett immediately identified as Sauvetyne and ignored with disdain. The other captive was Brent, shirtless and also tied to the pole.

Nate–looking through the same eyes–was horrified. It pained him greatly to see his boyfriend like this. He couldn't imagine how he could have ever assumed that his one true love was a treacherous, conniving son of a bitch.

~"Set him free! He hasn't done anything to you people!"~

The handcuffed brother rose from his wheelchair, limped a couple of feet forward to watch Brent. The young man, of course, could hear nor see Nate.

~"Please! I'm asking you, set him free!"~

Defiantly, Brent stared back, mentally bracing himself for whatever was going to happen next. Nothing apparently. It was puzzling, but not as puzzling as everything else he had experienced that day.

~"It's me! I'm looking right at you. *I'M HERE!*"~

'*Heh-heh-heh. I thought you might like the view better from up-close... This is priceless!–*' Pilchett enjoyed torturing his stowaway. In Nate's state of supernatural suspension he couldn't even lift a finger. He had zero power left.

'*–And o, so tragic. Boo-hoo-hoo! Think I'm going to pretend cry! The woeful end of a dainty romance. Only five feet away, yet forever apart.*'

~"*I HATE YOU!*"~

'*Hahah! You amuse me.*'

~"I swear, you are going down! You and your hermaphrodite brother!"~

"Are you in there, ghost of Noodascue?" Voegant asked, unknowingly joining the conversation. "Is he listening, Pilchy?"

"Yeah, he's listening. He says *Hi, I am a dimwit.*"

~"Sacks of hateful sick! Corrupt, repulsive scumbuckets!"~

Confusion once again spread across Brent's face. "My Nate is *inside* that guy?" he whispered to Sauvetyne. "How's that possible? It can't be!"

"Believe it," Sauvetyne responded in slurred speech. "You'll need all the luck in the world if you want to see him again."

Brent struggled to grasp this information. His only comfort was the knowledge that his boyfriend was a victim in all of this too. Nate wasn't to blame... Nate was still the fun-loving pacifist he knew. Innocent and sweet.

~"You're dead meat! *I WILL ANNIHILATE YOU!*"~

Pilchett chuckled and spoke out loud to include his brother in his merriment. "Tough words from a loser with nothing to back it up. You're an idiot. Voegant has been testing out potions on you since you left Portweald and you didn't even realize it."

~"What?"~

"You still haven't figured it out? Hah!"

Voegant cut in. "When did you became aware it was me, Pilchy?"

"After the lemon-flavored sleeping pill."

"That was quick, but you forgot the breath mint. That was the first time."

"Oh, right."

~"What breath mint? What pill?"~

'*Think back, stupid!*'

~"Just tell me!"~

Nate was too upset and angry to get a good lock on Pilchett's brain, which was already brimming with the answer.

"He still doesn't know!"

The two brothers both laughed at this. Laughter that would

have had a yeti run scared.

"Well, then," the future ruler of the world decided. "Let me show it to him."

Voegant transformed himself into another one of his incarnations. His plump, short body stretched upward. The shoulders expanded. Parts of the clothes tore as new muscles tried to fill the space. Bones twisted and grew and shifted. Someone else was breaking through. Someone handsome, virile, at the height of manhood…

29. Choice

"Surprise!"

~"*FLOCK!*"~

All the courtesans swooned from exposure to Kean Flock's splendor. They squirmed and groaned.

That's right!' Pilchett roared. *'Voegant was Flock the whole time, slipping you experimental potions because he thought he needed you to remember your past. But all that I needed was a potion to take over your body while you were sleeping and write the note.'*

Memories came flooding in that backed this up. Nate was overwhelmed by them. It was true! Flock was always handing him things:

It was Flock who had given him a breath mint right before that first lighthouse vision.

It was Flock who had offered him a sedative at the trailer park when Brent had just dumped him.

When Nate was taking a bath, Flock was there to pour in the bath oil, which triggered the second vision.

The strange tasting finger food and wine at the restaurant were Flock's idea.

And those were only the ones Nate could remember. Who knew how many other attempts there'd been. He connected the dots and it was a large arrow pointing at Sharminella's psychotherapist.

~"*EVERYTHING'S BEEN A BIG, FAT LIE!*"~

And always that knowing gaze, Nate now realized, that half-smile on the man's face suggesting he knew more than he led on. Cibyl had given him the same look.

Betrayed, mocked, abused… He'd been played for a fool.

Worst of all, Flock had pretended to care. He had asked Nate to confide in him. Just another underhanded way to find out if Nate was his long-lost brother.

"How is he taking the news?"

"He's mouthing you off."

~"LOATHSOME, EVIL, REPUGNANT BASTARD! I AM GOING TO-"~

"Hahahah. Don't keep it all to yourself, Pilchett. Let him take over your mouth for a second."

"-FLAY YOUR SKIN AND HAVE YOUR CADAVER RAVISHED BY STARVING RODENTS!"

It was an odd view. Pilchett stood totally still, but the mouth was all over the place. Nate had seldom been this furious.

"Double back at you, Noodascue," Flock said. "You've wasted a lot of my time and money."

"Wait a minute!"… A new alarming thought cropped up in Nate's virtual mind… "Sharminella's road manager didn't really ditch her in the middle of nowhere, did he? You forced him to abandon her at that pier so that you could introduce yourself as her new life coach."

"Guilty as charged."

~"Of course, you dolt! It was all too much of a coincidence."~ Pilchett added gleefully.

Nate's mouth exploded with rage. "You crushed a little girl's heart! She's just a kid. You are a MONSTER!"

"Now listen here, Noodascue," Flock said gritting his teeth. "You don't get off either. You killed Penelope. I will make you pay!"

"I didn't kill her! She fell off the building while trying to shoot me."

"Penelope was going to carry my special baby!"

"Well, she can't have been *that* special by the look of all these other knocked-up hussies."

Flock punched the face in front of him. Then he wiped his knuckles dry on his robe sleeve.

"*Aargh!*"

~"Cut it out. It hurts me too!"~ Pilchett added inaudibly, but it was just a reflex. The painkillers were working.

Flock walked back up the steps of the dais. "One of these wombs is going to bear my child," he continued. He looked more collected again, but the threat of violence lingered underneath. "And that child will become me. I will conceive myself!"

"*Wh-WHAT?*"

Nate couldn't believe Pilchett's ears. Brent, too, thought he must have heard wrong. He cast a glance at Sauvetyne for him to disagree, to ridicule it, but the man nodded his head. Anger was building up inside of him and was set to explode.

"You mean…?" Brent whispered. "He is going to *self-pollinate?* That's preposterous!"

"No. It's not." The tremors that had occupied Sauvetyne's aching hands were now spreading over his entire body. "Voegant wants to violate the sacred laws of nature and do the unthinkable!" His muscles tightened. Remnant traces of ladybug were breaking through. Potion or no potion, the back of the head widened and turned into a hard, dark shell. "Is there no end to your *ARROGANCE!*" he shouted at Flock. "Who do you think you are, tampering with the *Spiritual Blah-blah-blah?*"

Brent leaned back in fear of the head blowing off under the pressure. Suddenly the half-formed ladybug discharged a jet of orange ooze out of his exoskeleton. Flock took a dive. The toxic ooze missed him by mere inches. It flew on and out through the open oval window.

The guards hurled themselves on the prisoner… electroshock guns blasting away… They dunk the insect head into a bucket of green potion and made him empty it. When they were done,

Sauvetyne was back himself. Powerless.

"Leave him for now. Just another one of his pitiful attempts."

"Don't look so smug, Voegant," Sauvetyne wheezed. "I wasn't aiming at you, but at the window. My son is bound to have noticed the distress signal."

"Son?"

"Yes, I have a son. You're not the only one who can sneak in a spy to follow Noodascue around, you know. He will have seen the signal. He and the police are going to burst through that door and end your reign of terror.

"Bravo," Kean mocked, "You've changed quite a bit. You've gone one up from *sniveling coward*. I'm almost impressed."

"Three hundred years of being haunted by the barbaric things we did in the war has turned my way of thinking around."

"Doesn't matter. You've failed anyway. Who is the police going to arrest when they arrive? They'll find our dead bodies, Sauvetyne. The police can't lock up dead bodies, Sauvetyne!"

And with that bombshell Kean smiled victoriously and ordered a devotee to bring him more plates of red meat.

"You really think your son can save us?" Brent asked Sauvetyne.

"I hope he does. I hope he does... My son is a total idiot."

...

Outside on the sidewalk, some of the orange ooze had landed on Poledoris's head, causing tufts of his toupee hair to smolder. It didn't occur to him to take action. He remained immobile. The wide trenches on his forehead, however, deepened. There was some unidentified urge he wanted to satisfy. If only he knew what.

...

319

A shrub across the street from Poledoris jiggled a bit.

"Pssst, Duncetead? We have the freak in our sights. What do we do?"

The shrub next to it jiggled back.

"Well, Dirks. The freak is too dangerous to simply walk up to and arrest, obviously. He has lethal physical strength, you know? We'll have to use our cunning."

"Ah, good. Cunning. Gotcha."

In the safety of their stakeout shrubbery Dirks and Duncetead weighed their options. (The two policemen had in fact spotted Poledoris from the helicopter many hours ago, but had yet to apprehend him.)

"Maybe we should wait a little longer and see what happens?"

"Wait?... Good thinking, Duncetead. My pediatrician says I shouldn't exert myself too much."

"A pediatrician. That's a baby doctor, isn't it?"

"Yeah, you know. Still."

"Hand me the tranquilizer gun, Dirks."

"Tranquilizer gun?"

"Yeah, the tranquilizer gun."

"I didn't bring it."

"What d'you mean?"

"I didn't bring the tranquilizer gun. I thought you did."

"You thought wrong. Why would I have brought the tranquilizer gun?"

"I assumed you would."

"Then did you at least bring the darts?"

"Darts?"

"Yeah, the darts for the tranquilizer gun, Dirks!"

"I don't have 'em."

The shrub stifled a groan.

"How are we going to take him down then?"

"I don't know... Maybe ask him gently?"

The two were out of their depth. Usually the Officers were physically bigger than their suspect... They could then mess with the guy's head a bit, threaten him with some charges, and have a good time... But this Poledoris character was the size of them both combined. Such a thing demanded respect. It was an unwritten law in the *Big Book of the Belly Code*.

...

The urge wasn't going away. Poledoris couldn't place it. It was odd. He vaguely recalled doing someone a favor. Just because someone had asked him, he had done it. What was it? Brain neurons were firing... *'Keep an eye on Nate Noodascue.'*

Confusion set in, an unfamiliar concept. It didn't seem right to him that he would keep an eye on someone as a favor.

'I am Poledoris aka Dr. Brainzipper. I had an artichoke accident. Emotions are foreign to me...' Over the years his brain had assimilated the things people had called him and established them as truths. *'I am an anthropoid ape with less than a basic grasp of the social fundamentals. I am Poledoris, the quagmire of queerness. An ironic euphemism for disaster. The living and breathing placenta... doing someone a favor?'*

And then the goo of recollection descended. When the orange color reached his nose, he remembered who the someone had been. It was the one who had always been kind to him, no matter what. She would say things like "Hey, don't cry, 'douris. Were the other kids not playing nice? I'm here for you now. We'll go out for ice cream. How does that sound?" And the child Poledoris would wipe the snot on his T-shirt and smile up at her. (Well, he smiled as best he knew how.) He liked her antennas. They were funny. "You are not like the other kids," she would say to him. "You are a very special boy... because you are my son."

Her face broke through the fog. She was the only person in

his world for whom he would do everything and anything.

"...mommy?"

The orange goo was a defensive weapon, so she had to be in danger. Tears welled up in his science-defying, aberrant eye. The other eye feigned aloofness. Poledoris was obviously an *overgrown* man, but right now, in this moment, he was that unhappy boy again who wanted to run to mother. "*I AM COMING, MOMMY!*" He catapulted himself forward with great force, up the broad steps of the building. He pummeled the heavy oak door with his fists. *BAM! BAM! BAM! BAM!* Clearly, before long it was going to get ripped out of its hinges. *BAM! BAM! BAM!*

"*MOMMMMYYYY!*"

"He's on the move!" Duncetead shouted.

"He's trying to escape our superiority," Dirks shouted back.

"What do we do?"

"Take action is what we do!"

"Action... Us two personally?"

"Tell the reinforcements to come round the corner. It's go time!

"Yeah! I'll call the paramedics too, because people are going to get hurt. And with *people* I mean *Polewhatsit*, and with *getting hurt* I mean we'll be going medieval on his ass!"

"Good one!"

They leaned in to high-five each other and missed.

...

"Will somebody get the damn front door?"

The thundering blows were shaking the foundations of the building. It irritated Flock, because he'd been right in the middle of his stirring speech when he got loudly interrupted.

"Go! See who's there and make sure they keep out."

Several guards hurried away, their guns drawn. Those who remained set up position in the lair.

"Where was I? Oh, yes... I said, I will conceive myself! During the unbirth I will choose one of you ladies to harbor my soul cluster!–"

This was received with loud applause from the devotees and with someone remarking "Why don't you come over here and howl at my full moon, Wooflie?"

"–Which will propel *me*–I mean, me and my esteemed brother Pilchett, of course–into our final destiny!"

A roar of cheering and more applause followed. The women were elated.

"They say only gods can create themselves!"

This provoked disapproving shouts of "No!"

"That man cannot aspire to surpass the constraints of his own life cycle. This is untrue. After tonight *I WILL BE*–together with Pilchett, that is–*WILL BE IMMORTAL!*"

Another round of exuberant cheering. Flock ceremoniously poured a liquid into a crystal goblet marked with the symbol of an owl skull and crossbones. This triggered more euphoria. They were beside themselves with anticipation.

For the next bit, Flock turned back into the original shape of Voegant. One woman booed.

A nervous guard entered the room. Louder thumping noises and police sirens slipped inside with him. Plaster dust had snowed down on him. The guard was bringing bad news and he didn't look forward to breaking it to the boss. "Master, a police force of thirty have surrounded the entrance with patrol cars. And we think a battering ram is trying to demolish the front."

"Hah! Let them."

"Master?"

"I said let them. What do they want anyway?"

"A policeman is shouting through a megaphone. It sounds like *Surrender, polydomous!*"

"Surrender, polydomous? What's that supposed that mean?"

"Uh, I looked it up. It means *living in more than one nest.*"

Voegant stared at the guard.

"You know, like an ant colony?" the guard elaborated, his voice faltering midway.

"I see. Never mind the police. Just keep them out as long as you can."

"Yes, Master!"

Voegant turned to Pilchett. He raised the goblet above his head so that everyone could see. It was a cheesy move but a crowd pleaser nonetheless. "Are you ready, Pilchy?"

Pilchett nodded yes.

"Step onto the engraving with me. Do you trust me?"

Pilchett nodded again.

"A drink to our health–Oops! To our infirmity," Voegant grinned humorlessly. "Let's jump through the loophole!"

He drank from the deadly poison first. The whole room held their breath. The sizzling sensation of destiny hung heavy in the air. Voegant gestured to the guards. Sauvetyne was up next. They moved him into place. Sauvetyne had meanwhile become totally lethargic and he swallowed the poison brought to his lips without protest. The crowd applauded.

Then Pilchett greedily reached for the goblet. Nate resisted and pressed his mouth shut. ("No! Don't! *STOP!*")

~"Open wide! Here comes the airplane!"~

("*DON'T DO IT!*")

Pilchett briefly switched back to his own mouth and took several swigs. There was nothing Nate could do about it.

("*NOOOO!*")

Within seconds the substance entered the bloodstream and spread itself like wildfire. Every part of the body tingled, alternately piping hot and freezing cold.

"...You drank it! Just like that! You're insane! Now we'll die!" Nate's mouth said.

"Stop that prattle, Noodascue," Voegant bellowed. "We have unfinished business. You took my Penelope away from me. I demand satisfaction. A life for a life."

Somewhere a mechanism was set in motion. A little girl was being raised through a hole in the floor, presumably for dramatic effect.

Nate gasped. The panic in Sharminella's eyes said it all. She didn't understand what was happening. They had gagged and shackled her. She was in her bathing suit and crackly, dry mud covered her from top to toe.

"What's that smell?" Voegant asked.

"Chocolate," a guard replied. "She was at the Pinglop spa resort."

Nate couldn't stand it. "*LET HER GO!* She's got nothing to do with this!"

"A life for a life is what I said! You killed my Penelope. Now you must condemn one of your own to death. Who will it be? Tattoo guy or the kid? Give me one name. The other one I promise I will release. If you don't decide before the poison has done its work, you condemn them both."

Sharminella and Brent looked thunderstruck.

"This can't be happening! You're a sadist! *YOU CAN'T DO THIS!*"

~"This is awesome!"~ Pilchett chuckled. He got a real kick out of this game. ~"Take a stand for once in your life, you little wimp! Screw them both over, I say. Now that would be original."~

"Give me a name!" Voegant bellowed, "Whose trust are you going to betray? The one who *lubby-lubby-loves* you as much as you *lubby-lubby-love* him, or the brat you share an apartment with?"

"You can't make me! This is sick!"

Only the mouth was contorted. The rest belonged to Pilchett, who accompanied every word Nate said with mocking poses and facial expressions like a court jester.

"Don't you know compassion?"

"Decide, Noodascue! Which one gets it?"

"I refuse!"

"YOU HAVE TO CHOOSE!"

Nate was barely able to think. It was agony. Outside on the portico their rescuers were battering down the door, literally, but what good was that to him and his loved ones? The poison had taken hold... Pilchett's heart rate was dropping drastically... (In fact, half of the eighty-odd organs had already ceased functioning.) Nate desperately tried to protect them... tried to stave off what he knew was inevitable. ("I could spare Brent's life, but then could I forgive myself for letting Sharminella die? *NO, I CAN'T!*")

"Choose!"

"I won't do it!"

"Choose!"

("Sharminella is innocent. But I love Brent. This is too hard! Impossible!")

"Time is ticking away. Pick one!"

"Don't make me! *I WON'T DO IT!*"

"The poison is pumping through your veins. There's only a few minutes' juice left in you. *SO WHO WILL IT BE?*"

"*I CAN'T!*" Nate shouted. "I can't... I love them both with my whole being. I can't imagine myself without them!... You won't get that. You don't understand anything about true love because you're a corrupt, depraved, miserable–Pilchett, stop making those stupid jazz hands!–Don't make me choose!"

~"Tick tock, tick tock."~

"Nate, can I say something…?" Brent volunteered.

Everyone turned to look. Pilchett pounded his fist down on Brent's shoulder. ~"How nice. The precious sweetheart has something to share."~

"You really are somewhere inside of this guy, right?…"

"Yeah, I'm really here, Brent. Listen. I'm so sorry. I never meant any of this to happen. I should've told you about the ghost voice and all the other stuff. I was wrong to doubt you. I got you into this mess and now everything is…"

Brent's eyes started to water. Nate's eyes would have too.

"Choose for Sharminella to live."

"Wh-what?" Nate stammered.

"Choose for Sharminella to live," Brent repeated. "Save her. She's still just a kid and I've seen how much you care for her. She's the little sister you never had. Screw these psychos! We're meant to be together, Nate. If we have to die today, you and I will find each other again, on the other side. We'll be angels."

"Brent, are you asking me to-?"

"Be brave, Nate. Be brave for me and I will be too. Save Sharminella."

"No… no, I can't. That's madness," Nate mumbled.

The legs were starting to give out. The end was coming.

"Yes, you can," Brent said softer now. He tried to choke down the tears and failed. "It's okay for me. Save Sharminella."

"NO!… I won't-"

"Ssst… It's okay. Listen to me. Nate. We'll be together again. We'll find a way."

Only precious seconds remained. The soldier's dying body tipped over.

In his fall–through sheer luck or was it fate?–Nate's lips landed on Brent's. They stayed there for a last, quick kiss and then the body sagged to the floor.

"I choose… to save Sharminella," he said. The last words. His will was broken. Shattered.

The girl screamed through the gag and kept screaming. She understood what was happening.

"Took you long enough," Voegant sputtered. He no longer had a booming voice. The deadly substance had kicked in on him too. He staggered toward Brent.

"*I FORGIVE YOU, NATE! I FORGIVE YOU!*"... Brent struggled–*fought*–to free himself from the ropes. "I love you! Stay awake! *NATE!*"

A guard stabbed an electroshock blast into the young man's chest and then forced his mouth to stay open. Voegant poured the liquid in. With one gurgle it was done.

Down on the floor, Nate heard his boyfriend calling out, but could do nothing. He was paralyzed. Blind. At death's door. ("I changed my mind! Save Brent! *SAVE BRENT!*")

There was a violent commotion in the hallway. It started with the loud crack of the outer door being torn open. This was followed by gunshots and sirens and guards pleading "No! Please!" before being smacked aside, left and right, like pins in a bowling lane. The hefty individual thundered ahead, clearing himself a path.

So much was going on that nobody noticed the pitter-patter of cat feet coming up behind him.

Voegant knew he had only moments left to act. Feebly he motioned the guard to step away from the dais and he chanted "Seebil-muah-nicblimz-aumhinm-tula!" It was all he needed to complete the ritual. The goblet slid out of his hand and smashed.

Purple columns of smoke instantly surged up and out of the circles... flickering, churning, and infused with a black magic as ancient as it is was hungry. The smoke wrapped itself around the bodies, claiming them for its own.

A second later, Poledoris burst into the lair. "*MOMMY, I'M*

HERE!" And an entire police squad threw itself on top of him, with Officers Dirks and Duncetead bringing up the rear. The devotees plunged into hysteria. Pandemonium ensued. The remaining guards got knocked over or swamped.

But it was useless. The cavalry had come too late. Nate was dead. Pilchett and Sauvetyne too. Brent and Voegant as good as. It was a massacre.

A white blur rushed in, zigzagging around the many legs. Spatula had a critical mission to accomplish. Single-mindedly it bounded forward from one prone body to another, climbing higher and higher. It leapt into Sharminella's neck (who was still screaming into the gag) and gnawed off her necklace, fished out the hidden locket with its mouth, jumped off and plunked itself and the locket down onto the occult circles.

Spatula's tiny tongue lapped up the spilled poison, causing the kitten to explode into different forms in rapid succession: first into a different rabbit, then into another rabbit, and another ... *speeding up...* more rabbits... *going deeper into the past, into older incarnations...* Seconds later, it changed back into the form of a grown man with one leg.

Colonel Taytelly hissed at his mortal enemies for the last time and dropped dead.

Voegant–a death rattle on his lips and sprawled out beside the Colonel–watched it all happen. Taytelly was meddling with his plans! The locket contained Pilchett's name, so by bringing it inside the circles, the Colonel was deliberately botching up the ritual.

And the locket! He had missed that. He hadn't ordered his guards to strip-search the girl. Now, dying, he could do nothing to stop the damage done. His body no longer responded to instructions... '*OH, COME ON... NOT AGAIN!*' he thought and from one blink of the eye to the next, Voegant was dead too.

30. Unbirth

Bubbles...

Lovely bubbles.

Bright, vibrant bubbles everywhere, bubbling away like bubbly bubbles do.

Big bubbles, infinitesimally small ones, and bubbles of every size in between. A galactic ocean that held trillions of trillions of glimmering soul clusters, defying gravity and defying reason... This was bliss.

The departed–animal, vegetable, mineral... and miscellaneous–all crossed over to the ocean, their mutual place of origin, and amassed there in myriad quantities.

Whenever two bubbles bumped, they emitted a multitude of rays of every possible color in existence. This was spectacular in itself. And these type of collisions happened on innumerous occurrences between innumerous bubbles because there were so many of them. The sublime radiance of the whole was of an indefinable beauty.

Consequently, the ethereal traffic jam also generated an endless string of telepathic conversations along the lines of "Excuse me. Is this your bubble brushing up against me?" and "Oops! Sorry, my mistake."

Actually, it was the *only* conversational topic. No-one seemed to be wondering "Hey, that's strange. A moment ago I was a *basiliscus plumifrons* eating a snail, now I seem to be a small globule full of glitter."

There were exceptions, although they happened very rarely. The late Nate Noodascue found himself thinking "Well, what do you know? I'm a bubble!"

It had taken him a while to regain *super*consciousness. Now that he had, he didn't have a care in the afterworld.

Pilchett was with him, present as a second cluster of soulnubs inside the bubble, but apparently he wasn't awake.

The two were riding along on a current of bubbles as if they were in a cosmic roller-coaster. Nate was in wondrous awe. The currents alone were so huge that he wouldn't be able to grasp their eternal hugeness, even if he tried. They were indescribably stupendous. Streams of pure energy permeated everything.

Kindred travelers surrounded him. Just by looking at their soulnub clusters, he could determine what their past incarnations had been. "You were a pear tree. Those are sparrows, daffodils, a salamander, a school of snooks, dust mites, grass. That's a blackberry bush. Wasps... uh, termites, I guess... a spider. Wow! There are a lot of microbes, aren't there? Really a lot. *Reeeally* a lot!"

Nate's bubble shone brighter than of those drifting next to him and he had more soulnubs too. It was due to the unique, ritual-induced powers that he got this secret tour behind the scenes. He was free to float there where others were not.

This control, however, didn't make him think he was a cut above the rest. He felt connected with everyone. They all formed one current. Where the current was flowing was of no importance. It simply was flowing and they were all floating on it together.

Time didn't exist. Nate had no memory of when he had arrived. Nor did he need to. He wanted to stay forever. The place was so joyful. So familiar somehow. The harmonious chaos of gargantuan magnitude was home.

"What's this?"

Smooth avalanches of glistening soul particles were whirling down from above, trickling through the currents, and scattering themselves below over a vast meadow.

The meadow was crowded with an infinite number of more

shiny bubbles of all sizes, every single one anchored to the bottom by a long stem. The bubbles were gently swaying in the breeze like an never-ending panorama of dandelion clocks.

"It's magnificent!" Nate marveled. "This must be where the bubbles collect their soulnub particles."

In fact, he was in the presence of the birthplace of every living thing on Earth.

He went to have a closer look. Even though distances were incomprehensibly large, it took no effort to reach the meadow surface. "How exhilarating!"

He watched as a new stem sprouted up amid the throng of bubbles. The tip of the stem was encapsulated in a little bubble that rocked back and forth to catch falling particles. Once it had accumulated the right amount, it became *alive*. The whole bubble was now brimming with particles. Nate realized he was watching the birth of a centipede.

The horseradish plant next to it was waning. Its bubble broke away from the stem and was carried away on a passing current.

"Currents of the dead," Nate now understood. "They are like drainage canals. So pretty…"

Nate let his bubble rise. He wanted to find out where the dead were going. It took him no effort to find out.

Giant funnels hovered high above the meadow. They operated as enormous vortexes, sucking up nearby currents and spinning them around with such speed that their bubbles popped. After that, the gyrating blades inside the funnels broke every cluster up into its separate soulnub particles and something resembling a firework sparkler.

The particles were expelled out of the top of the funnels. They snowed down ceaselessly onto the meadow, to be recycled once more.

The sparkler, Nate understood, was the divine soul spark. It absorbed all the past life experiences from its particles and then rose up, to disappear through a tunnel of incandescent white light.

The whole process was astonishing. Nate was a privileged witness to this cycle of life and death. Privileged because he had the power to decide not to *meet the mixer* and not to have his cluster being ripped apart. And that was the difference. Under normal circumstances reincarnation meant he couldn't take his past live with him.

"But Voegant and Pilchett did it. Sauvetyne did as well. Multiple times!" Nate was stupefied by this insight. "They could because they were *unborn!* The three have gone back again and again with their soul clusters intact. And now that they've reenacted the ritual as intended they are finally *free to choose how!* They'll no longer get stuck being a ghost voice or an insect, not even a person of a different gender unless they want to be. They'll have free rein."

At last, Nate solved the last puzzle piece of the mystery: Voegant's intention was to search the meadow for one specific bubble, namely, the one of the baby whom he had conceived. He planned to force his own cluster inside of it. "He's going to spawn himself!"

Nate had been in a celestial lull, but now the sledgehammer of realization beat down heavily. "*I WAS MURDERED!*" he exclaimed. "And my boyfriend was too. I have to find Brent!"

BAM! A devastating shock wave rippled across Nate's residence. Someone's bubble had crashed into him. Multicolored discharges blasted out of the impact area.

"There you are, Pilchy!" Voegant said as if possessed. He resembled a snow globe on steroids, all bloated and veiny. "How about a brotherly *huuuug?*"

The spheres had half-merged with each other and were spiraling out of control, but Voegant did not let go. He was somehow *biting* into Pilchett, ripping nub particles out of his unconscious brother. Strands of them shot through the thin bubble film and flocked around Voegant's cluster; A cluster that was already fattened up from lifetimes of soulnub theft.

"We're getting sucked in!" Nate shouted. The linked bubbles were being propelled into the mouth of a funnel. "We need to work together!" Nate tried hard to move against the torrent. Voegant didn't lessen his cannibalistic grip. The pull of the vortex got too strong. Deeper and deeper they went into the colossal maelstrom of destruction.

"Can't you see we'll pop unless we get out of this hurricane thing?"

No reply.

Pilchett had woken up. He was utterly defenseless against the assault. "*STOP!... AARGH!...* Why are you doing this?! You promised me immortality!"

"You don't deserve it," Voegant snarled. "You're not leader material like me."

"But you promised!"

"We need to get out of the funnel, now!" Nate interjected. Nobody listened.

"*I* did all the work, all the research. *I* made it happen. You and Sauvetyne did nothing! I shall be the only one. I shall be omnipotent."

"I hate you. I always have! And another thing–"... Pilchett did not get to finish the sentence. Every last one of his nubs had been yanked out of him. His bare soul spark left their presence and started its journey toward the bright tunnel.

The revolving blades were dangerously close now. And bubbles, by the billions, around them were popping under the pressure, causing nub storms of epic proportions. Such baffling opposition made Nate decide to abandon the idea of breaking away and to counterattack instead. "I want you to die... again!" he yelled and he ground Voegant against the surrounding rubble, hoping that the friction would burst his bubble. "If there is any justice, you will pay for your crimes!" Nate hurled bolts of concentrated energy into his foe. Voegant just laughed. He didn't consider the young man a threat. If anything, he was going after Nate's particles next.

"*BRENT?*"ate was temporarily stunned. He'd caught a glimpse of Brent's bubble speeding past in the distance. The love of his life was adrift in the turmoil of debris, oblivious to the formidable blades. It was heartwrenching.

Voegant took full advantage of the distraction and rendered a blow Nate couldn't parry. He then latched onto Nate's cluster and started pumping him for soulnub. "I'm getting bigger and stronger, kid. Can you say *invincible?*" Voegant's bubble was looming large. It had swollen to about six times the normal size. Nate was being devoured by it, but he kept fighting back. He was determined to give everything he had. To the bitter end.

"I swear, Brent, I won't fail you twice! *ATTAAAACK!*"

All his rage and all his pain went into the next bombardment of energy bolts, boggling Voegant with its ferocity. The blast craters disrupted his surface tension. Nate kept casting bolt after bolt after bolt with all his might.

But Voegant retaliated and swiftly gained the upper hand. His appetite was ceaseless. He was extracting ever-increasing quantities of nubs.

"No! No! *RAAAAH!*" Rationally, Nate knew he had little chance of winning, but he wouldn't give up. He'd never give up. He had to beat the murderer.

Their wrestling match had brought them right up to the blades. They were being caught up in the perpetual blizzard of popping bubbles. They were about to get squashed unless a miracle happened. The mounting pressure alone was grueling.

Taytelly moved in and did the ethereal equivalent of a karate-chop to the neck. "Hi-ya!"

Voegant's surface rippled tumultuously, but didn't break. "Colonel Taytelly, my gap-toothed nemesis!" he boomed and instantly ignored Nate to redirect his assault toward the newcomer.

"Charmed to make your reacquaintance!" Taytelly said and banged his bubble like an obnoxious bumper car against his adversary. "Have at you, Sir! Here! Have at you!"

Nate's confusion about how Sharminella's kitten had been the military man all along had to wait. If he was to defeat the evil megalomaniac and reunite with Brent, then every moment counted. He joined in. "Two against one might even the odds."

"Make that three against one," Sauvetyne announced his arrival. "Hey, look! I'm circumagitating!" and he slammed into his brother.

Wreaking havoc in a place of total destruction could be thought impossible, but they succeeded at it.

Visibility was near zero. Inside the vastness of the twinkling dead, they got hit by a continuous surge of free-floating soulnub clusters. Still they fought on. It was a dirty fight with only one law: obliterate or be obliterated. Pulsating, convulsing... they collided into each other, threw crackling bolts of energy, savagely tore out particles... It was a full-on war not unlike a violent chemical reaction.

"*LET GO!*"

"*WHAT?*"

Sauvetyne's warning came not a moment too soon. In the heat of battle Nate had forgotten about the churning blades now directly above him. The pressure and pull they generated was huge.

Immediately he disconnected himself from Voegant's fat bubble, and followed Sauvetyne to a safer location. Easier said than done. Nate was in bad shape but he figured that if a ladybug could do it, so could he. "*COME ON, NATE!... MOVE...*

YOUR... BUBBLE... BUTT!"

Calling on every last bit of strength in himself, Nate made his retreat, slowly but surely.

The Barn Owl Captain and the Rabbitskin Colonel weren't so lucky. Stubborn as they were, they wouldn't allow each other to be released from their grip.

"Voegant, surrender to my superior banging!"

"Taytelly, you infuriating twit! I'll eat your other foot next!"

The blades had final say. The two bubbles collapsed–*Pop! Pop!*–and their glittery confetti got rapidly sucked up.

With that over, Nate was off like a bullet. Brent's bubble was still whirling around at high velocity. Locating him was surprisingly easy. Nate could see right into his sparkling soul. It was mind-bogglingly beautiful.

"Brent? Can you hear me? *Hellow?... CRAP!*" Despite his attempts to get his boyfriend to see sense, the bubble simply refused to change trajectory. "This can't be it! We still have so much to do together! *PLEASE, LISTEN!*"

Brent repeated on automatic "Sorry to bother you, but you appear to be poking my bubble."

"Move aside." Sauvetyne had turned up behind them. "I'm going to feed all my particles to him. He'll become aware, and then you can take him out of the flow."

"But then there'd be nothing left of you. You can't do that."

"I already am doing it. Consider it my present to you."

His soulnubs flushed into Brent. Sauvetyne emptied out fast.

"But why?"

"To atone for my past. I want to forget my army days and the crimes I've committed. It's like I said the first time we met in your apartment, I want to shatter into oblivion. It's for the best."

Sauvetyne, as a bubble, was everything she hadn't been in the flesh. Nate was amazed at how much more focused and to the point his ally was in this realm.

"So hurry, Noodascue. You must find the stems you two left behind when you died, and reconnect to them. Got it? It's the only way to get b-"

Sauvetyne popped. One moment he was here, the next, gone... Nate didn't get a change to say thank you.

The twinkling soul spark was being whisked away by an unseen force. Soon–same as every other spark in existence–it would move past the blades. Up, through the tunnel. Into the *Greater Unknown.*

Brent's bubble was gently sinking. Was he waking up? Nate didn't hang about to find out and guided him back to the meadow.

"Finding our stems in an ocean of stems should be simple," Nate told himself. "And then I guess reconnecting ourselves will be self-explanatory, like screwing in a light bulb... Yes, should be a straightforward job..."

"Man, I really hope this works..."

31. Family

Nate opened his eyes. He saw bubbles.

It was the carbon dioxide in a glass of champagne. Brent had smuggled it into the hospital and proudly offered Nate some. "Bravo!" he smiled. "And hurray for leaving today with a clean bill of health!"

"Thanks, I appreciate it. Although it's eight in the morning and I'll only be discharged at five this afternoon. Don't get me wrong, I'll be glad to get out of this hospital bed and get *you* into my own," Nate quipped and winked. A wink rife with suggestion.

The other patients in the room pretended they weren't eavesdropping on the cute couple.

"I imagine something to that extent can be arranged, Sir," Brent smiled again. Looking into his boyfriend's eyes he still went weak at the knees every time. He was absolutely smitten. Even after forty-six days of questionable hospital food Nate looked as handsome as ever. Charismatic too. He was almost glowing.

Brent was super grateful. People said it was a miracle that they had both survived the ordeal at all.

It certainly had been something of a miracle.

The paramedics had arrived in the lair in the nick of time. Brent and Nate were revived and their conditions stabilized.

Nate's recovery had taken the longest. Not only had he been poisoned, he'd also been shot and a large part of his soulnubs had been stolen.

To replenish the nubs, Brent had come up with an idea. After all, he understood the situation better than anyone, because he carried the knowledge of Sauvetyne's lives within him. He brought Nate a get-well gift: a whole flower shop's worth of potted plants (prompting the other patients in the ward to ask him for his autograph, just in case he turned out to be famous.) Surreptitiously, Nate slurped up the plant's particles and got better day by day. The nurses were stumped as to why all the plants kept withering.

But parts of Nate Noodascue were forever lost. "I'm thrilled I can go home again, alive and well. But I'm also sad that so many of my memories are gone. My head feels... hollow. I don't know how to describe it exactly. I can only hear myself think... I know, that doesn't make sense at all."

"Well, don't worry. We'll make many new fond memories, the two of us together. Now that you've got rid of that Pilchett guy."

"Who's this Pilchett you keep talking about?" Nate asked. He was sincere. He really didn't remember.

Brent decided to get into it at a later time. "I have exciting news," he said and announced the scoop with the accompanying sound of a drumroll. "The official papers have come in today. Now it's just a matter of going through the usual formalities. Congratulations! You're going to be Sharminella's legal guardian."

"Awesome!"

Nate was so happy with the news he jumped up and down on the hospital bed. Brent joined in. The other patients gawked at them, but the lovebirds didn't care. They were over the moon.

"Sharmy, isn't this great? We're going to be one happy family. We're going to have so much fun!"

Sharminella was sitting in the corner of the room, feeling embarrassed. She'd been put in a playpen she couldn't escape from. *A playpen* of all possible things to be afflicted with! Still, she made a halfhearted effort to cheer. "Whoopdedoo, Nanny!"

But, actually, it was perfect for her. She'd been thinking about ending her glamorous career at its peak anyway. To become an ex-beauty pageant queenie and be a brat like any other normal six-year-old.

Being part of a family was going to be a new experience for her. Sure, in the past she'd spent time with Mr. Holafinger and the makeup artists and such, but they'd been personnel, not real family. Whereas, with her roomie Nate, she'd always enjoyed herself: playing dress-up, singing the naughty versions of nursery rhymes, hiring a hand to bake her clay cupcakes for her... Nate was like an older brother. He looked after her and only occasionally borrowed her feather boa, although she couldn't imagine what he used it for. She thought Brent was an amusing mister too.

"So what do you say, Bubby?" she asked her Wanton Booboo doll. "Nanny for my gardener?" The doll stared up at her with its ever-goggling eyes. The girl pretended to listen to Bubby's reply. "...You're right. I think I like it also too. *YAAAAAAY!*"

Nate and Brent were kissing. They were two cuties making out. It was like one of those passionately kisses at the end of a romantic movie that went on forever. Their lips fit perfectly. Their embracing arms and hips were designed to form one whole.

At long last Nate had found his soulmate. Brent felt the same way. They were a match made in heaven. Their love was eternal. Everything was as it should be.

A siren went off, swiftly followed by the sound of breaking glass. A man–middle-aged, mortally obese and wearing a pale, loose-fitting garment usually bestowed on the criminally insane–was breaking out of the hospital's psychiatric wing.

The man taxied onto a large stretch of gravel, started wildly flapping his arms and... took off. Somewhat erratically at first, like a ladybug would.

"Hey, I didn't know Poledoris could fly!"

"Just ignore him," Brent said dreamily, "and kiss me some more."

"I can do that."

...

Somewhere, far away, in a sandbox in the center of a peculiar city built on top of a mountain, a strange plant was blooming doorknobs as it turned itself toward the sun.

Be a hero. Leave a book review.

You want to make the world a better place? Then leave a book review on the Amazon book page.

Here is why. You will not only support me, the writer, but also a number of **charity organizations** that maybe aren't as visible as the better-known ones but they provide vital services too.

Remember, I gladly donate **10% of my earnings to charity.**

Plus, other readers will be grateful for your review because it directs them to this great read, and they too will indirectly contribute to the charities. Neat, huh?

What other authors or books came to mind while reading this book? Tell the world and help out now:
amzn.com/B01AQZ319A (the direct link on Amazon.com)
goodreads.com/jonengleewell

You have my eternal thanks!
- Jonen

Excerpt from "Flamboyfriend"

Gleewell's next humorous novel will make its way into your heart shortly.

Cade Deveraux is seventeen and living on the outskirts of London. People tend to think of him as self-absorbed and delusional. He thinks of himself as having star quality.

Then, one day, he discovers Alli, a strange little girl sitting in a wheelchair in the flat next-door.

...

Mrs Wrye is standing in her hallway, looking furious. Seriously, the old woman has no decorum. She's always coming home when she's least wanted and welcome.

"Thiago! Why did you let that Deveraux boy in? You know people can't know about Alli! He can't be involved! He'll get Alli hurt!"

"Hurt her? Me?" I say. "The very thought!"

Thiago tries to reason with her. (You'd have better luck reasoning with a brick.) "It's alright. Listen, I've got wonderful news. Alli spoke to us and–"

"Don't talk nonsense! You know Alli doesn't respond. She never does and never will, but you won't listen." Mrs Wrye pushes him aside (to get a clear path to attack me, no doubt). Her hands are shaking so hard now, they are about to drop off. "You bringing the Deveraux kid in here has put her in danger. He is untrustworthy. A rogue! We have to protect her! She can't fend for herself, you know that."

"Wynflaeth, if you'd just reconsider for a moment–"

"Out! Both of you! Out! Out! Out!"

She's forcibly ejecting us from her flat. Thiago protests, but that makes her kick and slap us even harder. "Bugger off!"

For someone who is, like, a hundred years old, she has no trouble doling 'em out. Her slamming door hits us in the back.

Geriatric lunatic.

"What was that all about?"

"Don't ask me that. I can't go into it, Cade. What you need to understand is–"

A heavy thump almost knocks the hinges out of the door. Thiago and I exchange looks. It is the kind of thump produced when about eleven stone of meat says hello to a solid slab of stone.

"Are you alright in there, Wynflaeth?... Wynflaeth? Did you fall?"

When she doesn't respond, Thiago whips out his key, but the door is bolted. So the only way back in is to both go next-door, pass through my bedroom – I briefly ponder if we could stop to consummate our eternal love, but there isn't time – and then move along the fire escape and enter via Mrs Wrye's window. Sure enough, she is out cold on the hallway floor. Her body spread-eagled. Her face drained of colour. A white-knuckled fist is clutching the area where theoretically her heart would be. She has croaked! And I just know she will try to spin it like it was somehow all *my* vault.

"rgggr..."

Thiago is tending to her. "You hear that?"

"She's snoring. She must be alive then."

One part of me is actually relieved that she hasn't kicked the proverbial bucket. The other part, however, can't get over the fact how naff her knickers look. Beige, with fringes made out of doily cloth. Strange how the mind wanders in moments like these.

Thiago tries to wake her up, but it is of no use. "She may have a concussion! Her pulse is faint. I'm calling an ambulance. Cade, would you fetch a cushion for under her head?"

"Right away. Anything to help!"

I spring into action. Here we are in the middle of one of those tragic, life-altering situations, where we must pull through together... where strong bonds between men are forged.

In other words, a perfect opportunity to endear myself to Thiago with my virtuous bedside manner... and, if all goes well, sexy pillow talk later on.

I slide a cushion under Mrs Wrye's head and straighten out her skirt over the knees. Because the situation is already miserable enough as it is.

Nine minutes go by. Ten. Eleven. "What's keeping the ambulance?" Thiago grumbles. "It's taking too long. Royal Grace Hospital is only three blocks away, right?"

I agree. All of this is cutting into my precious one-on-one time with Thiago, Brasil's top export product.

Thiago. Look at him. Gorgeous sex beast. He is practically a saint. He refuses to move away from her, gently squeezing her hand, concerned for her well-being. He has such a big heart. I'd do anything to nibble on those delectable ears of his. Well, anything except performing CPR on Mrs Wrye. Bah! I wouldn't be any good at it anyway. Last year I failed CPR class, but it wasn't mind fault that the training dummy was just too ugly.

Where was I?

Ah, yes. Where *are* the paramedics? I look out the window. Thaw has finally set in–so much for a white Christmas–but traffic is still an unsightly bitch. Suppose Mrs Wrye is really in mortal danger. How much longer will society allow its elderly citizens to perish because there wasn't a budget for a snow plough? Is an old woman's fate merely a statistic to this city council? Am I to be denied my chance to get it on with Thiago's hot bod?

What is this world coming to?

About the author

In a parallel universe far, far too close for comfort...
Jonen Gleewell can be found writing in his den,
which contains a desk, a word-processing device
and an undisclosed stash of dark chocolate.

He began his career writing musicals and comedy
plays for teenagers (*Straight Undercover, Robin
Hood, Diamond Drift*). Currently, he is working on
his next novel "Flamboyfriend" with pertinacity and
with a dictionary.

Leave a review at:
amzn.com/B01AQZ319A (the book on Amazon.com)
goodreads.com/jonengleewell
or drop Jonen a line at jonengleewell.blogspot.com
He loves to hear from you!

Acknowledgments

My infinite gratitude goes out to:

God, Maarten Mylemans, Martin Gamble, Jasmine Vyas, Sibille Allgayer, Pamela J Alexander, Esthel Davidsenn, Marie Laenen, Kris Van der Heyden, Rosalie Delforge, Charlotte Delforge, Thomas Goyvaerts, Nicole Meys, Petra Raaffels, Marie McGinley, Martin Seeger, Kathy Sparrow, Carl Pansaerts, Jack Canfield.

My gratitude also goes out to those authors whose humor and creativity in their work have inspired me to write this book: Christopher Moore, Terry Pratchett, Douglas Adams, David Levithan, Neal Gaiman, David Sedaris, Brent Hartinger, Armistead Maupin, Robert Rankin, Joe Keenan, Oscar Wilde, Tom Holt, and many more.

Credits

Cover illustration by Alexandr Pushai.
Visit him at: www.behance.net/pushaiart
Typography by Jonen Gleewell.

Promotional consideration

The Stroll-Make™ **DeLuxe C5** model featured in this literary work. For your consideration.

Thanks to the Stroll-Make your four-legged friend will answer the call of nature in all its glory in the comfort of your own home.

Excerpt from the instruction booklet:

Your pet *(insert species here)* enters the Stroll-Make, triggering the switch *On*. Instantly high-definition landscapes are projected on the insides of the inner tube–a full 359 degrees 3D experience! Your *(insert species here)* will imagine itself running through a photo-realistic forest populated by birds and critters... or running through a lamp-post heaven... or a fresh desert of kitty litter stretching out into the horizon!

The self-cleaning grid on which your *(insert species here)* 'makes' is clinically tested titanium steel. The faeces can fall through the grid into a secured and odorless container for quick and easy removal. Hygiene is key!

Additionally, the grid is also a treadmill. It will promptly start moving when the motion sensors register that your *(insert species here)* is in pursuit of its holographic pray. In doing so, the Stroll-Make ensures that your indoor companion receives the active workout it so desperately needs.

But wait, there is more! To make the illusion complete, a rich mixture of scents are automatically released inside the Stroll-Make: the smells of tree leaves, lush meadows, chicken feathers, automobile tires, hedgehogs, concentrated rhino pheromones, territorial urine. Booster packs sold separately.

<u>Disclaimer</u>:

'*Caution*: Do not touch the collection tank with bare hands, elbow skin or inside of eyelid. It contains a strong disinfectant."

'Keep the Stroll-Make in a well-ventilated area. Ideally in garden or field.'

'Avoid direct contact with the receptacle. In fact, best to stay away from the tank altogether, you silly person.'

'Not to be used on human babies.'

'May permanently damage clothing if used for dry-cleaning purposes.'

'Unless expressly authorized in writing by the Ponkstram Corporation any use of the Stroll-Make by any person other than the buyer is strictly prohibited and punishable by law. And yes we are extremely litigious.'

'Do not ingest power cord.'

'Any resemblance between Mr. Yueng Chan's lower body region and our trademarked Scent Spout™ is purely coincidental.'

'Inside lamps cannot serve as a solarium.'

'May cause seizures in users prone to epileptic attacks: check with your veterinarian first.'

'Never replace socket board BIN54 with BIN98 to convert into a microwave oven.'

'In line with our new Preemptive After-Sales Strategy (*PASS*) all warranties became void the moment you left the store.'

'Advised to refrain from use in case of pregnancy or in the first week after neutering.'

'The Stroll-Make model has been proven to cause 0% infertility in male owners. (Researched by our laboratory on international waters).'

'Respect life. Cosmetic scents were not tested on animals.'

'The Ponkstram Corporation does not endorse nor encourage the use of the product for hallucinogenic purposes.'

'On purchasing the product you accept the terms and conditions of the sales contract, including liability for, but not limited to, any explicit, incidental, special, consequential, exemplary or hilarious damages, lost profits or other intangible losses as a result of improper use. Infringement of the terms and conditions may lead to the prosecution, imprisonment or the kneecapping of your family members by goons if we feel like it.'

'The buyer agrees to indemnify and hold harmless the Ponkstram Corporation, its subsidiaries, affiliates, officers, agents, that guy with the weird hair on floor six, partners, employees from any claim made on a faulty Stroll-Make product. Claims are contractually not admissible in court. So, there! And remember: the goons know where you sleep at night.